THICKER
THAN
WATER

LINDY CAMERON

Bywater
BOOKS

Cameron

...or MI 48106-3671
...ww.bywaterbooks.com

Bywater Books First Edition
First Printing August 2009

First published in Australia in 2003 by HarperCollins Publishers, Ltd.

Printed in the United States of America on acid-free paper

Cover designer: Bonnie Liss (Phoenix Graphics)

ISBN 978-1-932859-40-9

For Chele
My best friend and soul mate.

Acknowledgments

Several parallel universes of thanks to my precious family and friends, especially:

My mum, for still always wanting to be there; Fin and Steve for love and balderdash; Helen for the company, for the laughs and for Chele.

My host of treasured special-girl mates: Jen, Rob, Sally, Tricia, Jay, Kay, Trish, Jac, Jill, Kim, Ruth, Kerry and Ivy.

My finally found sisters, Penny and Donna, and wee nephews Noah and Bastian.

My fellow Sisters in Crime: Carmel, Viv, Sue, Cathy, Faye, Phyllis, Tanya, Robin, Kerry, Phillipa —Do we rule, or what! And Dr. Shelley R. for the forensic info (any errors are mine alone).

My wildly supportive hairy-scaries: Xena, Gabby, Ares, Emmett and Tess; and the never-forgotten Lucy, Rose, Taffy, Millie, Isis, Tuppy and Boofy.

My wonderful American publishers, Bywater Books; thank you Kelly, Marianne, Val, and Carol for offering me up to the rest of the world.

And for the all memories that live on in my heart, thank you Bill, Gus, Lorelle, Sheena and Miss Wood; and to Mrs. Dugdale who inspired the better side of Queenie Riley.

Chapter 1

One of the odd things about a human body that's been drained of blood is how ordinary it looks. The skin is not so much vampiric as simply pale and inanimate; more gray flannel than white cotton pajamas. If the deceased is face up with the eyes open, then the whites still look like boiled albumen surrounding a black-centered disk of dull-hued marble. The eyelids are grayish, the cheeks pale-grayish, and the lips slack and wan.

With some bodies, like this naked one, the chest hairs look like they've been badly transplanted by Hair-A-Go-Go; the concave nipples look like pâté, and the penis like a limp anemic slug. The groin and neck of this particular corpse was blue-black and bloody, but the rest of its outer dermal layer was just plain pallid. The only highlights were the pinkish-red puddles caught in the skin on the underside of the body where the dregs had settled in the lowest points, for even gravity loses interest in claiming what the heart can no longer push around.

"Five liters. It's not very much when you think about it."

"Pardon?"

"Five liters—or eight pints—that's how much blood the average human adult contains."

Jon Marek looked at his colleague and raised an eyebrow. "Not this one."

"Well, not any more. It's probably all there under him, though; that's a pretty big thing he's in ... on."

"Looks like a man-sized cake rack and baking tray to me," Marek noted, "but I trust you'll find out exactly what it is before you write your report, Detective Senior Constable. Now, have you seen O'Malley?"

1

"Who?"

"Katherine O'Malley, Melbourne's single-greatest finder of suspiciously dead persons."

"Really? What is she, a psychic or something?"

"No, Martin," Marek snorted. "She's more psycho than ..."

"I heard that."

"Ah," Marek noted, turning to acknowledge his once upon a long-time-ago partner, who was sitting at the bar. "There is *nothing* spooky about Kit O'Malley," he continued, "except her tendency to stumble over things like this." His sweeping gesture had started with Kit and ended with the deceased who was posed, dramatically, in the center of the dance floor.

"Oh," Detective Martin nodded, "then I guess Katherine O'Malley is the friend of the owner-chick who called us re: the 'bloodless bloke in the bar'. As you can see, she's over there trying not to throw up in her drink."

"I doubt it," Marek said. "And I wouldn't call either of them chicks," he advised, seeking a verifying gesture from Kit before clarifying his statement. "Well, *I* certainly wouldn't."

Kit smiled and swiveled on her stool as she listened to the two cops debate political correctness versus language trends, over the body of a man who may never have given the subject much consideration while alive but, given his druthers, would no doubt love to be able to chip in his two cents worth now.

Chick or bird, eh, Mr. Dead Guy?, Kit pondered, knowing that PC-bullshit had nothing to do with her preference for not being called anything that conjured the image of a huge-breasted, half-dressed, pouting girl straddling a Harley to advertise that great culinary excuse for a phallic icon—the chico roll. Or is that a phallic excuse for ... No matter!

And *druthers*? Where the hell did that come from, O'Malley?, she wondered, noticing that her ex was now strolling in her direction.

As the rest of this homicide crew weren't his, Kit knew that Jon Marek was not in charge of investigating the presence of a drained and denuded man in The Terpsichore's dance room. She also knew he wouldn't be in charge of the inquiry into the naked-man murder;

2

partly because of his recent promotion, but mostly because of his role in the ongoing Barleycorn Task Force. The latter meant that he *shouldn't* have a spare minute to scratch himself. Yet here he was with time enough to satisfy his curiosity or, perhaps, to check up on her. And by the looks of things, Kit tallied, he'd also had time for a haircut and was obviously still working his buff body at the gym—unless, of course, his exercise regime was now totally lust-filled and Erin-centered.

Marek took a seat at the main bar next to Kit, and opposite Angie Nichols, who was owner of the piano bar–restaurant–disco in which they were all loitering: he, because there was a homicide victim in a big metal dish in the other room; they, because they found said victim. Ordinarily, Marek wouldn't even be allowed in the place.

"Hi Angie," he smiled. "You okay?"

"All things considered, Jonno, no," Angie said. "And I'd like to state, for the record, that I had nothing to do with that thing over there *or* whatever the hell it's supposed to represent."

"I'd be surprised if you did. You know him?"

"Nope. Never seen him before—dead or alive."

Marek shrugged. "Don't s'pose you'd make some coffee?"

"Yeah, sure." Angie busied herself with the cappuccino machine, but kept glancing over at the unwelcome activity in her Red Room.

"I didn't think the sight of blood bothered you," Marek said to Kit, who was whacking the bottom of an up-ended tabasco sauce bottle.

"It doesn't," she said. Half the slurp went in her drink, the rest flicked over the bar and onto the clean glasses in the rack on the sink. Kit gave an unsurprised frown, stirred the tomato juice with her finger, drank the lot in one go, and then smiled at Marek. "I've just seen way more than my share lately. Besides, unlike you lot, I don't need to hover over the guy to make sure he really is dead. It's bloody obvious he's not going to get up again."

"Do you know who he is?"

"Nope." Kit emptied the rest of the tomato juice from the bottle into her glass and waved at Angie.

"Is that all you're going to tell me, Kitty?"

3

"That's all I know, Jonno. How come you're here anyway? I would have thought Bubblewrap Man would stop you being on-call for the duration."

"I'm not on-call. But I was in the office when I heard who'd rung in with this mess."

"Busybody," Kit sniffed, and then nodded towards Martin. "Who's your new floozie?"

"She's not mine. Well, she's on the squad, but ..." Marek shook his head. "Detective Senior Constable Cathy Martin is on Parker's crew."

"You are kidding!" Kit was horrified. "Please tell me that prick is *not* in charge of this investigation," Kit begged. "It will be embarrassing for all concerned—you know it will. I'm warning you right now, Marek, you can't do this, it's ..."

"A done deal, mate. His crew caught the job, you know how it works. *You* will just have to behave."

"Me?"

Angie returned with coffee and vodka just as Kit took up banging her forehead on the bar.

"Jesus, Jonno, what did you do to her?"

"Nothing. She's unbalanced, you know that."

"Angie, go press the fire alarm," Kit urged. "We need to clear the bar of these pesky cops, so you and I can drag that naked dead dude out into the middle of the main road."

"Why?"

"So none of *us* has to deal with Chucky Scumbag."

"And that would be who and why?" Angie asked with a shrug.

"You don't want to know." Kit was emphatic.

"I do if I'm going to have to, Katy darling."

Kit straightened up and peered through the doorway into the dance room, or "The Red" as it was commonly known, where the forensic pathologist was crouching and, for some reason, pulling faces at the corpse. The Doc snapped her fingers to get the police photographer to pay attention to her rather than to DSC Martin and a male detective, who were the only other people in that area of the crime scene. The Terpsichore seemed to be safely Parker-free—for now.

4

"What gives, Marek? He's got two crew in here, four outside and even *you're* here. So where's Chucky?"

"Good question," Marek noted. "He should've driven over with Crosby and Martin, but when she rang him about the job he said he was too far out to be picked up."

"Chucky Parker couldn't be *far out* if his life depended on it," Kit stated. "Unless he's on drugs now, which would only surprise me for a day." She did another visual sweep of the bar and turned to Angie. "You remember the last year I was on the job, I got caught up in that little hoo-ha over cops who were on the take over burglaries and insurance claims?"

Angie squinted. "You mean that horrible time when you had to testify against other officers? God, Katy, that was serious shit, not a little hoo-ha."

"Yeah, well two of those cops were completely innocent and proven so. But they'd been loaded up, along with three seriously bent detectives, in order to make it look like the corruption went way farther than it did."

"And that has what relevance to the dead dude in my disco?"

"None at all. But the man who is now Senior Sergeant Graham Charles Parker, and who will be heading the investigation into your dead dude, was then the Internal Affairs whip-dick who set-up a couple of extra cops to ensure his case against Jackson, Boxer, and Doghouse got enough attention to get *him* noticed. The bastard should not be around to tell the tale."

"Which of course he doesn't," Marek added. "Tell the tale, I mean. If he did, he'd have to admit to an impropriety that he denied at the time."

"Impropriety!" Kit snorted. "On top of all that, Parker's a sexist bully-boy."

"Given her *ex-cop* status," Angie said, "it's okay that Katy is ranting about this guy, Jonno, but should you be verifying her gossip? What if your colleague has to interrogate me?"

Marek gazed at the ceiling for a moment, and then gave a wicked smile. "I trust your discretion, Angie. Also, given the circs, I figure you *need* to know where Charlie Parker is coming from. Besides, the Princess of Rant sometimes needs clarification."

5

"True," Angie said, acknowledging Kit's green-eyed *who me?* "So, how did this cop get away with all that stuff?"

"Coz back then," Kit sneered, "it was seldom a case of what you knew, but whose arse you were on intimate terms with. It certainly had zilch to do with how good, or bad, you were."

"As several coppers discovered the hard way," Marek added.

"Chucky also had Brownie points with ..." Kit shrugged, "someone of the right-ranked brass, who conceded on his behalf that the end justified his completely despicable means. So what if a few reputations got sullied, the force managed to shed some bad bad boys."

"But surely if you have a bent cop on ..." Angie began.

"*I* don't have one," Marek insisted. "And besides Charlie's not bent, at least not *that* way; or your way either for that matter."

"Chucky is one of those dubious good guys," Kit explained. "A card-carrying member of the moral high-ground brigade who believes, absolutely, that he is always right, that his actions are always warranted, and that his methods are logically defensible. His is a small mind cloaked in a mantle of righteousness that conceals a twisted pile of his own scary shit."

"What? Like a TV evangelist with boy scouts in his basement?" Angie suggested.

"Yeah, except Chucky's not religious, or a pervert. He's more your redneck, Guns-R-Us, rabidly ambitious, chauvinistic, bast ..."

"Jeez you exaggerate, Kitty," Marek laughed. "He's an arsehole, but he's not that bad."

"Bite your tongue, Jonno. He is the Antichrist's podiatrist. And what's more, it was barely three weeks ago that you asked me why I hadn't shot him on behalf of the entire force before I left it to become a private citizen."

"Yeah, but ..."

"What I'd like to know," Angie said, through clenched teeth, "is how you two can sit around joking about irrelevancies, when there's a dead murder victim in my establishment?"

"A *dead* murder victim no less," Kit smiled.

"Kit tells me it's called gallows humor," Marek explained.

"No it isn't, Jonno," Kit contradicted. "What we are engaged in here is a diversionary tactic; we're trying to pretend that there *isn't*

6

a dead person within cooee of our irrelevant banter. Gallows humor is when you make amusing and tasteless remarks about the body itself, or about the crime scene, in order to laugh loudly in the face of death so that you don't scream or puke or go completely mental.

"Example. Under more blokey circumstances you might say: 'Wow, the first naked guy to get into Angie's infamous lesbian nightclub'—which in the yobbo mind illogically translates as hetero-male heaven—'and the poor bastard couldn't get it up if his life depended on it.'"

"I'd never say that," Marek objected. "Given that he's lying over a roasting pan posed like Vinnie Barbarino in *Saturday Night Fever*, I'm sure I could have come up with something far less blokey and much more clever."

"You're still doing it," Angie marveled.

"Yeah," Kit nodded, "Marek always mixes his characters and movies."

"No, you're still bantering."

"Ah," Marek said sagely. "This is because: a) O'Malley really doesn't need to see any more dead people; b) as this will not be my investigation, I can honestly say I'm here because I've always wanted to see inside Angie's infamous bar; and c) between us, Kitty and I are trying to keep your mind off your dead murder victim."

"It's not working," Angie stated. "And he's not *mine*."

"Why don't you ask her some important questions, then, Marek," Kit suggested.

"Um, I don't want to know anything?" Marek replied question-ingly, because either he was aware it wasn't a good response for a homicide cop, or he was suddenly distracted.

Kit followed his line of sight and glanced over her shoulder at Angie's only other patrons, sitting in the booth farthest from the crime scene. Nothing strange there, so she turned back to Marek with a palms-up shrug. "But you'll be a better judge of the facts than Chu …"

"Parker will do the right thing," Marek interjected. "I'll make sure of that. But I can't take over. I would, however, like to know who *they* are, especially the one with the tape recorder."

Kit swiveled around on her stool and took inventory of the

group who was sitting where they'd been told to sit and wait. When Angie had discovered the uninvited naked corpse in her disco, and had rung her friend the private investigator at home in an understandable panic three hours before, Kit had told her to make sure that anyone who was there stayed there, and to let no one else in until the police arrived.

"From left," Kit pointed, "Rabbit MacArthur, Booty Jones, Don't Know, and Sal ... um."

"Armstrong," Angie finished. "'Don't-Know' with the walkman is Carrie Someone."

"Rabbit, Booty, Don't Know, Someone," Marek repeated. "Don't they have real names?"

"Those names are as real as *mate*, mate," Kit smiled.

"Or Doggie and Biffer, or whatever you called those cops," Angie noted.

Kit widened her eyes. "So, Marek, why don't you take Angie over there so she can help you interrogate the witnesses? That way we can all find out who Carrie Thing is."

"Good plan," Marek agreed, taking the hint that it might also distract Angie.

"Scooter Farrell was here when we found the body," Angie volunteered, as she lifted a section of the counter top so she could get out from behind the bar. "But she had to go to work because she was relieving someone. Besides which, she had a cracker of a hangover and the thought of *him*," Angie cast a thumb towards the dance room, "was vomit-inducing."

Marek, muttering something silly about a compromised crime scene, escorted Angie over to the booth, whereon Rabbit MacArthur leaped up and thrust her hand out to shake his with all the enthusiasm of someone who had always wanted to be a real detective but had never bothered to join the police force in order to make the dream even a vague possibility.

Kit returned her semi-detached attention to Dr. Ruth Hudson and the two forensic staff who had joined her in the sound-proofed—when the doors weren't folded open—Red Room. She wondered whether the guy had been killed in there overnight, or had just been left for effect. Some bloody effect, she thought.

She rubbed her eyes and squeezed the bridge of her nose, then tried to view her favorite haunt from a cop/crime-scene perspective. The huge three-sided (one short, two long) bar, at which she was sitting was about thirty feet from the front door and divided The Terpsichore in half. The west side of the building, which looked out on St Georges Road—or would have if it had had windows—featured The Red at the rear, and ten booths lining the front half of the space. Kit turned around to face east, towards more booths and six pool tables adjacent to the long side of the bar, and where there was also a small bistro-servery. Chairs and tables, and a grand piano occupied the front, or southern end, of the building.

There were three ways in and out of Angie's: the front door through the entrance foyer, off which were the toilets; an emergency exit at the rear of The Red; and the kitchen door beyond the servery. The Red and the kitchen doors led into a side alley.

Well, that was singularly unhelpful, Kit thought, turning back to face The Red. Realizing she was too disturbed by the imminent arrival of Parker to give a rat's arse about how the killer got into the premises, she debated whether to run and hide, but realized how unfair that would be on Angie. Leaving her to deal with Chucky alone would be grounds for dismissal from the friendship ring.

Bah! Who needs friends? Kit asked herself. Bugger Angie! I do *not* want to go to jail for involuntary prickicide. Kit screwed her face into a serious pout. Bloody hell! It was bad enough that in the nearly four years of The Terpsichore's existence as a women's bar there'd never been any need to have cops on the premises—unless they were off-duty and women—but this particular need was beyond ridiculous.

The Terpsichore, commonly known as Angie's, was a nightclub, bar, and poolroom with none of the attendant problems. Until now. Until the first time an uninvited bloke gets in. Okay, Kit allowed, given his current condition the guy may not have *wanted* to get into Angie's, but … Shit! Of all the cops in the state to get the right to traipse his little feet through her home away from home, it had to be the traitorous Graham Parker.

Kit raked her hands vigorously through her short hair in a fit of frustration until she caught sight of the result in the evil mirror behind the bar, and tried to pat it back into its usual disheveled do. She closed her eyes, took a deep meditative breath, remembered she didn't have a clue how to meditate, and then jumped in fright as a hand gripped the back of her neck to render her incapable of movement.

"Do I need to gag and handcuff you?" Marek asked.

"No. Why?"

"Your favorite Martian is here."

"Don't insult the nonterrestrials," Kit stated, swiveling on her stool in time to see Senior Sergeant Graham Parker slithering through the front door like the snake he was.

Kit couldn't help the snorting laugh that escaped her control while her senses rippled with a minor revelation. Having been, only mildly, concerned she'd be unable to resist the urge to ram the open Tabasco bottle somewhere in Parker where the sun didn't shine, she'd forgotten to remember just how distorted the nasty things in one's memory can get over time. For here came the walking, breathing, insignificant proof: Graham Chucky Parker was so much less than she remembered. He was shorter, weedier, paler, and balder. He still dressed very well and it still didn't give him an ounce of style; and he still walked as if he had a prickly golf ball up his bum.

Parker gave Marek a curious nod, glanced at Kit without recognition, and continued on into The Red, where he consulted Martin and his other detective, and he was glared at by Ruth Hudson who waved him away from her space.

"Can I go now please, Jonno?" Kit begged. "I'd really hate to go to prison for squishing that slimy little slugger-bug. If there was more *to* him it wouldn't be such a waste of my future."

Marek looked at Kit quizzically. "He didn't seem to know who you were."

"Ah well, the last time we saw each other I was in the middle of my bad hair year."

"What do you call this, then?" Marek smiled, drawing a halo over Kit's head.

"Au naturel. Remember that long-haired perm that looked like a crinkle-cut skull-cap when I wore it in a bun for work, and which

10

went spackarse when it was loose. It's not surprising Chucky didn't recognize me as the snarling Medusa who threw hot coffee in his lap during our last encounter." Kit widened her eyes, "Speaking of snake heads."

"What are you doing here, Jon?" Parker asked. "Not checking up on me I hope, Boss."

"No," the boss stated, turning on his heel to face his colleague. Kit received Marek's follow-up *you idiot* by telepathy. "I'm having coffee with an old friend. You remember Kit O'Malley, I'm sure."

"Jesus! Um, yeah. You look ... different, O'Malley. How come ..." Parker ran out of words or wind or petrol, so he waved his hands around before anchoring them on his hips.

"Do you want me to brief you now," Marek asked pleasantly, "or are you going to tell me why it took you so long to get here?"

A surprised Parker hoicked his eyebrows at Kit while giving Marek a look that said either: "Steady-on, boss, not in front of the public—especially *that* member of it"; or "I'll get back to you when I've thought of a good reason."

Meanwhile Kit's insides smiled broadly as she counted three things she'd always liked about Jon Marek: he did not suffer fools, he made no allowances for dickheads, and, while he did believe there was an appropriate time and place for most things, there were some occasions when he just didn't *give* a shit.

"You can fill me in, if you wouldn't mind," Parker said.

"The bar ..." Marek began.

"A lesbian establishment, I believe," Parker verified.

"Yeah, not that that's relevant right now. The bar is owned by Angie Nichols, who is sitting on the left with those women over there ..."

Parker squinted. "Are they all women?"

Kit started squirming on her stool, so Marek squeezed the back of her neck where his hand still rested. "How about you take over, O'Malley," he said. "What time did Angie open up?"

"Twelve-thirty," Kit said, without spitting. "Which is later than usual because she'd been at a funeral ... in Bendigo ... where she'd driven yesterday morning. The others over there, plus one other *woman* who has since gone to work, were waiting to get in for

11

lunch unaware that lunch wasn't on today. Because of the funeral. Anyway, they all came in to help Angie set up."

"The patrons helped to set up?" Parker interrupted.

"The patrons who are also friends, yes," Kit explained, glad that Marek had hold of her. "Angie went around, as usual, opening windows to swap last night's air for today's. It was about fifteen minutes later that she got around to opening up The Red and ..."

"Red? What's wine got to do with this?" Parker asked.

Nothing *Chucky*, Kit said and thought to herself. "The Red is the dance room," she pointed. "Angie opened the doors and voilà: very dead man in very big tray. She called the cops, then me."

"Why you?" Parker asked with a bemused wiggle of chin and brow.

"Me friend. Me private eye."

Parker's chest spasmed with a short soundless laugh. "And are you a dyke too?"

Before Kit could move an inch, Marek slid his arm down over her shoulder and pulled her snugly back against his body. "Yeah she is, *Chuck*," he said, "but only on the full moon. And, mate, you should *see* her lesbian fur and fangs."

Kit held her breath, while Mr. Oblivious said, "Marek, please don't call me Chuck".

"Sorry *Charlie*, I forgot how much you hate it," Marek shrugged. "But do me a favor too, would you? Don't use the word dyke again. Or lesbian, for that matter."

"What?"

"Unless it is relevant to the investigation, the sexuality of anyone you come across in this establishment, or in connection with this case, is none of your business."

"What?" Parker repeated, casting his arms out to emphasize his astonishment. "You don't think these women are relevant?"

"Oh sure, the women may well be," Marek agreed, "but at this stage of the proceedings, I doubt the lesbians are."

"O'Malley!" bellowed one of the lesbians over in the booth.

"Yes, Rabbit?" Kit called back, as everyone turned in her direction.

"If we can't have beer, can Angie make more coffee, please? We're havin' withdrawals."

Marek beckoned Angie back to the bar. "We could all do with a very strong brew," he said.

Kit watched Parker watch the approach of the statuesque Angie Nichols. Interestingly, Chucky seemed to get smaller the closer she came, despite doing the small-man back-stretch to compensate. Like it would *make* a difference!

Parker looked Angie over—up to her head and down to her feet—taking in her large-boned but trim and taut frame, and her hair, which this week was silver and purple. His expression registered that she was, so far and without doubt, the likeliest suspect in the murder about which he knew nothing yet, apart from the fact that there'd been one and it was strange.

Angie gazed down at Parker with complete disinterest. "Espresso or cappuccino?"

"Flat white," he replied. "Then perhaps you'd like to give me your version of events."

"My version? You mean you want to know what happened."

"Yes," Parker said impatiently.

"Why? Who are you?" Angie asked, though it was obvious to Kit that she already knew.

"Senior Sergeant Parker. I'm in charge of the investigation."

"Oh, right," Angie drawled, as she slipped behind the bar again. "God, you took your time. I'd have thought the investigation was nearly over. Everyone else has been here for hours."

"Ruth wants you, I think," Marek stated before anyone else could get a smart word in.

"Who?" Parker asked impatiently. "Oh, Dr. Hudson," he amended.

"Sorry to interrupt you, Senior Sergeant," the forensic pathologist smiled, "but I'm about to leave. There's nothing more I can do until the body is delivered for autopsy. I've slotted it in for six this evening. Cathy and your new bloke will do the honors with me."

"That's fine, Doc," Parker nodded. "Anything you can tell me now?"

"Only the obvious."

"Which is?" Parker looked expectant.

"He bled to death, Chu … Charlie." Kit raised an eyebrow.

13

"Really, O'Malley? Well, if you don't mind, I'll wait for the expert's opinion."

"He bled to death," Ruth repeated straight-faced. "I'd say the vic was tied face down ..."

"Face down?"

"Yes. It wouldn't work otherwise, Senior Sergeant."

"What wouldn't work?" Parker asked.

Ruth smiled as she accepted the coffee that Angie offered. "Ordinarily," she said, "even *with* the major arteries severed, as they were in this case, a person would die before complete exsanguination. So, in order to deplete the body of most of its circulation volume before death occurred and stopped the heart pumping, a body—just like this one was—would have to be unconscious or restrained face down when his jugular and both femoral arteries were cut. The tray caught the blood flow, but moments before death he was rolled onto his back."

"How do you figure that?" Parker asked.

"There is a degree of lividity, but not much, in the gluteus max and in the heels, which are hanging lower than the rest of the body," Ruth explained. "That tells me that the heart was still beating—but not for long—when he was posed like ET phoning home."

"That's not ET, it's Disco Man," Marek offered.

"God, here we go again," Angie moaned.

Parker looked from Ruth to Marek and then puzzled: "It's a signature," he said.

"Of what?" Ruth asked.

"Hel-lo!" Parker crowed. "Am I the only one on-line here?"

"More than likely," Kit muttered.

Parker waved towards The Red. "This is obviously a secret ritual killing of some poor bastard by a bunch of raving bloody lezzos," he pronounced, giving Kit a cursory sneer before looking pointedly at his number one suspect—the rather surprised Angie Nichols.

Kit prepared a clench-fisted launch from her bar stool, until she realized that Marek's hold on her was only half-hearted. She settled down before he decided to let her go through with it.

"That's a moderately idiotic assumption," Ruth commented.

"You reckon?" Parker said.

"Oh Chuck, you ignorant little hetero," Kit sighed, in a tone so calm it was scary.

Marek released her completely and shoved his hands in his pockets, while Angie's low-voiced "Katy" was a definite warning—but for whom?

Kit smiled ... like a taipan. "I'm only going to explain this to you *once*, Senior Sergeant," she said. "By their very nature, lesbian rituals don't actually involve men in any way, shape, or form; nor in any condition—dressed, undressed, dead, or alive. That's the best thing about them, our rituals I mean, they are exclusively to and for women. They are the ultimate women's business—but there's *nothing* secret about that."

"Well, *I'd* like to point out," Angie smiled, "that it's also not much of a secret if one of the alleged raving lezzos calls the cops."

"On top of which," Marek said, "apart from being quite prematurely dead, Disco Man is not some 'poor bastard.' That there is Gerry Anders, head thug of the Riley clan and youngest nephew of Queen Marj herself. And he may be late, but I doubt he'll be much lamented."

"No way!" Parker exclaimed, scurrying back to take a better look at his homicide victim.

"You knew who he was?" Kit said. "So why did you ask us ...? Oh, okay; dumb question."

"Would someone explain why this pronouncement has got the little man's jocks all twisted," Angie requested. "What's the Rilycan?"

"The Riley clan," Kit enunciated. "You know, Angie: one of Melbourne's biggest, wealthiest, meanest, most notorious, um, dangerous ..."

Marek held up both hands, "Bad, bad, very bad ..."

"... families," Kit continued. "It's headed by the sixty-something matriarch Marjorie Riley—aka Queen Marj or Queenie."

"Nuh-uh, Queenie's in her seventies now, Kit," Marek corrected.

"Oh, I suppose she would be by now," Kit said thoughtfully.

"The Riley family business goes way back to Melbourne's boom years in the 1920s," Marek explained to Angie.

Unnecessarily, Kit thought, because her friend looked shocked rather than uninformed.

"But it was in the Depression and the war years that they really made it big. They grew rich on misery, or rather on helping folks escape the misery with gambling, opium dens, brothels, smuggling."

"Opium dens?" Angie exclaimed.

"Yeah. These days it's brothels, coke, and protection rackets. They've always maintained a host of legitimate businesses so they can insist, regularly, that having underworld connections does not make them criminals. But the Rileys *are* the Melbourne underworld; every serious bad guy in town is connected through them. Their decades-long, adversarial relationship with us has almost become a game with its own rules of engagement and ..."

"Stop!" Angie's voice was verging on the hysterical. "Are you saying I have a dead gangster in my bar?"

"Kind of," Kit acknowledged.

"Bloody hell!" was Parker's reaction from the dance room.

"That's a fucking understatement!" Angie declared. "Please, someone—anyone—tell me *what* a dead gangster is doing in my bar."

"I think that would be my question," Parker said, returning to the fray.

"Well don't look at me, Sunshine," Angie snarled at him. "*You* are the homicide detective; go detect something." She turned back to Marek and Kit. "Do you think you could get him out of here now, or soon?"

"Who? Chucky?" Kit smiled.

Parker's objection was overtaken by Angie's. "No goddamnit, the dead dude. Get him out before, before ... I don't know, before the other gangsters find out he's here. Here and *dead*."

"How about it, Ruth?" Marek asked.

"Who's in charge here?" Parker demanded. "Ah," he said a bare second later, when it obviously occurred to him that it probably wasn't him—outranked as he was by Jon Marek, acting Head of the Homicide Squad, and by Dr. Ruth Hudson FP, whose judgment alone could decide when the body was removed.

"Ruth?" Marek repeated.

She shrugged. "I'm finished; the autopsy is scheduled; the video and photos, as far as I know, have all been done; my team are finishing up; and I think Cathy is waiting for you."

"Or me," Parker said softly.

"Why don't you go find out, then," Marek prompted. He waited until Parker was out of earshot before smacking himself on the wrist. "I wish I could control myself."

"Why?" Kit asked. "He doesn't."

"True." Marek turned to Angie. "Dr. Hudson will arrange for the guvvy undertakers to remove the body asap. I'm afraid you will have to remain closed until Parker's crew is satisfied that the scene is secure. I'll get one of the other officers to take statements from your mates so they can all leave. Make sure you give some kind of contact info for the nickname who had to go to work, so that Cathy can do a follow up with her. Okay?"

"Yeah. Thanks, Jonno," Angie said. "How long will I have to keep the doors shut?"

Marek shrugged. "Unless there's anything suss, probably only until tomorrow. We'll see."

"I'd like to take your statement now, Ms. Nichols."

Aaghh! Chucky III—the Nightmare Continues, Kit thought.

"You're kidding!" Angie snapped at Parker. "So far I've *stated the facts*, as far as I know them, to the local cop who came first; then to the local CIB detectives, then to *their* Inspector. This was followed by a quite detailed statement to *your* Senior Detective Martin, then to Detective Inspector Marek—congratulations on the promotion by the way, Jonno—and now *you* want to hear the same thing again. Can't any of you read what the one before you wrote down? Don't you think this is overkill?"

"Compared to what? The deceased over there?" Parker queried, still trying to make some kind of point despite his passing look of horror at the disclosure that his prime suspect was on familiar terms with his boss.

"Lighten up, Charlie," Marek suggested. "She's right. If you need *more* information, I'm sure Angie will be happy to oblige later. Let's you and I go find out what else we need to find out now."

Kit watched them saunter back to the crime scene, where Parker stopped in the wide open doorway of The Red, unaware that they hadn't walked far enough away.

"I don't want to seem out of order, Jon," he said, "but I really think it's inappropriate that you talk to me like that in front of ... well, in front of anyone."

"Yeah, you're right; I'm sorry, Charlie," Marek apologized. "But, mate, you get what you give." Marek brushed his hand back and forth through his snowy-white hair.

Uh-oh, Kit thought.

"What does that mean, Marek?" Parker asked.

Oh goody, Kit amended. You asked for it, Chucky.

"It means that *you* bring every kind of grief possible on yourself, mate. You're an A-Grade wanker, Charlie, and you have to learn some manners or people will continue to treat you the same way you treat them—badly and rudely."

"But I'm a cop."

Marek shook his head in astonishment. "Chuck, that response is so stupid and irrelevant that I'm at a loss for ... You've lost me. I will say this, though: leave your prejudices at home and do not hassle or insult these women in any way, because I *will* hear about it; and while you are in charge of your crew, Senior Detective Martin is in charge of *this* investigation. You weren't here, so I made her lead investigator. Any problems with that?"

"None, Boss. It was her turn anyway."

"Good," Marek ushered Parker into The Red. "Now, why were you late?"

"Tell me," Angie whispered to Kit, "why *didn't* you shoot that moron on behalf of the entire police force all those years ago?"

"I'm not altogether sure now," Kit replied thoughtfully.

"It was an oversight on your part, I believe."

"There's *no* doubt about that," Kit agreed. "Who was the Carrie thing over there with Rabbit et al?"

"She's a newby. A brand new not-quite-sure newby, I gather. Her name's Carrie McDermid. She was here last night, for the first time; and came back today with Sal and Booty."

"What's with the tape recorder?"

"Dunno. You want me to find out?"

"Yeah, but later. I don't want to make a big deal about it, in case SuperChuck notices."

Chapter 2

"It was so gross, though, Booty."

"Yeah, Sal. But it was us who found it. We're, like, the key witnesses. How cool is that?"

"Not."

"Sal's right, Booty," Kit noted. "There's nothing cool about finding that dead guy. What's more, you're only a witness to the finding of it, so you're not really a key anything."

"Spoil our fun, why don't you," Booty grumbled. "Just coz you've seen it all before."

"That's how she knows it's not cool," Sal pointed out. "You can stop here, thanks, Kit."

Kit, who'd offered to drop Sal and Booty in Gertrude Street on her way home, pulled her car in behind a parked courier van to let them out, with silent relief. Usually intrigued by other people's response to unrelated-to-them real-life murder, Kit wished she'd forgone the previous ten minutes with the blow-by-blow repeat-queen of Fitzroy. While Kit fully understood the macabre fascination with finding a body, and knew it would give everyone at Angie's something to talk about for a long time, she was glad she recognized more of herself in Sal's reaction to the experience. Neither of them was reveling in the gruesome attention to detail that came with Booty's fifth recounting of their shared close encounter of the end kind.

But, unusual as it was, Kit wasn't going to hazard a guess about why Sal was not as enthralled as Booty, because even her own lack of thrall had nothing to do with the latter's been there, done that, tick it off diagnosis. Kit didn't dwell on it simply because she knew it wasn't good for her; but Sal only knew why Sal wasn't beside herself with interest. Actually, Kit didn't know either woman well enough to be sure how honest their reactions were. Sal Armstrong might in truth be seething with curiosity, but be too polite to show it, or too worried about how she might come across; while Mary "Booty" Jones could be in such a state of shock that all she could do was babble.

One thing Sal and Booty did have in common was that neither had arrived at the moment when the body became a person. The realization that *it* had been a *him*, with a life, was still to come; although, as they waved goodbye, Kit realized there was a chance that for them the two things might never connect. The dead guy they'd found might forever remain safely just "the body"—to keep it inanimate and away from them, to keep violent death away from their safe little lives.

To Kit, however, Gerry Anders—the body and the man—had to be one, and more than just a homicide victim. She could pretend all she liked to laugh Death right in his ugly old kisser, but if she suddenly found herself inured to the death of him, of Anders, then she'd have to question not only her reality but her purpose. Recognizing the dead was the only way she could fight the consequences of the bad things in the world that kept nudging against her place in it.

Jeez, O'Malley! What's with the psychobabble she wondered, turning left into Nicholson. Get a grip. You know that as far as you're concerned, shit just happens; and that from now on Sal and Booty's dinner-table yarns *will* begin "we found him, you know, that dead gangster." Yeah, she argued. But that will apply only to the *other* Gerry Anders, the one they're about to discover through the media when the newspapers and TV run this story into a marathon.

Kit shuddered. Oh, and are *they* ever going to have a rave with this one. It'll be the biggest beat-up of the year, featuring intimate, gory, scandalous details of the late Gerry Anders, nephew of Queenie Riley, whose naked body—his not hers—was found in North Fitzroy's soon-to-be ultra-notorious lesbian vortex of sex, bloody rituals, and other iniquitous goings-on. And the rumors! Rife, rife, bloody-rife will be the speculation about gay-Melbourne's

20

connection with every crook and criminal activity in town; while the *triple-merde* cherry at the top of every story will be the "exposure" of the city's secret lesbian vampire cult.

"Think I'll go to New Zealand until this blows over," Kit told her dashboard, then remembered a nice distracting something she'd offered to do for Del. Instead of making a homeward left turn into the broad expanse of Victoria Parade, she continued straight on into the city center grid, then hooked right into Lonsdale Street in an attempt to get near enough to Swanston Street for a quick walk to Slowglass Books.

This was not a simple process. It should have been simple, but it wasn't because in the city there was never a parking space where you needed it, *all* traffic everywhere was being diverted around and around the CBD for no reason whatsoever, and four-thirty in the arvo was an idiotic time to drive in Melbourne.

After circling several blocks, Kit finally gave up and parked at the north end of Swanston and jumped on a tram that took her back down past the green-domed State Library. Moments later she vented justifiable getting-*off*-a-tram rage towards the taxi-bastard who didn't think the huge green tram's STOP indicator applied to him and, as a consequence, scared her f/f-hormone into wailing *fright* by screeching to a halt one inch from her knees.

After regrouping—and vaguely wondering how, given that there was only one of her—Kit ducked into the sci-fi fantasy shop as fast as humanly possible. She took just enough time to pick up the fifth novel in a trilogy for Del, but not enough time to be seduced into spending all her money on those books that she didn't yet have, but really wanted.

Kit took a tram back to her car and then swore at the traffic all the way home to Richmond in between singing along badly to Roy, then Dusty, then the Pretenders. She finally turned off Swan and into her side street, pressed the button on her new garage door opener, and felt ridiculously pleased at the perfectly timed door-up car-in maneuver. Parking at the bottom of the outside stairs to her apartment, she noted, for the thirteenth time since its installation, that the thing her remote control opened was a misnomer incarnate, because there was no actual garage, just a door. Small things and small minds, O'Malley, she observed, and then noticed the time.

"Bloody hell! Twenty minutes to drive 4.2 kilometers! What a serious waste of a lot of important things like ... like time, oxygen, brain cells, petrol, life, Wednesday."

No, that was yesterday, O'Malley, she thought. Today be Thursday.

Kit glared at the challenge offered by the back stairs to her first-floor habitat and then, for the usual vertiginous reasons, turned her back on them in defeat. She had no choice. It would be so uncool for a grown woman, a professional woman, a private investigator no less, to freeze halfway up or down those evil planks, convinced that she could fall through—not off—but down through the gaps in the stairs. That's so illogical and, like, impossible she reminded herself. Again.

Katherine Frances O'Malley escorted herself out into the street, closed her not-garage door behind her, then shook her head as she was forced to concede: okay, one person *can* regroup. And, having done so, she strolled into Swan Street, then stomped in through the front door of Aurora Press and just stood there, arms akimbo, as if she had a dramatic announcement.

"Whoa," remarked the ever-observant Brigit. "A très-serious individual has arrived."

"Ah," Del mused, "but will this be a typical O'Malley gross exaggeration of a minor event, or is the sky really falling in this time?"

"You have no idea, Del Fielding," Kit exclaimed, holding up her friend's book, "how close I came to cactus, by running this wee errand for you. I was an inch and a nanosecond away from being taxied-flat in Swanston Street."

"Oh darling, I'm sorry," Del mocked. "Do you have bruises?"

"No," Kit grinned. "But I do have the lowdown on a late-breaking scandal in exchange for a cuppa and, ah, one of those cakes I see over there."

Del's partner in love and business leaped to her feet with such agility that Kit imagined that Brigit's ample body was made entirely of flummery. Brigie's reputation as a gossip junkie meant that, given the right incentive, she was capable of motion lighter-than-air and faster-than-light.

"Speak," Brigit demanded, placing a mug of coffee and a pastry on a plate on the corner of Del's desk in the same moment that Kit took a seat in the armchair next to it.

Kit obliged. "I have spent most of the afternoon at Angie's overseeing the consequences of our dear friend finding a naked, blood-drained *bloke* and *ex*-crook posed in a huge tray like," she flung her right arm up to demonstrate, "like ET on a feverish Saturday night."

Del was shaking her head to indicate something like ...

"What, who? Where did she find what?" Del asked.

... Ah, confusion, Kit realized.

"Angie found a dead man." Brigit was so helpful. "Where, Kit?"

"In The Red," Kit replied. "In a very big dish thing."

"In a what? Why?" Del asked.

"Buggered if I know," Kit shrugged.

"Well who, then?" Del asked.

"Gerry Anders: late of the notorious Riley family; nephew of matriarch Marj herself; estranged husband of Poppy Barton-Anders, herself a one-time Saturday Show dancer now weight-loss guru; father of three or four Gerry juniors; owner—woops, past tense— of the very hip Moshun Club; suspected killer of drug dealers Mike and Julie Sherwood; and, what else, oh yeah, currently under investigation for arson, kidnapping, and a lot of parking fines."

"Good God!" Del exclaimed.

"No such thing," Kit noted.

"Rewind," Brigit requested.

Kit licked custard off her fingers. "Which bit?"

"To the bit about the bloke being naked and drained of blood. In fact, from the start."

Kit filled them in on every little detail, suddenly feeling just like Booty the Crime Scene Queen but without her nose-studs and cowboy boot tattoo.

"Oh," Del sighed, "this is going to be a brutal QPRD."

"A what?" Kit asked.

"A Queer Public Relations Disaster," Brigit explained.

Kit laughed. "Also awkward for our Angie, who might be in a spot of bother with the law."

"Why? Angie didn't kill him," Del pronounced.

Kit shrugged.

"Don't be ridiculous, Kit!" Del reprimanded. "You can't even think it's a possibility."

"Didn't say I did, Del. But Detective Senior Sergeant Parker already has his own unique take on this bizarre little crime."

"But you said the Cathy detective was in charge," Brigit reminded her.

"Yeah, but Chucky's in charge of her and, ultimately, everything."

"Except Marek," Del pronounced.

"Except Marek. Thank um, who," Kit hesitated. "Thank the Police Commissioner; may she reign forever more."

"Is she one of us?" Brigit asked.

"Who? The Police Commissioner?"

"No, Kit," Brigit frowned. "The Cathy-in-charge."

"I've no idea, Brigie. She only gave her name, rank, and that's it. She didn't offer any other credentials and I didn't ask."

"And you couldn't tell?" Brigit was astonished. "Kit, I do hope that being in love is not affecting your gaydar."

"Brigie, honey, a woman in uniform is a woman in uniform—a fine sight to behold whichever direction she may head after work," Kit smiled.

"Yeah, of course," Brigit agreed, "unless she's got a face like a twisted old boot or the back end of a bus. Then even a uniform isn't going to help."

"Bite your tongue, Brigit Wells."

"I won't," Brigit declared. "Del, I don't care what you think, I refuse to kowtow to the kind of political correctness that denies me my aesthetic sense. Not to mention …"

"But you're going to anyway," Del interrupted.

Brigit gave her woman a snarly look. "Sooner or later we have to face a simple fact of nature that some women are just plain ugly. And accepting that doesn't mean that they can't be our best friends, unless they're ugly on the inside too, in which case we don't have to like them at all. But, damn it, if I can admit that I'm fat, then Barbara bloody Juniper can admit she's really fucking ugly."

"Who is Barbara Juniper?" Kit queried.

"Don't ask, Kit," Del sighed. "And don't go there, Brigit. I do not want to hear it again."

Brigit pouted, but gave Kit an "I'll tell you later" nod. "So, what can we do to help Angie?"

Kit shrugged. "The cops shooed us all out and told Angie to go home. She'll ring if she needs us, but Julia is due back from her Dad's tonight, so I think Angie will be fine, for now."

"Good," Del said. "And what about you?"

"Me?" Kit was puzzled. "I'm okay."

Her friend's headshake was supremely patronizing. "Your coffee's having its own private breakdown, then, is it?"

Kit looked at the mug in her right hand and discovered, to her surprise, that it was vibrating. Must be post-tram-and-traffic-rage, she thought. "Curious," she said.

"Curious my arse," Brigit noted. "You're in shock."

"From what?" Kit was genuinely clueless.

"You are hopeless, Katherine O'Malley," Del laughed. "The things you've been through lately would do a normal person's head in. And now you've just spent the arvo with another violently murdered person and you don't know why you have the shakes."

Kit held her empty hand out in front of her. Ooh, it *was* shaking. "I spent the afternoon with Angie, Marek, and the Scooter gang, minus Scooter, *not* the dead guy."

"That's not the point and you know it," Del said, standing so that all six-feet of her loomed over Kit. "Come on, you're coming home with us tonight. At least for dinner."

"Good plan," Brigit agreed.

"It's a lovely plan, thank you," Kit agreed, "but I can't. I'm meeting Enzo for dinner."

"What? Just Enzo?"

"Yes, Brigie, just Enzo. Alex is still in Sydney."

"There is a high level of weirdness in your current relationship, Kit," Brigit noted.

"Tell me about it," Kit nodded, getting up to take her mug and plate over to the sink to rinse them. Having a couple of Immigration agents tailing your new girlfriend's new husband and, therefore, quite often the girlfriend as well, was bad enough. But trying to

25

carry on some semblance of a courtship with the new girlfriend, while accommodating her new husband's predicament was confusing and frustrating. None of which had anything to do with why she was meeting Enzo for dinner tonight, but would no doubt confuse Bill and Ben the Feral Feds, who didn't seem to want to give up their suspicions about the divine Lorenzo McAllister not being a genuine husband to the gorgeous Alexis Cazenove.

"Yo, Kit!" The name-calling was obviously a repeat performance.

"Sorry, Brigie. What?"

"Why are you dining with Enzo, if Alex is not even in town?"

"Why not?" Kit asked. "Also, he might have a job for me." Kit raised a finger. "And, before you ask, no I don't know what it is yet."

Brigit closed her mouth.

Enzo McAllister, a picture of sartorial splendor in a Sean Connery-in-a-tuxedo-kind of way, sat elegantly in a Windsor Hotel armchair, deep in conversation with a spindly, skinny-nosed woman who was wearing too much jewelry and not enough lipstick. Enzo's slightly receding dark, with flashes of gray, collar-length hair, and his soft brown eyes and lilting Scottish-from-Lincoln accent combined to give him an air of distinguished trustworthiness. A historian and genealogist by occupation, he was also a concert pianist who preferred playing Broadway tunes and cool jazz—which he did, four nights a week at Dorothy's Caviar Bar. A Scottish-Italian, wannabe-Australian, recently married gay man, Enzo was also one of the most warm-hearted and honorable blokes Kit had met in a long time—in fact, ever.

She watched from a distance as he schmoozed his latest client by oh-so-respectfully charming her into feeling like his favorite aunty. Having never seen Enzo in action before, Kit was enviously fascinated by his technique. Actually she'd never considered there'd be this kind of in-action aspect to being a genealogist; but now that she knew better she wondered whether he'd give her lessons in the genteel art of sucking-up.

Not that she couldn't be all grace and politeness if she had to, she just couldn't maintain the charade if her heart wasn't in it. Any client who entered her world on a pedestal of self-importance, because of wealth or power or other related misconceptions of worth, would discover pretty bloody quickly that any kind of *attitude* would be ignored. After they'd signed her contract, of course. She'd give any rich bastard a chance, but expectations of more for less would be given short shrift; they'd get no more time or effort than she gave Joan Pinter, the pensioner next door, who regularly hired Kit to track down her no-good son.

All that being thought, she was prepared to behave herself for Enzo's benefit. She looked down at her bottle-green silk shirt, black trousers, and sensible leather shoes, and was therefore rather glad she'd decided not to challenge the old-fashioned sensibilities of the regular Windsor patrons—this client, in particular—by wearing her purple leather pants and runners.

"Ah, Kit," Enzo said, standing as she approached. He took her hand in his, kissed each cheek, and then turned back to Mrs. Skinny-Nose to make the introductions. "Sarah Boyes-Lang, this is my dear friend and," he lowered his voice, "private investigator, Kit O'Malley."

Sarah Boyes-Lang, who didn't stand for the handshake, stretched her mouth into something that looked a little less like a cat's bum and said: "This is quite something. I've never met a private eye before."

Kit smiled politely. At least Mrs. Beaky—*behave* O'Malley— hadn't added the dreaded gender-specific adjective, she thought.

"There can't be many of *you* in town," Mrs. B-L continued. "Women, I mean."

Oh-kay! Kit raised her eyebrows. "You'd be surprised," she said. "I actually know quite a few women in town."

Shut *up*, O'Malley!

Too late. Sometimes knowing stuff about someone before you meet them is really not a good thing. Especially because Kit knew she was just as prone as anyone to forming opinions based on cliché, rumor, and her own prejudices which, like it or not, she did have despite several DIY exorcisms.

But, honestly! Sarah Boyes-Lang could be mounted and exhibited as the cliché of affluent clichés. She was obscenely wealthy, without having done a day's work in her life; had disinherited her son for becoming an actor instead of a lawyer; had divorced three husbands because she was bored with them; had been a highly financial member of the political disaster known as the TrueBlue Party; was a founder of the Diana Club, a bunch of tally-ho women who routinely chased foxes to death; and belonged to the Wilma Foundation, a group of nutty, filthy-rich women whose idea of "community work" included thousand-dollar-a-plate dinners to raise money for the foundation's own spa and health resort in Daylesford. The head of the Boyes-Lang family was only 56-years-old, which, in this century, was way too young to be dressing, as she did, like a stitched-up vicar's wife. Mind you, there was the pig's ear and silk purse thing to consider because, to paraphrase dear Brigit, this woman was singularly unattractive and, oh, talking to her …

"What would you like to drink, Miss O'Malley?"

A slippery nipple, Kit thought. "A single malt would be lovely," she said taking a seat. "And please, *Sarah*, call me Katherine."

Kit smiled. She always kept a smidgen of politeness in reserve; mostly so as not to embarrass other people like the now relieved-looking Enzo McAllister, but only friends and humans got to call her Kit. She shrugged, grinned at Enzo, and waited patiently to be filled in. After a lot of very small talk while they waited for their drinks, Sarah Boyes-Lang finally switched from her superficially chatty face to her serious business face, seemingly just by stretching her neck and squinting, whereon Enzo sat forward and clasped his hands between his knees.

"Sarah would like to hire your services, Kit, Katherine," he began, "if you think they are appropriate for a rather delicate issue."

Sarah nodded.

"If *I* think they're appropriate?" Kit repeated.

Sarah nodded again. "If you think you can help."

"Oh. Okay," Kit smiled. Get on with it, she thought.

"Sarah's daughter, Vanessa, has been seeing an American who claims he's a descendant of the Russian royal family," Enzo explained.

Kit raised her eyebrows. "Do you mean *seeing* as in he's imaginary?"

28

"No dear, he's quite real," Sarah said. "We're just not sure about his lineage."

"Who's we?" Kit asked, somehow knowing it didn't include Vanessa.

"Lorenzo is checking his background for me."

Ah, the royal we, Kit thought. "Oh, Enzo, he's not saying he's related to Anastasia."

"No," Enzo laughed. "Says he's the great-nephew of a minor Russian duchess, who emigrated to America in 1917."

"Good timing. So this guy is, what, American of Russian descent with possible blue blood? I don't understand why you need me."

"Vanessa met Gregor while in Greece on her way to England two months ago," Sarah explained. "He was, he said, traveling the world before returning to New York to finish the studies he'd begun in Moscow, where he'd been living for six years. Nessa brought him home to Melbourne and they've been partying like there's no tomorrow ever since."

"Is that bad?" Kit asked.

"Good or bad is not the issue," Sarah stated, waggling her head until she stopped suddenly, as if a thought had entered it. "Oh my! Unless they're doing recreational drugs or …" She threw up her hands. "Oh, but that's not the issue either. What I want to know is *what* a 37-year-old foreigner would see in my 24-year-old daughter."

Kit laughed. She couldn't help herself. "You mean apart from the obvious?"

"Ah! You mean my money," Sarah agreed, pleased that Kit understood.

You selfish old tart, Kit thought. "I meant that Vanessa is an exceptionally good looking young woman," she smiled. And she wasn't just being polite. Nor was she guessing that even a fifty percent improvement on Mother B-L, had to at least put daughter on the plain side of good looking. Kit had, in fact, seen a photo of Vanessa Boyes-Lang at Enzo's place on the weekend, before any mention of this possible job had come up.

"Well, yes, she is pretty, but …"

"But you're worried about her nonetheless," Kit said, catching sight of the frown that was controlling Enzo's amusement.

29

"I am. There's the age difference, the fact that he is a foreigner, and, yes, I don't mind admitting there is also the possible gold-digger aspect to their whirlwind romance."

"Maybe it will blow over. Holiday romances quite often do," Kit said, giving a passing thought to Genevieve and Firenze and the rain and Genevieve and the passion and …

"They plan to announce their engagement next month," Enzo said, bringing her back to the Windsor and up to date.

"Oh," Kit said thoughtfully. "Why am I here?"

"I wish to ascertain whether he is genuine."

"Um," Kit shook her head, "I don't do fidelity tests."

"I wasn't expecting you to," Sarah looked confused. "I didn't know you could."

"I can't. I mean, I don't," Kit stated categorically.

Sarah raised her hands. "I meant, Katherine, that I didn't know there was such a service. I simply want to know if Gregor Tereshenko is the genuine article. If he is who he says he is, then I suppose I will *have* to believe that he loves my daughter."

Yeah right. Kit could almost see Sarah's cogs slipping around trying to figure out how one goes about fidelity testing a potential in-law.

"Does he have money?" Kit asked her.

"He seems to."

"Could he be royal Russian offspring?" she asked Enzo.

"Possibly. I'm still researching."

"So, again, why am I here?"

Sarah Boyes-Lang sighed a sigh that hinted it was a sad thing indeed that her world had come to this. "I'd like you to check him out, Katherine, to make sure that his own history is legitimate. Lorenzo is investigating the family tree aspect because it's part of Gregor's story, but I don't really care about his claim to royalty …"

Pig's bum, Kit thought. Sarah's lie had been delivered with the dead-give-away eye twitch.

"… but I do care about his *life*. I need to have it verified that he is the independently well-off only son of New York doctors; that he was studying in Russia; and that he was on the Grand Tour en route home to America. Is that an investigation appropriate to your agency?"

30

"Oh yes. My agency has a high success rate with cases like this." Kit rubbed her eye.

"I feel a great sense of relief knowing the two of you are on my side. Hopefully we'll be able to resolve this before any announcement is made. I do so hate being suspicious."

Kit pulled a standard contract from her briefcase. "Well, just think Sarah, if Comrade Tereshenko had come fully equipped with proof, then Lorenzo and I would *still* be needed to find out why he would go about the world with that proof in his pocket."

To help Enzo maintain his straight-faced impression, Kit began quietly explaining her rates of investigation to one of the richest women in Melbourne, while wondering why no one had yet invented a lipstick that *didn't* come off all over glassware and linen serviettes. Or if they had, why no one had told Mrs. Richer-Than-A-Supermodel about it.

Three hours later Kit lounged against Enzo's kitchen bench, watching him in his element—or rather one of them. They had dined together, sans their mutual client, at a Thai restaurant in the city and were now about to partake of coffee and exotic liqueur out on Enzo's eighth-floor balcony. Kit had agreed to venture outside only because the evening was unseasonably warm and on the condition that she was not required to approach the edge for any reason. After Melbourne's lack of summer—or rather enough hot days in a row to designate an actual season—most of the population now took every advantage of any sign of warmth to pretend that April and autumn weren't already dragging them towards winter.

Enzo handed Kit a coffee and a glass of something sticky and ushered her outside onto *Enzo's* balcony. Kit smiled. He was not exactly the association she usually made with this piece of overhanging real estate. Oh, no. Her true and lasting, tingling memory of this tiny terrace high, high above the street way way below, was that night in January; that first night; that hot, wild, sexy, trembling, breathtaking … stop it! She shook her head. Okay, O'Malley, she thought. Balcony, you, Alex, sex, vivid! But you can sit out here without the orgasmic flashback.

"Are you okay?" Enzo asked.

"Fine," Kit squeaked as she sidled into the nearest chair closest to the door.

"Tell me more about this crime family you're investigating," Enzo prompted, taking a seat against the railing and leaning his head back into the high night breeze.

"Enzo, I am *not* investigating the Rileys."

"But you'll have to, won't you, to find out who left the naked nephew at Angie's?"

"I'm not allowed to investigate homicides and I wouldn't want to investigate this one," Kit said emphatically.

Enzo looked puzzled. "But Kit, you do, you have. It was because of a homicide that you met Alex. Not to mention that mess in Collingwood earlier this month."

Kit shrugged. "I wasn't investigating that mess in Collingwood, I just ended up in it. And, technically, I met Alex because I was checking out a philandering husband."

"Oh, I see," Enzo smiled, "it depends how you word it."

"No. Private investigators are not supposed to get involved in murder investigations. Apart from which, they usually have no reason to. Me? I just keep turning up in the wrong bloody place at the most inopportune times."

"What if this cop starts hassling Angie because he has no other leads?" Enzo asked.

"Then Angie could hire me for any number of things, such as: to act as her bodyguard; to check the security of her premises to ascertain how an unauthorized person managed to gain access; to find out, very quietly, whether a recently deceased member of a prominent local family had any connections to any of The Terpsichore's patrons; or, perhaps, to see whether the now-departed had any designs—legitimate or ill—on the business, unlikely, or the site it occupies."

Enzo looked worried. "If the latter were the case, then Angie would have to know about it; and *that* scenario could prove incriminating for her."

"True," Kit acknowledged. "And that would also mean sussing out the Rileys, something no sane person would do without the backing of the entire Victorian police force."

"Or another crime family," Enzo suggested.

"Yeah," Kit said, as if that was a good idea. "Except it was probably another crime family that killed Gerry." She pursed her lips. "I could go undercover, forever, to find someone willing to cross the Rileys. But they pull so many strings in this town that it wouldn't even pay for their rivals or enemies to shop them, let alone their cohorts who'd know more.

"The best way to help Angie, should Chucky Parker get lazy and try blaming everything on her, would be to work out *why* the body was left at the Terpsichore."

"Was he killed there, or just deposited?" Enzo asked.

"Ruth Hudson, the forensic pathologist, reckons he was killed elsewhere. There were blood slops near the emergency exit inside and a couple of little puddles in the lane out the back."

"Blood slops," Enzo repeated, pulling a disgusted face.

"The guy had very little left inside him, Enzo. It had to go somewhere."

Enzo wiggled his shoulders as if to cast off a nasty feeling. "Well, my dear, it seems like you've given this murder case you're not investigating quite a bit of thought."

"Hey, I was there," Kit threw her palms up and grinned. "And I can't help myself, Enzo. That, and the fact that I'm *really* pissed off that someone trespassed in *our* space; that they left a dead naked male in our space; and that The Terpsichore seems to have been chosen specifically to draw maximum attention to … to I don't know what. And *that* pisses me off too.

"But, as I have no client and no facts other than a dead man in a place no man should be, dead or alive, then anything I might be mulling is half-baked and borderline ridiculous."

"Ooh, you're scowling, my precious," Enzo declared. "It's bad for the complexion. We need to change the subject. And we need more caffeine." Enzo sauntered inside and returned with the coffee pot. "Now, can young Hector really trace Gregor Tereshenko's movements?"

"Sure," Kit smiled. "It took Hector a couple of days last month to find the actual bloke in Adelaide that someone else was impersonating in Victoria, so I doubt he'd have trouble tracing the movements of a traveling Russian-American. Unless Tereshenko is a complete phoney."

"To be perfectly honest Kit, I found him to be quite charming. He appears to be smitten with Vanessa and she … What? Why are you looking like you've just had a thought worth voicing but haven't finished translating it yet?" he asked. He finished pouring the coffee.

"Because Enzo," Kit beamed, "I was thinking that we should ask those Feral Feds of yours to check on Gregor for us. They could be productive while they're watching you and Alex, when she's here, get on with your ordinary every-day married life."

Enzo groaned. "I just wish those silly bastards would get their own lives and leave us alone. They've been loitering in our affairs for months now; it's way too long."

"Yeah well, our *affairs* are probably the problem, Enzo," Kit laughed.

"You've got that right, honey, but how long are we going to have to hide them?"

"Don't know. I've never before been party to what amounts to a fraud perpetrated against the government of this great nation. So I don't know how long we'll be surveilled."

"God, Kit, I do hope we're not involving you in a crisis of conscience, or a moral dilemma from which you may never recover your … your morals."

Kit blew a raspberry. "When the man at the top of our pile of politicians can say 'I'm sorry' and explain the difference between a promise, a core promise, and an oath that isn't just bad language, then I'll start to worry about whether my actions conflict with what he says my morals should be."

"Katherine O'Malley," Enzo laughed, "you are without question one of my most favorite people."

Chapter 3

Sand palm tree tidal pool, crab scuttling from a crevice over crimson seaweed swaying in the shallows, not swaying spreading, liquefying blossoming out, coating the surface sticky red, reaching for incoming surf sounds awesome, threatening, howling yowling *Raoul Manuel* ... Kit sat bolt upright! Home, kitchen bench, radio, hungry meowing cat. Whoa.

"Thistle, thank you," Kit breathed, "bad dream that was." She leaned over so The Cat could affectionately head-butt her cheek. Thistle had other ideas: she bit Kit on the chin.

"You harlot!" Kit swore. "One of these days I'll bite you back."

Thistle turned her back and flicked her tail, allegedly giving serious thought to what she'd do next—*after* breakfast. She jumped off the bench and waited politely by her bowl.

Kit rolled her shoulders and stretched her neck a few times to remove the kink from having fallen asleep at the breakfast bar, again. She squinted at the kitchen clock—ten-thirty. Probably still a.m., she thought. She'd only dozed off for fifteen minutes this time.

"Thistle, honey," she said, getting up to feed the feline and finish making her first coffee for the day. "I hope you've been paying attention to how we humans do the phone thing, because if I fall off my stool after nodding off, and end up out cold on the floor," she shook some dry bits into the cat bowl, "then no amount of yowling in my ear for your breakfast will wake me. You'll have to pick up the receiver and *shit!*" Kit jumped as the phone rang. The second half of the milk she was pouring in Thistle's other bowl missed it completely, so she left the call to her machine while she cleaned up the mess—until she heard Angie's voice.

"Katy, if you're there could you pick up please? I need to speak to you and kinda need your help right now, on account of the fact that *Ma Baker and some of her sons*," she sang, "are here and ..."

"I'm here Angie," Kit said, snatching up the receiver after running, then skidding to a stop in her office.

"Thank the goddess, Katy, my love. Did you hear what I said?"

"Sort of," Kit said, "*Who* is there? And where?"

"I'm at the bar with Julia and Gwen and, ah," she lowered her voice, "a royal aunt and a couple of her henchmen."

"Queenie Riley is there?" Kit was astonished.

"Yeah. Do you think you could pop on over?"

"I'll be there in twenty minutes."

"You could bring anyone else who's around," Angie hinted.

"I'll bring reinforcements. Oh, Angie, do *not* argue with this woman. Make her coffee, answer her questions, do not get smart. See you soon."

Kit hung up and ran into her bedroom where she pulled on her jeans, swapped her shirt for a bra and a fresh T-shirt, and grabbed a shoe. She tore back out to the kitchen, threw several newspapers from the bench into the air before she found her wallet, keys, sunglasses, and phone, then crawled under her desk for her other shoe. So, Kit thought as she sat on the floor to put on her runners, Julia is back from her aunt's funeral in Bendigo and Gwen is ... Who is Gwen? Ah. Gwen the witch, one of Angie's mostly silent partners in the bar. But what the hell is Queenie Riley doing at the scene of the crime? Only one way to find out.

A minute later Kit was, as they say, hauling arse down the inside stairs to her upstairs apartment—oddly descendible at speed only because, in the case of emergencies, illogical fears *can* be over-ridden—and heading towards the second door along the ground floor corridor. The door nearest the bottom of her stairs, was the one to O'Malley Investigations; the other was the entrance to the hub of Del's and Brigit's feminist publishing empire.

Kit hoped like hell they were in and not busy. They were and they weren't, so they leaped to attention when Kit declared, "Angie needs us now. The gangsters have arrived. You lock up, I'll get the car and meet you out front."

◆◆◆

The large lawn in front of The Terpsichore had been taken over by a circus: a media circus; a police circus; a circus of protesters, already; and a lesbian support circus bolstered in turn by several drag queens who were probably just on their way home from last night.

Kit parked on the opposite side of the road so that she, Del, and Brigit could swear and shake their heads and wonder how on earth they were going to get through to Angie. Kit wondered if the Mob inside was as threatening as the mob outside; and voiced her amazement at the number of sightseers given there was nothing to see today, and that the murder had barely rated a mention in *The Age*—just all over the front page, half of page five, and an in-depth ready-written profile on the whole Riley clan on pages nine and ten.

"Then I imagine these folks are here," Brigit mused, "because of the barely off the verge of sensational coverage by all three commercial TV news programs last night."

"Ooh," Kit sneered as if she'd got a whiff of something foul. "I don't think *that's* good."

"Which part of all this very bad, is not good?" Del asked.

"That cute thirtyish redhead," Kit said. "Her name's Carrie; she was here yesterday."

"What's not good about *her*?" Del's tone signaled her visual appreciation.

"She's a maybe-baby dyke and she's talking to the press and that can't be good," Kit explained. "She won't have any insight into anything, except how bizarre it is to find a dead man on only your second visit to a women's bar."

"Odds on they'll make her the celebrity, then," Brigit foretold, opening the car door. "Come on. I think a bit of barging is in order."

"I knew Brigie's excursions to Mangle's gym would prove useful sooner or later," Kit commented to Del as they all got out.

"Please don't encourage her," Del begged, grabbing hold of Brigit's arm so they could flank Kit, but let her lead them through the throng.

"Yo, Kit!" It was Rabbit MacArthur, taking time out from stirring the Straight Virgin Christians, or whoever the protesters were, to draw everyone's attention to their arrival.

"Hey Rabbit, keep up the good fight," Kit called back, as she forged on towards the beleaguered-looking Cathy Martin. Kit nodded hello but waited while the Senior D had finished giving mob-control instructions to a uniformed officer.

"Good morning, O'Malley," Cathy sighed, with a smile.

"Bet you didn't think you'd have a carnival to contend with," Kit said.

Cathy pulled a "seen it all" face. "Murder, especially strange ones, always draws the nutty elements out for a perv." She lifted her chin towards the well-dressed, middle-aged couple standing on the sidelines, holding a sign with a crude sketch of an angel—or a pyramid wearing a frisbee—that promised: "God loves even the fallen—repent and know."

"Know what?" Kit asked.

"Beats me," Cathy replied. "But the reporters nearly had your mate for breakfast."

"Is Queenie Riley still here?"

"No," Cathy smiled. "She and her thugglies left five minutes ago. She came to see where Gerry had been found."

"What did you do?"

"I showed her," Cathy shrugged. "It's not like there was anything there for her to see. I drew the line at letting her talk to Ms. Nichols, who said she wouldn't unless you were with her, which is probably not a bad idea. No doubt Queenie will try again."

"Can we go in?"

Cathy glanced at Del and Brigit, who were loitering innocently behind Kit.

"Del Fielding, Brigit Wells," Kit pointed. As they stepped forward, unnecessarily, to shake the detective's hand, Kit finished the intro, "Detective Senior Constable Cathy Martin. We're Angie's next best thing to family, if that makes a difference."

Cathy smiled an okay. "I've already told Ms. Nichols she can have her bar back, but can't open again until tomorrow. So, if you could ask her not to let anyone *else* in until then," she glanced at Rabbit and her mates, "I'd be grateful. Oh, and before *you* go, O'Malley, can I ask you a favor?"

"You can ask," Kit agreed.

"Karen Farrell didn't go from here to work yesterday; and I can't find her. Could you …?"

"That's odd," Kit frowned. "I'll see what I can find out."

Kit had taken only three steps when she had to restrain Del from dragging *her* woman away by the scruff of her neck, after Brigie had quietly asked: "So Detective, are you a friend of Dorothy's?"

"Dorothy who?" Cathy Martin asked.

"Is there more than one?" Brigie queried, suggestively surprised.

"My mother's a Dorothy," Cathy said. "So is my landlady and my brother's cat."

"Brigit," Del snapped.

As Brigie turned on her heel to obey, Cathy winked at Kit, which meant no more than that she'd understood Brigie's impertinent question. Kit raised an eyebrow, rounded up her "reinforcements," and headed in to rescue Angie from a no-longer situation.

"It's about bloody time," she nonetheless exclaimed. "My yard is overrun with lunatics and perverts." Angie pushed a pile of pictures out of the way, then set out four cups on the bar.

"What happened to the gangsters?" Brigit asked. "I was hoping to meet the Queen Bee."

"See what I mean?" Angie pointed at Brigie. "Lunatics and perverts."

"Yeah, but *we* are the only ones that are allowed in," Kit said, as Angie half-filled the cups with espresso. "Where are Julia and Gwen?"

"Who wants cappuccino?" Angie asked, poised to pour the hot milk and ladle the froth. "Everyone? Good. Julia took Gwen home because she had to prepare a moon phase."

"Didn't know Gwen was that powerful," Kit noted.

"What? Oh. No, I meant …" she held up her hands. "I gather that we, as in the Earth, is/are in a perfect possie for an auspicious moon thing. Gwen's coven are chanting about it."

"Oh please!" Del moaned.

"Each to their own, Del," Angie insisted.

"Naturally," Del rolled her eyes. "But, given the circumstances," she stressed, "I do hope you didn't let any of those journos near your resident wicca expert. Your business partner being a witch is bound to send the lesbian vampire rumors into overdrive."

Kit laughed in agreement. "Yeah, I can just see the Hellmouth references in the headlines tomorrow. It's bad enough the reporters are out there interviewing Ms. McDerm ..."

Angie was shaking her head. "They're not."

"Yeah, they are. We saw them."

"Katy, they're not," Angie insisted. "*Carrie* is doing the interviews. She's a journalist."

"You mean she was here spying on us?" Brigit said, with fist-on-the-bar indignation.

"No, I don't think so," Angie said. She slapped a copy of the *North Star*, the local rag that covered Melbourne's northern suburbs, down on the bar. "I think she was here because she was here; but she got herself one hell of a story by being here."

"Yeah, but is she queer?" Brigie smirked.

"Darling?"

"Yes, Del? Oh, okay I'll shut up."

BLOOD-DRAINED MAN IN LESBIAN DISCO
by Carrie McDermid

"That's a screamer with a byline, if ever I've seen one," Del noted. "Read it please, Kit."

Kit took a breath. "Okay. *Alleged Melbourne crime lord Gerald 'Gerry' Anders was yesterday found murdered in a lesbian nightclub in North Fitzroy.* Crime lord?" she laughed. "That's a gross exaggeration of ..."

"O'Malley," Del interrupted. "Can you do it without the commentary? We can all get outraged afterwards."

"Yeah, okay. *The deceased's blood-drained body was found on a metal traylike box in the disco of The Terpsichore—a St. Georges Road bistro and dance club run by women for lesbians.*

"Aagghh! Sorry. *The dead man was found by the owner of the venue, Ms. Angela Nichols at 12:45 on Thursday afternoon. On discovering the body, which was suspended on a tray over the metal box which contained his blood, Ms. Nichols called the North Fitzroy police.*

"*According to local CIB Detective Ray Conway, the deceased— who was later identified as 47-year-old alleged career-criminal Gerry Anders—had bled to death. This was confirmed by the first Homicide Squad member on the scene, Detective Senior Constable Cathy Martin. The forensic pathologist Dr. Ruth Hudson declined to comment.*

"*Witnesses at the scene, when the body was discovered, claim they had no idea how the dead man could have got into the night-club, as it is only open to lesbians and other women. Men are usually not allowed in.* Do you suppose the idiot witness she quoted was herself?" Kit growled, before continuing.

"*Senior Sergeant Charles Parker, the man in charge of the murder investigation, stated that police already have a possible suspect*—the man's a fuckwit!—*that leads were being followed up and witness statements taken.*

"*The victim, Gerry Anders, who is a nephew of well-known Melbourne businesswoman Marjorie Riley, and husband of one-time Saturday Show dancer Poppy Barton, leaves behind his wife and three sons, Sean 25, Tom 22, and Mark 19.*

"*At the time of his death Mr. Anders was being investigated by Victoria Police over his role in the execution-style shootings of alleged drug importers Julie and Mike Sherwood. The bodies of the Sherwoods were found in their car in bush outside Woodend in late January.*

"*Anders was also about to face court on charges of assault against a patron of his popular dance venue the Moshun Club; and was recently questioned by the Arson Squad over his possible connection to three inner-city hotel fires.*

"*Anders spent five years in jail for armed robbery in the late eighties, and was arrested two years ago for the alleged kidnap-ping of Melbourne entrepreneur Alan Shipper. Those charges were dropped following the death of Mr. Shipper in a car accident before the trial.*

"*At this stage Gerry Anders' connection with The Terpsichore is unknown, but sources claim the late nightclub owner may have had a financial interest.* Bloody hell!" Kit finished.

"That's kind of what I said," Angie smiled.

41

"You want I should go out there and deal with the bitch?"

Everyone looked at Brigit Wells, considered her offer seriously, then snorted with laughter.

"Who on earth are these sources she's claiming?" Del asked.

"I have no idea," Angie stated.

"And you'd never met this Anders bloke before?" Del continued.

"Never," Angie threw her arms out. "Never met him, never seen him in passing, never spoken to him that I know of. I did not know he existed, until he didn't any more right here, most inconveniently, in my bar."

"And he has no financial interest in this business?" Kit queried, but only for verification.

"If you mean did he have a financial stake in our bar, then no, most absolutely not," Angie stated. "If you mean did he have an interest in *wanting* to have a financial interest in the bar, then, difficult as it is, you'll have to ask him because—never having met Gerry Anders or ever spoken to him—I wouldn't have a clue what he had an interest in. And now that he's quite dead, I'm not ever likely to find out. Nor do I care to."

"I gather you really didn't know him, then," Brigit noted.

"What about anyone on his behalf?" Kit asked.

"Who on his behalf of what?" Angie almost snapped. "Sorry, Katy."

Kit waved Angie's impatient tone away. "Has *anyone* shown any interest in acquiring or investing in or offering to develop either The Terpsichore, the building, or the land it's on?"

"In a word, no," Angie stated. "And if they did or had, you know I'd tell them where to go, especially if they contained too much testosterone without the required dose of queerness."

"Well," Kit shrugged, "that brings us back to the primo question: why was the body of Gerry Anders left in The Red?"

"And why was it drained of blood?" Brigie said spookily.

"It's my bet, the exsanguination," Kit rolled the word out of her mouth, "was done to increase the impact of a dead and naked man being found in a women's bar."

"But," Del raised a finger, "did whoever left him even know it

42

was a women's bar? Could they have just chosen 'a place' where they knew he'd be found sooner rather than later?"

"Maybe," Kit shrugged.

"But you don't think so," Angie said.

"Nope. I think there is a connection, somewhere, between Gerry Anders and The Terpsichore. It may not be obvious or direct; and it may not have any *meaning*, other than as a stunt to enhance the murderous deed itself. It may be an inconsequential link, an insignificant connection between Anders and his killer, or the killer and this bar ..."

"Whatever it is, it certainly results in some big words," Brigit commented.

Kit narrowed her eyes. "I'm thinking aloud, Brigie; I often use big words when I think."

"Well, I reckon *we* could find this mysterious missing link a lot sooner than the cops," Del proposed, in an uncharacteristic gung-ho tone.

"Especially if the cops are being led around by Chucky Parker," Kit agreed, but vaguely, because she was also thinking—uh-oh! She gazed at her friends and wondered how the hell she was going to head them off at the pass. As helpful, resourceful, and clear thinking as her friends always were, forming a posse under these seriously overshadowed circumstances would be totally *not* a sensible course of action. Get them involved, O'Malley, she thought, but with harmless sidetracks.

"Detective Martin seems okay, though," Angie was saying.

"You mean Five of Nine." Brigie waggled her eyebrows.

"Do I? Why?" Angie asked.

Brigie gargled a woo-hoo. "Five of Nine—you know, like Seven of Nine on *Voyager*, only Detective Cathy is not quite so sculpted with enhanced boobs and itty-bitty waist. And she's probably not as tall as Seven, but she *does* look like her. Don't you think, Kit?"

"Do we know what she's talking about?" Angie asked.

"*Star Trek*," Kit explained. "But, can we stick to this plot, please—whatever it is."

"Of course," Brigie nodded. "Plot stick away, Kit."

"Thanks. We need to find out if anyone that *we* know has any idea why the mortal remains of Gerry Anders were left *here* and not, for instance, in his own nightclub. We need to do this quietly and with care. We must consider who we ask things of, and to whom we tell any of the things that we know, or find out."

"By *we*, you do mean just the four of us?" Del clarified.

"Yes," Kit nodded. "We four, with strict boundaries, should do our best to find out who, if anyone, knows what. And Angie, you need to hire me officially, so I can act on your behalf."

"Righto, Katy, you're hired," Angie nodded. "Do I need to sign anything?"

"Yeah, but later; and *only* because a certain Detective Chucky Fix-You-Up is in charge of the murder investigation. Speaking of which, you must all remember that I am not, correction *we* are not—and I repeat—*not* investigating the murder of Gerry Anders. All we're trying to do is find a connection between Mr. Anders, the live businessman, and this," Kit waved at the bar, "one of his last resting places."

"What do you mean by boundaries?" Brigit asked.

"She means," Del injected, "we can talk to other patrons and people we know and we can talk to each other, but we don't talk to the press, including McThing, and we do not talk to any member of the Riley family. Right?"

"Right. Or any other crooks or crims or mobsters or strange people," Kit added. "Because of who Anders was, we are inadvertently dealing with some very bad people. We do not want to deal with them directly, and we certainly don't want them to know who we are, that we are interested in them, or that we care."

"What about Julia?" Angie asked.

Kit ran her hand through her hair. "Keep her informed and ask her to keep her ears open, but I suggest that she and the other owners keep a low and, if possible, silent profile."

"Especially Gwen and her woo-woo friends," Del added.

"What about Alex?" Brigit asked.

Kit sighed. They'd be calling on Rabbit and the Scooter gang to act as The Terpsichore Irregulars if she wasn't careful. Ooh, don't forget about Scooter.

"Alex is not due to leave Sydney until Sunday," she said. "Even then she may have to go straight to Adelaide. But, if there are no objections, I think we need her on the team anyway. At the very least, Angie may need a lawyer."

Angie pulled a sour face. "You think so?"

"Sorry, honey," Kit nodded, "but yes, I think so."

"Alex would also make us a proper famous five," Brigit stated, way too seriously. Before anyone could groan, which they all got around to in a flash, she threw her palms up. "Hey, I'm just trying to lighten the mood here. I mean, it's not like we knew the dead guy. We are simply caught up in someone else's shit here and, sure, while some of it is bound to stick on us, we do not have to lose our senses of humor."

Del stroked Brigit's shoulder. "I love this woman," she admitted. "No idea why, but I do."

"Speaking of mysteries," Kit sighed. "Cathy says she's not been able to find Karen Farrell."

"I heard her say that," Del said. "What does she want Scooter for?"

"She was here when I opened up yesterday, but had to go to work," Angie explained.

"She didn't get there," Kit said. "Do you know where she works?"

"An old folks home in Brunswick, since her school closed down," Angie said. "I told the cops that, and Rabbit told them where Scooter lives. I wonder where she is?"

"Was Scooter Farrell acting suspiciously?" Brigit queried, in a vaguely Sherlockian tone.

"No more than usual," Angie laughed. "They'd all been on the piss something chronic on Wednesday night apparently, so Scooter was not a well girl. It's not surprising she couldn't cope with the oldies after finding a dead man with the hangover she had."

"*That* then is the first thing on the agenda," Kit announced, turning to Del and Brigit. "Can you two find out where Scooter is recovering, loitering, or doing whatever it is she's doing ..."

"Easy," Brigit declared, sliding off her stool. "Toilet first, though," she added, heading immediately in that direction.

"... without arousing the curiosity of Rabbit & Co. outside," Kit finished.

45

"O'Malley?" Del placed her hand on Kit's arm and looked deeply and seriously into her sparkling-greens.

"Del," Kit acknowledged.

"Are you assigning us distracting chores so we'll keep our noses out of your official detecting business?"

"Yes," Kit smiled, "and no. I'm delegating less risky tasks to you, your girlfriend, and Angie, so that *none* of us gets too involved in the heart of this murder investigation. The Rileys are not nice people, Del. It's more than likely they did something extra nasty to another bad guy, that resulted in the over-the-top death of Gerry Anders."

Angie screwed her nose up in frustrated anger. "But *I* didn't do anything to the Rileys, or their cohorts or enemies; so why did some psycho-crook dump this shit in my lap?"

Kit gave an expansive shrug. "That might not have been the intention, Angie; but there's a thought. Can you find out whether your co-owners have any, even remotely, unwelcome connections to any underworld types or, failing that, whether *they've* been approached by anyone about selling?"

"Is that my job?"

"Yes, honey, that's your job," Kit said and then frowned. "But, as I said, please be careful, because I've just thought of another less-likelihood, but one that indicates just how dangerous the Rileys can be. Gerry Anders himself may have done something so wrong or unacceptable in the eyes of his own family that *they* did this to him."

"Oh shit," Del grumbled. "I may have to lock Brigie in the pantry until this is over."

"Why would Queenie want to see where he was found, if they'd left him here?" Angie asked.

"You're the one who called them lunatics and perverts," Del reminded her.

Angie shook her head. "I was talking about the god-warblers and the journos. Marjorie Riley was polite and seemed pretty upset this morning."

"Yeah?" Kit huffed. "That woman has been conning people her entire life, Angie; and she makes a hobby of lying to the cops."

Angie ducked her head in concession. "It could have been an act, I suppose. But to me it looked more like an 'I'm gunna get the bastard that did this to my boy' kind of deal. What I want to know, Katy, is why the hell she wanted to talk to me."

"Coz you found him. Dealing with her, however, is going to be my job, or one of them, okay? I saw enough of everything to answer Queenie's questions. And I'll pay *her* a visit so she won't have any reason to come back here."

Are you completely mad? Kit's mind screamed at her. Don't even suggest that as a last resort.

"Are you mental?" Del echoed.

"You know I am," Kit smiled.

"Will she remember that you were a cop?" Angie asked. "It might smooth the way."

Kit put on her best don't-be-ridiculous face. "Being a cop, even an ex, wouldn't smooth a bloody thing with the Rileys, Angie. Besides, I've actually never met the old tart. I saw her heaps, but never had a reason to talk to her, arrest her, interview her, or be introduced to her."

"And don't you dare do any of those things now, either," Del pronounced. "I mean, not on your own, O'Malley. Don't call on her without company or backup, without being wired or watched, or without telling us when and where you're going to do such a stupid thing."

"I wouldn't dream of it," Kit grinned, thankful that Del at least seemed to understand the seriousness of their collective situation. She hoped that would also translate into Brigie-speak so they'd be able to keep her out of any trouble-making too.

"So Kit," asked the devil herself, back from the loo, "what are *you* going to do?"

Kit started counting off on her fingers. "I'm going to try wangling more info from Detective Cathy, talk to Scooter when you find her, and, right now, I'm going outside to interrogate the shit out of Carrie McThing and find out who her alleged sources are."

Del snorted. "She's a journo. If she's remotely worth her salt, she won't divulge that info."

"Not even if I threaten to tell the other reporters out there that she and herself were two of her own quoted witnesses?" Kit proposed.

"You cannot out her, Katy O'Malley," Angie stated. "No matter what she's written."

"Unless she *is* a heterospy of course," Brigit allowed. "Then you can do anything you like to her. I'll help."

"Hey, you guys," Kit raised her hands in surrender. "If she is gay, I'd never out her—but *she* doesn't know that. So if she is, but I can't get her on side, then I'll just make noise."

"And if she isn't gay?" Del asked.

"Then I'll make a lot more noise."

"What if she is, but you scare her back into the terrible darkness of denial?" Angie asked.

"That's too bad," Kit said. "It'll be her own fault for smudging our rules anyway."

"We have rules?" Del asked.

"Of course we have rules," Kit said.

"What are they?" Angie queried.

Kit ran her right hand through her hair, then did the same on the other side with her left hand. "They're unspoken rules," she proclaimed.

"Ah," Del nodded. "That explains every-McThing."

"No," Kit said, sliding off her stool to pose with her hands on her hips. "It explains why she only smudged the rules. I am now going outside to set her straight."

"O'Malley," Del warned.

"Not that kind of straight, Del."

"Speaking of O'Malley, O'Malley," Brigit began, and then continued because everyone, including Kit, looked at her blankly. "How come Detective Cathy calls you O'Malley and not Kit or Ms. O'Malley or Katherine?"

Kit shrugged. "Why shouldn't she? You guys do sometimes."

"Yeah, but only if we're trying to get your attention when you've vagued-off; or because we're mad at you. Not that we're ever mad at you, Kit, but you know what I mean."

Kit pondered the original question for a moment, then shrugged. "Obviously my old habits have resurrected themselves," she said. "I always preferred fellow officers to call me O'Malley because, in my callow youth, I thought it sounded tougher than Kit. But it seems that, without even thinking, I also ask it of new cops I meet—like Cathy, yesterday. Marek was the only one who ever called me Kit; though more often it was Kitty—which was mildly annoying then, but kinda nice now."

"Interesting," Brigie noted, as if it really was, while she poked the pile of pictures that Angie had pushed aside when they arrived. "What's with the pics?" she asked.

"Julia, Gwen, and I have been discussing the theme for a new feature wall."

Kit glanced over Brigit's shoulder at the photos, before grinning at Angie.

"I knew *you'd* approve, Katy," Angie said, spreading the photos out. "We agreed, a process no doubt clinched by the masculine infringements of the past twenty-four hours, that the time has come for a bit of myth-making and a pictorial tribute to our favorite butt-kicking icons."

"It's about time," exclaimed Kit, who had groaned a year ago when the partners had finally given in to the sporty-dykes and had begun the Athletes Wall—still a work in progress—behind the pool tables. In the end, of course, she had to admit that Cathy, Tatiana, Yvonne, Dawn, Susie, and all the other splendid bods she didn't know from Eve, looked pretty spiffy up there. *This*, however, was her idea of the woman as hero, and was also a perfect extension of the bar's other collages, which featured the world's estrogen-powered movers and shakers.

Angie had just indicated the large expanse of purple but otherwise undecorated wall beyond the piano; the only vertical space yet to get The Terpsichore treatment. All the other lacquered walls, from the entrance and left around by the booths and on past The Red, were covered with photos, articles, and paintings of real-life women, who had inspired, led, or featured in every kind of human endeavor ever recorded in or left out of history—from music, literature, art, and acting to science, politics, humanitarian work, and exploration.

The new wall was to be dedicated to the imagination: to the

world of goddesses, mythical she-beings, the female heroes of legend, and, *woo-hoo*, contemporary pop culture.

"I only know half of these mythological and fictional women," Angie was saying, "so your special-girl is not going to recognize many of them at all, is she Kit?"

"Hey, we're getting there," Kit said. "But introducing a grown woman with no concept of TV or movie culture to our known universe is a very slow process. Alex does recognize Xena, Gabrielle, and Buffy now, so it's a start."

"There she is Angie—that's Seven of Nine," Brigit said, tapping a Women of *Star Trek* photo. "That's a great one of Emma Peel, ooh and Ripley."

Kit was torn between curiosity and a job or two that needed doing. Bummer, the jobs won.

"I'm going out to tackle the media now," she announced.

"Be nice Katherine," Del prompted.

"I'll do my best, Delbridge," Kit nodded, bracing herself for the thirteen-ringed circus outside. On her way out—just for luck—she stroked the perfect, left bum-cheek of one of the four life-sized stone caryatids whose eternal task it was to hold up the cupola over The Terpsichore's ridiculous foyer fountain.

Chapter 4

As she did a bit of careless leaning against a large tree of a species she couldn't identify, Kit pondered the only use she could think of for being a smoker: it gave good cover. Being exiled to the great outdoors to inhale fresh air with one's ciggie, while the nonsmokers inside were breathing the ever-mutating germs recycling through air-con systems that only operated at minimum efficiency now that they didn't have to expel smoke, meant that anyone with a cigarette in their hand had a valid reason for standing around pretending not to stare at people. Being a nonsmoker, however, meant that Kit had to appear nonchalantly disinterested without a handy prop, no small task when Journo McThing kept glancing at her, possibly tossing up whether it was safe to approach yet or not.

Make a note, O'Malley, she thought. Buy a packet of smokes so you can intentionally loiter anywhere with no apparent intent. She also noted that the sideshow crowds outside Angie's had thinned a little. Only half of Rabbit's band of curt-remarksters were still there firing jibes at the fewer-in-number but still chanting HeteroGodsters, and the two remaining uniform cops were trying to ignore the reduced jackal-pack of reporters. Cathy had apparently made good her escape, and the DQs had gone wherever camp divas go in the noon-day sun.

Kit turned her attention to their interloper, the possible spy, the dubious-dyke. McThing was full-figured but not overweight, about five-five tall, naturally redheaded if the fair skin and freckles were any clue, and dressed in black jeans, boots, white shirt, and green jacket.

Kit didn't think she'd fessed-up to being a PI within Carrie's ear-shot yesterday, but felt sure—given the circumstances—that her profession would've been on Rabbit MacArthur's customary low-down on all things in the community. Rabbit was a formidable presence: tall, large-breasted, trunk-thighed, and loud. She was also a treasure, once you got beyond the somewhat scary spiked hair and demonic tattoos crawling from the sleeves of the tight T-shirts she wore under her trademark black overalls. She had a heart of gold and a mission to make everyone feel welcome; so there was no doubt the questionable queer knew everything there was to know about everyone she'd seen in these parts in the last two days.

A journo worth her salt, Del had said of McThing, would not reveal her sources. Well, ditto for a PI when confronted by a journo marching up to demand what the PI knew about everything. So why hadn't McThing demanded it already? Why was she still seemingly searching for whatever it was she needed to gird those young loins? Oh. It dawned on Kit that the PI might have frightened the reporter. Yeah, sure, O'Malley. You're not that scary. Just because she—well, everyone actually—heard you berating the deluded duo offering the frisbee-ride to redemption, doesn't mean a thing.

On the other hand, Kit acknowledged, Ms. McDermid's attention *was* ping-ponging between her and the couple who'd relocated with their dodgy sign to the other side of the lawn *after* Kit had asked them who the fallen were and what would they know if they got up.

"The women who gather together in this place have fallen from grace," Mr. Dogmatist had informed her. "Unless they repent their ways, the Lord will forever look on them as the abominations of his gift of life."

"Why?" Kit had asked.

"Without the guiding hand of a mortal man, made in God's own image, these women are forever damned and excluded from his light," *Mrs.* Dogmatist elaborated.

"The light of man or the light of god?" Kit had queried.

"The light of God through man," Mr. Doggydoo proclaimed.

"Really?" Kit frowned. "I don't know about this spooky male-light business, but I have been in the dark of true evil, pure and bloody, and I can tell you it was totally *man* made."

"Where there's dark, there's light," God's image insisted.

"I doubt that's scientifically true, but if you want to believe it, go right ahead. I'll let you in on a secret, though: there are more goddesses in that place," Kit pointed at The Terpsichore, "than there are genuine representatives of any half-way-decent god out here on this lawn."

Mr. Doodoo recoiled. "This is a house of sin; a faithless den of sex, debauchery, harlotry."

"Harlotry?" Kit snorted. "Listen, mate, it can only be your secret stash of porno magazines that would generate that kind of wishful thinking."

"This is indeed a *den*," Mrs. Doo had wailed, as if "den" was the really important word. She crooked an accusing finger before continuing, "frequented by fornicating lesbians."

Ah, "den" goes with "fornicating"; that makes it a noun to be reckoned with, Kit thought, amazed at how creatures so chockers with bile could look so much like normal humans. How come the church, any church, never burned twisted nutters like these at the stake?

Mr. was still at it: "Nakedness and licentiousness, sex and ..."

"Blimey!" Kit had exclaimed, "you God-fearing breeders are amazing. All you ever think about is sex. Believe me, very little naked fornicating goes on in that piano bar.

"And where the hell are your priorities anyway, you lunatics? The *married man* whose dead body was left in there was a known philanderer, a drug dealer, and a murderer, yet you two are out here protesting against us. Do you have any idea how ridiculous that is and how petty you are? That's actually a rhetorical question. Please don't answer, because I really don't care to be assaulted by anything else that might be festering in your sad little minds."

Mr. and Mrs. had endeavored to make another sad point, but Kit had crossed her wrists in front of her face and backed away, growling: "No, aagh; get away, strange people."

Returning to the here and now, Kit realized that McThing's face was responding questioningly to the stare that she was unconsciously leveling in the reporter's direction. Ooh, we are getting bold, she thought, offering a tiny affirmative raise of her chin. Carrie's standing-start to racing-walk response was immediate; as was Kit's negative finger-pointing motion aimed at dissuading the tag-along photographer.

"Kit O'Malley, right? We met briefly yesterday," McThing said, still on the approach but on her own now. "I'm Carrie McDermid."

"Carrie," Kit nodded, shaking the offered hand. "You weren't a journalist yesterday."

She had the gall to look puzzled, then the grace to look apologetic. "I was, I just didn't tell the police that."

"Or me, or Angie."

"You didn't ask," Carrie shrugged. "And, likewise, you didn't tell me you were a private detective, Ms. O'Malley."

"Everyone knows that about me, though," Kit said, playing along.

"Everyone who knows you, you mean."

"Yep," Kit nodded. "And now that you do, drop the Ms. It's just O'Malley." Strange, she noted, that habit's having quite a revival.

"So, were you here undercover yesterday?" Kit asked.

"No, I was here for lunch."

"What about Wednesday night?"

"Wednesday? Oh. Um, I was here to, ah ..." Carrie fiddled with her hair.

"Check us out?"

Carried nodded. "I suppose."

"Are you writing a feature on great eating places, alternate lifestyles, or hip venues for the sexually curious?"

Carrie laughed. "No. Until yesterday, when I couldn't have lunch here, I wasn't writing anything related to this place at all. I was checking it out, as you say, to see what, to see if I'd want to come back, or ..."

"Are you gay?" Kit asked bluntly, but quietly.

Carrie's face mutated through three expressions—startled, unsure, indignant—before she spoke. "Is that any of your business?"

Kit sighed. "Given the state of affairs—and by that I mean the whole dead guy thing coinciding with you being here, twice, *and* you being a reporter, and us, as in you and me, technically still being on our premises—then yes, it's my business."

"And if I choose not to answer?" Carrie queried.

"You don't have to," Kit smiled. "But you may find it difficult to get worthwhile info from anyone who frequents this bar or has any affiliation with it."

Carrie looked incredulous. "Are you saying that if I'm not gay, no one will talk to me?"

"No," Kit laughed. "But this tendency of yours to get things arse-about is a worry. I meant that if you're not honest with me, with us, then some people may not want to talk to you coz—and this may be an alien concept to a journalist—they won't trust you. Quite frankly, my dear, we don't give a damn what you are, as long as you *are* it—whatever it is."

"Oh," said Carrie, shaking off the serious huff she didn't need any more. "I don't suppose there's any chance we could go inside and talk about all this, O'Malley?"

"No," Kit smiled. "Only family is allowed in there today. Police orders."

"But you're not family, are you?"

Kit shrugged. "As a concept that word needs redefining," she said enigmatically, "but not for you by us today. We're still trying to get over the startling melodrama in which you encased the banal in order to support your dubious facts."

Carrie screwed up her face. "What are you talking about?"

"You beat it up, stretch it out, make it fact by claiming it is, quote the anonymous, then reduce everything to the lowest common denominator kind of reporting."

Carrie was about to protest, probably too much, when Kit raised her eyebrows and continued, "Unless of course, as they tend to do, your editor laid a heavy and brutish hand on your story; and it *wasn't* you who described Angie's as a place run by women for lesbians."

"Why? What's wrong with that?" Carrie demanded, putting on her huffy hat again.

"It's stupid and it's not accurate." Kit decided she was tired of standing, so sat down cross-legged on the grass before continuing, "And it's almost tautological."

Carrie sat down beside her. "You've lost me."

"If you must use a superfluous qualification to emphasize the nature of this establishment, then at least get it right. The Terpsichore is, in reality, a bar run by lesbians for women."

Carrie still looked lost.

"Carrie, Carrie," Kit shook her head. "To say that women run the bar for lesbians implies that only lesbians are allowed in. What's more, by saying that, you'd *already* overkilled the point you were hammering, so much so that the follow-up 'men aren't usually allowed in' was in the really-fucking-obvious department—don't you think? Or don't you think?"

Carrie assumed a contrite visage. "Could we start our relationship again, O'Malley?"

Kit pretended to assess the request by examining Carrie's reasonably attractive face, noting that her pale-green eyes featured specks of brown. "Will you be wanting to get back into Angie's in a completely *non*-professional capacity?"

"Yes," Carrie smiled.

"Then we'll have to start over," Kit shrugged, "because I promised my friends in there that I'd be nice to you if you turned out to be genuinely gay."

Carrie sighed deeply. "What if I'm not sure."

"Was that why you were here? To find out, because you think you might be?"

"Yes."

"That's okay, then."

"It is?" Carrie looked bemused.

"Of course it is," Kit explained. "I told you this was a place for women—gay, straight, bi, transgender, even Liberal-voting at a pinch; not to mention newbies who get sidetracked by a dead guy on the premises while they're trying to find their inner special-girl."

"Bet you wouldn't let her in," Carrie indicated the wife of God's-image-incarnate.

Kit's raspberry said it all. Well, almost. "Sadly, we might have to," she sneered. "She *is* the female of her species after all."

Carrie laughed, then decided it was time to get serious. "So O'Malley, will you talk to me about what happened here?"

"I don't know any more than you do, Carrie," Kit stated. "In fact, it's possible I know less than you. Will you tell *me* who your source is?"

"No. You know I can't tell you that."

56

"Aw, come on Carrie," Kit grinned. "I don't want to break my promise to be nice. Who's the source who told you that Anders had a financial interest in Angie's?"

Carrie slapped her hand over her mouth; so Kit got to her feet with a sigh. "I don't want to do this, Miz McDermid," she said, "but I think it's my civic duty to trot over there and give that steroid-filled TV reporter the name of *your* 'witness at the scene when the body was discovered'. What do you think?"

"You wouldn't!" Carrie was horrified.

"Hey! If you can't write *all* the truth, then don't bloody exaggerate," Kit snapped. "Sorry, I forgot I was being nice." She grinned to make up for it.

"Are you for real, O'Malley?" Carried stood up and jabbed her fists defiantly into her hips. "I cannot reveal my source—end of story. Do your worst."

Damn, Kit thought, bluff called already. "Okay," she changed tack, "can you tell me whether you've managed to have the allegation verified?"

"What do you mean?"

"What do you mean, what do I mean? Good grief, woman, how long have you been a reporter?" She held up her hand. "Bottom line here, Carrie, is that Gerry Anders had no financial interest in The Terpsichore, unless it was in his own now-dead imagination. So, if you're planning on reprinting that nonsense, you should check out its likelihood."

"O'Malley, my source is nothing if not reliable."

"No such thing, Carrie, but it's sweet that you believe in something."

"Okay, if you *must* know, Mrs. Riley herself verified it this morning."

Kit snorted. "Oh yeah? And what did she say? Exactly."

"She came up to me, introduced herself, and invited me to call on her to do an interview. She said, and I quote, 'we must talk about this financial interest of Gerry's and this sad business.'" Carrie's expression said: "so there—exclamation mark."

"Marjorie Riley approached you?" Kit said. "Had you met her before?"

"Yes she did, and no I hadn't," Carrie replied.

"But she knew who you were?"

"Yes," Carrie smiled, as if this was a good thing.

"Shit girl, she wants to know what you know. She didn't verify anything."

"That's an interesting take on a discussion you weren't party to." Carrie's lips were actually pursed.

"You are a dead woman." Kit threw the comment away.

"What are you talking about?"

"Oh, sweetie," Kit moaned. "Euphemisms aside, Carrie, you described Queenie Riley as a well-known Melbourne businesswoman in the *same article* that you called her dead nephew a career criminal, an ex-con, a murder suspect, and a crime lord."

"So? What's wrong with making that connection? They are related."

Kit squinted at her. "You're not from Melbourne, are you?"

Carrie looked surprised. "No, Perth. Why?"

"Because," Kit rolled her eyes, "while Gerry Anders is, *was*, indeed most of the things you alleged, he was also a thug. And not the top thug. His sweet Auntie Queenie is the crime lord, Carrie; and your bloody editor should've known *not* to let you connect those particular dots."

Carrie frowned.

"So if you do go to interview her, don't go alone," Kit stressed, "because, unlike like me, that nice old lady will not hesitate to rip your toenails out to find out who your source is."

"Well, it won't do her any good to know who it is," Carrie stated.

"Why not? Is your source already dead?"

"No," Carrie was appalled. "He's …" she stopped herself just in the nick of.

Damn, Kit thought; and then she flinched and looked to the left and right, as did Carrie, to see whose mobile was ringing.

"Mine," Kit said, pulling her phone out of her pocket to answer it. "Excuse me a sec."

"O'Malley?" It was the liquid-gold voice of the sexiest woman in the known universe and Kit's heart and stomach exchanged places in a tingly somersaulty-type motion which put her momentarily to

58

the left of center, until her organs oozed back to their rightful spots. Judging by Carrie's worried expression, Kit's face must have looked pretty peculiar.

"You okay?" Carrie mouthed.

Kit nodded, held up a finger, and moved away to talk to Alex Cazenove in private. All in all, a lag in response time of about 3.4 seconds.

"Alex, honey," Kit breathed.

"Hello, darling."

Kit melted all over again, but was almost ready for it this time. She wondered when this internal waterfall thing was going to stop happening; then reneged on that thought because she was quite certain she never, ever, wanted it to stop.

"Please tell me you're home," Kit said.

"Wish I could, Kit, but I'm still in Sydney. What is going on down there? Your message was weird, and I believe I saw The Terpsichore on a current hysteria show on TV this morning."

"Serious shit is going on down here, Alex. But what's with you? Since when do you even recognize a telly, let alone turn one on?"

"There are strange dead men at Angie's and you want to know why I turned the TV on?"

"There was only one dead man, Alex, and he's gone now." Kit filled her in on all the gory details, minus the actual gore, and then asked why it'd been so long between calls. Thirty-eight hours to be precise. Not that she was counting.

"Katherine O'Malley, are you asking where I was last night?"

Kit could imagine the amusement in those gray and beguiling eyes so "Yes", she admitted, but sheepishly, because she didn't want Alex to think she thought she had the right to ask.

"Let's see, I had drinks with the irritating clients in a bar at The Rocks from five to seven, then dined with some ..."

"Alex," Kit tried to interrupt.

"... old friends at their house, and I drank ..."

"Alex."

"... way too much, so I slept on their couch and had to dash to my meeting this morning via the hotel ..."

"Alex, I don't *need* to know everything."

"Why not? Aren't you interested in what I've been up to?"

There was definitely a smile in that tease, but Kit still couldn't admit there was nothing in the world that she was more interested in than everything that Alex Cazenove did.

So why can't you come clean, O'Malley? she asked herself. *Because*, she replied, it would be pushing the boundaries, asking for trouble, expecting too much from something so new and so ... new.

She changed the subject. "Well, *I* had dinner with Enzo last night, after he generously shared one of his new clients with me."

"Is that the case of the royal Russian?" Alex asked.

"Yeah. And those bloody Feral Feds sat in their car *outside* the restaurant this time, eating Maccas I think. The silly bastards will probably file a report that implies Enzo and I are having an affair now. I swear, Alex, it's time we did something about these guys. This can't be normal."

Alex sighed. "I've heard of cases where the Feds continued to spy, on and off, for months after the wedding."

"Bloody hell," Kit swore. "I'm beginning to think the federal Immigration espionage sector must be solely responsible for the increase in employment that I thought the government *lied* to us about on a regular basis. I mean, if Bill and Ben the Flowerpot Feds have been solely on Enzo's case for the four months, then the Lurking and Accountable-to-no-one Department must have a gazillion spooks on staff just to watch all the bad bad people who want to become legit Australians."

"O'Malley?"

"Yes, Alex?"

"Are you a little bit stressed?"

Oh wow, Kit thought, she still hardly knows me, yet she can sense stuff.

"A little," she admitted, "but only because of ... well, everything really."

Alex laughed. "I have an idea. What are you doing tomorrow night?"

"Nothing," Kit said.

"Good. I can't get out of this damn follow-up trip to South

Australia, but I could swing a late flight to Melbourne tomorrow, and a Sunday red-eye to Adelaide. How about you meet me at the Tullamarine Hilton tomorrow evening?"

Oh yes, oh yes, oh yes! Kit thought. "Oh yes," she said. "Tomorrow, that's Saturday, right? When, what time, what room?"

"Whoa, darling. As soon as I organize it, I'll let you know. Okay?"

"Good plan," Kit nodded.

Excellent plan, she cheered. *And* she's still calling me darling, which can only be good. You are such an idiot, O'Malley, she added.

Chapter 5

"Yo, Kit."

Kit jammed her phone in her pocket and turned to the yo-ing Rabbit MacArthur, who was heading her way with Del and Brigit in tow. It took her a moment to realize that Carrie had escaped her remonstrating by nicking back to the relative safety of the press pack.

"If I can help your investigation into this mess, you just call me, okay?" Rabbit offered, giving Kit a one-armed, around-the-shoulders hug that nearly folded her in half lengthways."

"Thanks, Rabbit," Kit squeaked, aiming a questioning squint at her sidekicks. "But what makes you think I'm investigating any-thing?"

"D and B said you were after Scooter. I figured that, you know … aren't you?"

"No," Kit fibbed. "It's the cops who want to talk to Scooter, not me. They need a witness statement like the one you gave. I said I'd help find her that's all."

"Rabbit reckons she'd be at work now," Brigit said.

"That's where she was supposed to be yesterday too." Kit turned to Rabbit. "Any ideas why Scooter didn't turn up for work, even though she left here to go there?"

Rabbit performed some serious-thinking callisthenics with her bottom lip. "Nope. She *was* pretty cactus, but."

But what, Kit wanted to ask; instead she said, "With a hangover, right?"

"Yeah, but it wasn't a hangover hangover, Kit. It was more your lubed-up, slip-sliding, long late night kind of hangover—if you catch my drift."

Kit narrowed her eyes. "I hate to appear dense, Rabbit, but your drift escaped me."

"Sex," Rabbit shrugged. "Lots of it."

"Oh. I didn't know she had a girlfriend," Kit admitted. Like you'd notice, O'Malley.

"It's all new pasho and fairy moans," Rabbit explained. "You know, ringing out for pizza coz they don't want to leave the hotel. But," she whispered, "it's also a hush-hush secret."

"Well, the secret's hush-hush anyway," Kit said, raising her eyebrows.

"And why is it?" Brigit the Curious asked.

No one, it seemed, was going to ask Rabbit to elaborate on the moaning fairies.

"Actually, *it's* not a secret," Rabbit stated. "I mean everybody—except you lot apparently—knows about it. But the girlfriend herself, by which I mean her identity," Rabbit squinted meaningfully, "is a huge secret." She shoved her hands into the pockets of her overalls, which apparently indicated the end of her statement, until she eventually realized that everyone was expecting more detail. "Oh," she continued, "and the reason for the secrecy would be because she's married. The other woman, I mean, not Scooter."

"Scooter Farrell is having an affair with a married woman?" Brigie seemed impressed.

"I take it this woman is not out anywhere, then."

"Kit," Rabbit shook her head dejectedly, "*I* don't even know who she is."

"That's *some* secret affair, then," Del noted.

"It's a right bitch, lemme tell ya," Rabbit winked.

Kit ran her hands through her hair. This was all nicely juicy, but not useful for anything except slaking Brigie's thirst for goss. She gave Del a time-to-leave nod and the Big R's arm a gentle farewell slap. "Gotta go, Rabbit mate, but if you see Scooter, please tell her she has to call Detective Martin at the Homicide Squad. If that's too scary for her for any reason, then tell her to call me and I'll explain why she has to."

"Sure thing, Kit. Have I got your number?"

Kit smiled. "I don't know, Rabbit, have you?" She pulled her wallet out of her back pocket and extracted two of her business cards. "One for you and one for Scooter."

Kit was halfway to her car before she checked that Del and Brigit had Scooter's address.

"Yes," Del nodded, "but we don't need it Kit. It really *is* the police who want to talk to Scooter, remember, not us."

"But we *could* interrogate her," Brigit suggested cheerily.

"About what?" Del asked.

"About who her married woman is."

"Why?"

"Because I want to know."

"And your reason?" Del asked Kit, as they all got into her RAV.

"I thought if she was local we could swing by on the way to wherever we're going and tell her to front up before the cops get suspicious about her for no valid reason."

"Where *are* we going?" Brigit asked.

Kit shrugged and looked at Del who said, "Scooter lives in Williamstown."

"Oh. Wrong direction. So we're not going there," Kit said, taking St. Georges Road.

"Thank goodness," Del commented. "Because as charming as Williamstown is, it's not on the way to anywhere I want to go today."

As the place Del most wanted to go was back to work, Kit dropped her friends off at their office, then tossed an imaginary coin to choose between going to see Erin Carmody at the *St. Kilda Star* or Jon Marek at police H.Q. The coin divined that she'd get more of relevance by visiting Marek's office, because that would increase the likelihood of bumping into the hopefully helpful Detective Cathy again. Also, it wasn't really necessary to see Erin in person, except that actual visits to her office usually resulted in cake, which was always good. But not today, Josephine, she thought as she pulled up three cars back from the Punt Road intersection.

While waiting the usual two weeks for the left-turning drivers ahead of her on Swan Street to get their cars into go-forward mode, Kit jammed her phone's earpiece into her earhole and called the *St. Kilda Star* because, in person or not, she did need a favor.

She had no idea whether it was possible, but hoped that Erin might be able to apply something in the right place to ensure that a certain northern-suburbs' journo didn't end up in the Maribyrnong River wearing concrete runners because she was too intrepid for her own good.

The phone rang and rang and rang. Kit rotated her shoulders and growled as a vaguely felt hysteria that *nothing* was happening *anywhere* fueled the impatience caused by her still waiting-waiting for the last car ahead of her to get a bloody move on. Ring. Ring.

"Oh shit, shit, shit!" she swore as she realized that now she *wasn't* going to St. Kilda, she didn't even need to be in the no-choice-but-to-turn-left-lane. "Life would be simpler, Katherine O'Malley, if you'd decide before you drive. Ah, finally!" She made the now unnecessary turn and headed south on Punt Road. Ring, ring …

"*St. Kilda Star*, Simon Veducci speaking."

Oh no, not Mr. Loopy. "Hi Simon. This is Kit O'Malley. Remember me?"

"Do I?"

"Um, I don't know, Simon. Is Erin there?" she asked.

"In a word, no," said the guy she'd last seen crouching on top of the office storage shelves—out of reach of the nogglers and scary rats. Erin had suggested he take a long holiday, which he did, but from which he now seemed to have returned.

"Do you know where she is?"

"That's Kit the PI, yeah?"

"Yes, Simon."

"Okay. I can tell *you* that Erin has gone to a meeting, and is incommunicado."

"Inco … really? Would you tell her I rang, then, please, Simon."

"Of course. I don't suppose I can help?" he asked hopefully.

"Maybe," she replied. "Are the *St. Kilda Star* and the *North Star* related?"

"Yes, Kit. Both newspapers are owned by the same quartet of stinking capitalist bastards. They also own the *Eastern Echo* and the *Westerly*."

"Thank you, Simon."

"My pleasure entirely, I believe." He hung up.

"Bye, then," Kit said, lifting the sunvisor to take a squiz at the Nylex silo clock. "Two-fifteen and, and," she said, "come on, ah—twelve degrees. That explains the temperature."

Fool! came the afterthought, as she crossed the Yarra Yarra by the negligible Hoddle Bridge and made a right turn onto Alexandra Avenue to follow the river's course beside the Royal Botanic Gardens. The Yarra wasn't looking its best this arvo, she noted, but then it really had nothing to reflect today but gloomy gloom and an overcast sky. Kit tried Erin's mobile number, just in case her friend was unreachable only when it came to Simon Veducci, but as the call went straight to voicemail she had no way of knowing whether that was the case or not. She left a message asking Erin to call back.

The Homicide Squad, when it was in, worked out of the Police Complex on St. Kilda Road, along with the Arson, Drug, and Organized Crime squads. It took Kit such a ridiculously long time to travel the very few kilometers to its thereabouts opposite Melbourne Grammar, that the flying crows who'd set out at the same time had died of old age by the time she got there.

She signed in, waited for her escort, took the lift to the ninth floor, and stepped out into the familiar chaos of a busy squad room. Most of the Ds she passed on her way to Marek's office ignored her, one glared suspiciously, and another hailed her warmly. She couldn't see Cathy Martin anywhere, but she could see that Marek was pacing his office like a man with only two directions in life—back and forth—until he saw her; and that stopped him in his tracks. He beckoned her inside where, surprise-surprise, she found the not-really-missing Erin Carmody lounging on Marek's over-stuffed couch, drinking coffee.

"I'd love one of them," she said to Marek, as she plopped herself down next to Erin and gave her a kiss on the cheek. "Hi, honey."

"Hello, cherub," Erin smiled.

Marek handed Kit a coffee. "For the record, this is not a café. What are you doing here?"

"I was just walking by," Kit frowned, "you're the one who invited me in."

"Oh good, it's smart arse day," Marek huffed, collapsing into his own chair with an air of such resignation that it would have worried Kit, had she not seen this act a hundred times.

"Really, I was just passing," she insisted, offering up one of her best no-ulterior-motive, butter-wouldn't-melt kind of smiles, knowing he wouldn't buy it—not even for a second. "What can I say, Jonno? Obviously I'm on a digging expedition. I was hoping to get some stuff from Detective Martin *and* I was looking for Erin."

"What made you think she'd be here?" Marek asked.

"If you're talking about Erin, I didn't; if you're talking about Cathy, she works here."

"And what stuff could Martin possibly have for you?"

"I don't know yet," Kit said thoughtfully.

"Everything in this office is classified," Marek stated.

"Since when?"

"Since you walked in. I'm warning you right now, Kitty, I do not want you out there finding any more dead bodies while you're not investigating the one you found yesterday."

"You found *another* one?" Erin exclaimed.

"Where have *you* been?" Kit frowned.

"At home, on holiday, since Tuesday."

"Simon the Mad said you'd gone incommunicado to a meeting."

"That was *last* Friday," Erin rolled her eyes. "So, spill. What have I missed?"

Kit took a breath to begin the lowdown, but ...

"Did you not hear me say this isn't a café?" Marek swiveled his chair, massaged his hand on his spiky-short hair, and let go a serious long-suffering sigh.

Oh dear, Kit thought, there *is* something wrong. "How about you and I go somewhere for something," she suggested to Erin, as she stood up. "Unless you've only just got here, in which case I'll go and look for Cathy."

"What? Why?" Erin frowned at Kit, then glanced at Marek, and, by the looks of things, saw something there she didn't recognize. She reached up to make use of Kit's offered hand. "Let's go get cake. I only dropped in to invite Jon to dinner and I've done that."

As she stood, Erin's soft black velvet skirt dropped in waves like, well, soft black velvet from her previously semi-revealed knee down to her well-turned ankles. This, combined with the flick of her wild red hair over her shoulder, produced an interesting—and never-before-seen-by-Kit—effect on Detective Inspector Jon Marek. Kit noticed that while his eyes softened in a smile, his chest expanded suddenly as if he'd been caught unawares by something truly worth noticing. Ooh, love stuff, Kit thought, pleased that two of her dearest friends had found it together.

"Sorry, guys," Marek apologized. "This just isn't the best time for socializing."

"Or the right place, either, Jon," Erin said. "We understand. Come O'Malley."

Marek walked them to his door, lightly touching Erin in the small of her back as he ushered them out. He then caught hold of Kit's elbow, "Cathy is in interview room four, for the peace and quiet, if you really want to talk to her about any 'stuff' that isn't classified. My advice—which, of course, you won't take—is not to get caught up in this one, Kitty. *Nothing* the Rileys have done is worth you getting in their crosshairs."

"Of that, I am aware," Kit smiled. "But thank you, Jonno."

"The Rileys?" Erin whispered as she followed Kit, closely.

"Yeah, *the* Rileys," Kit said, stopping outside the interview room. "Erin, honey, would you mind waiting out here. I'll fill you in, I promise, but I doubt the nice Detective in Charge of Dead Gerry will tell the private eye very much at all if she comes armed with a reporter."

Erin scowled and pouted, but sat down on the bench seat opposite the closed door on which Kit was knocking. When it opened, Detective Senior Constable Cathy Martin, who didn't look quite surprised enough to see her, stepped back casually and waved her in.

Kit noticed the phone on the desk. "He rang ahead."

"He did," Cathy shrugged. "Have a seat and tell me how we can help each other."

"We can?" Kit sat.

"Play your cards right, O'Malley, and this *could* be the start of a beautiful relationship," Cathy said, trying not to laugh. "What do you need?"

"Nothing specific," Kit grinned. "Angie Nichols has hired me just in case she needs a forward scout in the ruck."

"A scout in the ruck?" *Now* she was laughing.

"Sorry, my sporting analogies are woeful," Kit said. "I'm not even sure what a ruck is. I *am*, however, worried that Chucky—sorry, Detective Senior Sergeant Parker—will make Angie your public prime suspect by either deliberate or accidental implication."

Cathy ran a finger through her blonde hair. "I am the lead investigator," she reassured her.

"I know, Cathy. But I also *know* Chucky. We go way back, sadly. Anyway, that's why Angie hired me. I assure you, however, I am not investigating the murder of Gerry Anders."

"Good. Coz you're not allowed to."

Kit grinned. "I'm also not investigating anything else that's not allowed or foolhardy."

"What *are* you doing then?"

"I'm looking into how a certain Mr. Anders came to be where he was found."

Cathy offered Kit half a smile. "What do you want, O'Malley?"

Kit widened her eyes, waited for the other half of the detective's smile, then said, "Anything you can tell me, between now and when you do solve his murder, that relates to or affects Angie, our friends, or the bar, in return for *everything* I discover in my quest to find out what, if any, connection Gerry boy had to The Terpsichore and/or all who sail in her."

Cathy leaned back on her chair and considered Kit's offer thoughtfully; or checked her out from head to foot, depending on whether subtext was playing *any* part in the future of this beautiful new relationship or not. Kit waited politely.

"The Boss, as in Marek not *Chuck*," Cathy raised a brow as she threw up her superior's name, "said I could use my judgment in what I give you because you won't go blabbing anything I ask you to keep to yourself to the wrong people; like your reporter mate out there."

You mean Marek's reporter mate, Kit thought. "That sounds like a perfect relationship."

"Good. First things first, then. Have you managed to find Karen Farrell? And if not, should I be worried about that?"

"No and no," Kit said. "She allegedly has a new lover and therefore probably has no idea you want to speak to her. But I'm still looking. Do *you* have any clues or ideas as to why the body of Gerry Anders was left in The Terpsichore?"

"No clues and no ideas, yet. But Charlie ..." Cathy stopped herself for a moment, perhaps to reconsider how much she really should tell Kit. She obviously got the go-ahead from herself, because she continued, "um, Charlie was organizing for the Doggies to keep an eye, or rather continue to keep watch, on a couple of Gerry's known accomplices and a foe or two. While he has been—I *think* jokingly—mouthing-off that 'those women' did it, Charlie does agree with the rest of us that it's more likely the murder has something to do with Gerry's hit on the Sherwoods."

"Chucky's not joking," Kit snorted. "He would just love for one, nay all of us women to be responsible. But if Gerry's demise is related to those nicely now-dead drug dealers, why would his killer leave what was left of him at Angie's?"

"I really don't know the answer to that," Cathy said. "But if I discover there's a reason that makes any sense, I'll let you know— if I can. What about you?"

"Yeah, sure," Kit agreed. "I've got feelers out to see if any of the regulars have connections to the Rileys or, more importantly, to anyone who hates the Rileys."

"Or just Gerry," Cathy suggested. "He did a lot of shit on his own, O'Malley. I've heard that Queenie was forever threatening to squeeze his favorite bits in the nutcracker she allegedly keeps for exactly that purpose. His arson stuff, for instance, was apparently not a Riley deal. The word is that it was either a scam, or business competition over his nightclub."

"Yeah, well you can't believe every word," Kit reminded her. "That idiot reporter Carrie McDermid from the *North Star* claims Gerry had a financial interest in The Terpsichore."

"Yeah, I read that too," Cathy laughed. "Don't you think we should regard that as fact, given it came from the woman who also called Gerry a crime lord?"

Kit smiled. "Well, aside from the *not* true aspect of it, have you heard anything similar? Or, do you happen to know who McDermid's source is?"

"No idea about the source, but we *have* heard rumors that Anders had an interest. Not an actual financial stake, but an interest," Cathy qualified. "But already it seems that no one is sure whether they know this because they read it in the paper or because they know it for a fact. I've got someone working that angle just in case; the same officer who's investigating *any* possible links between Gerry and your mate Angie, and/or her business partners."

Kit scratched the back of her head and frowned.

"You know I have to," Cathy added.

"Of course," Kit acknowledged. "It's just that it's all too ridiculous for words. If Angie had any connection with Gerry, the Rileys, or their enemies, why …?" Kit turned her palms up.

"Why would she kill him somewhere else, then take his body back to her own bar and call the police? You're right, it's crazy," Cathy agreed.

"So, you're sure he was done elsewhere?" Kit asked.

"Oh yeah. There were no blood splatters to indicate that someone had their most important veins sliced open on the premises, at any time, and there were zero signs of a struggle. In fact, if not for Gerry himself, there'd be almost no hint of a crime happening there at all."

"Do you know how the perp got in, post-murder?" Kit asked.

"The pantry window from the side lane. One louver was removed and one was broken. Then he or they opened the fire door in the disco and just wheeled poor Gerry inside."

Kit foraged around in her mind for any details that could generate more questions. "What about Alan Shipper?" she suddenly asked.

Cathy looked puzzled. "He's dead, isn't he?"

"Yeah, I know he's dead. But who killed him? That could be the question, Cathy," Kit proposed. "If it *was* his alleged kidnapper, Gerry Anders, who did him in, then the late Mr. Shipper—a previously ordinary, apart from being filthy rich, family man—may now have some understandably angry relatives roaming the mean streets looking for payback."

71

"I thought Shipper was killed in a car accident," Cathy frowned. Kit reacted with her seriously dubious face, so Cathy narrowed her eyes and added, "But I'm sure we're looking into that possibility." She pulled a stack of manilla folders into the space on the desk between them and changed the subject. "Would you do me a favor, O'Malley? Take a look at these surveillance pics and tell me who you think *shouldn't* be there."

Kit flipped through a couple of dozen photos taken outside Angie's earlier that morning, and pointed out the religious protesters, Mr. and Mrs. Godsimage, a few sightseers, all the reporters, three cops, and one lone and terribly unfortunate-looking bloke standing closer to the ex-church next door than The Terpsichore, so he may not have been *there* at all.

"Hmm," Cathy hmmed. She did a bit of shuffling, opened another folder, and tapped the top photo, in which was captured for posterity what looked like a surreptitious deal going down between two more-than-likely crooks.

Bloody hell, Kit moaned silently. With bastards like these haunting the edges of my old life and, it seems, threatening to enter my current one, it's no wonder I have inexplicable creepy nightmares, instead of dreamscape adventures with gorgeous Amazon warriors.

"It's the same guy," Cathy was saying.

"So it is," Kit said, peering at Unsightly Man, who featured in both photos. "Who is he?"

Cathy shook her head. "I was hoping you'd know."

"Sorry. I do know who the other bloke is. Unfortunately," Kit volunteered. "But not him," she said pointing.

"You know *this* guy?" Cathy was surprised.

"Yeah. Don't you?"

Cathy shook her head. "It's not my file. This was one of the photos that Charlie laid out for the uniforms this morning, so they'd know which of Gerry's associates to keep tabs on."

Kit was intrigued. "Really? Which of these two did he want them to follow?"

"I don't know," Cathy said, as she examined the picture more closely. "I wasn't paying attention at the time because, at that stage, I hadn't seen these photos from The Terpsichore. Who is he? A friend of Anders, or an enemy?"

"Either, neither, both; I don't know," Kit shrugged. "I can vouch that there's no love lost between *him* and a good twenty percent of the current police force—*one* detective in particular—as well as several retired cops, including me."

"Goddamnit, O'Malley, who is he?"

"Edward Paul Jackson; affectionately," Kit sneered the last word, "known as Pauly-J. Ex-cop, *bad* ex-cop. Taken down, and right out, a few years ago by a toecutter named Graham Charles Parker."

"Charlie was internal affairs?"

"Cut his teeth and earned his dubious stripes by ridding the force of Pauly Jackson and a couple of his way-bent partners in crime."

Cathy frowned. "I wonder why Charlie didn't mention his name this morning?"

"The doggies would already know Pauly-J." Kit sighed deeply. "I've got to admit, Cathy, I really don't like it that Chucky *and* Pauly-J are now, and concurrently, impinging on my personal landscape when I've had nothing to do with either bastard since I left the force. It's like the bad elements in society have been regurgitated into my neck of the woods just for the hell of it." She got to her feet. "It's spooky, and enough to make a girl go home and hide."

Cathy seemed amused by Kit's verbal eruption, but said, "Just like that?" when it was over.

"Yep," Kit responded. "Encountering the Chuck yesterday was bad enough, but this is an unpleasant coincidental blast from my past, and I *hate* coincidences. So, I'm going now."

"I don't get you, O'Malley," Cathy remarked, with another half-smile that meant Kit couldn't work out whether she was disappointed or baffled.

"What's to get?" Kit shrugged. She pulled out a business card and placed it on Cathy's desk. "Thank you. If you need anything, or have anything for me, please call."

Kit was at the door before Cathy reacted. "There was one thing you didn't ask, O'Malley."

"Only one?" Kit said mockingly.

"Yeah. The *when* did Gerry Anders die question."

"Okay. I'll bite. When did Gerry's severe loss of blood result in his no longer being alive?"

Detective Senior Constable Cathy Martin raised her eyebrows, and kept them there. "Ruth reckons last weekend—as in six or seven days ago. His body had evidently been kept on ice."

"Oh, that's charming," Kit remarked. "Who the hell would want a dead Gerry Anders lying around in their freezer?"

"He wasn't frozen, he was stored somewhere just cool enough to keep him fresh."

"Oh, now you see," Kit noted, "that is way more information than I needed."

Cathy laughed. "And it, *all* of it, O'Malley, is for your ears only, okay?

"Oh yeah," Kit agreed, as she opened the door. "And thanks, Cathy."

Chapter 6

"So?" Erin demanded as Kit emerged from the interview room. "What have you found out?"

"About what?" Kit teased, walking by the squad room towards the lift and chocolate cake.

"About whatever it was you were in there to find out about," Erin said seriously.

"Erin, honey, this is a two cappuccino story, at least. And I'm not going into any details until we're sitting in some café with the appropriate …"

Bang!

"… ambience," Kit finished.

Seven cops, from three or four crews, working a host of still-to-be-solved murders, raised their heads in a united squad reaction to the slamming of a single door. All eyes, Kit's and Erin's included, were on the detective standing alone and stunned outside Jon Marek's office.

Marek himself paced inside his office, then back to his door, wrenched it open, and crowded the much-heavier-built-than-him detective back against the hall wall. "I don't want any more bloody excuses, Harper. Find that sick little creep, ask him the questions again, and get us something we can use. If you can't manage that, then I'll manage you a transfer out of this squad."

"Right boss. Whatever you say, Marek."

"Like there'd be any other way to do it!" Marek stepped back into his office, picked up a phone book, and hurled it at his chair, which sent it crashing into the back wall.

Harper glanced at his colleagues, who returned their collective attention to everything else around them, and headed down the hall in the other direction.

"What's going on?" Erin whispered. "Do you think Jon's okay?'

"No, I don't actually," Kit replied. "Listen Erin, I'm supposed to meet a couple of guys you know at Leo's in an hour. Do you want to wait for me there? I think Marek ..."

"Go, Kit," Erin insisted.

This time as Kit reached Marek's door, he stepped out and scowled at her. "Now what?"

"We need to talk," she said quietly.

"Not now, O'Malley."

"Yes now, Marek. Please?"

"What about, for Christ's sake? Can't you see I'm busy?"

"Can we go in here?" Kit asked, indicating the room behind her, which had no windows to the rest of this interior world.

"You do not want to go in there," Marek stated.

"Is there anyone in there?"

"No."

"Then that's exactly where I want us to go." Kit opened the door and all but dragged Marek into the room. She shut them in, but he switched the light on and then crossed his arms defensively over his chest and gave her a look that said, "well, get on with it, then." Actually, on closer examination, Kit realized his was a typical how-come-you-never-listen-to-me? stance, and his expression was more of a "you asked for it."

Kit looked around at three cork-boarded walls, covered in the crime scene photos of what could only belong to the Barleycorn Task Force—the homicide investigation into the murderous activities of the person the press had dubbed the Rental Killer, but what those in the know regarded as the serial nightmare of Bubblewrap Man.

"Do you still want to be in here?" Marek asked, coldly.

Kit held on tight to a shallow breath, and walked a horror walk around a pictorial gallery of torture and mutilation beyond description, which showed, from every possible angle, the ghastly images of once-were-women—stolen, starved, brutalized, and murdered. Kit looked at the photos, at the victims, not to prove she could and certainly not because she wanted to—the devil himself, the bastard, knew that wasn't so—but because *this* was what was wrong with her friend.

76

Day and night, for nearly four months, Jon Marek had been enduring the depravity wrought by this *barbarian* as he'd called him. And Marek's job on this investigation was not a case of applying work time and professional energy to solving one or two beyond-awful murders. This was a thirty-hour a day offering-up of his mind and psyche to find the killer of two, then three, then ... It was now five women who'd been starved, raped, beaten, and had their hearts cut out while still, but barely, alive. Five victims, who had then been encased in bubblewrap and left in empty rental houses.

Erin Carmody had been involved in finding victim number three, which was partly how Kit knew as much as she did about this case; and that was way more than the average woman on Melbourne's streets, who knew only that there was a serial killer loose amongst them. They could only surmise, from what the media were allowed to reveal, that this was a killer who worked to no apparent rhyme and with no reasonable pattern, there being nothing similar about the victims—not their age, their hair or eye color, their job, their marital or financial status, their religion or ethnicity, their car, their gym, their vet. Nothing—except their gender. The random nature of the Rental Killer's choice of victim made him all the more terrifying, because any and every woman in the city was at risk until he was caught.

And each time, since the phone call that led Erin and the police to the body of Susan West in an otherwise empty house in Elwood, Bubblewrap Man had called a different journalist to inform them where, in their neighborhood, he'd left his latest victim.

Marek sighed deeply and dropped into one of the orange plastic chairs placed at the huge table in the center of the room. "Get the hell out of here, O'Malley," he advised.

As Kit's attention shifted from the crime scene photos to the multitude of evidence bags that covered the table, she was overwhelmed for the first time in her life by the oppressive, age-old, and female-only surge of cowering anxiety spawned by a perceived powerlessness. Shit! *That's* an awful feeling, she shuddered. Thank something, however, the already-dissipating flush of nameless panic did not make her feel afraid, or leave a residue of dread. No.

You're *not* getting me, Kit scowled, feeling righteously angry and fighting mad. All she wanted now, was to draw her broadsword and cut this murdering bastard to pieces.

"O'Malley, please?" Marek's eyes sadly searched hers. "This is no place for ..."

Kit squatted down, balancing herself with her hands on his knees. "No place for whom?"

"For anyone."

"Who are you talking to about this?"

Marek harumphed. "No one. The crew—which means no one, I suppose. Oh, except you. I talked to you about it. Remember?"

Kit shook her head. "Marek, that was nearly a month ago. There's been two more since ..."

"Tell me about it!"

"No, *you* have to tell someone; you've gotta get this out of your head, Jonno. Go see the department shrink or de-briefer. There must be one assigned to a case like this, or you'd all," she waved in the direction of the squad room, "be losing it by now."

"Some of the others have been talking to the Doc, but ..."

"But what, Marek? You do *not* have to be tough and totally in-control machismo-man, you know. You won't be any good to anyone if you take the denial route to self-destruction."

"You don't get it, Kitty ..."

"No, you don't get it Marek," Kit interrupted. "I saw a side of you out there a moment ago that I've never seen before and, despite *all* your previous and thoroughly hideous cases, never thought I would. You have to get this case off your lone and sagging shoulders. Use me if you want. Hell, I've heard, and now seen enough to at least have a clue where your head is."

That's right, O'Malley, she thought. Volunteer for nightmare watch. Like you need any more visions that aren't your own already. Kit's gaze wandered over the body of evidence gathered on the table: hundreds of bags containing great and small clues and, no doubt, more than a few irrelevancies. There were easily identifiable things like bus tickets, necklaces, feathers, and underwear; strange what-on-earth things, like little pieces of metal and wire, small bits of green stuff, and tiny colored fibers; and gruesome

78

things like a tooth, hair, and thumb-cuffs with spikes on the inside.

"This is not even the worst of it," Marek said softly. He was standing beside her, staring, like she was, at all the evidence that had so far gotten him nowhere.

"Please get some help, Jonno," Kit begged, "before it's too late—for you. Or before you lash out and accidentally deck one of your mates out there."

Marek let go a short laugh. "Harper *is* actually an imbecile."

"That may be, Marek, but he still doesn't deserve the brunt of your bad shit," Kit stressed, realizing she'd been fiddling with one of the plastic bags. "What is this?" she asked.

"Don't know, Kitty, but put it down; you *really* don't know where it's been."

That's better, Kit thought, welcoming the return of Marek's gallows-side smirk. "My big question for the day," she smiled, "is why you let off steam at poor Harper when you've got up-Chucky in your squad? He is, after all, an unmissable target worth hurling your invective at."

"That's true," Marek smiled. "And if I beat the crap out of *him*, I won't need the shrink."

Kit gave him a disapproving frown.

"I'll make an appointment this arvo, I promise. Now, will you get out of here?"

"For you, anything." Kit opened the door.

"Do me a favor, then? Tell Erin I'm not prone to violent verbal outbursts."

"She knows, Marek."

As Kit waited for Hector to return with his bugs and Enzo to get back from the loo, she glanced around Leo's Spaghetti Bar and wondered how it was that so many people could be just sitting around socializing at only four-thirty on a Friday arvo. Does everyone in St. Kilda get off work early; or is this a secret life for those in the know? You're here working O'Malley, she reminded herself. Maybe they are too.

"More coffee?" queried the out-of-thin-air waitress, startling Kit quite unnecessarily.

"Ah no, I'll have a Cascade and a foccacia with sundried tomatoes and cheese, please."

"Are your friends coming back?" The waitress began clearing the
table of coffee cups.

"She's not," Kit pointed to Erin's now empty chair. "But the
other two are."

Kit returned to the deliberation of her next move, or moves—
she did have two cases on the go, after all—now she was at least
satisfied that she'd done her best to prevent anything untoward
happening to Carrie McDermid, either through naivety or inexperi-
ence. Like it's really any of your business, O'Malley, she thought.

Which was kind of what Erin had muttered when Kit had asked
the favor of her. Actually, Erin had said, "why do you care?"—with
the emphasis on *you* not *care*.

Someone has to was a lame reason, but apparently good enough
for Ms. Carmody because, after she'd been filled in on the little Kit
knew about the death of Gerry and its consequences so far, Erin
called her counterpart on the *North Star*. She pointed out to "Barry,
sweetheart"—in no uncertain terms—that apart from using "his
alleged common sense, he had a duty of care to ensure that his
young reporters were properly briefed on the pros and cons of
dealing recklessly, or in *any* way, with Melbourne's biggest crime
family, goddamnit!" She had rung back a heartbeat later, to say:
"and don't you dare take her off the story to cover your arse."

Erin had then left Kit and the boys to rush home and prepare a
romantic banquet for her *spunk monkey*; a term of endearment
that Kit could not reconcile with Jon Marek no matter how she
tried—which admittedly wasn't very hard, because she really didn't
want to begin to imagine what it might mean.

Kit spotted Enzo, wending his way back from the gents via cheery
chats with several people who apparently knew him and vice versa,
then spied Bill and Ben the Feral Feds *in situ* near the glass dessert
cabinet. Enzo hovered behind his government antagonists, while
they pretended to be wooden chairs, and then he continued on to
another table, where he whispered in the ear of a guy who looked
like a refugee from a seventies' rock musical.

All of which prompted Kit to contemplate the men in her life: first by acknowledging the activity as an alien concept and wondering whether she'd *ever* done it before; and second by laughing that it wouldn't take long, as there were only three of them. As she rarely saw her crazy brother Michael, or old workmates like Nick, she didn't include them in the tally.

Worth counting, in many more ways than one, however, were Enzo McAllister, Jon Marek, and Hector Chase—men who had little in common with each other, but for whom Kit would do anything; and, hopefully, vice versa. They were dear friends she'd scored through fate, good fortune, great management, or, as she most liked to believe, because they deserved each other. While she often had these thoughts about her women friends, it dawned on her how wonderful it was to also have these three guys on her balance sheet.

A quick calculation told her that she'd known Jon Marek for thirteen years now, since she'd joined the force. He'd been her senior-ranked partner while in uniform, her colleague in the fraud squad when she'd made detective, and then her partner again during her brief stint in homicide before she left the job. The divine Enzo she'd known for only a few months; but Kit recognized valuable treasure when she came across it. And then there was Hector, a juvenile-d she'd once arrested for a bottle shop robbery; but who, even then, had more integrity and maturity than most adults Kit knew. He also had the will, and the sheer grit necessary, to overcome his shitty life start and make something of himself. He was now twenty-three, a computer game designer, all-round technowhiz, and Kit's semi-official sidekick.

And now two of her boy friends were about to discuss *work* with her here at Leo's, while others played. Enzo had found a plausible way for her to check out Gregor Tereshenko in person but, as they couldn't discuss their job while Erin was still there, Hector had dashed home to pick up his new surveillance toys.

The waitress delivered the beer and food at the same time as Enzo and Hector returned to their seats, whereon they placed their own drink orders and agreed to share Kit's foccacia.

"Given the chance," Enzo confided, "my long-haired friend Dean, at the table behind Snig and Snog over there, will accidentally-on-purpose make a mess all over our spooks."

"Oh shit, mate, are they still tailing you?" Hector asked.

"They emerge from their cocoon every other day to remind us how excellent their absence was. But I can't go on like this. I'm thinking about hiring some ruffians to, to ruffie them up."

"Just give the go," Hector laughed. "And I'll get some mates to ruffie them good and proper."

Kit, who'd been checking out the long-haired guys at *all* the other tables behind the Feds, patted Enzo's arm and queried, "How can you know so many Dean-things in the one place?"

"Woo," Hector noted. "It'd be good if *that* question made sense. You been smoking something funny, O'Malley?"

"Don't be silly, Hector." She pointed. "There's a hundred hippies sitting back there."

"Uh-uh," Hector shook his head. "I refuse to look."

Enzo did, however; turning back to Kit with an expression that said he'd only just noticed the strangeness of the crowd. "They're thespians," he said, as if that explained everything.

"They're blokes, Enzo," Kit stated.

"Th, th, thespians Kit, not lespians," Enzo grinned. "They belong to Foreplay, and they're doing a gay *Godspell*."

"Why?"

"Because they can, darling."

"I am *so* not going to look," Hector stressed, widening his baby-blues until Kit's now-curious inspection of him, made him put on his uneasy face. "What?" he asked, cautiously.

"Hector. You've had all your hair cut off. And you're all wet."

"Really, O'Malley? And, it's pissing down outside."

"Hmm," Kit noted. "Should I assume from that somewhat patronizing tone, Hector, that you've been without ponytail for longer than, say, today? And if so, why didn't I notice?"

"I had it cut yesterday, O'Malley, so you're not completely unobservant." Hector ran his fingers back and forth through his brown, now nape-length locks. "Why you didn't notice when I was sitting here earlier, though, I *don't* know; but then why would you?"

"Why *wouldn't* I?"

"You don't notice things like that."

"Yes I do. I just did."

"She hasn't noticed your tips, I'll wager," Enzo commented.

True. So? Kit thought, admiring the blond bits now they'd been pointed out to her.

Hector turned to Enzo. "Last week I watched Lillian perform acrobatics in her kitchen to draw O'Malley's attention to her new hairdo. Did she notice either the do or the show? No."

"I assure you I noticed," Kit said. "I just didn't comment on her latest variation of the same thing. Unlike my hair, which Mum is partly responsible for, hers *always* looks good."

"Yours is wonderful, Kit; it has character," Enzo proclaimed.

Kit laughed. "Thank you, Enzo, but my hair looks like some mini youse—as in tiny Scotsmen, not sheep—are flinging Highland-like through it, on speed. Now, do you guys think we could get down to business? Please."

Enzo responded immediately, with an eloquent flourish of his right hand that delivered an envelope into Kit's. She opened it and pulled out two official invitations to ...

"Oh no, what on earth is a Metro Blaazt?" she asked.

"You're kidding!" Hector exclaimed, excitedly and with demonstrative wriggling. "It's only the coolest nightclub in Melbourne, O'Malley." He almost snatched the gold-embossed cards from her hand, but decided to lean over the table to ogle them instead. "Oh, mate! These are for the grand opening; they're for then, for that, for ..."

"For you, Hector," Kit smiled. "One of them is, anyway; so don't say I never give you anything. I'm not even going to ask how a place yet to be grandly opened, can already be the coolest in town. But Enzo," she groaned, "when you said 'an opening' I thought you meant an art gallery. I hate nightclubs."

"Honeylamb," Enzo shrugged, "these invitations are not unlike hen's teeth. The junior-duke Gregor and his lady-love Vanessa, *will be* at this Blaazted thing, because come Sunday it will be the place to be. As I've no desire to be within miles of a thing so gauchely straight, I figured you and your sideshoot could trot along there and spy on our star-spangled lovers."

"If they're so rare how did you get them?" Kit queried.

"Comrade Tereshenko himself *gave* them to me yesterday, when

I lunched with him, his paramour, and her Mummy-not-so Dearest."

"I feel like I'm in a daytime soap," Hector said morosely; whereon Kit and Enzo filled him in on their job for Sarah Boyes-Lang.

"Cool," Hector said, turning the invitation over and over to check for extra perks or hidden agendas. "Now, I have something for you, O'Malley. Hold your hand out."

Kit did as she was told and Hector dropped a tiny clear plastic doodad into it. "Oh, that's lovely Hector, but you shouldn't have."

"Stick it in your ear, O'Malley."

"Really? Or is that like an insult?" she asked, putting the logical end of the extra-soft thing in her right ear … *'Thank you Enzo, but my hair looks like some mini-youse—as in tiny Scotsmen, not sheep …'* Kit's own voice said to her.

"Whoa!" she pulled the doodad out of her ear and stuck it in Enzo's. "Where's the mike?"

Hector drummed his fingers on the table. "Is this a ring you see before you?"

"Good God," Enzo said, raising his hand to his auricle.

"No such thing, Lorenzo," Kit sighed. "So where's the tape recorder?"

Hector unclipped a beeper-sized device from his belt and handed it to Kit. "It's a mini-disk not a tape, O'Malley. The mike to recorder range is about fifteen meters, so you can either wear it like this and get in close like I've been; or you can hide the recorder nearby, even outside a window. You place this bit," he pulled a tiny silver device from the center of his ring to demonstrate, "in the best spot for picking up whatever it is you want.

"It's noise activated and will pick up immediate-vicinity dialogue with ripper clarity. It'll also record voices or sounds for up to a five-meter radius from the mike, as long as there's no ambient noise like music, or too many voices like there are here. As you heard, our chat was crystal clear, but we couldn't pick up Spick and Span over there."

"I'm full of amaze," Kit grinned. "And *so* glad I've got you to find and understand all this stuff for me, Hector. So I don't ever have to. In fact, I'm officially retreating to the O'Malley Investigations Techno Vacuum, coz in this area I have no skills and I fear I'm one step away from future-phobia. Except, of course, that the future is sitting on this table."

Hector squinted at her. "Did someone beam your mind out, O'Malley? You can't be future-phobic, you're a science fiction fan."

"Yeah, in the abstract," Kit agreed. "As in the *fi* part, not the *sci* stuff; as in warp speed and transporters, not as in how TVs or mobiles work. And as for *this*, this spooky stuff of yours—or, you know, electricity." She pointed at a small leather-cased thing, "Like I thought that, which is huge by comparison, was your new 'little' listening toy."

Hector grinned, unzipped the case, and pulled out a sleek silver thing, no bigger than a pack of cards. "This, my Captain, is my new little *watching* toy. It's a digital video camera."

"Okay, that's it. I'm going to live in a cave."

"It's so cute," Enzo laughed. "Ooh, do me a favor and take a picture of Ding and Dong."

"Haven't you done that yet?" Hector asked,

"No. Why would I? *I'm* the one being investigated."

Hector ran his thumb along one sleek, narrow side, flipped open the world's tiniest screen, and placed the camera next to Enzo's glass. Glancing down casually, he adjusted the camera's position slightly as he spoke. "So, O'Malley, we have a date at the Metro Blaazt on Sunday?"

"A date indeed," Kit nodded. "Before that, however ..."

"I know," Hector raised his palms, "you want me to trace the Russian's international movements. Man, I feel like the spy who came in from the rain."

"I do want you to do that, yes," Kit agreed, "but I was also wondering if you're doing anything tonight. I mean this evening for an hour, or so."

Hector scratched his head thoughtfully. "I'm meeting a friend for dinner later, but I can do whatever with you until seven-thirty, as long as it takes no more than half an hour to get home from wherever we're going. Does that help?"

"It's perfect. I need backup when I pay a visit to Queenie Riley."

Enzo raised his hands dramatically and said, "Um?"

"What?" Kit queried.

"What indeed!" Enzo declared. "What have you done with the Kit O'Malley who, just last night, said that checking out the Rileys was something no sensible person would do without a whole force of nice police persons covering their cute little arse?"

"Ah well, you see, that was last night before Queenie herself paid a visit to The Terpsichore wishing to talk to Angie about what she'd found. The cops wouldn't let Ma Riley do that but, in order to prevent a repeat visit, I'm going to head trouble off at the corner of Wessex and Vine, by dropping in on the sweet old thing myself. I can answer any questions she has about the finding of the very dead body of her sweet nephew Gerald."

"O'Malley?" Hector said, extra-cheerfully. "I'm sorry, but I believe I've just remembered a prior, earlier, important engagement."

Chapter 7

Chez Riley, while not quite a mansion, was nonetheless very large. Set on a double corner block and back from the low brick front fence, it lay in wait amidst a long-established garden of willows, roses, and gigantic hydrangeas—a typical old Hawthorn residence of brick and rendered concrete, with bay and high-casement windows, and stained-glass panels on either side of the wide front door. Kit could almost smell the timber picture rails and oversized skirting boards she knew would be a feature of the interior.

The house fronted Wessex Street, which was lined with the traditional around-these-parts oak trees; while Vine Street, which ran down the side of the residence, was narrow, treeless, and lined with parked cars. Vine provided access to the Riley garage, which was set into the high brick fence that shielded and surrounded the rest of the property.

It was 6 p.m.

"Are we waiting for anything in particular?"

"No."

"Let's go, then. Your faithful but rather unsettled backup boy still has constraints on his time, O'Malley. And I'm getting wetter."

"Okay," Kit flared her nostrils, sniffed as much air as she could, and huffed it out. "Right, let's go." She turned off the windscreen wipers, and got out of her car to join Hector on the footpath. Then she led the way through the gate and down the rain-soaked path to the front door of the home of that "well-known Melbourne businesswoman," Marjorie Riley.

Hector prodded the doorbell button.

"Hi, there," Kit smiled at the muscle on muscle who opened the door, "I was wondering if Mrs. Riley is home?"

"Depends," said Will.

Well, Kit assumed his name was Will because his MoShun Club staff T-shirt said it was. His physique, on the other hand, implied his surname was Thumpya.

"On what does it depend, Will?"

The man looked momentarily doubtful, either about his name or Kit's question, then replied, "It depends on why you're wondering."

"Ah! Strange as it may seem, Will, I'm wondering because if Mrs. Riley *is* home I'd like to see her."

"Are you the reporter?" he asked.

"No."

"Yeah, right."

Kit shrugged. "If you think you know who I am, why did you ask?"

Will scratched his ear. "Good point. Okay, you are the reporter." He took a few steps back, opened a door just inside the hallway, and waved Kit and Hector in and towards it.

Before they could do anything about the fact that Will seemed to be ushering them into a closet, he shoved them both from behind and slammed the door. When they stopped tumbling and ouching, probably breaking and definitely bruising quite valuable parts of their bodies, they lay at the bottom of, roughly, nine steps—with Hector on top and not moving.

"Hector?"

"Yes, O'Malley?"

"Can you get up, mate?"

"Dunno. I thought I'd just stay on this soft thing."

"I'm the soft thing."

"I know. But your smart-alec repartee with that dense but professional boofhead just got us thrown down a flight of stairs into the dark so, as I said, I'll stay on this soft ..."

"Get off me, you idiot."

Hector rolled groaning away into the dark, where he swore, knocked something over, and swore again. There were some irritating scraping sounds before the room, or whatever they were in, and Hector's face were lit up by the flame of his cigarette lighter.

"O'Malley?" he said suspiciously. "Why are you looking at me like that?"

"Because this is how I look?" Kit suggested, raising her shoulders and her brows. "And, because I can see the blood that's about to ..."

"Shit!" Hector exclaimed, as a smidgen of his good-stuff oozed from his eyebrow, slid through his lashes, and plopped onto his cheek. The flame flicked out, then back to life, by which time he had blood smeared all over his face and the back of his hand.

"Light," Hector pointed. Kit obediently turned, then got to her feet and flicked the switch.

Lots of light!

Not much free space, though, Kit noted. But at least it wasn't a closet, or a room routinely used by the Riley clan to torture their enemies. Not unless they packed their equipment neatly away in lots of boxes between sessions. It was simply a storage cellar with lots of wine racks running off to the right, and a variety of boxes stacked floor to ceiling to the left. Having plenty of wine to drink and no rack to be stretched on didn't make being thrown into it any better, but it did make the situation less threatening.

Unless, of course, Will Thumpya plans to leave us down here forever, Kit thought.

"Hector, you don't smoke," she said. "How come you've got a cigarette lighter?'

"For emergencies," he muttered, giving Kit a curious trying-not-to-smile look.

"Emergencies like what?"

Hector widened his eyes and waved around the room to indicate their predicament.

"Oh yeah, like this happens on a regular basis."

"I'm also seeing someone who happens to smoke," he said.

"You're seeing someone?" Kit was intrigued. Surprised and intrigued.

"Yes, O'Malley. I do have a life outside your sphere of influence, you know."

"Come on, tell me. Who is she?"

Hector gave Kit a look that implied that this was not even *remotely* the time or place for a discussion of this kind. "You're a lunatic, O'Malley," he pronounced. "We're locked in a basement owned by the city's biggest crime family, I'm bleeding to death, and you want to know about my love life!"

"Is it love, Hector?" Kit grinned.

"O'Malley," Hector moaned. "Bad guys. Basement. Head injury. Possible death."

"Oh don't be silly, Hector," Kit said, pushing his hand away from his forehead. "It's just a flesh wound. Put some ice on it and you won't even have much of a bump."

"Ice?"

"Yeah. Later," Kit acknowledged. "I'll check if we're actually locked in down here." She scooted up the stairs, grabbed the door handle, realized her hand hurt, and then returned to Hector. "We're locked in."

"Shall we split up to see if there's another way out?" Hector suggested.

"Good plan, meet you back here." Kit headed off to the right. She counted twelve wine racks, each taller than she was and about three meters long, standing perpendicular to the wall. There was just enough space for two people to walk abreast alongside them or stand between them. There was no other exit; neither door nor window, escape ladder nor handy coal chute.

Kit grabbed a nice bottle of red, and on the way back to the stairs counted 3411 webs, the shed skins of fifty-three huntsmen, one live and fat black house spider, and the shitty evidence of a large family of mice.

"Hector, we have to get out of here," she called out.

"Suddenly you're in a hurry," her sidekick noted, returning with a handful of C- or DV-Ds.

"The place is infested with huntsbastards. We have to get out," Kit stressed.

"I'm lucky, I found pirated movies," Hector said. "What have you got?"

"A bottle of Grange Hermitage, 1959. Have you got an emergency corkscrew, or doesn't your girlfriend scr ..." Kit hesitated, "drink. How do you know they're pirate DVDs?"

Hector glowered at Kit, but not very well. "Because this martial arts film," he explained, waving the disc, "hasn't even been released

90

at the pictures here yet, let alone on DVD." He stuffed the evidence down the front of his jeans, and dropped the other disks into Kit's jacket pocket. "Just in case we get out of here," he said. Then he reached into his own back pocket and unfolded the corkscrew from his pocketknife.

"Were you a boy scout, Hector?"

"You *know* I wasn't, O'Malley." He handed the open bottle back to her.

Kit took a swig, and rolled her eyes in delight. "Oh, wow. Not exactly how I imagined the so-unlikely chance of me ever imbibing a little Grange, but what the heck."

"Is this *good* shit, then?" Hector asked.

"This is most definitely good shit." Kit handed him the bottle, then pulled her mobile out of her belt pouch. "Oh lucky us, it's not broken. Oh shit, the battery's dead."

Hector was screwing up his face. "It tastes like red wine."

"Yeah," Kit said, her tone implying the extra-bloody obvious.

Hector sniffed and relinquished the bottle. "It's red, it's white, it's wine, it's boring."

"It's probably worth about $600 a bottle," Kit grinned.

Hector remained unimpressed. "That's about $40 a mouthful then, O'Malley. But while we're getting expensively drunk, there are two things I want to know. One, considering I've given you about fifteen different chargers, how the hell can your phone *ever* go dead? And two, how the hell are we going to get out of here now?"

Kit ignored his second, presently unanswerable, question. "Don't give me a lecture on technology, Hector. Where's yours anyway, Mobile Man?"

Hector looked sheepish. "In your car."

"You were saying?" Kit said.

"Hey, O'Malley, you got us into this crapola; guess whose job it is to get us out. Ooh, hang on, I think I hear voices." Hector bolted up the stairs, held his hand up to dissuade Kit from making any kind of noise, then pressed his ear to the door. A second later he bashed the door with his fist, yelled "Oi," whacked it a second and third time, then turned and glared down at Kit with what looked a lot like displeasure.

"Get it over with, Hector."

Descending the stairs as he spoke, he said, "Elvis has left the building, O'Malley. I just heard a woman saying: 'for God's sake, hurry up, Will.' To which our friend the meatax said, 'but what about the reporter, she'; whereon the woman interrupted him and said, 'she missed her chance, and we are now late.' This is not good, O'Malley. The bad guys have gone out."

"Well," Kit blustered, "we'll just have to wait."

"For what?"

"For them to come home again. Just as well we've got something to drink, isn't it?"

"Aagghh."

Kit was woken at one in the morning by Hector, who was making a racket opening boxes because he couldn't sleep; at three because she had a pain in her back; and at four because Hector's leg cramp produced a lot of bloody swearing. When she woke again, at seven, she found herself slumped in the corner at the bottom of the stairs, with a sleeping Hector's head on her lap. He had obviously propped her against the wall, after rolling up his jacket and giving it to her as a pillow. They were sitting and lying on several layers of cardboard which, while not in the least bit comfortable, had reduced the chill rising off the concrete floor.

"Hector," Kit croaked. "Hector mate, wake up."

"I'm there already," Hector mumbled. He rolled over and sat up. "That was fun."

"I think we can try banging again. I heard a door slam up there."

"Oh goody," he said, getting to his feet and offering Kit a helping hand up.

Kit grabbed a bottle of wine from the nearest rack and they both limped and groaned their way to the little landing at the top of the stairs. "You hear anything?"

"Nope," Hector said. "Wait. I can hear singing. And it's an actual person. Isn't that nice?"

They both started banging and shouting, "Hey, oi, help, let us out!" until Kit held up her hand. The singing, which for a moment had been getting closer, had stopped abruptly and now there was … nothing.

Kit pushed Hector gently back against the wall. Holding the bottle by its neck, she swung back and then smashed it against the bottom of the door. A good portion of the wine surged out underneath, hopefully securing the attention of whoever was, hopefully, still outside.

There was a muffled bellow—which explained a few things, like just how thick the cellar door was—then thuds, shouting, and … silence. Shit!

Kit prepared a hefty backswing just as the door was flung open by a vase-wielding spiky-haired girl, wearing a mini-skirt and imposing boots. She also had serious backup from an aging "Anne Bancroft" dressed in a red silk dressing gown and armed with an umbrella.

The momentum of Kit's about-to-whack-the-door motion propelled her out into the foyer; with Hector right behind and grabbing hold of her arm so she didn't land flat on her face. The women took two steps back, understandably given that Kit was still clutching the neck of the now broken wine bottle.

"Oh. I forgot," said Will Thumpya, who had just re-entered the picture from the hallway.

"You forgot?" Kit shouted at him.

"Who are you?" the girl demanded, waving the vase. "And why are you in Gran's cellar?"

Kit cocked her head and narrowed her eyes. "Gimme that!" She snatched the vase and chucked it down the cellar stairs.

"Hey!" the girl objected, as the vase bounced once, then crashed its way to the bottom.

"Hey yourself," Kit snapped, winding up her bravado. "My friend and I made noises just like that vase when that knuckle-dragging imbecile there," she pointed at Will, "pushed *us* down into your Gran's cellar …"

"What?" Marjorie Riley demanded, of both Kit *and* Mr. Thumpya.

"… yesterday," Kit finished, through clenched teeth.

Queen Marj, pushing her thick gray-black hair behind her ears, did a fine impersonation of confused. "Explain yourself properly child, or I'll call the police."

Child? Kit was livid now. "You? Call the police? That's rich," she laughed. "We've been in your charming dungeon for," she looked at her watch, "thirteen bloody hours."

"O'Malley, for Christ's sake!" Hector begged.

"I really don't understand," the lady of the house declared. "Who *are* you?"

Kit was too mad to be nervous, which made her reckless, which, she was vaguely aware, wasn't entirely sensible. But bloody hell!

"We were," she said, "simply paying a courtesy call on you, Mrs. Riley, when this merde-head, excuse my French, threw us into your cellar."

Shit-for-brains flexed his whole self and said, "I tried to tell you about the reporter before we went out last night, Queenie."

"What reporter, Will?" his mistress asked.

"Her. There. The reporter you was expecting, and asked me to take care of."

"I tried to tell him last night that I wasn't the, or even a, reporter," Kit said.

Queenie Riley was saying, "She's not the reporter I was talking about Will, and even if she was I did not tell you to shove her, or anyone for that matter, into my cellar. 'Take care of' means invite them in and offer them sherry. How did you get to be such a foolish man?"

"It's in his genes, Gran," said the granddaughter, still eyeing Kit and her bottle warily.

"But Queenie," Will said, "I thought …"

"Please don't!" Queenie gave him a backhand whack in the chest, which fazed him not at all, although it did shut him up. "It's obviously beyond you."

"I'd really like to go home now," Hector muttered.

Queenie turned to him and smiled. "Would you, young man? Perhaps before you do that, we could start over. First, I offer my profuse apologies; second, if you'd care to introduce yourselves to *me*, and explain why you called," she cleared her throat, "yesterday, then we should be able to clear up this little misunderstanding."

"I'd love to," Hector said, speaking loudly over the top of Kit's vexed "little misunderstanding?" which was only a tad shoutier than the granddaughter's, "she's armed, Gran, they're probably nutters."

"I am not a nutter," Kit stated, dropping what was left of the bottle. "I'm just irritated."

"Perhaps you'd care for some breakfast, then. Would that make you feel any better?"

Kit sighed. Who could refuse such a politely offered invitation from the head of a ruthless crime family? "Coffee would help things a lot," she nodded.

Hector whimpered.

"Come," her royal matriarchness commanded. "Sasha, make a pot of coffee and some crumpets, please. We'll be in the sitting room."

"What do you want me to do, Queenie?"

"You can bugger off, Will, you've caused more than enough trouble this week. Go to work, or the gym, or, better still, go play in the traffic."

Everyone who belonged in the household set off in different directions, so Kit and Hector followed Queenie, at a distance, down the hall.

"What is *wrong* with you, O'Malley?" he asked, under his breath. "How come you're suddenly the Princess of Over-reaction? Last night you were nervous about entering the lioness's den and today you're poking the big cat with a long pointy stick."

"I'm pissed off," Kit snarled, following mama-lion into her homely den, which was furnished with antique sideboards, cabinets, bookshelves, and a luxurious floral lounge suite arranged around a glass coffee table. Note the giant nutcracker on the mantelpiece, O'Malley.

Queenie waved them towards one of the couches as she lowered herself carefully, no elegantly, into an armchair. Hector sat, Kit hesitated, Queenie smiled.

"Sit, child. I promise I won't bite. No matter what you may have heard to the contrary."

Kit did as she was told. It seemed the best thing to do. For now.

"Okay, I know who you are not, so perhaps you'd like to tell me who you *are*."

"Do you want me to answer, O'Malley?" Hector prompted, elbowing Kit, who was busy giving Queenie Riley the once-over.

Actually, Kit figured, she was returning Queenie's compliment; as the once-over was precisely what the older woman was doing to *her*, while wearing a curious smile.

"I can manage, thank you, Hector," Kit smiled at him, before returning her gaze to their hostess who, she noted, was remarkably fit for seventy-something. Queenie's skin was amazing, with barely a wrinkle or blemish; and, despite being well able to afford it, the look didn't appear to be artificially acquired. The woman simply had great bone structure. She also had big, clear brown eyes; dark brows; her own teeth; and thick, gray-streaked but still mostly dark hair, styled in a straight shoulder-length cut, parted on the right.

There *was* actually quite a bit of the wonderful Ms. Bancroft about her; but, on closer examination, Kit realized it wasn't so much the whole face, as just the eyes, the hair, and the take-no-prisoners attitude. Queenie Riley was slim but not skinny; straight-backed but not church-pew uncomfortable; and her hands, which were now removing a cigarette from a silver case, were slender and still dexterous.

"Hope you don't mind," she said lighting up, "I'd give the bastards up if I enjoyed them only half as much. You were saying?"

"My name is Kit O'Malley, and this is my friend and associate Hector Chase. I am a private investigator …" She hesitated and raised her hands when Queenie's face adopted an oh-shit look. "It's okay, I have information for *you*," Kit assured her.

"Oh, really?" Queenie huffed, with an *I might have known* roll of her eyes. She was now not so much suspicious as annoyed, or bored. "And how much is it going to cost me, this information I'm sure I just have to have?"

"Nothing," Kit frowned. "I'm a friend of Angela Nichols, who runs The Terpsichore, the piano bar where your nephew was found."

"Oh," Queenie said, her interest reignited.

"Angie told me you visited her yesterday and wanted to speak to her, but the police wouldn't let you. So I offered to drop by—in retrospect, I should've called ahead—and answer any questions you might have about this sad and sorry mess. I was there, at the bar, for most of Thursday, so I know everything there is to know; that is, anything about it that you might want to know."

"And, no doubt," Queenie smiled, "you were also hoping that as a consequence of your visit here, I wouldn't bother your friend again at her place."

"Yes, that too," Kit smiled back, then glanced up as the grand-daughter entered the room, carrying a coffee pot and a plate of steaming buttered crumpets.

"Ah, brekkie," Queenie sighed. "Kit O'Malley, Hector Chase—this is my precious Sasha."

"Gran," Precious groaned, as she set the tray on the coffee table and sized up the intruders again, now that they weren't threatening her with a broken bottle. "And *they* are?" she asked, nonchalantly, as she retrieved four cups, saucers, and cake plates from the sideboard.

"She's a private eye; and he is her friendly associate," Queenie explained. She poured while Sasha used small tongs to serve the crumpets onto individual plates, which she handed around. She then took her serve and propped herself on the arm of her grand-mother's chair.

"Well, go ahead, Ms. O'Malley, tell me what you know about my nephew."

"Please, call me Kit," requested the same PI who, not two days before, had stated quite categorically to herself that only friends and humans were invited to be so familiar.

What's wrong—no, what's *right* with this picture? she wondered, as she filled Queenie Riley in on nearly everything she'd seen at Angie's on Thursday. It must be the whole silk dressing gown, messy hair, coffee, crumpets, and darling granddaughter thing, Kit thought. Lulling alert, O'Malley! This is a bogus sense of security. Do not be fooled by this cozy-family routine; and don't believe, for a second, that Queenie didn't know that you, or *someone*, was locked in her cellar all bloody night.

"So what you're saying," Queenie sounded sceptical, "is that no one that you know had any reason to harm my nephew?"

"Certainly no one I know," Kit verified, "and so far, no one that I know *of*, either. And, while I'm not naive enough to state

97

categorically that there's no connection between your nephew and possibly more than one patron of The Terpsichore, I do have my doubts that any woman who frequents the piano bar on a regular basis would voluntarily involve the establishment in this kind of adverse publicity. It is our refuge from the world; our home away from home."

"Is that how you see my uncle's death? As adverse publicity?" Sasha asked.

"Yes," Kit admitted. "And I'm guessing your grandmother can recognize it as such too."

When Queenie shrugged, Kit continued. "The tragedy of his death aside, and for that you have my deepest sympathy, the scurrilous publicity surrounding where and especially how he was found, has made the circumstances of his death even more public than they were destined to be—given who he was. That same where and how have even, to a sad and certain extent, overshadowed the fact that he was so brutally murdered by persons, so far, unknown."

You are so full of shit, O'Malley, she thought; aware, however, of the tiniest of smiles on Queenie Riley's face.

Sasha snorted, then glanced expectantly down at her grandmother.

"Kit is quite right, Sasha. At least about the unfortunate nature of the publicity," Queenie affirmed. "Your uncle's body being found in a gay women's bar is not good for anyone's business; particularly, I'm guessing, for the gay women. It is, of course, of no benefit to the family, either—not even your aunt. The media attention has made a grim spectacle indeed of a tragic and already too-public happening."

"I suppose," Sasha said, reaching for her coffee.

Okay, Kit thought. I have given, now let's see if I receive. "Were you aware of your nephew's alleged financial interest in The Terpsichore, Mrs. Riley?"

"Oh, for goodness sake!"

Whoops, wrong question!

Then again, maybe not, because Queenie was smiling as she placed her plate on the table. "Young lady, I am not now nor have

I ever been Mrs. Riley. I am Miss or Ms. Riley, Marjorie, Marj, or Queenie. I could have been Mrs. Puig," she sneered, "had I taken my husband's name; but I did not. Given that mad Jim and I were wed for only a year before he drove his car off the Great Ocean Road, I'm rather glad I stuck with Riley—unusual as it was to do so, at the time. I'm especially pleased I retained my maiden name, as the only good thing JP ever did for me was give me my beloved Helen, who in turn gave me Sasha."

Life in a nutshell, Kit thought, catching sight of Sasha, who seemed to be surprised at what, or how much, her Gran was saying. "On a similar note," Kit smiled, "I've never been a lady."

"Duly noted," Queenie laughed. "Now, *child*, your question. No, I was not aware of any financial interest Gerry had or *wanted* to have in your friend's business. That's not to say he didn't; I am simply not aware of anything."

"The local paper ..." Kit began.

"Ah! The press, as you know, lie like snakes in the grass."

"That's exactly what I thought," Kit said. "Although, at least one reporter claims to have a source that's totally reliable."

Queenie looked sceptical. "Does this reporter—and I take it to be the young woman that my idiot chauffer *didn't* lock in my cellar—does she also belong to the flying pigs club?"

"More than likely," Kit grinned.

"Pigs being the operative word there, Kit," Queenie declared. "Given the speed with which Ms. McDermid acquired her spurious, no let's be generous and say 'questionable' information, I'd say she got it from the cops. And you know, I'm sure, how they just love to exaggerate."

Kit shrugged, not wanting to buy into that argument, likely or not. But, it was now crunch time. Trouble was, never having met Queenie before, Kit had no way of knowing whether the crime queen was in a good and generous mood, or simply exercising primo-lulling techniques on a person who'd spent the night not sleeping well on the cold concrete in *her* cellar. Kit glanced at Hector, who seemed strangely resigned as he stuffed half a crumpet in his mouth.

Bugger it, she thought. One thing we do know, O'Malley, is that this might be the only audience we'll ever get, or want, with this woman.

"Queenie, may I ask you a few other questions?" she requested. Hector's elbow jab in her arm was very pointy. "Oh, sorry. May I call you Queenie?"

"You may call me anything you like, dear, as long as it's not *Mrs.* anything. And, while I may choose not to answer your questions, feel free to ask."

"Thanks," Kit smiled, conscious that Sasha was studying her like a bug. Kit decided to look at *her* while she spoke; taking in the spiky hair, the tiny ruby nose stud, the fact that she was dressed to go nightclubbing at seven-thirty in the morning, and that she was probably closer to twenty than the sixteen or so Kit had first estimated.

"Without implying anything at all about your nephew and his business interests," Kit said carefully, "I'm wondering if you think it's possible that Gerry's murder might have something to do with either the deaths of Mike and Julie Sherwood, or the kidnapping of Alan Shipper?"

Queenie raised her eyebrows and waggled her head as she weighed up her answer, or whether to answer. "Either of those possibilities, Kit," she replied, also speaking with care, "are as likely as his strange, sorry, estranged wife having a hand in his murder; *or* any one of his nightclub rivals taking him permanently out of their equation; *or*, and this is the most probable, one of those no-good Barker bastards, just doing what they do."

Kit looked puzzled. "Barker bastards?" she queried, choosing to follow-up on that allegation rather than the too-obvious reference to the niece-in-law.

"A member of the Barker family of bastards," Sasha explained.

Oh yeah, Kit thought; the Barkers—they of the genus *lesser crime family*, and one of the many tribes who faced the Rileys as arch enemies.

"Tell me, Kit, why do you wish to know this about Gerry?" Queenie was asking. "Are you investigating his murder?"

"No," Kit said emphatically. "Of course not."

"Why not? I mean, if your friend is implicated."

Kit gave an expansive shrug. "My friend's *building* is implicated; and even then, only as a repository, or is it a depository." Shut *up*, O'Malley. Too much info.

"Both, perhaps," Queenie smiled. "I take it, Gerry *wasn't* killed there, on the premises?"

Kit screwed up her face. "No. And that *is* a fact, Queenie."

"So, why are you asking these questions," Sasha echoed.

"I'm simply trying to clear air that's been seriously smogged by media reports which have been variously misleading, downright wrong, and majorly hysterical—both in the funny and in the menacingly provocative strife-inducing sense of the word.

"I'm also trying to make sure that the cops, or rather one in particular, don't lay an easy rap on my friend for something she could not possibly have done, being as she is motiveless and not in town when it happened," she explained.

"You're sure?" Queenie asked.

"Positive," Kit said. "She was in Bendigo, for a funeral, oddly enough."

Almost true, Kit thought. Angie definitely wasn't in town when the body was left in The Red. But where she was when the murdering deed was done a week ago, is anyone's guess.

"So who's this cop you don't like?" Queenie smiled.

"What? Oh," Kit said. Idiot, she thought. "Just an old nemesis who loves to find the easy way to the top of everything. It's a personal gig; we *really* don't like each other," Kit half-explained, hoping it would satisfy Queenie. She didn't want to accidentally sick the Rileys onto Charlie Parker; well, not unless she could find a justifiably good reason.

The matriarch shrugged. "What else would you like to know?"

"Given that you mentioned it, Queenie, what about Gerry's business rivals? I don't suppose you'd give me a few names."

Why do you want them, O'Malley? Come on, *think*, woman! A good reason would be ...

"Because, it's just occurred to me," she continued, "that perhaps it wasn't *Gerry* who has an interest in Angie's bar, but one of his rivals. This whole thing could be an elaborate two-birdies-with-one stunt by *them*, to take out your nephew and eventually acquire The

101

Terpsichore. You know, after waiting for the adverse PR to create a buyers' market." Ooh, that's good, O'Malley. Where the hell did that come from?

"They're Gerry's rivals, Kit. You're more than welcome to know who they are. Top of the list is Stuart Barker, who owns the Zeplin Club in Richmond and two pubs in the western suburbs. There's Mickey Stano, who runs Swiggers in Prahran and Harley's in Toorak; and John, no he's dead, Peter Cochrane, who has a trio of clubs in the city and Frankston."

"Are they business rivals or, um, enemies?" Kit asked, hesitantly.

Queenie adopted an owlish expression and waved her right hand. "Far be it from me to influence your opinion of these legitimate business people, Kit."

"Fair enough," Kit smiled. "What about this new Metro Blaazty place? Who owns that?"

"Uncle Gerry," Sasha replied. "Sort of."

"Really?" Kit said surprised. "I thought his was the Moshun Club."

"Gerry also co-owns," Queenie sighed, "owned the Blaazt. The new nightclub was a joint venture with his cousin Adrian and a couple of other associates. His oldest boy, Sean, will be the manager." Queenie frowned. "What made you mention that nightclub, specifically?"

Kit shrugged. "Last night before I came here, and spent the night, a friend offered me *his* invitations to the grand opening on Sunday."

"What's wrong with *him*, then?" Sasha asked, as if giving up tickets to the Blaazt was the most baffling thing she'd heard all morning.

"He's a 46-year-old gay man," Kit smiled. "He didn't think it would be his scene."

"Is it yours?" Sasha asked.

"Don't know yet." Kit returned her attention to Queenie. "What about Gerry's wife?"

"She's a lunatic of the first order."

Kit grinned. "I often say that about my mother, Queenie, but I'm almost certain she wouldn't murder anyone. Do you really think Poppy could have done that to Gerry?"

Queenie gazed at Kit thoughtfully for some moments, deciding, as it turned out, to change the subject—a little. "What if I were to hire you to find out who did murder Gerry?" she posed.

"Gran, don't be ridiculous! You don't know anything about her."

"I can't anyway," Kit stated, adding a serious shrug.

"You can't or you won't?"

"Um," Kit was still flustered by Queenie's left-field offer. No she wasn't; she was flabbergasted. "Both, actually," she said.

"Oh man," Hector muttered.

"At least you're honest," Queenie noted. "What if I double your normal rates?"

"That's very generous Queenie, but *really* I can't," Kit said. Thank *Thistle*, she thought. "My PI license doesn't license me to investigate murder. I'm simply not allowed to."

"Yet she's here doing just that, Gran," Sasha pointed out. "Aren't you?" she asked Kit.

"No, Sasha, I'm not actually. I'm here hoping to verify that there was no good—as in relevant—reason for Gerry's killer or killers to leave him in my friend's bar. It's *so much* better for me, for her, for all my friends—and for you Rileys as well—if his body was left in *our* nightclub for no other reason than to generate a huge amount of demented publicity."

"If that's the reason, and you're probably right," Queenie said, "then there's no question it's working."

"I'm assuming," Kit said, trying out a trusting tone, "that you *really* don't know why your nephew's body was left at The Terpsichore."

"I really don't know," Queenie stated.

"Would you tell us if you did?" Hector queried.

"Oh, he speaks," Queenie noted with amusement. "Yes, I believe I would, Hector; if I thought it would help to find out who killed him. Now, Kit, you say you can't investigate Gerry's murder because you're not allowed to, but why won't you?"

Kit raised her eyebrows. "Because, and not to put too fine a point on it, Queenie, you're the bad guy."

Sasha leaped to her feet in indignation, but Queenie Riley roared with laughter. "I do believe I like you, Kit O'Malley," she exclaimed. "Yes I do, I like you very much."

Oh, shit no, Kit thought.

Chapter 8

"I gather from your loudly non-committal silence, Hector, that you think I'm crazy."

"My uncommitted state has nothing to do with your level of sanity, O'Malley; I already know you're deranged." As Hector held the front door open for her, he glanced into Aurora Press and noted, "Brigie and Del aren't in yet. And my bout of silence was related only to a condition called thinking. I was wondering what you meant."

"I meant," said Kit, removing a note from her office door, "that I address myself when I think." The note commanded her to "Ring Rabbit" on a given mobile number.

Hector shrugged, again. "Yeah, so? Most people talk to themselves."

"Yeah, but do you say things to yourself like, 'Oh that was a fab idea, Hector. We should think about that you and I, *Hector*.' Do you do that?" She unlocked her office.

"O'Malley, I wouldn't use the word 'fab' in a psychedelic bean bag. So that is a worry—that you do, I mean. As for me talking to myself and using my name, I have to say, I don't think so. At least not often enough to say it's something I do. What's that?"

"Dunno," Kit said, picking up the envelope that had skidded across the floor when she opened the door. She ripped it open, removed the contents, and then put on her baffled face. "Still don't," she said. She checked the envelope. Yep, it was addressed to K. O'Malley. That was all it said, though, which meant it had been hand-delivered.

"It's a newspaper clipping," Hector explained helpfully.

"Oh, so it is," Kit gave him a look. "It's an article from *The Age*,

February 11, about a fire in Geelong. But with nothing else in the envelope, I've no idea who sent it or why."

"There's writing on the back that might enlighten you," Hector pointed.

"Or not," Kit said, deciphering the scrawl. "It says, *Go back 3 years: 3VR 379.*"

"That's very helpful," Hector nodded confidently. "What does it mean?"

"Still don't know; *really* don't care." She handed him the clipping, opened the adjoining door to Aurora Press, and waved at Brigit who was coming in the front door. Kit checked the kettle for water, turned it on, and began spooning coffee into the plunger.

"Good morning, lovely friend," Brigit hailed as she dumped a pile of stuff on her desk.

"Morning, Brigie. Is Del coming?" Kit asked. "Hang on, it's Saturday. Why are you here?"

"We've got a deadline, sweetie. We're working tomorrow too. And Del's bringing cake."

"Oh, *mate*," Hector's tone was rollercoaster-suggestive. "I think you might like to care about this." He rattled the paper at her. "This warehouse fire in Geelong wasn't February just gone. It was nine years ago."

"So?"

"Listen, to this," Hector cleared his throat. "Blah, blah, ah: *Such was the ferocity of the blaze, the furniture warehouse was already a smoldering shell by the time firefighters arrived at the scene. There is believed to be an eyewitness to the inferno, which erupted following an explosion at 4 a.m. The warehouse owners, the Stano family of Norlane, estimate the fire caused nearly three million dollars worth of damage.* How spooky is that?"

"Why do I know that name?" Kit asked.

"Queenie, not an hour ago, mentioned *Mickey* Stano. He runs Swiggers in Prahran," Hector reminded her. "But that's only the half of it, O'Malley. The spooky gets weirder."

"Hector," Kit snarled.

"Settle, child," he grinned. "*According to the arson squad members investigating the site several hours later, there was little*

105

doubt that the fire had been deliberately lit. Although the officer in charge declined to reveal the similarities with January's furniture warehouse fires in Werribee, Williamstown, and Altona, Detective Senior Constable Graham Parker," Hector heaved the name out, *"did confirm that they are believed to be connected."*

"Well I'll be ... more confused than ever," Kit exclaimed. "And I do so hate these anonymously sent cryptic clues." She was still standing staring at Hector, with her arms akimbo, and a pathetic expression on her face when Brigit sidled up to her with a huge grin.

The grin vanished. "Shit, and good grief!" she swore. "Have you been fighting again, Kit? And who with this time?"

"Fighting? No. Why?"

Brigit cocked her head and then looked startled as Hector stepped fully into view. "Oh my great grandmother's kippers! Have you been fisticuffing each other?"

"What *are* you talking about, Brigie?" Kit demanded.

Brigit, unusually speechless, simply held up both palms to indicate there was something about Kit that wasn't quite right.

Hector meanwhile was saying, "Gotta go now; me," as he backed towards the exit of O'Malley Investigations.

"You, come back here," Kit commanded. She leaned left and looked at herself in the small mirror on the wall next to the sink. "What the ...?" Her left cheekbone was blue and purple. Oh, and a little bit green. Strangely enough, it wasn't swollen or, now that she touched it, not really sore; a little tender perhaps but—great granny's fish indeed!—it was colorful.

"Damn and blast it," Kit moaned. "How come I always have a black eye when I'm about to see Alex after being apart for a while," she asked no one in particular. "There is no answer to that question; but, you could have told me, you bastard," she said to Hector.

"Hey, I figured if it started hurting you'd know soon enough," Hector claimed, trying to remain straight-faced. Then he pointed at his own eyebrow, his black-and-blue forearm, Kit's bruised left knuckle, both their knees, and lastly her face, before adding, "Besides, all of this? *Your* fault, O'Malley."

"Righto wimp-boy," Kit mocked. "You wanna be a private eye, but can't take the bumps, is that it?"

"Katherine O'Malley," Brigit snapped, "Why did you beat up young Hector?"

Kit turned to Brigit with her hands on her hips. "I didn't," she asserted. "Kinda wishing I had, though, now. But, in reality, a large moron threw us both into a cellar."

"That's okay, then," Brigit nodded at this most ordinary of explanations. "How about *I* finish making the coffee while you tell your story. Or should we wait for Del and the cake?"

"Better wait," Hector suggested.

An hour later, Kit stood under the shower, luxuriating in a super-hot pummel of her back, shoulders, and head, as the water soothed all the aches and some of the bruises. Ow! Not the face, though, she winced, and turned the water off.

"Mlertle?" The Cat asked from her shower-watching spot beside the hand basin.

Kit shook her head, stepped out onto the mat, and grabbed her towel. "It's okay, you don't have to worry, Thistle honey. I did bring it on myself. Sort of."

"Graank," Thistle remarked, leaping to the floor so she could lick Kit's toes.

"Typical, you think? Thanks a lot, buddy," Kit said. She wiped the fog off the mirror, smiled at the laminated Xena and Gabrielle in-action poster reflected from the wall behind her, and then took a good look at her own battle wounds.

Ha! Being shoved into a cellar by Queenie's backward right-hand thug was a pretty ignominious way to score a few bruises. "Make a note, Not-So-Warrior Girl," she said. "Mr. Thumpya *will get* a return bout."

As Del had said earlier, given that Kit, and certainly Hector, hadn't even come close to threatening Will—while asking to be taken to his leader—*his* response was unquestionably in the way-overreaction basket, and therefore unacceptable; and not Kit's fault at all.

While Kit appreciated Del's support, she did wonder how soon her mouth was going to get her into the kind of serious shit that it would then not be able to get her out of. As *that* had been Hector's

107

point over the coffee and cake downstairs, Kit now pondered her own disposition and whether it needed realignment; because while it wasn't *her* to be silent or reserved when vocal or smart-arsey was available, she had to admit that lately she couldn't stop herself from being the latter.

Bah! she thought, fronting up to her open wardrobe. Tomorrow, Scarlet. Let that one ride for now. Concentrate on the things you can figure out; like what to wear. Blue jeans and white T-shirt, loose green rugby shirt—to match the face, which also went with the purple socks—and one black runner later, Kit looked at her overall effect in the full-length bedroom mirror and decided that that too would have to do. She then set about dealing with the Highland flingers in her hair, first by bending over and trying to shake them out, and then by running her hands every which way including loose amongst them. She ended up with the same look she'd started with and, so equipped for the day, she headed for the kitchen to feed the starving Thistle, who'd missed out on dinner the night before.

That done, she poked her answering machine, then headed down the three steps to her lounge to retrieve her other shoe from under the coffee table, while the messages played.

Alex: "Hi darling. I'm flying in at … What, now? Damn. O'Malley, I'll ring you back."

"Oh no," Kit swore.

Lillian: "And if I could just remember where I left it, things would be much easier. Oh, and Michael has gone flippy again; what do you think we should do?"

"Put both of you in care, Mum," Kit suggested.

Enzo: "If you get home before nine tonight, could you give me a call? Ciao lassie."

Kit raised her eyebrows. "Très bien, laddie mate."

Alex: "Hmm. So where are you? Your mobile's not answering either."

"Locked in a cellar all night, my love."

Lillian: "Don't call me tomorrow. Connie and I are going to the Sunday place a day early."

Kit rolled her eyes.

Alex: "Okay, it's midnight Friday and I'm going to sleep. You mightn't be able to get me tomorrow, coz I'm lunching—and this is work, believe it or not—on Joe Brindle's yacht. My plane gets into Melbourne at six-fifteen tomorrow afternoon. I've booked us into Room 917. I miss you."

"She misses me," Kit sang, and did a rumba around the lounge and back into her office.

Vaguely familiar female voice: "O'Malley, this is Cathy Martin. I have some goss you might find interesting. Any sign of Karen Farrell yet?"

Totally unfamiliar male voice: "The fire, O'Malley. It's worth looking into."

Kit sat in her desk chair. "Yeah, but how come you talk like you know me, Fireman?"

Completely uncalled-for male voice: "Charlie Parker here. I need an insight into your, ah, friends in order to proceed fairly with this case. Thought you might oblige me in this matter."

"It's not your bloody case, you dickhead," Kit said to the answering machine.

Alex: "It's eight on Saturday morning. I'm just about to board the boat, the reception's fenagilerts where on earth argubeno oof forget bergel love Virgin happonatch 917."

"Alex, honey, I hope you were talking about Virgin Airlines," Kit said.

That was it. Messages heard and mostly accounted for. Kit picked up the receiver, and hit the autodial for Alex's mobile. No luck. She rang Homicide and asked to speak to Cathy. No luck there either, as the detective was unavailable. Glancing at the kitchen bench to verify she had put her phone on the charger, she left a message for Cathy to ring her on the mobile. She couldn't ring the mystery Fireman back to find out who the hell he was and why he was bothering her, and had no intention of giving Chucky an insight into anything, so she retrieved Rabbit's note from the corner of her desk and rang her.

"Yo. This is Rabbit, you can speak."

"Gee thanks, Rabbit."

"That'd be you, Kit."

"It would indeed. I only just got your note, Rabbit. When did you leave it?"

"Only 'bout two hours ago. Listen, Kit, I know you said you didn't need my help and such, but I found Scooter for you and I'm hangin on to her coz she's real reluctant to talk to the cops. She reckons she'll talk to you, though."

"Why is she reluctant?"

"Dunno; she won't tell me. Will you Scooter? Nope, she's still shakin' her head."

Kit sighed. Like I need this, she thought. "Okay, Rabbit. Where are you?"

"Just up your street in the front bar of the Vaucluse Hotel."

"I'll be there in five. And thanks."

Kit pushed open the pub door, received the requisite olfactory dose of beer and chips, and made her way through a small lunchtime crowd to the table by the window where she'd spotted Rabbit and the no longer missing-in-action Scooter Farrell.

Rabbit, in T-shirt and black overalls, looked just the same as she had yesterday, which was par for her course; while Karen Farrell, nominal head of the Scooter Gang, looked as alluring as ever. Apparently, even when possibly hiding out from the cops, she still liked to look her best—as in young, slightly butchy, almost-femme, definitely fatale, and leader of the pack-type cool. Scooter—age about twenty-four, height around five-seven—had a knockout smile, short blonde hair, and blue, blue eyes. She was the fantasy lay of a good seventy per cent of the baby-dyke population of Melbourne, and a fair number of the grown-ups too. And she knew it, and she loved it; and, while she wasn't in the least bit up herself, she'd never been known to turn down a good offer. There were even rumors of a notched belt.

By the time Kit edged her way through the suits and skirts and sat down with them, Rabbit had already poured her a beer from their jug.

"Nice of you to join us, Kit," Rabbit nodded.

"Thanks for the invite," Kit smiled. "Okay, what's with you, Scooter?"

"Do I have to talk to the cops, Kit? I'd really rather not."

"What are you worried about? They just want a statement. You didn't see anything that Rabbit and the others didn't see, did you, so what's the big deal?"

"Exactly. What's the big deal?" Scooter seemed more nervous than she should.

Kit shrugged. "Just state what you saw. Say it, sign it, over and done with. No biggy."

Scooter frowned, went to say something, frowned again, squeezed out a little whimper, and finished by looking helpless.

Kit's phone started ringing at the same moment that lights of various kinds dawned, flicked on, and did the whole *oh I get it* thing in her mind. Kit gave Scooter a don't move, don't speak hand signal while she wriggled to get her phone out of her pocket.

"O'Malley," she said, not taking her eyes off young Scooter, who now looked like she was hoping aliens or netballers would rush in and abduct her.

"Yeah hi, it's Cathy."

"Oh, hi mate," Kit said cheerfully suggestive. "Where are you?"

111

"Just passing the Tennis Centre heading towards the city. Why?"

"Great! Hey, why don't you join me for lunch at the Vaucluse Hotel in Swan Street."

"Do I want to?" Cathy queried.

"Oh *yeah*. It'd be great to catch up."

"Message received. I'll be there in as long as it takes." They both hung up.

Kit twirled her phone on the table, still looking at Scooter. "You did see something else."

Scooter looked fit to burst, but kept her mouth firmly shut.

"No, that's not it," Kit smiled. "You *know* something else."

"I know," Scooter closed her eyes for a moment, "I *knew* who it was. When Angie opened up The Red and we found the body, I knew then it was Gerry Anders."

Kit did a double take on that unexpected admission. "Do you know who killed him?"

"Of course I bloody don't!" Scooter shouted. "Sorry," she added softly.

"It's okay, mate," Kit stroked her hand. "Did you know him, or just know who he was?"

Scooter fiddled with her bracelet as she contemplated the distinction. "Sort of both. I mean, I didn't like know him to talk to or anything; but, I *know* him."

Blimey, Kit thought, this is like getting your own blood back from a vampire.

"Scooter, I need help here," she said. "Did you leave Angie's because you were, I dunno, upset because the guy was dead?"

"Shit no!" Scooter hissed. "I wasn't upset at all. Gerry Anders was a prick."

"Well, what then?" Kit begged. "If you didn't care that he was dead, and you don't know who killed him, why the hell are you so freaked out?"

Scooter sighed. "It's a family thing. A very complicated family thing."

"Aren't they all?" Kit noted. Okay, it's a family deal. She squinted at Scooter but discarded the likelihood even as she asked the question. "You're not related to the Rileys, are you?"

"Hell no!" Scooter exclaimed, but with a look that suggested Kit was on a parallel track.

"Scooter, mate, I am this far," Kit used her thumb and index finger to indicate just how close that was, "from thumping you, ever so nicely, or walking. So speak, or I'm out of here."

"Okay, okay," Scooter surrendered. "My cousin, who is also my bestest friend, is having a secret super-classified relationship with Gerry Anders' son, Tom."

"That's it?" Kit said.

"What's with you Farrells and your secret screws?" Rabbit smirked. "Who else is doing the naughty besides your cousin and ..."

"Shut *up*, Rabbit," Scooter snapped, before returning her attention to Kit.

"Sorry," Rabbit sulked.

"No, Kit, that's not it. But that over-my-dead-body secret, is the simplest part of a shitful mess. I've no idea whether this means anything to you, but it will to the cops. Cousin Suzie isn't a Farrell, she's a Barker; daughter of Stuart, granddaughter—as I am—of Papa Leo."

"Who's head of the Barker family of bastards," Kit stated, immediately gesturing an apology for the insult. "That's what Queenie Riley and *her* granddaughter call your lot," she explained, while thinking: New Zealand is looking better by the hour.

Scooter's shoulders slumped. "I so wish they weren't my lot. Except for Suzie, who I love to death, I rarely have anything to do with my Barker cousins. I hadn't seen Uncle Stuart in three years until my mother insisted I go with her to visit his unconscious body in hospital."

"What's he doing there?" Kit asked. "I mean, apart from being unconscious."

Scooter sighed. "This is where the shitty mess gets complicated. At least I think it does and that's why I don't want the cops to know *who* I am. Talk about me being in the wrong place."

Uh-oh, perfect timing for that statement, Kit thought, spotting Cathy in the doorway. And she couldn't pretend the detective was anything else, because Rabbit might not play along.

Kit shuffled her chair closer to Scooter and put a protective arm around her—so she wouldn't be able to take off. "My friend who's about to join us is the cop in charge of ..."

Scooter tried to lurch away. "You bitch, O'Malley."

"It's okay. *She's* okay, I promise. Let's see if we can make a deal here. You may be the only one who can shed any light on this mess."

"I don't want to shed anything," she snarled.

Although Scooter relaxed a little, apparently recognizing a lost cause when she was in one, Kit kept hold of her as Cathy took the empty seat at their table. Kit gave Cathy a suggestive look, while offering undercover intros. "*Cathy*, this is my friend Scooter Farrell."

"Nice to meet you at last, Scooter," Cathy smiled.

Ms. Farrell grunted eloquently, so Kit said, "Scoot was just telling me how she knew who your late friend was ... on Thursday ... before you got there. It seems her cousin ..."

"Kit!" Scooter snapped, "When I said 'over my dead body,' I wasn't kidding."

"Trust me, mate," Kit gave Scooter's shoulders an extra squeeze.

Oh, and I can't believe you said that, O'Malley.

"Her cousin, one of the Barker clan," she continued, "is doing a Romeo and Juliet routine with one of Gerry's sons."

"Oh really? That's nice," Cathy said, as if Kit had said Dimmey's were having a g-string and sock sale. "Is that why you've been," she searched for a word, "unavailable, Scooter?"

"Sort of, *Cathy*," Scooter waggled her head.

Cathy shrugged with disinterest. "Unless you or your cousin or her Romeo know anything about his father, then I couldn't care less about their love affair."

Scooter, the tip of her tongue clenched between her teeth as she shook her head in disbelief, finally whispered, "Cathy, I don't give a rat's arse whether you know or care about it. But now that you do, what I *am*, and only ever was, worried about is that Papa Leo Barker or Queenie fucking Riley will find out. You do get the possible ramifications of Kit's astutely arrived-at Romeo and Juliet reference, don't you?"

"Of course, Scooter. And as I said," Cathy held up her hands, "no interest here. Therefore no need to repeat those facts to anyone. Unless …"

"Let me guess," Rabbit jumped in. "Unless they turn out to have bearings on the case."

"Couldn't have said it better myself," Cathy acknowledged.

"Scooter was just getting to the other reason why she wanted to hide from you," Kit said.

"I'm going to get you for this, Kit," Scooter promised, although it seemed, now that it came down to it, she was relieved. "The thing that makes this web more tangled, I *think*, is that my Uncle Stuart, the rotten-arse father of my cousin *Juliet*, is in the Alfred Hospital. He's been there for four weeks, but only came out of his hit-and-run, bullbar-induced coma on Friday. *Last* Friday, not yesterday."

"Hit and run by …" Cathy said questioningly.

"A large, dark car. And no, he didn't see who it was. Or at least he claims not to know who ran him down as he crossed The Strand from the Williamstown Yacht Club. The thing is, it's natural, like in their DNA, for the Barkers to assume it was the Rileys."

"Why is that?"

"I couldn't even begin to explain it, Kit," Scooter admitted wearily. "I'm not really sure I know how the feud started, but feud it is, and often bloody. I do know it was already a major quarrel when Papa Leo was a kid, and he's nearly eighty."

"So your fear, and by that I gather you don't know anything for sure," Cathy smiled, "is that Gerry was payback for Stuart."

Scooter pulled a face. "I really hope not."

"If you answer some other questions for me now, Scooter, we can forgo the statement I was after. For now at least."

"Yeah?" Scooter said in disbelief. "Go ahead, ask away."

"Where did you go when you left the bar on Thursday?"

"Great. The one question I don't want to answer."

"Should we assume you were with *your* hugely secret inamorata?" Kit said helpfully.

"Fucking wonderful! Let me guess which bucket-mouth you got that from."

"Hey," Rabbit self-incriminated. "That's all I said, Scoot; seein' as how that's *all* I know."

"Which it seems, Rabbit, is so much more than enough," Scooter growled at her. "Look, where I went has nothing to do with any of this," she explained. "I swear. Yes, I left the bar because I didn't want to be there when you guys arrived; but I simply met a friend I'd been going to see after lunch anyway. I just got there early."

"Fair enough," Cathy said. "Can you tell me who in your uncle's family might be the most inclined to take action for his run-in with a moving vehicle; if, in fact, revenge was the case?"

"No."

"Is that a no you can't, or a no you won't," Kit asked.

"Yes," Scooter replied mockingly, looking at Kit and then Cathy as if they were both mental. "I actually can't because I wouldn't have a clue *who* would, *if* they were going to. On the other hand, if I knew for sure, and it *was* a family member, not only would I *not* tell you, but you wouldn't see me for dust. On my third hand, if any of this *is* so, then the return gig could've just as easily, so I gather, been handled by a sub-contractor."

"To keep the distance?" Cathy asked.

"Well, yeah."

"If I keep quiet about your Shakespearean tragedy in the making, will you let me know if you hear anything at all that you think you can tell me?"

Scooter squinted. "Yeah."

"Thank you," Cathy said. She gazed thoughtfully at her potential snitch, before noting, "I get the impression there's more to you than just a temp worker in an old folks' home."

Scooter smiled humorlessly. "I was an English lit teacher, but I was retrenched when the community school I worked for closed down. Can I go now?"

Cathy pulled out a business card and handed it to her.

"I'm not walking around with this," Scooter declared. "Here, write your number on the back of Kit's card."

"Strange woman," Cathy commented, as she and Kit watched Rabbit and Scooter wend their way through the lunchtime drinkers.

A guy in a suit was about to do what guys in suits in pubs do to cute girls who push their way through packs of guys in suits until he noticed Rabbit, covering Scooter's rear, and smiling her special cheesy bodyguard smile. Whatever the guy was about to leeringly propose, got drowned by his hurriedly swallowed half glass of beer. Scooter was oblivious, Rabbit just nodded thoughtfully, and they both kept on walking out into Swan Street.

Chapter 9

A squall, for it couldn't claim to be anything else, swept its way past the pub window. And then did it again. One minute, sunshine; next second, leaf-laden urgent wind with horizontal rain. Then sun, bluster, and, oh, hail—all at once. Bizarrely typical, thought Kit, watching a few Swan Street perambulaters morph into track stars as they dashed for cover. Other shoppers, qualified for Melbourne's autumn, narrowly avoided taking out the eyes of strangers as they snapped up their umbrellas. A courier used the thing he was delivering to keep his head dry; and a blue ute skidded to a stop to avoid the sandwich board that tried to kill itself by leaping onto the road.

"Another drink?" asked her companion, apparently noticing nothing untoward outside.

"No thanks, Cathy," Kit replied, returning her attention to the inside world. "I've done nothing but drink coffee and beer since I had breakfast with Queenie Riley this morning."

"You didn't!" Cathy seemed impressed.

Kit grinned. "I had no choice, having spent the night in her cellar. Or rather, she felt she had no choice, after her granddaughter let me out."

"W … why? Or shouldn't I ask?"

Kit recounted the night's adventures, in between having to move her chair twice: first to let a woman, as round as she was tall, squeeze by; and again, so several burly blokes didn't have to break formation to get to the bar. "So, it was a case of mistaken identity," she finished. "Queenie's thug-boy thought I was Carrie McDermid; though I'm still not sure whether Queenie knew I was there all night or not."

"I can't believe you drank that wine," Cathy laughed.

Kit shrugged playfully. "I thought it was worth about six hundred bucks so, in retrospect, I'm glad I hid the empty, coz Del rang a wine auction place this morning and the '59 Grange is valued between thirteen and sixteen hundred."

"For one bottle? How can any wine be that good?"

"Oh it *was!* But, had I chosen the bottle next to the one I did," Kit said, now-knowingly, "I suspect you'd be dragging me from the Yarra, coz the 1951 vintage I waved my hand over is worth a mere forty grand."

"There are some things in life that I just don't get," Cathy confessed.

"Uh-huh," Kit said. "So, what's this gossip you had for me?"

"Oh yeah. That guy from one of Charlie's photos, you know, standing with the guy that you didn't know, well he's dead."

Kit shook her head. "Sorry, which one is dead?"

"The guy you knew, the ex-cop Edward Jackson."

"Pauly-J, really? When, how?" Kit asked.

"Cancer, July last year. It was obviously an old photo."

"What about the other bloke, then? The ugly mutt who was also at Angie's?" Kit asked.

"He's a rent-a-headbanger by the name of Sid Ralph." Cathy's eyes lit up. "Most recent employer—Stuart Barker."

"You're kidding!" Kit exclaimed and then thought, Yep, Rotorua, here I come.

Cathy suddenly looked dubious. "It couldn't be *that* easy, though, could it?"

"Doubt it," Kit agreed. "I mean, I doubt your case, with such a carefully staged and grotesque opening scene, will be that easy to close; though the reason might be easy to nail."

"And *your* reasoning for that?" Cathy prompted.

Kit considered the obvious. "If ordinary family feuds—by which I mean squabbles between law-abiding kith and kin—can begin over silly slights or misunderstandings, then it probably defies *our* understanding what kind of insignificant incident, relatively *and* comparatively speaking, could have started this on-going war between rival clans who not only, as a matter of course, work and play outside the law, but who also fiddle a fast and loose tune with other areas of civilized behavior as well."

Cathy looked confused, then bemused. "Like throwing you into a cellar?"

"For starters," Kit nodded. "And it's more than possible, given the evolution of conflicts of this nature, that the whole affair is based on suspicion, mistake, wild assumptions, or unproven accusations. But, regardless of its root system, just imagine for a moment *how much* ingrained rivalry and pointless hatred, not to mention inbred stupidity and blinkered reasoning, goes into a blood feud that's at least three-score-years-and-ten in the making."

Cathy smiled. "So, O'Malley, you reckon if Stuart woke from his coma last Friday, and Gerry got the gong on the weekend, that Barker-inspired retribution *is* the key to all this."

"Oh yeah," Kit agreed emphatically. "Coz the other thing about revenge is that while it might make a tasty gazpacho, it's more often served boiling hot from the battlements; which is why it's self-perpetuating and, so very often, screamingly foolish."

Cathy sighed. "All of which makes this whydunit bloody obvious. But the exact *who*dunit, given Scooter's sub-contract theory, leaves us in about square two."

Kit nodded. "Unless Gerry's murder in square one was payback for the dead Sherwoods. Mind you, there is the chance that Uncle Stuart was actually run over by a drunk yachty on his way home to anywhere, and that Gerry was done-in by a gay vampire."

"There's that too," Cathy laughed.

"While we're covering topics of a far-fetched nature, you better take a look at this," Kit said, sliding the Fireman's newspaper clipping across the table.

Cathy's puzzled frown remained in place as Kit detailed the connections—as she understood them—between the Stano family of Norlane, Mickey Stano of Swiggers Nightclub, the late Mr. Anders and therefore Queenie Riley, and, therefore again, the Barker family. "Beyond that I'm clueless," she stated, retrieving the clipping before Cathy could read the scrawl on the back.

"And then there's Charlie," Cathy pointed out. "What's with that, do you reckon?"

Thank Thistle, *she* brought it up, Kit thought; then said ever so casually, "Chucky? He's always been a coincidental kind of bloke. But you don't think he is significant do you?"

Cathy's eyes were wide. "I bloody hope not."

Half an hour later, and making a run for it between two Antarctic-generated mini tempests, Kit dashed back down the street and threw herself into the foyer of her building—with three strangers right behind her and closing fast.

"Sorry," they all said as they stumbled into each other, and then marveled at their pursuing downpour, through which they now couldn't see the other side of the street.

"Don't worry, it'll be gone in a jiffy," Kit predicted. "See! There it goes." She turned and headed for her office, to be met by a skulking hulk at the end of the hall. Actually, he wasn't hiding so much as getting up from where he'd been sitting on her steps.

"At last! I've been waiting forever," he complained.

"Have you come to apologize?" Kit asked.

"No."

"Then, get lost." Kit unlocked and entered her office, leaving the door open as she wandered over to give a purposeful hoy to Del and Brigit through the other door.

"Look, I was sent ..."

"You still here?" Kit said, standing akimbo *and* glaring.

"All right, bugger me! I'm sorry I threw you and your friend down the stairs."

Kit shrugged. "What do you want, Will?"

"I don't want nothin. Queenie wants you to read this. Please."

Kit accepted a floral envelope, pulled out an also-floral card, lavender scented, and read:

> *Dear Kit, Please consider taking on a small task for me. I will pay you $2000 to escort my granddaughter to the opening of my nephew's nightclub. As this was an event you were planning to attend anyway, you could regard it as more of a favor—if you prefer. Queenie.*

A favor? Who's she kidding? Kit's mind shouted at her—loudly! Do a favor for Queenie Riley, and the next thing you'll be pricking your finger and swearing a blood oath just to save yourself from having your tongue removed so you can't blab to anyone.

"Do you know what this is about?" she asked Will.

He sniffed. "Someone rang and threatened, like, the whole family—you know, one by one."

"So why me? And why didn't Queenie come in person or ring me?"

"This is her version of in person," Will explained.

"And I gather Sasha refuses to miss the opening and the other bodyguards are booked?"

"Something like that."

Kit shook her head, shook it again for good measure, then pointed her unwanted guest in the direction of gone. "Tell Queenie I'll think about it; and I'll ring her at five today."

"Okay. Will do."

"Of course you will, Will. Now piss off." She closed the door behind him.

"You are stark raving bonkers!" Del stepped in from her office. "Brigie should take you over to Dimmey's to help you pick out a pretty hat to go with your new cement thongs."

"What can I say?" Kit handed Del and Brigit the card. "Queenie likes me. A lot."

"Ooh, you're in the sticky this time, aren't you?" Brigie noted. "Are you going to do it?"

"Don't know," Kit replied wearily. "I *am* going to this shindig, so I s'pose I could keep an eye on young Sasha. But it's asking for trouble; I just know it."

"And if you say no?" Brigit asked.

"To Queenie Riley?" Del added pointedly.

Kit waved her hands around. "Much the same outcome as saying yes, but right now I'm going to suss out the Zeplin Club up in Bridge Road. Wanna come with?"

"You bet," Brigit jumped. "Why?"

"Oh, save me," Del begged, returning to the safety of her publishing deadline.

"It's okay, Del," Kit called after her. She turned to Brigit. "Stuart Barker, one of the Riley rivals, owns the Zeplin Club. I just want to take a squiz and it'd be better if I had company. I'll drop you back afterwards on my way to the airport."

Previously unknown to a certain local PI, Richmond's famous—infamous?—Zeplin Club was stashed among the clothing shops in Bridge Road. The entrance was a small no-nonsense black door, set slightly back from the footpath, under a blue and yellow awning.

No sooner had Kit and Brigit stepped inside and registered the smoky and atmospheric gloom, except for the spot lights illuminating the bar and ten card tables, than they were given the bum's rush by a flubbedy old woman in a square skirt, cardigan, and black stockings.

"Competition day, no visitors allowed," she mumbled, and closed the door in their faces.

"Interesting," Kit remarked. "So what did you notice in there, Brigie?"

Brigit adopted her special remembering face. "Only one woman, no ventilation—they'll all die of respiratory failure long before the lung cancer gets them—that tacky beveled orange glass at the back of the extensive liquor selection behind the bearded barman, and a lot of guys playing, I've no idea what. Go Fish maybe?"

"That pretty much sums it up," Kit agreed. "Sorry about the aborted expedition."

"I could stake out the joint, if you want," Brigit offered.

"No thanks, sweetie," Kit chuckled. "It's not at all necessary."

"What were you hoping to find?"

"No idea. I thought it was a nightclub, so it was different, if nothing else."

"I think that's a nightclub next door," Brigit pointed.

"How do you know? It's got no name at all."

Obviously a minor detail for Brigit, who was already on her way and announcing, over her shoulder, "In that case, it's gotta be related to the den of canasta cardsharks next door."

"Sharps; and why does it?" Kit said, catching up. Oh, but this *is* more like it, she thought, as they entered another gloomy but this time large space with a bar down one side, high stools and tables clustered at the front, and a dance floor at the back. Unlike next door's gloom, this kind was provided by the minimal lighting that indicated it was not yet open for the day.

To prove the point, "We're not open yet," came a voice from the dark at the end of the bar.

"So I gather," Kit said, heading towards the woman anyway. "We're in Melbourne just for the weekend, you know, for shopping and eating and drinking, but we're confused. This is the Zeplin Club, right? We went next door by mistake."

"Strangeness in there," Brigit declared.

"You got that right," the woman laughed. "A bunch of guys playing competition rummy for little plastic trophies; go figure. We lost our sign in that storm earlier, so it's no wonder you're confused. The same people do own both places, though, so we share the name. This is *The* Zeplin nightclub and next door is the Zeplin Club. We open at six but only for tapas type food. The band tonight is Bruce, and our DJ is Gigawatt. It's the place if you wanna dance."

Kit squinted. "Did you get them round the wrong way?"

"What? Oh," she chuckled. "No, I didn't. The band really is called Bruce."

After dropping Brigit off, Kit had nipped upstairs to feed The Cat and change her clothes—twice—only to end up wearing a version of what she'd taken off. She'd tried ringing Enzo and Alex again; and had warily rung her mother to find out what Sunday place she'd gone to on Saturday. Enzo still wasn't answering, Alex's phone was off, and Lillian hadn't returned from tomorrow yet. She'd then done a third time-check, at five-forty, and announced, "I s'pose we could just go to the hotel early, Thistle, and have a drink in the bar if they won't let us in the room. Me, I mean, baby-puss; they wouldn't let you in, you being a cat and all."

She'd then repacked her overnight bag and headed out, to where she was now: sitting in her stationary car on the elevated Bolte Bridge—with the housing commission highrises off to her left, the CBD to her right, and the river down below—waiting, waiting, wai- aaaggh! All things being equal, what with the Citylink system

124

sometimes being what it was cracked up to be, once Kit had hit the Burnley Tunnel it *should've* taken her thirty minutes max to get to the Melbourne Airport Hilton. No traffic lights all the way out to Tullamarine. What a joy.

Ha! It was just as well she loved this view of the city skyline embossed against a five-shades-of-gray cloudy sky, at twilight, on a Saturday, in April, because she'd been looking at it for fifteen minutes now, while the ubiquitous *they* cleared the mess off the road from a four-car tailgating accident in the two left lanes. Kit had even, without giving a damn, had time to wonder what sport was happening at the madly illuminated Colonial Stadium.

Kit sighed, groaned, swore, then adjusted her phone's earpiece by poking it farther in. She picked up her mobile to dial the number written at the top of Queenie's scented card, and turned down Vanessa Amorosi, who'd been singing her wonderful lungs out at top volume.

Five rings, and then a voice tinged with trepidation. "Marjorie Riley. Hello."

"Hi Queenie, it's Kit O'Malley."

"Ah, that's a relief. I thought you might have been another crank."

"How many calls have you had?"

"Just the one that Will told you about. But the phone hasn't rung at all since then."

"Queenie," Kit said, unable to help the ironic tone, "you don't really strike me as the kind of woman who'd get rattled by a menacing phone call."

"Kit," Queenie replied, "I'm a 76-year-old woman with a cherished granddaughter whose life has been threatened. Doesn't matter who else I am."

"Point taken," Kit acknowledged, as the traffic was finally waved forward.

"Where are you?" Queenie asked.

Where am I? Kit's mind echoed in translation. "Why?"

"Sorry; bad habit, I know," Queenie admitted, or covered. "I like to know where people are when I'm talking to them on the phone."

And at all other times, no doubt. Kit wondered if Queenie had asked her crank caller where he was when he rang. "I'm in a water

125

taxi on the Yarra," Kit lied, as her speedo, and she and the car along with it, reached 100 kph and the start of the Tullamarine Freeway.

"I've never taken one of those river taxis," Queenie said, as if that was truly strange.

Me neither, Kit thought, then cringed at what she was about to rush headlong into—on the phone, not in the car. "I've considered your request Queenie. Hector and I will play escort, or bodyguard, for Sasha tomorrow night. But *only* the once and on one other condition."

"And that would be?"

"That you *also* give a thousand bucks to the Lort Smith Animal Hospital. Today."

Queenie cackled. "Deal."

"So, do you want us to pick her up, or just watch over her at the club?"

"I'd like you to collect her and bring her home, please, Kit. It's the only way I'll let her go."

"Righto. I'll ring you, or her, tomorrow to make arrangements. I'll talk to you then."

At six-thirty precisely, Kit parked her RAV in the multi-storey airport carpark, then took the lift to the Hilton Hotel lobby, where the concierge informed her that Ms. Cazenove had already checked in. Moments later, and fairly brimming with anticipation, apprehension, sexual tension—*"it's just emotion,"* she sang—as well as inclination, affection, and all the other "ions" she'd been battening down for the week, she knocked on the door to Suite 917.

In the very next nanosecond, three midgets on wheels came howling down the hall at speed, lost control for long enough to knock Kit on her arse, and kept right on going. Kit was still sitting there frowning and looking like a complete goose when the door to Room 917 opened before her. She cocked her head and smiled beatifically, as her gaze traveled up from a pair of bare feet, ankles, and shins, to the hem of a fluffy white bathrobe, and on up to the—*oh*, and again, *oh-so* seductive, and gorgeously suggestive slightly gaping V where the robe didn't quite meet between breasts that Kit could tell were otherwise naked. And then up, up to the tousled auburn hair and that smile, *the* smile, and those laughing gray Cazenove eyes, and—*hooley-dooley*—Kit's mind set about arousing every *other* part of her body with delight, desire, amazing heart-expanding passion and, there was absolutely no doubting it any more, love. This really *was* it. Love of the *in*-it variety, with a capital L and all the trimmings.

Wow! she thought. "Wow!" she exclaimed.

She of the molten and sexy, amused and inviting voice said, "What are you doing down there, O'Malley?"

"Would you believe I'm just sitting here so I can admire you?"

"No," Alex laughed, reaching out her hand.

"Then it's likely you won't take to the idea of me being run down by midgets either," Kit smiled, allowing herself to be pulled into Alex's enfolding arms and back into the room.

Alex pushed the door shut and Kit up against it, then covered her face and neck with kisses. And Kit let her do all that, because she now had no choice as her legs had gone all shaky and ridiculous and because there was nothing in the whole world better than Alex's mouth on her neck … except for, ah that: Alex's mouth on hers.

Kit reached up, placed her hands gently on her woman's face, and turned *her* back to the door, so she could explore that mouth, her tongue, and, "You're all wet," she noted.

"You got me out of our bath," Alex whispered, taking Kit's hand, and all the rest of her, to lead her through the lounge room, then the bedroom, and on into the ensuite, where a giant bubble-filled spa awaited.

"I am *all* yours," Kit declared, yanking off her rugby shirt.

"I truly hope so," Alex smiled, "because I plan to do things to you that no one else should be doing." She placed Kit's hands inside her robe, so *she* could remove the rest of Kit's clothes; in between kisses and caresses, and then more of each.

When Kit was naked and helpless with want, Alex shrugged that robe off and stepped into the spa, holding out her hands in invitation. If the bath had been big enough, Kit would have dived in head-first and then slid up Alex's body. But it wasn't, so she stepped in and slid down it instead, pulling the world's most gorgeous woman on top of her into the bubbles.

Chapter 10

Kit stood, her forehead and the palms of both hands pressed against the cold window, staring out at the starry cloudy night. She marveled—no, she didn't have enough energy for that—she vaguely appreciated the Melbourne city lights, way off in one direction; and wondered about the state of mind of the designer of the huge and peculiar concrete structure that was the airport control tower, which rose in the other direction behind the old Ansett terminal. Poor old Ansett, she thought. The more things change, the more they bloody move along.

"Kit? What's up?"

Kit flinched, but leaned back into Alex's embrace. "Nothing," she shrugged. "Don't know. Can't sleep."

"Obviously you can't sleep, darling. But you were asleep, so what woke you? And is this normal or just something that happens every time we're together?"

Kit turned in her arms and looked puzzled. "Does it?"

Alex smiled. "Most times."

Kit frowned. "Don't know what it is."

"Well, is it bad dreams? Indigestion. What?"

"*Strange* dreams; not bad ones, not really. When I wake I'm always cold."

Alex ran her hand back through Kit's hair. "Cold? That would explain your other habit of getting out of bed and standing naked in front of a window, then."

Kit offered a crooked smile. "Cold inside," she explained. "Like a deep down core cold."

Alex led her back to the bed, piled the pillows so they could sit up, and then got in and gathered Kit into her arms under the covers. "Okay," she said. "Let's take a look at what's going on in your waking life that might be giving you nightmares."

"They're not nightmares, Alex," Kit denied. "They're more like colorful bits of dread."

Alex laughed. "Redefining the word doesn't make them something else, Kit."

"But there's no scary monsters, or evil bastards; no one is chasing or threatening me, or ..."

"But you wake up scared and cold," Alex said.

"Who said scared? I didn't say scared."

Alex raised an eyebrow.

"Okay," Kit agreed reluctantly. "But they don't make any sense— at all. None."

"So in the immediate aftermath what do you think about when you stand there starkers, staring out the window?"

"This time, I was thinking how much the traffic control tower looks like a giant golf tee."

"O'Malley, be serious."

"I was. Thinking that, I mean; *and* being serious. I'm tired of it, though, you know? I always have to be so fucking serious, coz I have to tend to so many awfully serious things. I swear my only salvation is that I *have* a sense of humor, warped and misplaced as it often is. But if it wasn't there, I'd be in a round room somewhere screaming at the walls."

"Wouldn't we all? Maybe you need a holiday."

"Oh yeah, cool. But, I've got all these *things* to do, Alex. There's Angie and the bloody dead guy in the bar; Enzo and his alleged Russian count; Queenie and her grandchild in jeopardy; Michael's gone strange again; Mum's stuck in tomorrow somewhere; and Marek," she blew a raspberry, "Marek is *really* not dealing with his Bubblewrap loony. Then there's Chucky, and Carrie McThing, and the irritating Fireman with his ludicrous note ..."

"Stop already," Alex interrupted. "And who's Michael?"

"My brother."

"Oh, well you're allowed worry about him. But Marek's case is his problem, not yours."

"Alex, I'm not talking about his case. I'm talking about Marek.

He's not coping with it, psychologically or emotionally. That's not like him. And I don't know how to help."

"Maybe you can't."

"But it's my job, Alex."

"Yours? Why?"

"He's my friend."

Alex sighed deeply. "Oh, Kit darling, it doesn't work like that. It's not your job."

"Yes it is," Kit insisted. "Well, it's not like a career-type job, but it is what I do, Alex. And Jonno's stuff is one of the evil bads I can't walk away from." She sighed. "This is me, my life, my stupid Emma Peel, Warrior Chick, O'Malley-to-the-rescue, frustrating, fulfilling, can't help myself, meddling, motivating life-force *thing*." She held her hands up like empty claws.

"Okay, darling, I get it. But you don't need to take the full weight of Marek's burden to be able to help. No matter how much your imaginative little mind would like you to be, you are *not* a super-hero. Just be there for him, if he needs you."

"He does now, I think. Angie too, at the moment. Michael might, if he applied any kind of clear thinking to *his* life; and then there's Mum." Kit waved her empty claws in frustration.

"What's wrong with Lillian?" Alex asked.

"You've met her," Kit said, as if that was explanation enough. "And there's the Fireman and the Russian and the skating short-people who I'm *sure*, now that I think about it, bowled me over on purpose."

"You mentioned the Russian and the Fireman already. But, are you saying it really *was* midgets on skates who knocked you down and beat you up?"

"Rugrats they were, Alex; you know—kids. And knocked down, yes; beat up, no," Kit clarified, and then looked perplexed. "What? Did you think I just fell over out there?"

"Yes," Alex laughed. "Sorry, Kit, but you do have a tendency, at least when I'm around."

"Ah well," Kit grinned at her.

"Are you going to tell me who did this, then?" Alex queried, brushing her fingertips lightly across Kit's bruised cheek.

"A crime queen's cerebrally challenged gofer-thug mistook me, and Hector strangely enough, for a short redhead of the female sex and journalist persuasion and, having done so, celebrated by tossing us into a cellar."

"This story requires a drink." Alex slid out from under Kit and headed for the fridge.

"So you see," Kit said a little while later, having recounted every little thing that had happened to her and everyone they knew, since Thursday morning, "you just have to stop going away; coz every time you do some bastard beats the crap out of me."

Alex laughed. "I can just see how my not being here results in your face being rearranged."

"And my knuckles," Kit showed her. Alex kissed her hand better. "And my knees," Kit added, flinging off the bedclothes to point to her legs. Alex shifted down the bed and kissed them too, then sat up again, all without spilling a drop from her glass.

"Have you had any space for you, since I've been away, or at all in the last few weeks?"

"Space for me?" Kit killed pulled a face. "Whatever do you mean?"

"I mean, time out for Kit. What about your book? Have you been working on it?"

"What book?"

"The crime novel that your other friends allege you are writing."

"I am?"

"O'Malley!"

"Sorry," Kit grinned. "I've kinda lost interest in it, lately."

"Why?"

Kit widened her eyes. "Coz real life's a bitch; and she keeps getting in the way."

"Oh my love, you really do need a holiday."

Kit glowed. "Am I really your love?'

Alex cocked her head and endowed Kit with one of her enigmatic smiles.

"I know, I know," Kit ducked. "I'm exasperating."

"Yes, you are. And I find you most intriguing."

"Me? No." Kit was astonished. "I'm an open book, Alex."

"Of course you are, darling." Alex tried not to laugh; and then did. "Kit, I often get the sense that *you* don't have a clue who or where you are; so how am I meant to figure you out."

Kit considered her comment. "That's quite true, Alex. But then I said a book, not a street directory." She suddenly felt worried, so she pouted. "Don't you think I'm honest?"

"Uh-uh, now I did not say that," Alex declared. "Truth be told, Katherine O'Malley, you're one of the most honest people I've ever known; but that is not the same as being open."

"Hmm," Kit said, although she didn't get what Alex meant, in relation to her anyway.

Alex smiled. "Is there anything else bothering you?"

"Apart from the ongoing wackiness of you and Enzo and the Feral Feds; and the whole you-keep-going-away stuff. No."

"I'm here now," Alex smiled.

"Yes, but you're going again in the morning."

Alex raised an eyebrow. "And I'll be back on Monday night."

"Really? You said Tuesday."

"I just changed my mind."

"You can do that?"

"Of course I can, O'Malley. You are seriously messy, aren't you?"

Kit pouted and squirmed uncomfortably. "I just get all stupid and convinced that you're only going to come back to tell me you're leaving again and not coming back."

"Why would I come back to tell you that? Why wouldn't I just leave?"

Kit looked horrified.

"Kit, darling."

"Yes, Alex?"

"I love you."

"Really?"

"Yes, really, you fool. You do understand that I organized this sleepover tonight because, even though I was coming back on Tuesday—now Monday—*I* couldn't go one more night without seeing you. Without," she leaned forward and kissed Kit deeply and passionately, "doing that. Not to mention everything else we've been doing."

"So," Kit smiled, "you only want me for my body."

"Yes," Alex acknowledged, "but only because I'd get lost in your mind right now, wouldn't I?" Alex kissed her again, then wrapped her in her arms and held her tight.

"You are the only thing that keeps me in the here and now," Kit whispered.

"Well, step back into our moment with me, then, Kit. We'll deal with everything else *together* when I get back on Monday."

When Kit woke at nine in the morning Alex was long gone, leaving sparkling and delicious memories, a lingering lusty scent, and a love note on the pillow. Kit laughed out loud when she read it because that's precisely what it was—a note that said "love." She found another one stuck to the bathroom mirror when she went to take a shower, that said, "order breakfast; it's already paid for." So she did. She ordered bacon and eggs and tomatoes and toast and juice and coffee, because she was ravenous.

She checked all the cupboards for stuff before she left, even though she hadn't opened any of them before then; and found a third note in her shoe, which said, "I adore you."

K.F. O'Malley sang and danced all the way home. Well she would have, except she didn't go home, and—as she told herself—you shouldn't really dance while driving. But she did sing and jig to every song on the radio whether she liked them or not and, in two cases, when she didn't even know them. And she did this all the way to Williamstown's Blue Strand Hotel.

And why here, why now? she asked the world at large.

"Coz I feel excellent, and not even work on a Sunday can hold me back or drag me down. Oh *man!* No, not even that," she declared, spying the interloper as she fluked a car park on The Strand, opposite the Barker-owned Blue Strand pub, and two cars along from a redhead called Carrie.

Kit got out of her car and took time out to drink in the last moments of her *placido domingo*. "Ah," she sighed, taking in the view across Hobsons Bay towards the distant Station Pier, with the seagulls and a solitary pelican dipping into the deep dark-blue wet, and a massive bank of threatening and accumulating nimbus overhead.

"Right, that'll do." She strode up the street and rapped on the boot of the little blue Torana, thereby frightening Ms. McDermid's peaceful Sunday right out of her alleged mind.

"Hi," Kit said, bouncing up to her driver's side window.

"Shit! And bloody hell, O'Malley!" Carried shouted.

Kit grinned. "What are you doing out here? Surveilling the patrons or casing the joint?"

"Neither. I just got here, if you must know. And what the hell happened to your face? No, let me guess; you were being nice to someone other than me this time."

Kit pointed at her own face. "This, you little tart, is your fault."

Carrie clambered out of her car. "Like how?"

"Like, Queenie Riley was expecting you when I knocked at her door. So I got thrown down nine fucking stairs and into her cellar, where I spent Friday night. All of Friday night, until seven yesterday morning."

Carrie was laughing.

Typical. You go out of your way, O'Malley, to ensure nothing happens to this snotty little snipe, and she laughs at your misfortune. "Want one just like it, Carrie?" she asked cheerily.

"No," Carrie pressed her lips together, "but thanks, O'Malley. I'm fine like this. Besides I wouldn't want to outshine you with a fresh one."

"Ha bloody ha," Kit scowled. "Shall we go together incognito-like and suss the place out?"

"May as well," Carrie agreed. "How come *you're* here, though?"

"I'll tell you my tip, if you tell me yours."

"Why not," Carrie said agreeably. "We might be seeing a bit of each other for a while."

Kit squinted. "I was thinking more of a quick chat over a drink and then goodbye forever."

The Blue Strand was a very old hotel, renovated to look like a new and trendy old hotel. The interior wore a coat of so-called distressed blue, the actual bar in the public bar had been sanded back to look like it had been, ooh, sanded back, and all the chairs and tables were retro-futuro chrome and leather, and chunky stressed-out timber.

Kit planted her bum on a bar stool, patted the one next to it to encourage Carrie to sit and stop staring so blatantly at the other clientele, and ordered a VB.

"You?" Surly the barman asked Carrie.

White wine, Kit predicted silently.

"A glass of chardonnay," Carrie requested.

Bingo! "So, how did you find out about this place?" Kit asked her quietly, while she scanned the patrons herself, with a slightly higher degree of subtlety than her comrade. There were about fifteen tables, most of them occupied with young and groovy Sunday lunchers. Kit frowned, realizing groovy was a word too much like fab to be remotely groovy. Whatever! All the tabled drinkers and diners, whatever their state of being, were in couples or mixed groups. Propping up the bar, as they do, were five single blokes or, rather, blokes on their own. *You* can talk, O'Malley—about bar-propping, not solitary drinking.

She noticed that while getting their drinks, the grumpy barkeep, with his teensy patch of bum-fluff on his widdle chin, was talking to a blond with a square head, who was seated near the cappuccino machine. Carrie and Kit were the only single women in the place— single, in this case, meaning unattached to or unaccompanied by a chunk of masculinity.

"I may be newish in town, O'Malley, but I do have a few contacts," Carrie was saying. "It didn't take long to get the lowdown on the rivalries involved in our mutual," she hesitated as the barman returned with their drinks, "interest. It's …"

"You mean your editor filled you in," Kit interrupted.

"I mean my editor filled me in," Carrie nodded, without missing a beat. "And this place is but one enterprise I'll be checking out in an attempt to get the lie of the land, for myself."

"Well," Kit said, taking a swig of beer, "I don't recommend the lowland of Mistress Marjorie's cellar. And speaking of your mythical contacts, Carrie, are you going to tell me who told you about the *non*existent, except where alleged by you, connection between dead whatshisname and my mate Angie?"

"No." Carrie fiddled with her hair and the stem of her wine glass.

Hmm, ambidextrous, Kit thought. "Queenie's got a theory which *she* doesn't like much."

"And what would that be?"

Kit leaned in nice and close. "Given as how she also knows it's not true, she figures it was a cop who told you, in order to spice up the brew that feeds this old conflict."

Carrie McDermid would not a poker player make. "And why would he do that?"

Oops. "Because he knew you'd print it as god-given. Which you did. Consequently, for example, our friend the matriarch would love to know *which* cop it was," Kit explained. As would you, O'Malley. "So I wouldn't be going anywhere near the old dear, if I were you."

"You would say that, wouldn't you, to keep the story to yourself."

"Hello! Earth to Carrie. I'm not after a story. Remember? O'Malley be after the truth."

Carrie sniffed, then unnecessarily re-tucked her light-blue shirt into her slightly darker blue calf-length pants. "Don't suppose you'd be willing to deal?"

Kit narrowed her eyes. "What kind of deal?"

"An info exchanging kind of deal-type arrangement," Carrie proposed succinctly.

"We could work something out," Kit agreed tentatively. "But only if you start with one name, Carrie, to convince me that you're kosher."

Carrie sighed, and whispered, "Senior Detective Charlie Parker."

Like you didn't see that one coming, O'Malley!

Kit whispered back to her, "Chucky Parker is one of the great fabricators of all time. I know him, Carrie. I know this about him, as an absolute fact. He lies to get things moving, to get things done, to … he just lies. Do not trust him."

Carrie looked disappointed. Understandably. "I did wonder," she admitted.

"You wondered and you still printed it?"

"Hey, if you can't trust, you know, *them*, then who can you trust?"

"Not trusting someone you don't know from Adam, no matter who they are is—like wow, sweetheart!—the best advice I can give you for your line of work, quite apart from it being a thing that should've been drummed into you by your parents or jailers or psychiatrists from a very early age."

"Now you're just being rude. No wonder people throw you down stairs."

"The dickhead threw me down those stairs because he honestly thought I was you."

"Okay. All right, already."

"Aw now, you two chicks aren't havin' an argument, are you?"

Streuth! Kit thought, then remembered they were in one of the bad guys' domains. She curbed her natural instinct to insult and turned to the square-headed blond, who'd relocated from farther up the bar to display his concern, and smiled sweetly; just in case he could be helpful. She doubted it, though, as he looked barely old enough to be in a licensed premises.

Carrie the Clueless, meanwhile, said, "Rack off, you nob."

Whereon Kit put on her apology-face and said, "Sorry, as you can see, my *sister* and I are most certainly having an altercation."

"Sisters? Wouldn't have taken you for related."

"She's adopted," Kit snarled. "And you are?"

"Pete Barker, night manager. Off duty, obviously."

"Obviously," Kit grinned. And obviously older than he looks. And see how it can pay to be nice to the yobbos. She ignored Carrie's flabbergasted expression; just like a sister would.

"Can I buy youse two a drink?" offered young Pete, of the Barker family of bastards.

"If you like; that'd be great," Kit agreed.

"Sure," Carrie said, joining the game.

"Oh, *now* you're nice," Pete said to her, not missing a trick.

"I didn't mean what I said before, Pete," Carrie said. "I am *really* pissed off with my sister, but that was no excuse to be rude to you."

"You are forgiven," Pete grinned, indicating two more of the same and whatever his usual was. "Come sit, join myself and the view, over by the window."

Kit and Carrie followed Pete, and a moment later the now-not-surly barman delivered the drinks to their table by the huge open window. It was a touch cool, but the air was briskly fresh and the view across the inner waters of Port Phillip Bay was still perfect.

"Intros," Kit began. "I'm Gabrielle, and this is my little sister Renee."

Pete, all blond crewcut and goofy grin, politely shook their hands. "So, was that a private argument you were having or could anyone have joined in?"

"Private-ish," Kit said. "But maybe you could give an outsider's objective opinion, Pete."

"Yeah? Lay it on me, Gabrielle."

Think fast, O'Malley. "Okay. I've just quit my high-stress, highly-paid job coz I got way fed up with the shit going down at work, right."

"Yup," Pete nodded, paying a lot of attention.

"Now, Renee thinks I'm completely mental coz I've got a mortgage and car payments and stuff and, here's the clincher, I paid for a two-month holiday to Europe in June."

"Ah," said Pete, "you're still going overseas, but Renee thinks you're irresponsible."

"She *is*," Carrie asserted, adding her two cents to the charade.

As that was her only contribution, Kit had to continue. "She keeps giving me the, 'What are you going to live on in the meantime, Gabrielle? What will you use as spending money over there, if you have to use it all here first, Gabrielle?' Get the picture?"

"And you're the *younger* sister?" Pete said, giving Carrie an incredulous look. "Man, what's the world coming to?"

"That's what *I* said," Kit cheered.

"Why don't you just get another job, until you go overseas?" Pete suggested.

"Who would take someone on for just a few months?" Carrie chipped in helpfully.

"I dunno. It depends. What do you do, Gabrielle?"

"I'm a bio-chemist," Kit said. Good grief, where did that come from, she wondered. "I was working for a monster multinational pharmaceutical company."

Yeah right, O'Malley, you and whose brains trust?

"I get the short-term gig problem, then," Pete nodded sagely. "So do something else."

Good thinking Pete. "Like what? Do you wanna give me a job?"

"I'd love to," he shrugged.

"Really?" she asked. Good boy, she thought.

138

"Yeah, why not? I'd have to okay it with my Dad, him being the owner and in charge of all hiring and stuff. But we always need barmaids."

"That's very generous, Pete, but I've never been a barmaid."

"There's nothing to it, Gabrielle; I can teach you. That's *my* job after all."

"Would I have to have an interview with your father, or what?"

"Ordinarily, yes. But *I* like you, so I'm sure he would. Besides, I'm kind of in charge at the moment, coz he's in hospital."

"Oh, I'm sorry," Kit soothed. Yes! she thought. He's even the right branch of the Barker bastard family tree. "Is he okay? I mean, I hope it's nothing serious."

"It was touch and go for a while. He was in a coma after getting hit by a Range Rover—just out there," he pointed, "about a month ago."

"Really? The poor man," Kit exclaimed. "But he's okay now?"

"Yeah, he's coming home on Tuesday. On crutches, but he's fine."

"I hope the driver's been charged, if he hit your Dad bad enough to put him in a coma."

"No," Pete sneered. "It was a hit and run. The cops haven't found the prick."

"Pete," Kit remarked, "the cops couldn't find their *own* pricks."

Pete guffawed. "Man. How true is that!"

"So this guy, I assume it was a guy, he's still out there, then."

"Yeah," Pete shrugged. "Unless God got him, I mean gets him."

"God?" Kit looked surprised.

"Yeah, you know, as in what goes around, comes around; that whole Lord-dude workin' in creepy ways and such."

Kit put on her amazed and quizzical face and whispered, "Pete, correct me if I'm wrong, but I get the feeling you know who did it."

"Me? Nah," he denied to the stranger before him, but with a small smile and a knowing look. "Though we reckon it was a purposeful act."

"You're kidding? You mean, it was intentional?" Kit whispered, while looking aghast. "Shit, Pete, that's awful."

"Yeah, it sucks."

◆◆◆

"Okay, I'm impressed. That was incredible," Carrie said.

"What was?" asked Kit as they stood halfway between their cars, opposite the Blue Strand where Gabrielle the biochemist, was to start work as a barmaid, on a trial basis, next week.

"That whole getting info routine. You're a master, a mistress, a sight to behold."

Kit gave Carrie a look that said, *huh?* then another that said, *oh, I get you.* "Flattery will get you nowhere that I'm going," she said.

"Are you always like this?" Carrie asked.

"No. I've been a bit to the ragged-left of center lately. I *was* really good this morning, until I got here, and found you."

Carrie pulled a face but otherwise ignored the insult. "A month ago," she said, "the guy who owns Swiggers Bar and Nightclub in Prahran had a knock-down, drag-out fight with our late friend Gerry. There was shouting and punching, kicking and gouging, the works. I even heard rumors that knives were drawn."

"Really?" Kit said. "It just so happens that Swiggers was my next port of call."

Carrie raised one brow, then both.

"Really," Kit smiled. "I was going from here to pay a visit on Mickey Stano. Shall we go together or take our own cars?"

"I'm not getting into a moving vehicle with you," Carrie stated.

"Whatever," Kit grinned. "I'll meet you there, then."

Chapter 11

Kit had been sitting on her own in the joint known as Swiggers Bar, the nightclub part being closed at two on a Sunday arvo, for nearly ten minutes before her date stuck her little red head in the front door to see if the coast was clear. Or there.

Carrie gave a wave and made a detour to get herself a drink, while Kit continued to stare into hers, there not being much else to look at. A scant three other customers did not make for good cover; and as this was the third drinking hole, not of her choosing, that she'd been to in the last twenty-four hours she wasn't particularly interested in the decor. That thought brought up the specter of the Blaazt, not the least for its idiotic spelling, and her mind began to whimper at the prospect of attending the launch of the coolest nightclub in town tonight.

"Who are we this time?" Carrie whispered as she sat down opposite her.

"Us, unless a situation presents itself, which seems unlikely," Kit waved at the room.

"I wasn't going to ask," Carrie said, preparing to abandon her resolve, "but I *have* to know. You'd already done a recky in that other pub and sussed out who Pete was, hadn't you?"

"Nope. Never set foot in the Blue Strand until I was two steps in front of you."

"But you knew who *he* was, and your cover story was ready, yeah?"

Kit shook her head. "I thought he was an underage yob, and from then on it was improv."

"Yeah sure," Carrie moaned. "*Bum!* I should've known you wouldn't really deal."

Kit laughed. "Honestly, Carrie, it was guesswork and play acting, pure and simple."

"So tell me how you did all that so easily."

"Practice," Kit shrugged. "And intuition, I s'pose. We were the only single sheilas sitting at the bar and we're not bad looking, so it was odds on that at least one of the blokes also sitting at the bar was going to try to pick us up."

"Yeah. But it—he—could have been anyone."

"True. We got lucky, we hit pay dirt, we scored the *perfect* Barker DNA. But, even if we hadn't, if he'd just been a yob on the make, we still might have learned something because, in my experience, guys who sit *at* the bar are usually the regulars."

"And? So?"

Kit sighed. "When we first walked in there and you were scoping the place like a startled pigeon, what were you looking for exactly?"

"I don't know," Carrie shrugged. "Villainous types, maybe."

Kit snorted. "And would you have approached any of these villains for info?"

"No way! They might have ..." she shrugged again.

"What? Villained you?"

"Now you're making fun."

"Of course I am," Kit admitted. And it's not hard. "Regulars *know* stuff, Carrie. In most investigations the best people to use, and I do mean *use*, to get info of a general or, if you're lucky, specific nature are the employees: you know, the staff, the underlings, the wage slaves. Ditto for lesser family members, neighbors, or colleagues—especially disgruntled ones.

"These connected bystanders nearly always have a grievance, or gossip they're just busting to share, or something to get off their chest or simply wonder about out loud. They're also the best homing pigeons for planting facts or *mis*information. Apart from journos, that is."

"Hey!" Carrie was winding up for a good old snarly rebuff, when ...

"Well I'll be damned! If it isn't Katherine O'Malley, the private dick, *dock*," came a booming male voice, approaching from Kit's left. "And still diving for clams, I see."

Kit closed her mind for but a second—a full, shit-coming-back-to-haunt-her second; a what-the-hell moment; a no-way *not another* coincidence interval—and then looked up, into pale-brown eyes located a sensible distance, *yep there it was*, above the blond moustache and below the subtly receding hairline. He was tanned, fit, Ed Harris-handsome, and, as usual, way too pleased with himself. Some things, sadly, *never* change.

"Boxer Macklin, you absolute bastard!" Kit declared. "Oh but look, I see that your brain is still as developmentally challenged as your dick."

"Ha!" Macklin said, taking a seat. "Should you talk like that in front of your girlfriend?"

"She's not my girl, Boxer. And I don't recall inviting you to sit, here or within cooee of me or my shoes," she retorted, while desperately wondering what the heck was going on. Was it old home week, *This is Your Life*, or a force no-longer with you reunion, or what?

"You got no choice, O'Malley," he was saying. "I manage this dive, it's my place."

"You do? It is?" Kit asked.

Macklin's face reflected her surprise. "Yeah. So if you don't like me you can, like, leave."

"Well, I don't like you, Boxer," Kit declared, "but do I *have* to leave?"

Andrew Boxer Macklin, ex-cop, ex-*bent*-cop, now manager of *he*-only-knew what kind of trouble, smiled a generous smile. "You pay, you can stay. I don't give a stuff."

"I thought you'd high-tailed it to Queensland to hide after your public and unceremonious dumping," Kit said to him, and then turned to Carrie. "Boxer used to be a cop, but not a very good one," she explained, as if she was talking about a naughty little boy.

"Shut up, O'Malley," Boxer laughed, with a too-amicable familiarity. "And you can stop the malicious shit-spreading okay. I am so over all that, and you should be too. And don't you listen to her, whoever you are," he winked at Carrie, "coz half my life's been pure bullshit made up by someone else."

"Aw, I was innocent," Kit intoned.

"No, I wasn't," Macklin stated. "But I did do undercover for so fucking long, I didn't have a clue where the light was any more."

Kit gave a mental pout. She really, *really* hated that. She hated that there was once a cop she'd quite liked and admired, who turned out to be bad to the bone, who took others down with him, who she had to hate *then* because it was her duty and coz he was so worth hating; but who she, right now, realized she still quite liked. Well, at least she still liked the things about him that she always had.

"You're a deadset prick, you know that, don't you, Boxer."

"It's good to see you too, Kit," he smiled.

"What the hell's going on?" Carrie asked.

"If she's not your squeeze, who is she?" Boxer queried. "And is she going to be around long enough for me to care?"

Kit smiled. "Andrew Macklin, manager of this, meet Carrie McDermid, journalist; and ah, ipso squid," she waggled her introducing-finger between them. "Seriously, Boxer, last I heard you were living on the Gold Coast. What are you doing here? And I mean here, here," Kit pointed at the floor.

Boxer gave her a curious look. "Did not like the heat, and it's bloody wet up there, Kit. Went to Adelaide for a minute, didn't like the architecture; tried Sydney, but mate, the crims up there are shockin'; so I came home. I fuckin' love this city. Been back six months and I'm running this place for a mate. And let me tell you, I earn more and get a lot more respect around here, than I *ever* got on the job."

"That's coz around here you can be honest," Kit grinned, "about being a crook."

"You always did have a smart mouth, O'Malley."

"Tell me about it." Kit indicated her bruised cheek. "So you really are the manager here."

Now he looked perplexed. "Yeah, but you know that."

"I do?" she said. No I don't, she thought.

"Course you bloody do. Jeez, O'Malley! Do you think I just crawled out of a train wreck?"

How would I know? Kit wondered, trying her best to look innocent but not stupid.

"Okay, I'll play," Boxer said, with a frown and resigned shrug. "How about, I knew *you* would turn up here sooner or later, the moment I saw your gorgeous ugly mug on the TV."

"What? I was on TV? When?"

"In the crowd outside your mate's bar. Don't panic, it was only a fleeting eyeful, that won't spoil any pending clandestine investigations you might have on. I reckon only intimate friends, your mother, and me obviously, would have recognized you—and only then because your mouth was working overtime, as per. It, ah, kinda looked like you were hassling some olds just for carrying a sign."

"Oh shit," Kit laughed.

"On top of which, I read the papers," Macklin added, turning his attention to their mostly silent companion, "including *your* little piece of amped-up hysteria. I bet you fifty bucks, Carrie, that it was fuckin-Chuck who lied to you about that dead wanker's interest in a dyke bar. Sorry O'Malley, didn't mean to be rude or un-pc."

"That's not rude Boxer, it *is* a dyke bar. For women," she added, for Carrie's benefit. "And of course you're correct about Chucky the Fabricator."

"*O'Malley!*" Carrie objected.

"What?" Kit said. "He lied to you, Carrie. What do you care if Boxer's suspicions are verified, given he just validated for you what I said about that lying bastard earlier."

"Thank you both very much, I'm sure," Carrie said scornfully.

"So, you saw me on the teev and you can read, Box, but how does that add up to me coming here? Or rather you knowing I would?"

Boxer the Baffled, or perhaps Disappointed, said, "You mean apart from figuring you'd check Gerry's business connections? No, wrong word; coz 'connections' implies agreement."

"*Apart* from investigating inter-family business rivalry?" Kit said. "What else is there?"

"O'Malley," Boxer frowned. "I really thought you were quicker than this."

Righto, Kit thought. It's me he's disappointed in, with. What am I missing?

"The brawl between Gerry and your, I assume, *boss* and mate Mickey Stano," Carrie proposed, "would have to be a significant factor in the equation, wouldn't it?"

Boxer pulled a maybe, maybe-not face.

"I mean it stands to reason," Carrie continued, "because the moment *I* told O'Malley about that fight she just had to come here. Though she claimed she was coming anyway."

"The fight is a good point, Carrie, but kind of in the middle of the story," Boxer shrugged, "coz the Rileys and the Stano family have been ..."

The Stano *family*. Of Norlane! Well, yoo-bloody-hoo, O'Malley! Could you be any more dense? Kit mentally whacked her own head with a house brick.

"... years," Boxer finished saying, so he could take up grinning. "Ah, it looks like you've finally worked out how to drive that little red wagon, Kit."

"*You* sent the newspaper clipping," Kit said. "But why the cryptic, Boxer? I *hate* that. Well I'm here now, so fill me in, elaborate, *explain* for goodness sake."

"Nuh-uh, no way," Boxer declined. "I *am* one of the bad guys, Kit," he said, with a smile of comfortable self-awareness, "or rather I work for them and do business with them, so I won't hand anything to you on a platter. Ever. But if you suss out what I have given you, I won't be unhappy about what you find. Neither will *you*, of course, which, from your point of view, is way more important. But, ah, don't waste the chance to get even. Check out that Law Report I tipped you to."

"Is that what that scribble meant?" Kit said.

"Der," Boxer nodded.

"Do I know what you're talking about?" Carrie asked.

"No," Kit said, "but then neither do I." She glanced at Boxer, who gave the slightest of nods. "If you're a good girl, though, you may get a story out of whatever it is."

"Well, that's me done, I gotta go," Boxer stood up. "Nice talking, Kit," he smiled.

"That's it? You're not going to tell me anything else?"

"Come back when you've got questions."

"I've got questions," Kit insisted.

"Okay." He leaned over to listen. "What?"

"Do you know who killed Gerry?" she whispered.

"No."

"Do you know who ran Stuart Barker down like a dog in the street?"

"No. At least not for sure."

Kit smiled. "Do you think Gerry is payback for Stuart?"

"It's possible, Kit. But I *really* don't know who did Gerry. That whole 'bloodless in a gay bar thing' seems too weird for the Barkers."

Kit squinted. "Tell me about Doghouse Dixon, Pauly-J, and the other two."

"Why?" he smiled.

"Hey, they're my questions."

"Okay. Pauly-J is dead. Got the big C about two years ago and carked it last August."

"July," Kit corrected. "What about Mason and Mapp?"

Boxer pulled a face. "From what I heard, Deon didn't take the fallout from the trial at all well, so he quit and went opal mining in Coober Pedy. As far as I know, Sheryl Mapp is still on the job. As for Doghouse?" he gave a short laugh. "He retired to the beach. He's got a woman and a boat and a little boat business. Haven't seen him in nearly three years."

"You don't keep in touch?"

"No. Why would I?"

"You were mates, you were partners," Kit shrugged. "In law *and* in crime, if I recall."

"Yeah, well, Doghouse was a mad bastard, and fun; but once we got 'dumped' as you say, *we* had nothin' left."

"Except the dumping and the reason for it."

"Which provided no context for a lasting friendship, especially when Doghouse is also a complete wanker and three tinnies short of a six-pack."

Kit smiled. "Last question. Do you know a reptile-ugly rental by the name of Sid …"

"Sid Ralph," Boxer interrupted. "He's a truly nasty piece of excrement. Dunno who he's working for now. Last job I heard about was a one-off for Stuart B., about two months ago. You remember that brutal bastard, Colin Manderson?"

"Oh yeah," Kit sneered. "I helped the old team put him, and that little creep Jimmy Kerman, away in January."

"Well, next to Sid Ralph, commonly known as Toad," Boxer said, fingering his moustache, "Colin Manderson is a sook. So, you stay clear of him—Toad, I mean. Don't look for him, Kit. Do not play *any* kind of surveillance game with him, and if you see him coming—especially if it looks like he's coming for you—then *run*. Fast."

Carrie walked Kit back to her car to get the complete lowdown on some of Melbourne's very-late-twentieth-century lowlifes—cops *and* crooks. Kit explained, off the record, her own historic connection with Boxer, Chucky, and the other cops, good and bad, who'd been stung all those years ago. Or rather, she divulged just enough to sidetrack Carrie from a private quest to find or, more likely, forge links between any of the names she'd heard today and her so-far shallow investigation into the murder of Gerry Anders.

This was mostly because Kit understood that the truth, what and wherever it was, seldom got in the way of a good journalistic beat-up. But she also figured that Carrie's first port of recall, whether she now believed he was a liar or not, would still be the highest-ranking mouth on the subject; and that no good whatsoever would come of that. Chucky Parker's memory of his internal affairs inquiry that led to a major court case would be far from objective. And while it was old-old news, a new journo in town might see it differently, and therefore put a fresh spin on it simply by implying a connection with current affairs.

So what, Kit thought, if some of the names remained the same? Coincidence, even in the plural, rarely equaled fact. And speculation was a troublesome, even dangerous, offspring of coincidence; so Kit was hoping to kneecap Carrie's interest before the reporter could even begin to imagine where it might lead her.

"But where does this terrible-sounding Toad character fit in?" Carrie asked, still lingering with intent beside Kit's car.

"The Toad character," Kit replied, deliberately not using his real name, "was allegedly seen in the vicinity of The Terpsichore on Friday; the day *after* all you guys found Gerry."

Hmm, curious, Kit thought. Ms. McDermid co-found Gerry.

"Ah! Does that mean," Carrie enthused, "I mean, do you think it means *he* killed Gerry?"

"No. I think it means that he was allegedly seen there the next day," Kit smiled.

"You're not very good at sharing are you, O'Malley?" Carrie noted.

Kit pulled a *you're kidding* face. "I don't know anything else about him, Carrie. And what the hell do you expect for nothing? Your exchange rate so far is pretty low. Oh *man*, hang on," she slapped the heel of her hand into her forehead. "Speaking of finding the body, as I did, I've just remembered someone I didn't talk to about their connection to dead Gerry."

"Who?" Carrie queried expectantly.

"You."

"What?"

"Well? *Did* you know the deceased prior to him being in that condition?"

"No!" Carrie proclaimed. "Didn't even know *of* him, let alone him, himself, him. Alive or in any other state."

"You got a good story, though, huh?" Kit noted. "And you just happened to be there?"

"No, O'Malley, happenstance it wasn't. I organized it the night before."

"You organized it?" Kit studied her with amusement. "Are you saying, that as a precursor to leaving the body there, you—the murderess—organized to meet the Scooter gang for lunch so they'd be there with you—the reporter—when Gerry was found?"

"Don't be bloody ridiculous," Carrie's laugh was minor-league hysterical.

Kit grinned. "So you just organized to meet for lunch."

"Yes. No. I mean," Carrie waved her hands in frustration. "The others talked about meeting for lunch, I organized with them to join them. It was Rabbit's idea. I think."

"And when did you tell them all about being a journalist? Or did no one know, until your howling *blood-drained man in lesbian disco* front-page excuse for a news story came out."

Carrie sneered while she thought, or vice versa. "Collectively speaking, I don't think I did tell *all* the women that I met at Angie's; but, I certainly mentioned it to some of them. It's not like it's a secret or anything. For instance, it came up in conversation on Wednesday night with—let me see—Booty, Sal, Scooter, and a couple of other women who *didn't* go for lunch the next day, because Sal's niece has just got herself a cadetship."

"Oh, good for her," Kit noted. "Well, I gotta go now."

Carrie scowled. "You're awful, O'Malley. It's beyond me why I think I might end up liking you."

"Damn," Kit sounded disappointed. "And I've been trying so hard to piss you right off."

Carrie laughed. "Where are you going now?"

"To see Lillian."

"Is that important to the investigation? I mean, can I know? And, can I come if it is?"

"It isn't; but, you're welcome to come and visit my mother if you *really* want."

Katherine O'Malley stood on Lillian O'Malley's front porch for about three years, waiting, not just for the door to be answered but for an explanation. On discovering that her key did not unlock the wire security door, Kit's first thought, being mildly paranoid, was that she had gone peculiar—she herself, not her mother—and was at the wrong house, ringing the wrong bell. Having reassured herself this was indeed her childhood home, Kit pushed the button again.

Still no response, despite the presence of Lillian's old green Rover, parked in front of Connie's new maroon Toyota, indicating that there should be humans in the house. She couldn't recall doing anything that would cause her mother to change the locks on her; but, now that she had so much time to study it, she realized it wasn't a new lock, it was a new door; and while it was locked, the actual front door was open. She sent a yoo-hoo up the hall.

A moment later, but apparently having heard nothing, her

mother's willowy best friend emerged from the guest bedroom and headed away from the front door towards the kitchen.

"Connie?" Kit said, whereon, and with a bellowing "whooahh," the usually placid and graceful Constance Forest flung herself back into the hatstand. Whatever she was carrying—oh, a pack of cards—hit the wall, then the floor in 52 pieces, give or take a joker or two.

"It's only me," Kit said.

"Oh my!" Connie said, with a flimsy wave. "Hello, Kit dear."

"What, what, what?" came Lillian's voice, on the run. "For goodness sake, Katherine! Why are you scaring the beegees out of Connie?"

"Like that was my intention, Mum. I've only been standing out here bell-ringing and yodeling for a decade. You wanna let me in? And what's with the door?"

"*Ondréa* the Giant, while leaving last week, chose to demonstrate a stretching exercise of questionable benefit. She ripped the old door clean off its hinges," Lillian explained. She let Kit inside, then returned to help Connie with the cards. Kit joined them on the floor.

"Who?" Kit asked. It helped to keep abreast of her mother's roll call of friends, if only to pretend she knew them when Lillian mentioned their names again, in passing, in two years.

"Andrea silly-britches Watson, from our group." Lillian stood up. "That's all of them."

Connie accepted the cards and they all headed for the kitchen. "You have a good nose, Kit dear; you're just in time for coffee and chocolate slice. I hope you haven't just eaten."

"I can't resist your slice, Connie, so even if I'd just stuffed myself to the any-more-would-be-regurgitated stage, I'd make room."

"I sent her to a very good school to learn how to speak like that," Lillian noted.

Connie rolled her eyes at Lillian on Kit's behalf, then said, "I'm going to be staying here with your mother for a while."

"She might even be moving in full time," Lillian said over her shoulder.

"Really? What a great idea," Kit said enthusiastically, as she and Connie sat down next to each other at the kitchen table to wait.

Kit often wondered why divorced or widowed grown-ups, at least those with no dependent children, didn't take up the house-sharing concept with more gusto. Learning to share again had to be better than being lonely or isolated. And Connie and Lillian, life-long friends, spent most of their time together anyway. They'd done so even before Connie's adored husband, James, lost his life—in bliss, it must be said—on a short par five the year before.

"We think it will work for us," Connie was saying.

Lillian turned to agree or comment, but stopped and gave them both a look instead. "Already in cahoots, I see. Do you expect me to wait on you both hand and foot, feet?"

"Yes," Kit and Connie said in unison.

"Fine," she gathered three mugs and the coffee pot and joined them at the table, where the milk and sugar and chocolate slice were already waiting. "Now, I'm going to ask this time, Katherine, so that you don't have to pretend it isn't there. Tell me about the bruise."

Kit did as she was told, but left out all the bits of the story that might worry her mother for some time to come—like Queenie Riley, Will Thumpya, the stairs, the night in the cellar, and the drinking of the fifteen hundred dollar bottle of someone else's wine. The story of the bruise, therefore, came down to accidentally whacking herself in the face with the car door *very hard* while getting into it in frustration after someone had decided he didn't want to tell her something she needed to know.

You are such a liar, O'Malley!

Connie said pretty much the same thing by thumping her on the thigh, under the table, while Lillian observed, "It's a very strange business you're in, my darling."

"It is that, Mum. So what was the Sunday place you two went to yesterday?"

"Church, of course," Lillian stated, as she poured the coffees.

Kit waggled her head. "Church? Of course. Why didn't that occur to me?" She looked to Connie for a sensible explanation.

"It was more of a chapel than a church," Connie said.

No help there, then.

"Mum, you don't go to church on any day, let alone Saturday. So what … oh no! You haven't been recruited by some door-to-door god-bangers, have you?"

"Don't be ridiculous, Katherine. The converters wouldn't have a hope of getting either of us, would they, Constance? We *never* listen. Even that one time, when I invited them in for …"

"You didn't?" Kit was horrified.

"Let me finish, darling. We invited them in for coffee. But when I told them *I* was God, and Connie was my priestess, they couldn't get out fast enough. They haven't been back since."

"I'm not surprised," Kit laughed. "Okay, I give up. Church, chapel, why?"

"Adam Burgess, from our group …" Lillian began.

"Our theater group," Connie elaborated, "not a strange religious cult or anything."

Lillian pushed her graying, honey-colored hair back behind her ear. "Adam, and his partner of twelve years, Jules, are having a commitment ceremony next month, to which we have been invited. They asked Connie and I to reconnoiter a few chapelly-type reception places to find a suitable one."

"Is Jules a male or a female partner?" Kit asked.

"Yes," Connie answered.

"Both," Lillian elaborated.

"I see," Kit nodded, picking up her mug. "So have they told you which Judy Garland song you have to sing at the wedding yet?"

"What?" Lillian said, in horror. "I don't sing."

Connie thumped Kit's leg again.

Chapter 12

"NCA, O'Malley," Kit said aloud. "No Coincidences Allowed, in this consideration. We'll call them, ah, parallel or circular happenings. Okay?"

Righto, Kit agreed with herself, as she pulled up outside Hector's and tooted the horn.

So what *do* we have? she thought, getting her fingers ready for the count.

A trio of bent cops: one dead, one retired, one feeding you info. An old photo linking the dead cop, Pauly-J, to a vicious thug called Sid, known as Toad. A new photo placing not-nice Toad outside Angie's, a day after dead-for-a-week Gerry turns up there. Toad's last known, by both cops and crooks, employer was Stuart Barker, operating head of the Barker family and sworn enemy of the late gangster, Gerry, and his clan of Rileys. Lastly, or perhaps firstly—definitely *somewhere* in the circle—Gerry got to be an *ex*-crime lord (not) by leaking all his vital fluids into a big pie plate, undoubtedly against his will, and soon after Scooter (*absolutely* NCA) Farrell's uncle, Stuart Barker, emerged from a month-long car-induced coma.

Questions, O'Malley: Did Stuart get Gerry, once and for all, for getting *him* in the first place? Or did Papa Leo order a hit the moment his son came to and verified what they all believed anyway—that the Rileys did it. Why did Gerry run Stuart down in the first place? If, in fact, he did.

And, if all this is true, what will Queenie Riley have to do to salvage *her* family honor? Will she accept that Gerry started it this time—if he did, and if his act wasn't already payback for another ... Oh boy! Kit groaned. Keep going—you've gotta work this through. *Can* Queenie let it go at that? Or will Stuart now have to be taken out properly—by a tank this time—in order to restore balance and keep this bloody feud on an even keel? Is Queenie even interested in the truth? Are any of them? Do they even know it's out there? What is keeping Hector?

Kit pressed the horn again. And what of Boxer's clues? She couldn't even imagine the relevance of a three-year-old law report, let alone a warehouse fire nine years ago. Oh, Kit laughed, now *there's* something you didn't check, O'Malley. Does the cryptic clipping have anything to do with the death of Gerry at all?

"Oh you tease, Boxer; of course it doesn't," she said aloud, as she watched Hector dash out his front door, turn with flapping arms, and run back inside.

"I swear that boy gets stranger by the day," Kit remarked.

Don't waste the chance to get even, Boxer had said. That could only mean *getting* Graham Charles Parker, the prick, coz there was no one else in the world they'd both like to shoot. Kit tried to get inside the mind of Andrew Boxer Macklin—scary thought—and figure his logic.

If he saw *her* on TV, then he probably got an eye-full of his old foe Chucky as well. He would then, and not unreasonably, assume that Kit would *have* to stick her nose into the Anders investigation to protect her friends; thus putting her in regular contact with upChucky. And knowing that encounters with Parker, while universally unpleasant, would play like a bad acid flashback for Kit who'd been there, done that, and tried to tick it off already, Boxer would bet that dealing with Chuck would make her more inclined to check out *his* thing; without giving much thought to its relevance to *her* thing. But "thinking" she was, and with each new consideration, Boxer's thing was looking oh-so unrelated to the Case of the Bloodless Gerry.

And, hello, why wasn't Boxer dealing with his thing himself? He could hire hitpeople by the truck load if he wanted.

Kit put her hand on the horn for one, one, then three seconds while undergoing a vague and passing faith-restoring event. Maybe ex-Detective Macklin wants a legal kind of retribution, but his alter ego, the Box, is too far over on the dark side these days to secure it for him.

155

Okay. So let's look at Boxer's clues. Nine years ago Charlie Parker was investigating the latest of four fires in the western suburbs and Geelong. All were alleged arson attacks and more than likely were related. Nine years ago also meant that Chucky's arson squad stint predated his time with Internal Affairs, where his crowning achievement was to uncover an insurance scam, and bring down Boxer Macklin and his pals. Charlie Parker: promotion secured, but at the expense of his relegation to complete-bastard status because of the methods he'd used.

Boxer's suggestion that she also check out *3VR 379* from three years' back, implied that *after* his own drumming out of the force, a case of some interest to him went before the Supreme Court of Victoria.

A law report of that case, and others of its ilk for the annum, was then bound into the third of the volumes known as the *Victorian Report*, or VR, for that year.

Kit took a breath as she saw Hector emerge again, this time on the run through the rain to her car, and began to wind up the meeting with herself. Supposedly, should she choose to look it up, she would find something interesting, intriguing, or relevant to Boxer-knew-what, on page 379, in volume three, of a three-year-old *Victorian Report*. But *would* she check it out? Could she be bothered?

By the time Hector leaped into her passenger seat, shaking himself like a wet dog, Kit had made her decision on that matter. Then she sighed because, apart from it now all being in a different order, she had *exactly* the same info in her head as when she'd started. And, except for uncovering Boxer's possible trickery, she had not enlightened herself about anything.

"You look fab," Hector grinned.

Kit cast a nodding look over her lilac shirt, purple leather pants, and black boots. "I do, don't I? Don't know what it is lately, I just can't help myself." She started her car, waited for three cars to pass, then headed up Carlisle Street and took a left into Brighton Road.

Hector stroked his silky black shirt, then smoothed his black jeans. "What do you think?" he asked. "I've been told that black is the new black; so I thought I'd blend."

"Very groovily black indeed," Kit complimented, catching the green light through St. Kilda Junction to head up Punt Road. "I'm sorry it's me you have to go to this Blaazted thing with. Believe me, if it wasn't work I would've given the tickets to you and your smoking girl."

Hector sniffed derisively. "She dumped me."

"What? Already? I mean, why?"

"You were right with the already," he said. "And it was coz of Friday night."

"Oh Hector, you didn't tell her you missed your date coz you spent the night in a cellar with another woman did you?"

He snorted. "No. It was only our third date but, and you have to get the full significance of this, I let her down. I let her down in front of her parents; although not literally, coz I wasn't *there* to do it front of them—that being the biggy. Undependable-boy, that's me."

"Your third date was with her parents?"

"Yeah, well," Hector said dismissively.

"But you implied love."

"No. You inferred love from my use of the expression 'love life.'"

"Yeah," Kit nodded.

"Come on, O'Malley. I'm a guy. Sex is always love."

"Is it?"

"Yeah, until you find out that you've got lots in common with her; then it becomes just sex because love is way too scary; then it becomes just love, because you don't want it to be all about the sex; which is really silly because, of course, sex *is* always what it's all about."

"Does this happen to you a lot?"

"Every other girl," Hector shrugged. "Although I know some guys who go through it every other *day*, you know, just walking down the street."

"That must be quite confusing. And exhausting," Kit mocked.

"Only on Wednesdays for some reason," Hector grinned. "Okay, before we get to the club to spy on the comrade-dude in person, I can verify he is the only son of two medical doctors, Gregor and Irina Tereshenko; that he was born in New York; and they *all*

157

have money. Lots of money. I'm still checking his own education credentials and his international movements."

"Wow! That didn't take long."

"Ah, Captain Luddite," Hector sighed. "I merely used my way-scary techno-shit for the task you assigned me; and also to research those old fires for you."

"You did?" Kit was impressed. "Way to go, Initiative-boy."

Hector grinned. "The first fire was a shoe factory in Altona, the second was a forklift manufacturer in Werribee, and the Williamstown fire razed a car auction place. The owners were, in order, a chick named Margaret *Barker*; a guy called *Leo* Barker; and a dude named Nigel—I kid you not—Pippineetal."

"Interesting," Kit nodded.

"Yes," Hector agreed. "Then came the Geelong fire, of the newspaper clipping, in a furniture place owned by Mickey Stano's parents. That was followed by two more fires the following month, with less damage but the same MO; one at a Geelong band venue owned by a Bruce Cramer; and the other in the back half of a Barker-owned pub in Footscray. There were a few other similar fires but, given the pattern, I think they were camouflage."

"Camouflage for what?"

"The pattern," Hector repeated. "Um, I mean to cover the existence of, and therefore the reason for, the pattern; as well as the involvement of several well-known criminal identities. In each case the incendiary device used to ignite the blaze was the same, the propellant was the same, the time was the same, the planets were probably aligned the same, *and ...*"

"The insurance company was the same?" Kit guessed.

"No. The insurance *broker* was the same: a probably well-tanned and definitely filthy-rich dude, now living the life of Skase in Spain."

"Name?"

"Neil Porter—aka Nathan Pittock, Nino Piantoni, and, yes, Nigel Pippineetal."

"How did you find all this out?" Kit asked, making a right turn into Victoria Street to run the stop-start gauntlet through Little Saigon.

"Well, as my weekend was not full of sex as planned, I did some surfing and some hacking *and* I took an actual trip to an actual library to look up old newspapers in the archives."

Whoa! Should *not* have come this way, Kit thought, dodging trams and cars, pedestrians and shopping carts, and something that looked like an aardvark on a leash.

"Hacking?" Kit pounced on the word as soon as it registered. "Hacking what?"

"Um, old arson squad files. You don't want to know."

"You are so right," she agreed. "But, Hector mate, it's good you know how to use your legs too, coz there's a walking-into-a-library-to-get-info-type-job I was going to ask you to do tomorrow. So it's good you've been practicing."

"Yeah?" Hector smiled. "Yikes! Look out! Oh, it's okay. What do you want me to get?"

"I'll explain what and why later, but you may need a suit. Do you have one?"

"A suit of what?"

"Clothes, Hector. You know, a man-suit. Otherwise the librarian at the Supreme Court Library in Williams Street may not think you're fit to look at anything. Did you find out how the fire insurance scam worked?"

"Yeah, sort of. They all insured their places through Neil Porter for massive amounts, like two or three times what they were worth, and with a variety of insurance firms. The firebug—who was never caught, by the way—then practiced his craft and they each made claims.

"Porter, as the broker, processed those claims and the money; with Neil himself, naturally, getting his commission. Then, as Nathan Pittock and/or Nino Piantoni—the client-broker go-between—he also claimed a management fee, aka a *huge* cut, when handing over the still-big payouts to the Barkers, the Stanos, and to his very own other self, Nigel Pippineetal."

"So when did all these NPs piss off to Spain?"

"They, he, didn't. He was already living the expat life there and making business trips to Melbourne. He'd do the contracts here, return home to Spain, come back for the 'assessment,' and then rush back to the old hacienda. He also just outright nicked the policy contributions of heaps of businesses who didn't make claims for anything, let alone deliberately lit fires; which is just as well coz they had no actual cover."

"Okay, but if all this is known, how come the Barkers and the Stanos didn't go to jail or run off to Majorca with Noggin Pillow?"

"Because with *them* it was all innuendo and speculation, and you know how a good lawyer deals with that. And because Noodle Pillock covered himself, and therefore also his partners in crime, by doing the right thing by enough prominent and respectable people—some of whom had claims and some who didn't—that no actual winnable 'conspiracy to commit fraud' could be leveled at any of the city's big crime families."

"Hmm. But not the biggest family? Not the Rileys at all?"

"Nope. Not that I could find."

"That's strange, given Gerry's own propensity for arson-related shenanigans. I must say, you're getting very good at this, Hector. Perhaps I should send you to PI school."

"Who needs school? I'm a natural, O'Malley."

"That is true," Kit agreed, pulling up out the front of Queenie's house. "Shall we go stick our heads in the mouth of that old lioness again?"

The official invitation to the by-invitation-only launch of Metro Blaazt said the doors would be opened to those with invitations from 7 p.m., and not at all, to those without at any time tonight. From tomorrow, the Blaazt would be open to all-comers, bouncer-approved of course; but entry to the gala event was for the chosen few hundred only.

Sasha Riley was obviously aiming for them all to be fashionably late, however, because she was still getting dressed. On the other hand, given that Queenie had already educed a swag of O'Malley Inc. info regarding the investigation into Gerry's personal business—as in Anders-related not Riley-approved—Kit figured that the old girl had given the young one the go-slow.

Queenie smiled generously, therefore, when Kit—after also veri-fying that, yes, she did know that the pathologist suspected poor

160

Gerry had been dead for days before his remains were left at The Terpsichore—finally said, "my turn now."

"If, as the police believe, Gerry *was* murdered some time last weekend," Kit said, "how come no one reported him missing? Where did you all think he was?"

Queenie reached for her cigarette case, did the polite offering around, and then lit the only one that was to be smoked. "I didn't know he was missing until I was informed of his death. Gerry didn't live under my roof, so I usually only saw him once a week or so.

"Next—the painful Poppy. Gerry's wife, allegedly, didn't know he was missing because *she* was. She spent Monday to Wednesday playing hide the cocktail frankfurt with her new aerobics instructor. Tacky, I know, but that's Poppy in a nutshell."

"But what about the weekend?" Kit reminded her. "If Gerry had been dead since then, how come Poppy didn't notice he was gone before *she* went?"

"They are estranged, Kit," Queenie explained. "Their house is ostentatiously huge, and they moved into opposite ends of it years ago. Poppy claims that Gerry mentioned in passing, quite literally I gather, that he was going fishing for the weekend."

"And?"

"And," Queenie gave a reluctant nod, "it's true enough. He was supposed to do just that, as he often did, with his best friend Matthew Hunt. But also, as often happened with Gerry, he didn't turn up, so Matthew went on his own. Between Matthew thinking nothing was strange and Poppy being strange, no one noticed that Gerry wasn't anywhere he should be, until we all discovered that he couldn't have been, even if he'd wanted to."

"But the man was about to open a new nightclub," Kit said perplexed. "Why wasn't he missed by anyone there? By his business associates, or his cousin, um, Adrian, is it?"

Queenie nodded. "I suppose that also seems a little strange; but more so to an outsider than us. You see, Gerry was helping to bankroll that venture, but wasn't going to take an active role in its operation. It was more for his sons, in partnership with Adrian and his son. I'm sure that Sean, Gerry's oldest, probably wondered where he was, but even he would only have started to worry on

Friday, as we all would have, if his father hadn't turned up for our weekly family lunch. Even Poppy doesn't miss those. Of course by Friday, we all knew exactly where he was, even if we've yet to find out where he'd been."

"From that, I assume, he *did* make your family lunch last week?"

"Oh yes, and he was in fine spirits."

"Was that the last time any of you saw him?"

Queenie looked thoughtful. "Matthew, with whom he was to go fishing, organized that with him by phone on Friday afternoon, but never actually saw him again. Sean and Tom caught up with him later that night at the Moshun Club, that's his ... oh you know that. And Poppy, whom we believe was the last of the family to lay eyes on him, said it was around eight on Saturday morning that he mentioned the fishing trip."

Kit took a sip of the lemon barley drink that had been poured for them on their arrival, and watched her hostess thoughtfully while Queenie answered, with a negative, Hector's question about whether she knew either Neil Porter or Nino Piantoni.

What things, what dastardly things, have you been responsible for over the years, Queenie Riley? Kit wondered. Are you the Big Bad in Granny's green-silk tracksuit? Or is that a reputation made of myth and mirrors and bloody good bad-PR?

"Do you happen to know who used a very big car to knock Stuart Barker into a four-week coma?" Kit asked, snapping Queenie's attention back to her.

"Do you think I should?" Queenie said, recovering her wits quite nicely.

"No, not necessarily," Kit shrugged. "I just thought you might have heard."

Hector, who was suddenly being unnaturally brave in the question-asking department, said, "Paraphrasing what O'Malley said yesterday about us not making any assumptions about your nephew's businesses and rivals, um ..."

"Yes, Hector?" Queenie smiled.

"If your Gerry, while cruising around town in his car, had kind of—I dunno—*run into* Mr. Barker in the street, would you tell us?"

Queenie laughed. Uh-oh, Kit thought, she likes Hector too.

"If you recall, young man, I asked you and your charming colleague, if I could employ your services to find out who murdered Gerry."

"Yeah? So?" Hector glanced at Kit, perhaps for reassurance, then cocked his head at Queenie. "I was asking about your knowledge of a hit and run, um *accident*, not a murder."

"Of course you were, Hector," Queenie agreed. "But you see, if I knew that Gerry had been driving around the neighborhood knocking people down, then I could probably figure out for myself who then took to him with a sharp implement and deprived him of his life. Do you see where I'm going with this?"

Kit laughed this time. "What? And you don't think it's possible, and therefore enough, that the Barkers just *think* Gerry ran Stuart down; whether he did or not?"

"I'm sure they do, or did. But as far as I know, Gerry didn't. And, as far as I know, the Barkers did not, this time, commit an act of murder."

"And you're sure about that?"

"Good heavens no, Kit," Queenie exclaimed. "But I've never been one to make rash assumptions, to act prematurely, or to take revenge when the heart and mind is on fire with the desire for it.

"If I and the other elders behaved like every Stuart, Mick, or, I'm ashamed to say, Gerry, then our streets would've been awash with the blood of families ruined over trifles." Queenie reached for and lit another cigarette, then peered at Kit and Hector through the smoke. "Oh don't look so surprised, you two. I wasn't planning to speak in euphemisms forever."

"Give us the plain English lowdown then, please, Queenie," Kit said.

Queenie nodded. "I do not believe that Stuart or Leo Barker ordered a hit on my nephew. Plain enough?" she said. "Of course it doesn't mean they didn't."

"Does that mean there's also a chance that Gerry *was* the driver or organizer of Stuart's hit and run?" Kit smiled.

Queenie shrugged, then raised a hand to hold the conversation there, as they all heard the strange clackety approach of several people wearing spiked shoes.

Oh, no it wasn't. It was one Sasha, wearing red patent-leather, high-heeled, and thigh-high boots. And, as if they weren't statement enough, she had matched them with a white vinyl mini skirt and a sleeveless top, horizontally striped in pale red and black.

Blimey, Kit thought, as her own fashion sense fled the room. She looks like an escapee from a tacky sixties' record cover for the best of British pop.

"Oh my God, Sasha, you look like a trollop!"

Or that, Kit silently agreed.

"Thanks, Gran," Sasha grinned.

"That wasn't a compliment, darling."

"I know," she said cheerily, then turned to face Kit and Hector and clock-in with her official petulant sigh. "And here you are, my big brave bodyguards."

"Actually, I'm the wicked witch your granny hired to lure you into the woods and lose you forever," Kit said. "Or sell you to a troll."

Sasha's posture was making the transition from smart-arse to huffy, when Queenie exclaimed, "Oh excellent, Kit! I was about to tell you not to take any shit from my sweet granddaughter; but I see the advice is unnecessary."

"That's charming, Gran," Sasha said. "You're supposed to be on my side."

"I am, darling. That's why I'm letting you go out to this nonsense tonight *with* Kit. You should be grateful she agreed to escort you— the alternative being Will, or not at all."

Sasha pressed her hand to her heart and turned to Kit. "In that case, I can't thank you enough for saying yes. Shall we get going then, before we miss all the fuss?"

"Oh let's," Kit said enthusiastically, leaping to her feet and dragging Hector after her. "We've only been waiting here for half an hour, but we should rush now."

"This is going to be such fun," Sasha noted, walking over to Queenie, who got up to give her a hug.

"Sash dear, can't you wear something with more bottom coverage than this belt?"

"It's a skirt and I love you too, Gran. Don't wait up."

"Have a nice time, darling." The matriarch of the ruthless Riley crime family sighed, and added, "If there is any kind of problem, you are to do *exactly* what Kit or Hector say. Got it?"

"Yes, I promise, Gran. But I still reckon *they* are my problem."

Queenie gave her granddaughter a long-suffering look. "Oh they *are*, Sasha dear; that's why I hired them."

As Sasha led the way to the front door, Kit could hear Hector behind her, humming the baseline of *These Boots are Made for Walking.*

Chapter 13

The Metro Blaazt. And what a blast! All chocolate-brown and stainless steel, and light and dark, and super-shiny floor, and mirrored ceiling and dance floors everywhere among the couches of chocolate-brown and stainless steel and walls of glass. Well, plexiglass so that it looked good but drunks couldn't fall through it and sue the management.

If one were into this sort of place, the Blaazt would no doubt be the bees-bloody-knees of places to be into. If one weren't, then it was just an impressive-looking space with repetitive couldn't-really-call-it-music loudness and too many humans.

As the noise and color and movement swirled around her, and while keeping most of her attention on Sasha, Kit edged her mind out of this smudge on the space-time continuum, to take half a moment for herself.

Oh crap! Is that all you can manage? she sulked, realizing now that she'd hedged when Alex had asked when she'd last taken time for herself, because she couldn't remember. Well, who bloody could? Jeez O'Malley, think about who you've been mixing with in the last month or so. She took inventory: loopy letter writers, a serial killer, one utter wacko, the worst rock band in the world, several dead people, a footballer, some actors, and too many politicians. Then, there was this week's dead gangster, his crime family, their rivals in the crime stakes, several ghosts of lifetimes past, and now the in-crowd of a nightclub with the most mind-numbing music in history. No wonder her dreams were creeping her out.

Hector reached through from his region of space-time and handed her a lemon squash. She pointed out Sasha and a guy with strange hair on the dance floor, and sighed.

Still no time for Kit. There was none available, and none to take. As for her novel, the one she'd almost forgotten about coz it'd been so long … Now that's odd. She hadn't given Flynn's adventures a thought in weeks, so why now? Was it just the link with Alex's question? No. That's not it, she frowned, realizing her book-thoughts were being manipulated by a bit of real-world woo-woo; namely the lassoing of *her* subconscious by an emanation to her right. Wonder about the vagaries of the human mind overtook her puzzlement for a nanosec until she diagnosed the cause: scary indecision was oozing from the scrawny guy at the next table. His inability to get his act together was subliminally reminding Kit of how hard it often was to get her characters to do anything.

Oh boy! What *are* you on about, O'Malley? Kit laughed. Forget Pete Barker's lord-dude. It was the human mind *alone* that worked in spookiness.

Kit shook her mind to make it stick to one thing at a time; to *the book*, perhaps, and its secrets still hidden in the depths of her increasingly peculiar psyche. Sometimes, she'd write a seamlessly natural or efficient passage to get Flynn Carter from the kitchen to the bedroom, or from one side of Melbourne to the other, *without* feeling the need to describe the decor or the scenery en route—sometimes a chair is *just* a chair, O'Malley!—but then, in the next chapter, she wouldn't be able to get her off the damn couch.

And now, here in the coolest nightclub in the continuum, life was imitating art; or rather Mr. Fidget, alone at the next table, was fast becoming the personification of a hiccup in the creative process. He so wanted to go ask the girl in the little black dress for a dance, a drink, or hot sex, but was attached to his table by a short imaginary bungee rope. Kit watched as he kept going to move, going to move … only to be snapped back on his stool, before he'd even made it into the upright position.

Oh, Aphrodite! This is unbearable. Kit got up, strode over to him, and asked him his name.

"Um, Paul."

"Back in a sec, um-Paul," she said, and then approached the brunette in the LBD, placed her hand innocently into the small of her back, and said, "Excuse me."

The brunette gave the smile of a single soul on the hunt for company, and said, "Yeah?"

"Don't look now," Kit shouted in her ear, "but the nice-enough looking guy at the table behind us has been trying to get up the courage to ask you for a dance. I don't know him, but if you're interested, his name is Paul. What's yours?"

Ms. LBD glanced casually behind Kit, then back at her. "I'm Claire. Is he your friend?"

"Nope, don't know him from Humphrey Bear. It's up to you now, you can wander over there, or run and hide." Kit returned to Hector, for an update on Sasha's position in the room.

A moment later Claire looked Paul's way, in a casual way, and he unhooked his bungee rope enough to offer her his stool.

"What did you say to them?" Hector seemed highly amused. "And why?"

Kit shrugged dismissively. "It was too sad. Some people just need a kick up the bum."

"Yeah, right. And there's not a romantic bone in your body, Katherine O'Malley."

Kit changed the subject, but only to get the lowdown on Hector's chat with Gerry's oldest son. As arranged, Sasha had introduced them to him on their arrival. "What did Sean say?"

"First up, I'd like to say how peculiar it is that it *seems* so easy to talk to this wacky family of career crooks. Second, unlike me, Sean's vibe is like super-reliable-guy. People kept barging into his open office with problems and he just dealt calmly, and returned to our chat. He's pumped about this gig tonight but not stressed by the hype, except he thinks it lacks respect, under the circumstances. I sensed he was really cut about his dad; and if it had been up to him, he'd have cancelled this spectacle. But, now that it's running, he wants it to be perfect. And he wanted to get back to things out here, but not to escape my questions."

"Good profile, Hector," Kit nodded. "And the facts, man?"

Hector grinned. "He says he's got no idea who killed his father, but reckons it probably wasn't the Barkers. But, just like Queenie, he doesn't rule them out. Actually, what he said was, the melo-drama of it was way too imaginative for those arseholes.

"He said that when he last saw his father, around ten-thirty at the Moshun Club last Friday night, Gerry mentioned he was going fishing with Whatshisface for the weekend. There was also a dark-haired woman trying to pick him up, pick up Gerry I mean, or vice versa that night. Sean said that wasn't unusual, even when his parents had still been talking to each other, so he didn't pay much attention to her and has no idea what came of it."

"Is that it?"

"Not quite. Gerry's fifty percent stake in this venue is an investment in Sean and his brothers, rather than a business venture with the cousin."

Kit nodded her thanks. "So, Hector, is this place cool or what?"

"Oh yeah," Hector said, realizing in the nick-of that it probably wasn't cool to give an actual thumbs-up to show his approval.

Kit shook her head at him, he grinned at her, and they both returned their attention to …

Shit no, Kit swore. Where the bloody hell? Oh, there she is. But that's not the same bloke.

"That's a different guy," Hector shouted.

Kit was up and onto the dance floor and, with a slide here and a nip and tuck there, was at the side of Sasha Riley and her new dance partner—a vaguely familiar young man with short dark hair and wide brown eyes—in a flash and a bit. Just as well she rushed too, coz that scar on his dimpled chin could well be the mark of a hit gone wrong. Just coz he *looked* adorable didn't mean he wasn't a hired killer; especially as he and Sasha weren't really dancing and his body language was so very earnest.

The look on Sasha's face, though, put a whole different spin on things—as did the hands on her hips and her, "What the hell are you doing, Kit?"

"*What* did I say, not fifteen minutes ago?" Kit scolded, adopting her own Shintaro stance.

"But he's my cousin," Sasha snapped.

Aha! Probably *is* a hired killer, then.

"Don't care if he's your once-conjoined twin, Sasha," Kit growled. "Rectify that *I* don't know him *now*. And, you do this again, the next guy's face will be girl-rammed to the floor."

Sasha curled her lip. "This is my cousin Tom Anders. Tom, this is a very annoying person."

"You want me to have her thrown out?" Tom asked. And he was serious.

"In your dreams," Kit laughed, now noticing the security mike and hearing device in his left ear. "Queenie hired me to irritate Sasha as much as possible tonight."

"Oh, okay," Tom nodded. "Can I get you a drink, then? On the house."

"Just got one, thanks. But can I talk to you for a sec?"

Sasha was gobsmacked. "Hey! What is your deal, Kit? Have you got some kind of mojo that works on everyone but me?"

"It has the perfect effect on you, Sasha," Kit smiled. "Table. Now."

By the time they got there, Sasha had spotted someone else she just had to catch up with.

"Who?" Kit asked.

Sasha pointed towards the couches between the next two dance floors, to a group of four—one girl and three guys. Kit couldn't see all their faces. She sighed.

"Who do you know? All of them?"

"Just my hairdresser friend Tina and her yucky old yob boyfriend, the flexing one."

Kit squinted. She could see only the back of the muscly poseur with the spiky-blue hair; and of Tina, hanging on his arm, all she could make out was: slender, animated, short blonde bob. "You absolutely *have* to say hello to your hairdresser?" Kit asked Sasha.

"My hairdresser *and* my friend Tina—*if* that's all right with you!"

"Go. But do not move from there, without coming back here first."

"How about I take Hector with me?"

Hector stood up. "I'm warning you, Sasha, I'm nearly as mean as O'Malley."

Animated—that's it; that's why Tom had seemed familiar. He looked like his father, only alive. He also resembled Gerry more than Sean did, and was better looking than both of them.

"Are you crowding Sasha because of the phone threat?" Tom asked.

Kit nodded. "Any ideas who it might be?"

170

"Not a clue," Tom said. "With our bloody family, it could be anyone. And it could be for real, or just some shit stirrer."

"Do you think it could be connected to what happened to your father?"

"Same answer, Kit," Tom screwed up his mouth. "My Dad inherited and *made* a lot of enemies. Shit, half the time I reckon he went looking for them."

Kit looked puzzled. "Did you two get on?"

Tom shrugged. "I guess so, but like any father and son who don't have much in common, you know. I'm the middle brother, the kind of nowhere-son. And I've got my own plans, my own life. I'm studying architecture, so I can get the hell out. Sean and Mark are happy in the life, you know. This place to them is heaven, and the family business is, you know, family."

You know, Kit's mind echoed. And, either Tom Anders didn't get or value the concept of the crime family code of face-value togetherness, or Queenie's employment of her and Hector had sanctioned them for insider info. Uh-oh, what did that make her in Tom's eyes?

"Is coddling cousin Sash a permanent gig, or just till this threat comes true or blows over?"

Ah, Kit realized. It makes you one of them. He thinks you're a bad guy, O'Malley, which goes some way to explaining the career-crook blabber-mouthing that Hector had commented on earlier. "It's just for tonight," she explained. "Sasha wanted to come here, but Queenie wouldn't let her out unless I played bodyguard."

Being considered "bad" was good for getting info from the lesser family members, she reminded herself, but what does it mean in the dodgy pattern of life's every little thing? Probably that she and Hector were now accessories, after-the-fact, to every single one of those little things, that's what. Oh goody, Kit's mind laughed, coz that would include murder, mayhem, arson, thuggery, burglary, drugs, thieving, armed hold-ups, prostitution.

We are so *in for it*, she thought. "I'm actually a private investigator," she confessed.

"Really? Wow," Tom said. He removed his security headset and stuffed it in his pocket.

Kit shrugged, then leaned in close. "Can I ask you about Suzie?"

Tom Anders, handsome young uni student, wanting a life outside family crime, *possibly* with his "Juliet" of the House of Barker, turned white as a fridge. A heartbeat later he put on his Anders–Riley fighting socks, or Romeo's cautious britches, and said "Who?"

"Tom, I'm a friend of Scooter Farrell's. It's only a weird fluky-thing that I'm watching over Sasha tonight, coz I'm really investigating why your father was left *where* he was."

Tom's confusion was big. "What's that got to do with this Scooter person?" he asked.

Kit smiled. "You mean apart from her being Suzie's cousin? She frequents the place where your father was left, and was there when he was found. She freaked out, because she thought that once the cops found out who she was, her 'being there' would somehow have an adverse impact on you and your girlfriend. You know, your girlfriend of the Barker clan."

"Shit! Oh man, oh shit!" Tom said eloquently, then glared at Kit. "What do you want?"

"I don't want anything, Tom," Kit assured him. "Except the truth, if there is such a thing in this world you inhabit. That bar, where your Dad was left, happens to be owned by a friend of mine, and all of this stuff implicates her by association."

"So that's it? You just want to know what I know. You don't want money or anything?"

"What would I want money for? Apart from all the things one usually wants it for."

"This isn't blackmail?" When Kit gave a surprised and emphatic headshake, Tom looked apologetic. "Sorry, but hey, you're the one who mentioned the kind of world I inhabit. Go ahead, ask me what-ever."

"How long have you and Suzie been an item?" Kit asked.

"About eighteen months. And yes, I love her. She loves me. We love each other."

"Does anyone else in either family, besides Scooter, know about your relationship?"

"No. Unless you're really Queenie's spy; in which case we'll be leaving town now."

"I swear I'm not a spy," Kit assured him. "And if no one else knows, then it's unlikely that your personal situation had anything to do with her father's accident or your father's murder."

"Christ, I bloody hope not," Tom was appalled.

"Do you think that what happened to them is connected in any way? One to the other, I mean."

"Possibly, as with everything that happens in this town between us and them, and the Stanos. But I don't think so." Tom fiddled with his ear. "'And why?' you'll no doubt ask next. 'Because of how and where my Dad was found,' I'd reply."

"Too creative for the Barkers?"

"Just a bit," Tom snorted. "And while we're on the subject of that place, your friend's bar I mean, I don't know anything about Dad being interested in it. What the hell would a middle-aged macho womanizer want with a gay women's joint?"

"I know a few narrow minds who'd just want to see it closed," Kit noted.

"Nah, not Dad," Tom smiled. "He was all he-man rugged, tight-arse straight, and pretty chauvinistic, but strangely enough he wasn't homophobic. One of his life-long best mates is his gay car mechanic, whose partner is a drag queen."

"Really?" Kit laughed. "Well, what about just plain old interest in the venue or the site, rather than for the existing business?"

Tom pushed out his bottom lip. "Not that I *know* of. Which is not really saying much."

Okay, last long shot, Kit thought. "Do you know of a bloke called Neil Porter?"

Tom stared at the ceiling, or himself reflected in it, then shook his head. "Don't think so."

"What about Nathan Pittock or Nino Piantoni?"

"Nathan? That name rings a vague bell," Tom frowned. "Dad, at least I think it was Dad, could've been Adrian, mentioned a Nathan in connection with ... what? Think. Nah, it's gone."

"Oh well, it's not important," Kit lied, just as Hector returned with Sasha in tow. She, however, merely made a pitstop to inform Kit that she was now going to dance with her friend Tina, who was loitering over by the dance floor.

On only slightly closer inspection, Kit could make out that Tina had a few good years on her friend Sasha, that it was unlikely she was a real blonde, and that she favored split level mascara, blue eye shadow, and a ridiculous number of bracelets, anklets, and necklets. Kit watched as they danced, out onto the floor with matching moves and identical steps, to something with a beat-beat but no tune-tune within the range of human hearing.

"Hector?" she shouted, after introducing him to Tom and leaning back so the two blokes could bond by exchanging manly hand-sweat. "Am I getting old or is this just noise?"

"You're old, older, oldest, O'Malley," Hector grinned. "Hey, guess what I just found out?"

"You missed your lobotomy upgrade this morning?"

"Ha-ha, not!" he sneered. "Sasha knows Vanessa."

"That's nice, Grasshopper. Who's Vanessa?"

He endowed her with the idiot's look, as in *she* was the idiot. "The real reason we're here."

"Oh yeah. Maybe her cousin does too, then." Kit turned to Tom, as Hector said something she didn't catch. "Do you know Vanessa Boyes-Lang?"

"Everyone in clubland knows Nessa," Tom nodded, looking around. "She was just … Ah, there she is, drooling over the Yankee Tsar."

Kit followed Tom's pointing finger to the couple sitting at a table that was so conveniently close to theirs it could have been planned, had she even remembered why they were really here. A stunning figure in green, with shoulder-length blond-tipped dark hair, exquisite cheek bones, and eloquent hands, Comrade Tereshenko outshone the fairly attractive Vanessa in the details; although Ms. Boyes-Lang also had that noticeable *something*. Whatever it was, Kit thought, Vanessa's mother certainly didn't have it; nor did she seem to recognize it in her only girl child—the one who was going to inherit half the squillions that old Mrs. B-L apparently didn't want her daughter to share with *anyone*.

Kit realized Hector was giving her the look. "What?" she said.

He pointed to their quarry. "I was about to say, *and there they are*."

"Learned something by asking the other bloke," she explained. "Or I will in a sec."

Kit directed Hector's attention to Sasha on the dance floor while she took a moment to observe Gregor and Vanessa making old-fashioned love to each other: holding hands, making with the eyes, laughing when neither had spoken, him kissing the tips of her fingers, her brushing his hair back, and so on and so forth, etc. Get a room, for Ethel's sake!

"What do you mean everyone in clubland knows her?" she asked Tom.

"She's a nightclub junkie," he said. "Or she was. She used to do them nearly every night, but now it's a weekend thing. She still spends big, dances heaps, and is generous with her friends when they're hanging."

"Does she, I mean how does she maintain the momentum?"

Tom narrowed his eyes. "Wouldn't know, Kit."

"I'm not making any judgments, Tom. Just wondering what the attraction is."

Tom shrugged. "The music, the mood, the pace, the rush, the shoes? Who knows. Whatever it was with me, it wore off before I turned twenty. But then I was raised in joints like this. I get paid to be here now, otherwise I'd be home watching the Sunday night movie.

"But with Nessa and her friends it's a lifestyle; or maybe a life," he shrugged. He leaned in even closer. "I don't *think* she takes, except maybe the occasional eccy. With her it always seemed to be the dancing and the boys, and I mean *boys*, until old Count Cossack showed her his roubles."

"You don't like him?"

"I don't know him. Not enough to give a shit, anyway. But, if that Yankee wanker and his overplayed Russian accent," he said, rolling the Rrrussian, "is anywhere related to a royal anything, then I'm a Queen's corgi."

Kit reached out and fondled Tom's ear. "Nice doggy," she said.

Tom's astonishment, as he glanced at Count Gregor, was replaced a second later by an expression more like *bloody hell!* as an elsewhere-happening grabbed his attention.

"What's up?" Kit asked, although it was unlikely she'd get an answer as Tom, having retrieved and replaced his headset while leaping off his stool and about ten feet away, now seemed to be demanding a full security alert. The situation was apparently grim and urgent, at least defcon five or six, because he was snapping orders to … what? seal the hatches and throw the women and kiddies overboard first? All she did hear was, "How the hell did he get in?" and "Get him the fuck out now, and fire that dickhead on the door."

Tom returned to Kit, with an apologetic wave. "Gotta go help deal with a creep who shouldn't be …" he let the rest hang. "You really *are* watching out for Sash, yeah?"

Kit nodded. "Yeah. Tom, who …" but he was gone. As Kit hadn't seen anyone strange or any trouble, she wondered whether his performance was simply an act to get away from her.

"Wow! D'you see that?" Hector exclaimed. "Three nine-foot bouncers just surrounded a way too-old for this place, but otherwise ordinary dude, and escorted him thataway without so much as an eyebrow raise," Hector stated. "It was a beautiful thing to watch."

One-thirty a.m. Monday. Katherine O'Malley loitered with intent, laced by irritation, in the fine feathery drizzle out the front of the Metro Blaazt. Ten or so other bods were hanging around the hotdog stand; strolling straight, gay, and pan-sexed club-goers were to- and froming the other Commercial Road nightclubs; Hector had gone for the car; and Sasha had gone—for a moment, she'd said. Back inside, for just a sec, she'd said.

Kit was about to dispatch Hermione Munster, the door bitch—equal opportunity ruled at the Blaazt—to retrieve her recalcitrant client, when two dozen raving lunatics were disgorged through the front door simultaneously. Sasha Riley was in amongst them. And then she wasn't. Okay. Kit jumped up, bent down, leaned left, bent right, pushed her way through the crowd that was now nothing but a hindrance, then returned to her spot at the corner of the building.

Shit. The corner of the building, beside the lane. Yep, there was

176

Sasha. Oh, shit again! What on earth was that girl doing now? And with whom? And all the way up there?

Sasha was backing away from the main street. What light there was, was on *her* face and the back of an advancing-towards-her person. Kit resisted the urge to shout out, just in case the person had a weapon of the sort that could be used from a distance of five feet, and began a quick and quiet approach up the darker side of the alley instead. As Kit jumped a puddle, she did wonder why Sasha hadn't called for help, and why the little pest was smiling.

"God, Jason, you're a bloody liar. Adam's not here at all is he?"

Oh, that explains everything, Kit thought. Sasha knows this one too.

Kit was about to relax her warrior-gal to the rescue response, so she could throw the anger one at Sasha instead without feeling the need to deck her, when the situation changed again.

A shape ... Bugger that! A *bloke* emerged from the dumpster behind Sasha, grabbed her round the mouth and waist, and slammed her against the wall. Jason, the bloody-lying-lure, turned and ran for it, only to come a cropper over Kit's flung-out foot—a move made while she ran towards clear and present *danger*, Will Robinson.

The closer she got, however, the more Kit wanted to hightail it after Jason. She certainly didn't want to know for sure what she suspected; that—oh, shit!—*both* those awful cracking sounds had been Sasha's arm.

And, what was it Boxer Macklin had told her? If you see him coming for you, then run—fast. Well she *was*—but in the wrong bloody direction.

At two meters and still closing, Kit let out a howl. She leaped, higher than she thought possible, braced her hand against the wall next to Sasha, and jammed her foot, accompanied by her full weight, down on the assailant's knee. Mr. butt-ugly Sid Ralph bellowed and crumpled, but Kit was not going to let him drop and roll. Regaining her balance, she swept his injured leg back and around, so he faced her for a second, then she punched him hard in the chest, using her fist and his own momentum to ram his back into the side of the dumpster. He hit the ground—right knee first, then his arse. Kit punched him in the balls, for good measure, then jammed her thumb and bent-index finger into his throat and squeezed his windpipe.

"Hello, Toad," she snarled. "Not a good idea to mess with my friend."

Toad gurgled. He may have said, "who the uck are you?" but Kit wasn't really interested.

"Way to go, Kit!" Sasha said, getting to her feet. She was crying, but getting over it. Fast.

"Very bad idea to mess with Queenie's granddaughter," Kit added.

"Can I kick him? Please," Sasha asked. She was cradling her right arm, and there was blood and tears on her face, but she was otherwise fine. Ropable, but fine.

"Be my guest," Kit said.

Sasha took a step back and delivered a perfect goal-scoring drop-kick right into Toad's ribcage. He grunted; she said, "Can I kill him now?"

"No dear. Run along and find Hector, so we can take you to the hospital. Then I'll explain to your Gran how you brought this on yourself."

"Okay, Kit," Sasha said agreeably, heading off down the lane.

Woo, Kit thought. Add mental derangement to the broken arm. Queenie *will* be pleased.

Toad tried to move, or faint, so Kit squeezed his important breathing apparatus again to get his attention. "Who hired you, you stupid bastard?"

Mr. Ralph flared his nostrils.

"Do you want me to call her back, and watch her kill you?"

"Dead, if I tell you," he mumbled, "so get fuc ..."

Kit finger-flicked his toady wet-lipped mouth with her free hand. "Don't be rude. How about you just nod, or shake your head?" She knelt in his groin.

"Aaggh, kay, okay."

"The Barkers?" Kit asked in a whisper.

Toad shook his head.

"The Stanos?" Negative response again.

"Another family?"

"Wrong bloody side. Bitch."

"Wrong s ...? Cops?" Kit went cold.

No reaction, let alone response.

"A cop?"

"Don't wanna be dead."

"Toad, you messed with the Rileys: that makes you a fuckwit, " Kit pointed out. "So, one way or another, you're going to die; and probably sooner than you planned. I suggest you get outta town before the good or bad cops, or the Rileys, or my feral cat find you. In fact, I'd start crawling, before Sasha's cavalry of bouncers get here."

Kit smacked his head back into the dumpster, to ensure he couldn't enact the lunge of every thriller's frighten-the-shit-out-of-you penultimate scene, and then stepped over him and went looking for her charge. And her sidekick.

Ms. Munster and two bouncers passed her on the run, just as Kit's fighting adrenaline surge segued into clammy-shaky fright and the need for a nice lie down. No, throw up first.

Oh, that feels better.

She possibly still had work to do, so she waited for Hector to find her; and Sasha. He could take charge for a while, while she collected the bits of herself that usually made sense.

Chapter 14

Patty cake, patty cake, poke your eye. Kit batted the little paw away. The Cat biffed her on the chin.

"Thistle, baby, go away."

"Lerrkle."

"I don't think so," Kit said, putting the pillow under her head, so she could roll on her back. She glanced at the clock radio, groaned, and then stared wide-eyed at the ceiling until the view was obscured by black cat-in-face.

The phone rang. Thistle leaped off the bed, as if the ringing tone contained a special feline call to arms, then ricocheted off a shoe and back onto the bed; possibly because her human's reaction was a swearing one, not a leaping out of bed and feeding The Cat on the way to stop the ringing noise one.

Having arrived at this analysis of Thistle's behavior in the time it took her to reach for the bedside phone, Kit decided she'd been spending too much time alone with The Cat. "Yeah?" she said into the receiver.

"Morning Kit. Don't suppose you could drop by my gin joint. Like now?"

Wake up brain, match the voice with your database. "What, why? No," Kit objected.

"But," he began.

"Boxer, I haven't even had brekkie and you're giving me indigestion."

"You haven't? It's eleven already."

"So?" Kit stroked a purring Thistle's tummy, hoping to receive the mythical feline healing-vibes in return. The Cat bit her hand. "I was in Casualty until three-thirty this morning."

"Oh. Are you okay?"

"Yes," Kit replied. "I was escorting the casualty, not being it for a change."

"I've got a little problem, mate."

Mate? Kit thought. "I hate to break it to you, Box, but that's old news. What's more, you've been dealing with yourself by yourself for years without my help; so leave me alone."

He sighed. "It's just that I was kinda hoping you'd get here before I call the cops."

Kit tossed up for a second whether she was game to ask, "Why would you do that?"

"Because," Boxer said, "my little problem is of the deceased human kind, as in prematurely dead, and quite obviously by a hand other than their own or god's."

"In that case, I'm sorry, mate," Kit laughed, "but with that I cannae help. Marek explicitly told me I was not allowed to find any more dead bodies."

"But you didn't find it, O'Malley. I did. It is, however, someone we know."

Kit closed her eyes. "I think I'm sure I didn't want to know that. But, if it's someone *we* know Boxer, then odds are it's not a friend of mine. So do I care?"

"Yes."

Kit exhaled a long low growl. "Twenty minutes. And by the way Boxer, there *is* no god."

Half an hour later, Kit stood in the four-space, employees-only parking area at the rear of Swiggers Bar in the rain. Again, in the rain. Boxer was holding an umbrella ineffectively over her head, as they stared in silence at the dead body of not who Kit had expected.

Access to the carpark, which also accommodated two dumpsters, lots of crates, a collection of gas bottles, and what had possibly once been a quite serviceable spaceship, was via the cobbled laneway which ran behind Swiggers and the shops and cafés on either side. The body that wasn't Toad Ralph was propped between the dumpsters, legs splayed out in front and with an ugly rain-soaked gash from throat to breast-bone. Probably the cause of death, Kit thought, but you can never be sure.

"You okay, O'Malley?" Boxer asked.

"Yeah," Kit nodded. It was possibly a lie, but she was too busy realigning her sensor array to allow for this anomaly in her expectations to know whether the scene had any effect on her, other than surprise. But bloody hell, this past-life bullshit is getting a bit much, she thought. When a girl assumes she's going to see a dead thug, especially one she'd assumed had been taken out by vengeful relatives or hirelings of the thug's last-known victim, then it was extra-specially weird for that girl to find herself staring at a murdered police officer. Again, especially because this was yet another person whose name had been mentioned to and by Kit in the last few days, but whom she had not thought of or seen for so many years that she'd had to look twice to make sure it was her.

Kit sighed, wiped her eyes, and ran her hand back through her wet hair. Detective Senior Constable Sheryl Mapp lay before them, dressed in, of all things, a crimson sequined evening gown and matching high-heels. She would've looked stunning had she been alive. Kit turned to Boxer, not caring that he'd know her eyes were wet from more than just the rain, coz she knew he wasn't completely together himself. It wasn't so much that they were shedding a tear for someone they knew well, as releasing emotion for an old and well liked comrade, now fallen. But …

"Andrew Macklin!" she stamped her foot. "What the hell is going on?"

"Wish I knew, Kit," he said, no doubt worried about how this would come back on him.

"And you found her?"

"Yes, I found her. I came out to empty a bin and *voi*-bloody-*là!*" he gestured towards Mapp. "I was the first out here today. I mean from Swiggers. I unlocked the back door."

Kit looked at him suspiciously. "How come there's no cars parked here?"

"The council has yet to repair the crater that's barring vehicle access to the entire lane."

"And you *have* called the cops?"

"Yes. I spoke to Jon Marek himself. He and the squad should be here any …"

"He's here." Kit felt a hand clamp down on her shoulder. "Why are you?"

"Hey there, Jonno," Kit faked a grin.

"Don't you dare 'hey there' me," Marek warned. "I swear Kitty, I'm just going to save time and charge you with every homicide in the state."

"But I've got an alibi," Kit swore.

Marek turned to Boxer, hesitated a moment, then offered his hand. "G'day Macklin. Long time no see. Nice weather for it."

"Yeah," Boxer agreed, shaking Marek's hand, "if you like dying in a shit-heap in the rain. Was she still working undercover?"

Marek smiled. "I can't answer *your* questions, mate. You've gotta do the talking."

"Jonno," Kit said. "I hope you brought Cathy with you."

"Why?"

"Coz I think this might be connected to Anders."

"Really?" Marek said, in a tone that suggested Kit wouldn't know a connection if it had a visible join. "And why would you think that?"

"Because," Kit began and then told them about the previous night's encounter with Sid Ralph and *his* insinuation that it was a cop who'd hired him to mess with Sasha Riley.

"And wouldn't he just love *that* little piece of bullshit to do the rounds," Marek noted. "And what are you *on*, Kitty? You knew Mapp; she was one of the most honest Ds around."

"Vouching here," Boxer agreed.

"You shut up," Marek said.

"For goodness sake, Jonno," Kit exclaimed, "I didn't mean I thought Sheryl hired Toad, you fool. I'm not even saying what he told me is true. But, given that he *did* tell me that, then he probably gave the same story to whoever got to him in that alley after me."

"And who do you think that would've been, exactly?" Marek asked.

"Don't know, but I doubt it was the Red Cross."

"You *really* beat him up?" Boxer said in amazement. "Man! I tell *you* how dangerous Toad is, in order to warn you off and keep you out of trouble, and the very same day you take to him with, what, your insanity?"

Kit put her hands on her hips. "Hey, sometimes you've just gotta go with the flow. I took him by surprise, Box, it wasn't difficult."

"And warning O'Malley off a thing is like telling her she *can't* do it coz she's a girl," Marek laughed. "Plus, and you've obviously only just realized this, Macklin, she's a mental case. Speaking of which, Kitty, if you're not implying Mapp was Toad's employer tell me again why you think this is connected to Gerry boy."

"Der, Jonno," Kit said. "If the Rileys think it was a cop who hired Toad to hurt Sasha, what do you think they're going to do if they see a cop, in a ball gown, in the vicinity, in April?"

Marek snorted. "I doubt they'd start by taking out the first cop they see, on the off-chance of getting the right one. Especially when they're not likely to know or assume she *was* a cop."

"And take it from me," Boxer pointed at Mapp, "the Rileys *never* retaliate this quick."

"Okay, apart from those reasons," Kit nodded, not really wanting to put Queenie, who'd said pretty much the same thing only yesterday, in the picture for *this* murder. "But we are only several hundred meters from the scene of Toad's attack on Sasha last night. It's possible someone recognized Sheryl and ..." she waved her hand vaguely.

Sure, O'Malley. Just coz you're still coming to grips with this not being Toad, doesn't mean the only other known murderers of your acquaintance are responsible. Kit spent an unsuccessful moment tracing the logic she'd first used to arrive at the assumption that this body would be Sid Ralph's; until she noticed Boxer flinch, or perhaps flex his muscles.

"Shit, no," he complained. "What's that prick doing here?"

Kit and Marek looked up to see, of course, Charlie Parker under an umbrella and picking his way around the puddles towards them.

"You asked for Cathy, right?" Marek said. "Well, she comes with excess baggage." He told Boxer to "stay," then dragged Kit by the elbow out into the lane.

"What's with the manhandling?" Kit asked.

"Two things," Marek said, "and for your ears only. Go easy on Charlie, for today at least."

"Why, on earth?"

"Coz Bubblewrap Man gave us number six on Saturday. And Charlie kind of knew her."

"Oh no, Jonno," Kit reached out and clasped his forearm.

Marek tipped his head back to get the rain full in his face, then he held Kit's gaze and let out a weary breath. "She was twenty-two. Her family and friends thought she was on holiday in the Grampians; the people she was supposed to be with thought she'd changed her mind."

He wiped his face on his sleeve. "The down time between each vic is getting shorter. The bastard's not keeping them as long as he did in the beginning. This one—jeez Kitty, she had such a sweet face …" He swallowed. "This one was only chained for maybe five days."

Kit's well-being shivered as her memory cast up the hideous crime scene photos. "Jonno, please tell me you spoke to someone about this the other day; and that you'll do it again."

"Yeah, I did," he smiled sadly. "And I will. I'm also making sure everyone else who's involved in this nightmare, is too. No exceptions."

"Good. Now Chucky, what's with that? I mean, how?"

"She was one of Charlie's trainers at the gym he goes to *and* she went to the same church as him. And yes, he really does attend gym. He also knows her father a little, so it's more than just a passing acquaintance. So be nice, or at least try not to get up his nose.

"The other thing, apart from the statement I require of you regarding your presence *here* this morning, is that it has come to my attention—through the earlier use of your own big mouth—that I'll also need you to come to H.Q. and give Detective Sally Evans a statement regarding your altercation with one Sid Ralph, aka Toad."

"Why?"

"Because he was fished from the Yarra early this morning. And he wasn't breathing."

"Oh dear," Kit grimaced.

"Understatement of the day. Now, take Macklin inside with you and give your statements about this mess to Cathy. But do not leave until I say so. Okay?"

"Yes, Jonno."

Four hours later Kit sat twiddling her mind, while waiting for ... Hmm, she'd been waiting so long for it she'd forgotten what it was. The new-to-the-squad Detective Evans had popped back into the interview room some time ago and given her coffee and a sandwich, but even they were old memories now.

Kit had learned a few things during her statement-giving session with Detective Martin back at Swiggers, but not a lot from her technical incarceration here at homicide H.Q. When Kit had told Cathy that none of the Rileys seemed to think any of the Barkers were responsible for Gerry's murder, despite Stuart's hit and run, Cathy had confirmed that her crew had come to the same assumption. Not conclusion, she'd emphasized, as no one wanted to preclude the so-very-obvious as a possibility. She'd also said that while it, too, hadn't been ruled out completely, they'd pretty much shelved the likelihood that someone connected to the once-kidnapped, now-deceased Alan Shipper was responsible. There apparently wasn't anyone out there with an interest vested enough to take revenge on his behalf.

Cathy already knew about Gerry's failure to go fishing and about Poppy's aerobic sex sessions, but not about the woman who may have picked Gerry up from his own club on the last night he was known to be alive. While tabs were being kept on the wife, the sons, and even the best mate, just in case, the squad still regarded a payback deal for Gerry's double killing of the Sherwoods as the most likely reason for his death.

Cathy was curious about Kit's run-in with the now also-dead Toad, because of *his* interest in Gerry's resting place at Angie's; but the only real news that Cathy had was that Papa Leo Barker had been admitted to the Alfred Hospital early that morning, having suffered a stroke.

Kit's session with Detective Sally Evans at police H.Q. had played out quite differently. When she'd given the detective a statement

186

about her stoush with the *very much alive* Sid Ralph, Evans had wanted to know exactly what damage she and Sasha had wrought upon the ostensibly living Toad. This fine detail, the detective claimed, was needed in order to help the forensic pathologist distinguish between any injuries Kit's "*alleged* pre-homicidal attack may have caused, and the condition Mr. Ralph's mangled body was in when pulled from the river".

They'd been *her* words. That's exactly what this homicide detective, who didn't know Kit O'Malley from Buffy Somers, had said. *Alleged pre-homicidal attack.* In other words … No, those words were too stupid, Kit thought. And what kind of phrase was that anyway? At the very least it was ambiguous, because who could tell whether the *alleged* belonged to the word "attack" or to the idea of "pre-homicidal." The former questioned Kit's veracity, or perhaps her ability to beat the crap out of Toad Ralph; while the latter was definitely a worrisome "in other words." Yep and, shit, Kit acknowledged. That's what Detective Evans was implying all right—that she, Katherine O'Malley, was suspect numero uno in the actual homicide of Sid Ralph.

The door opened, allowing the return of Evans and another officer. She sat opposite Kit, he stood by the door. Kit decided to get in first.

"You should really be liaising with Cathy, um Detective Martin, about Toad's demise."

"Why?"

"Because Detective, it's possible that bad and malicious drug overlords hired Sid Ralph to murder Gerry Anders in retaliation for Gerry's killing of their couriers, the Sherwoods; and that they, the nasty drug people, then took Toad out themselves; to keep things tidy."

Yeah, Kit thought, sounds possible, plausible—lame. She shrugged mentally. Well, Toad was seen outside Angie's, and there are drugs in this city, and he is dead.

"Or," Evans proposed, "someone disposed of Mr. Ralph's body, for you and your little friend, after you beat him to death."

"Or that," Kit nodded, calmly, while flexing her tummy muscles to squelch the rising hysteria so it wouldn't reflect in her face or voice. "Except, of course, I don't know anyone who'd do that for me," she smiled. "If I had done that to him, I mean."

"Really?" Detective Evans' tone was chockers with disbelief. "Even though you'd just saved the life of Marjorie Riley's grand-daughter?"

"Yes," Kit said, emphatically. "Nice of me, wasn't it?"

Ho-ly *shit* no! Kit swore, as a horror breached her sluggish mind. I *did* kill Toad. I must have. I killed him, or he died coz I killed him, I mean hit him; and the Blaazt bouncers—aka employers of the Anders therefore Riley clan—tossed his remains in the Yarra to cover for me. Oh crap! Oh crap and bugger! Queenie owns me, or I'm going to jail.

Evans stood to make her arrest. "DSC Martin wants to talk to you before you leave."

"What?" Kit asked. "I can go now?"

"After you've spoken to Cathy," she smiled. Like a viper. "Tony will escort you."

"That new detective of yours thinks I bumped off Sid Ralph," Kit said to Cathy, sitting opposite the lead detective in the Anders case.

"Yes. That would be because you are the only known person to have ever come away, unscathed, from a fight with the vicious thug and prison prize fighter known as The Toad."

"Prize fighter?" Kit said. "Even *I'm* impressed now." And hind-sight-terrified, she thought.

"What on earth were you thinking?" Cathy asked.

"I wasn't thinking, I was acting," Kit explained. "I was doing the old Latin *factis non verbis* two-step; but I swear I didn't kill him, Cathy. I may have broken his knee; I did punch him, and I even hit him when he was down, but that's it."

Cathy smiled. "We know, O'Malley."

"You do?"

"Of course."

"So why was I kept in that room with, and without, Detective Suspicious for three hours?"

"She was getting someone to check your story."

"And?"

188

"And the nightclub bouncer who led the pack up the lane after Sasha Riley sounded the alarm didn't find anything. No Toad," she added, in response to Kit's baffled look. "They did see a panel van peeling off up the lane from the spot where you'd left him, so either he drove with his broken knee or he had a getaway driver."

"There was someone else there?" Kit said, suffering another aftershock. "But, but," she stuttered, "in that case who killed him?"

"Beats me," Cathy shrugged, "and don't tell anyone, O'Malley, but I don't really care." She studied Kit's face with amusement. "Don't go thinking he drove himself away, and then went for a concussed little wander by the river where he fell in and drowned."

Woo, mind-reader, Kit thought. "I shouldn't think that then?"

"Not unless he also half-severed his own arms and legs before taking a dive." Cathy reached for a red folder. "Wanna see?"

"No thank you, Cathy," Kit smiled. "Seen enough severing for today."

Cathy sighed. "Speaking of Detective Mapp, that's why I wanted to talk. But what I'm about to tell you is for your ears only."

"I'm getting that a lot today," Kit noted.

"That's because *we* all know who you've been mixing with lately." Cathy ran a finger up and down the edge of the folder as she spoke. "We've got two homicide crews investigating four apparently separate murders, but which we consider may be connected."

"Gerry, Toad, and Sheryl," Kit stated, and then frowned. "That's only three."

"Yeah. The fourth is a small-time dealer. Anyway, because of Bubblewrap Man nearly everyone has been seconded to the Barleycorn Task Force, except for us and one-and-a-half crews rotating through permanent on-call. And, while we're not entirely convinced our cases are linked, we are handling the four murders together because they do overlap and it makes sense to share our limited resources."

"And why do I need to know this?" Kit asked. "I mean, why do *you* think I do?"

"Sheryl Mapp was working undercover, investigating a high-end drug trafficker," Cathy divulged. "She'd spent two years infiltrating his organization, making it all the way to the top. Last night she accompanied him, his semi-legit cohorts, and their socialite friends to a charity ball—hence the glamorous outfit she was found in."

"Who is him?" Kit asked.

Cathy fiddled with her earlobe. "That I can't tell you," she said, "except to say he is head of the well-oiled machine that employed that nice married couple Mike and Julie Sherwood."

Spooky, Kit thought. "I just mentioned them to Evans, in relation to Toad."

"I know, I was listening," Cathy confessed. "We *really* don't know how or even if Toad fits in, but we are pretty sure that Gerry did. But this is about Sheryl Mapp. In order to flush out the killer, we will be treating her, as far as the press is concerned, as a Jane Doe."

"But surely you know who killed her," Kit frowned. "I mean, it blows the hatch on *my* wacky theory, but isn't it logical that Sheryl's cover got blown and she was killed by your secret Mr. Big Bloke, the trafficker?"

"Of course it is," Cathy agreed. "The Drug Squad are ferreting around like old chooks, or even ferrets, trying to get word off the street about just that. But, even if it is the case, we don't want Mr. Big or his drug cronies to know for sure, if they ever did, that she was a cop. Because, apart from Big Bloke, there are still the Anders, Riley, Barker, and dead-Toad links."

"And the curious fact of how she got where she was," Kit noted. "Why do you suppose she was dumped behind Boxer Macklin's joint? Where was the fundraising do she'd gone to?"

"In Albert Park," Cathy said. "But, after attending their soul-redeeming charity event, most of Sheryl's dealing-party went nightclubbing to a place about halfway between the Metro Blaazt and Swiggers. So if, as you suggested to Sally during your interview, someone from the Blaazt—namely a Riley, an Anders, or a family thug—took Toad's 'a cop made me do it' confession as true, and then one of them saw Sheryl in the almost-immediate vicinity, and somehow recognized her, then ..."

"Stop," Kit interrupted. "That means several planet-sized chunks of coincidence collided on Commercial Road, in a single night, to rob Sheryl Mapp of her life for no good reason at all. So it's not bloody likely. Besides, you're the one who said the Metro Blaazt bouncers didn't find Toad in that alley."

Cathy shrugged. "Yes, that's what *they* said."

Kit shook her head to realign the info that was rattling around inside. It didn't help. "Um, Cathy, if you don't think they were telling the truth, then I *must* be a suspect."

Cathy grinned. "Of course you are, O'Malley. You're just not *the* suspect. They are. Or the Big-Bloke's mob."

Kit scowled in confusion. "Do you guys actually know anything at all?"

Cathy pulled a not-really face. "Not a lot. Except that Sheryl's body wasn't dumped. The forensic pathologist—oh, you know Ruth Hudson—she reckons Mapp was killed there behind that night-club. The one run by ex-cop Andrew Macklin."

Kit narrowed her eyes. "Is Boxer a suspect?"

"Detective Senior Sergeant Parker doesn't regard him as a suspect," Cathy said slowly. "He's convinced he killed her."

"Chucky despises Boxer," Kit explained. "Actually it's mutual; they hate each other."

"I picked up on that," Cathy smiled. "And Marek filled me in, a little. Anyway, I doubt your mate had anything to do with it. He was the one who called it in, after all."

"For the record, he's not really a mate. But how are you going to keep the 'Sheryl being an undercover cop' secret when so many people, Boxer included, know who she is, was."

Cathy threw her hands out. "Macklin agreed to keep quiet. It's a risk, we realize, and one that Chucky—god, now you've got me doing it—a risk that Charlie went ballistic over. But Marek took Macklin at his word, so guess whose judgement I'm going with."

"But Sheryl was more than just a cop, Cathy. What about her family and friends?"

"Her family and closest friends, and colleagues of course, have been or will be informed of her death. Her parents have agreed with the necessity of keeping her identity anonymous for a few days. We want as much intel as we can get before it's revealed she was a member, let alone undercover."

"I can't begin to imagine how hard that will be for them," Kit noted. "So, is that all you needed from me? Just to keep my lid on too? And if so, can I go home now?"

"Yeah, to all that," Cathy smiled.

Kit stood up to leave. "Oh, one last question for me. Has your spy found any connection at all between Gerry and Angie?"

"No. Have you found anything?"

"Diddly," Kit replied.

"The situation looks good for your friend, then," Cathy smiled. She reached for her ringing phone, but held up her hand to ask Kit to wait.

Yeah, Kit thought, it *looks* good. And come to think of it, if there *is* no link between Angie and Gerry, and the cops-that-count don't believe she's involved, then this job is over. Case closed. There's nothing left to do, is there? Pay attention. Gerry Anders was melodramatically offed, in order of obvious likelihood, by either Sheryl Mapp's Mr. Big Bloke as payback for the Sherwoods; by a member of a rival crime family; or, at a stretch, by his own aerobically occupied wife. That means Angie, your only real client—are you listening O'Malley—is in the clear.

Right. So why doesn't it *feel* over? Too many red hot irons in the proverbial, that's why, O'Malley. Just remember, you only seem to be busy but none of it means anything, because: a) investigating the murder of Gerry Anders is not part your job description; b) bodyguarding Sasha Riley was more trouble than it was worth; c) being interrogated for hours over a murder you didn't commit was a waste of time; and d) looking into Boxer's biz will no doubt attract more unpleasantness. It is, therefore, time to reverse out of the rest of this tangled mess before a nasty drug baron also cottons-on to who you are, and takes offense at your meddling; or Queenie Riley really does adopt you into her crooked clan.

Chapter 15

Cathy provided Kit with an escort from her den because, apparently, someone else wanted to talk to her before she left. Please not Chucky, Kit thought as they headed through the squad room towards—phew, Marek's office. The Acting Head of Homicide, however, was not there.

"Hi, honey-bun," said Erin, who was.

"Ditto," echoed Carrie McDermid, who ditto.

Cathy smiled. "The boss wanted you all to *leave* together, after he personally reminded you of the injunction on everything you happen to know. Especially you two," she waved her hand at Erin and Carrie. "Which means you shouldn't even talk to each other about what you know in case one of the others doesn't know it."

"You are aware we have a free press in this country," Erin said cheerily. "At least I think we do. I'm pretty sure we're allowed to speak our minds. Would you like a piece of mine?"

"Yeah. Just leave it in my in-tray," Cathy said. "The thing is, guys, we also have a lunatic serial killer—and I am aware that's possibly a tautology; plus a few other highly sensitive murder investigations at the moment. I realize you're the press, and not," she glanced at Kit, "but we really need your co-operation. You've all been briefed, in different ways, so if you could oblige us for just a few days ..." Cathy left the request hanging.

"Easy," Carrie said. "I don't appear to know anything anyway. Not even what I thought I did."

"Is this the latest in state-sanctioned torture, then?" Kit queried, taking a seat in Marek's chair. "You lock people who know stuff into a room and ban them from communicating?"

Cathy shrugged. "Go ahead, communicate to your heart's content;

193

as long as it's about something irrelevant, like sushi or *Neighbours* or Peruvian harpists."

"I *had* just started telling Erin about O'Malley's special underling theory of information gathering," Carrie said helpfully.

"See, that's good," Cathy said, "whatever it means. Unless it's code. It's not code, is it?"

Kit, too, was looking at McThing blankly, as if she was a strange individual indeed—but only because she liked to see a redhead squirm at least once a week.

"You remember," Carrie scowled at Kit, then turned from her to Cathy and Erin. "She has a theory on how lesser family members and employees, especially disappointed or irritated ones, oh, and regulars, are the best sources of information on a crime; or anything, I suppose."

"Of course they are," Cathy agreed. "Stay away from disgruntled postal workers, though, they tend to be unreliable."

"Did you say wrigglers?" Erin queried, as Detective Inspector Jon Marek strode into his own office only to stop suddenly when faced by four women, all of whom ignored him, especially after he'd crossed his arms over his chest to give an impression of superiority and displeasure.

"No. Reg-u-lars," Carrie enunciated. "You know, pub regulars or club members or café frequenters; they make good eyewitnesses."

"No they don't," Kit, Erin, and Cathy all said at once.

"Okay already," Carrie threw up her hands. "What's with the ganging up?"

"Nobody makes a good eyewitness," Marek stated, turning to the slim woman who took three steps into the office and proffered a clipboard. He signed something for her and she left again. "And no two witnesses ever see or remember the same things."

"But," Carrie began.

"There's no but, Carrie," Kit explained. "I said that family and staff gave good info, not that they were reliable witnesses."

"And even good info does not mean reliable info, and it certainly doesn't mean fact or truth," Erin stated.

Marek pointed at Kit. "You, out of my chair. And you," he turned on Carrie, "who the hell are you anyway?"

"Carrie McDermid, Sir, I mean Detective. Of the *North Star*. Ah, newspaper."

"Of course you are." Marek winked at Kit behind Carrie's back, as he reclaimed his throne. "So Carrie of the *North Star-ah* newspaper, give me a description of the woman who entered this room shortly after I did."

"What woman?" Carrie asked.

"She was mousey," Erin said, "plain, pale brown, and petite."

"No, only her clothes were pale brown," Kit said, "her hair was dark."

"What woman?" Carrie repeated. "You're having me on now, aren't you?"

"Nope," Cathy said, and then smiled at Marek. "Who was it boss?"

"Who?" he said, not expecting to be put on the spot himself. "One of the admin staff."

"Jenny Porter?" she suggested.

"Yeah," he nodded, until he registered his colleague's expression. "No?"

"No. Liz Nash."

"I knew that," Marek stated.

"Her hair was definitely light brown," Erin insisted. "She had a mole on the back of her left hand and she wore a white shirt under her brown cardy."

"Hmm," Kit frowned, "now that I think about it, you could be right about the hair, Erin, but it wasn't a white shirt, it was a brown twin set. And I do believe, that when she bent to tie Marek's shoelace, I noticed a wood duck tattooed on her left buttock."

"What bloody woman?" Carrie demanded.

"Have you given them my lecture?" Marek asked Cathy, who nodded. "Okay, you can all piss off out of here now. Nicely, I mean."

Kit, Erin. and Carrie emerged from the Police Complex on St. Kilda Road into blinding sunlight—for just a moment, though. This was Melbourne in autumn after all, and the sun's best efforts lasted for mere minutes at a time, before being diffused by a passing cobweb of cloud, then devoured completely by a sky-sized canopy of dark-gray formlessness. Kit put her leather jacket on, Erin struggled into her long coat, and Carrie shivered while admitting, unnecessarily, that she still wasn't used to Melbourne weather.

A whiny voice, carried on the chill breeze from the footpath, nay the gutter, sent a different kind of shiver up Kit's spine. She acknowledged, with a small wave, the *"Oi, O'Malley"* that had been launched at her by Chucky Parker, who was standing between the open passenger-side doors of an old tan Holden that was idling in the No Standing zone. Kit had a black-and-white TV flashback to George and Leonard in the opening sequence of *Homicide*; and then groaned, because she didn't want a Chucky moment to ruin that fond memory.

Be nice, Kit instructed herself as she wandered over to talk bantam with the Chuckster. "Oi yourself, Charlie," she said, offering him a cheesy pageant-smile.

"I'd still like an insight into your friends at that bar so I can proceed fairly with my case," he said apropos of absolutely nothing in the vicinity.

"Still?" Kit asked, putting on her *I don't get it* face.

"Yes," he said seriously. "Still. Two days after I left a message on your machine."

"Machine? Oh, sorry, Charlie, I seldom listen to that thing," Kit shrugged. "I only have it so I can ring in to fool my cat into thinking I'm home." As she watched him mentally adding another thing to his list of reasons not to like *her*, Kit noticed two odd things about him. First, Chucky's hair was getting très thin in the small remaining patch on the crown of his head; and second, the usually dapper dude was dressed way down in old trousers, a red flannel shirt, and a khaki army jacket.

"Perhaps, if you had time tomorrow we could go over things."

"Things? Sure," Kit agreed. "You don't want to do it now? Or are you undercover, or going bear hunting or something?"

"No, I'm off duty now, and we're about to go fishing."

"Fishing?" Kit noted, because she could. "Who's we?" she asked.

"Guy," Chucky pointed to the driver's side, at the same time as a voice from inside the car announced his presence by saying "Charlie and me."

Kit bent down to acknowledge the "me" of the equation, partly because it was the polite thing to do, but mostly because she didn't think Chucky had any friends, so she was mildly curious. And then, she just couldn't help herself, "Yep, that's a guy all right, Charlie."

"That's his name, O'Malley."

"Oh," she said, smiling at the also red-flanneled and very anemic bloke drumming his fingers on the steering wheel. "Hi, Guy."

"Hi, girl," he nodded, with a disinterest in their exchange that bordered on rudeness. As hers had done.

Night fishing, huh? That explained Guy the guy's pallor, Kit thought. But what about their mutual moods? His and hers? Guy's and Girl's? That would be Chucky's EM field, O'Malley, she told herself. It obviously creates discord in *all* the people around him.

"Was that all you wanted, then, Charlie?" she asked.

"For now," he nodded.

"Good. I'll give you a call about your case, then," she said over her shoulder as she walked away. Then being, of course, when penguins fly north; or anywhere, for that matter.

"What did he want?" Erin asked.

"Not sure. I think he might want to know what lesbians do."

"What?" Carrie was appalled.

Kit shrugged. "He wants an insight into my friends at the bar. What else could he mean?"

"Do you want me to tell him?" Erin offered.

"Are you ..." Carrie began, then looked mortified at her own effrontery.

"No, she isn't," Kit said. "But she *is* a journo, which means she's got a vivid imagination and a PhD in Bullshit Artistry."

"I've had that degree framed too," Erin grinned. "So, now what, girls?"

"Nothing," Carrie stated, "unless we want to swap stories about sushi or Patagonian harpists over coffee. We're not supposed to communicate with each other, remember."

The saddest thing about that statement, Kit noted—and Erin too, judging by her wrinkled brow—was that Carrie appeared to be serious.

"They do that to us all the time," Erin said. "To me and Kit, I mean. Don't they, dear?"

"Oh yeah," Kit nodded, making like it was more than just that one specific time.

"Do what? I don't get it," Carrie said.

"They *want* us to talk, compare notes, and keep digging," Erin explained. "We might come up with something they've missed. While they really don't want us to *print* whatever they've put a reasonable embargo on, Cathy and Jon would never expect us to lay off completely."

"So, let's go to my place and talk peregrine harpies over a stiff drink," Kit suggested.

"I don't know where you live." The tone of Carrie's confession was laced with frustration.

"I do, so you can drive me," Erin suggested.

One thing Kit loved about her previously single lifestyle, or rather the living alone thing, was that after a hard day's dealing with bad guys, cops, and corpses she could retreat alone to her comfy cave with no one but the demanding cat making demands on her time or energy. One thing she hated about that life was that too often alone was just lonely. Many more times than occasionally she'd therefore wished for someone to come home to—or be home for. Hmm, she thought, as she climbed to her home at the top of the stairs, with Erin and Carrie close on her heels, there was a chance if Snick and Snack ever gave up spying on the divine Enzo, that the gorgeous Alex might be the one she'd return to be with each day. Not that living together had been discussed, but the possibility was there. Or at least the desire for Alex to be that possibility was there.

One of the things Kit loved about her friends was that they all felt enough a part of her life to visit at any time, and even let themselves in, whether she was there or not. That meant that a very good thing about single living, was that no one had to be consulted—not even her—about anything. Kit didn't, for instance, have to ring ahead (but hopefully to Alex when she did have to) and announce, "I will be home soon, honey, and I'm bringing some mates".

Kit was therefore not surprised when she opened her front door with Erin and Carrie in tow to discover, by the sound of it, that there were already people in the lounge room of the flat she inhabited with no one but The Cat. On tripping up the five steps inside her front door, however, she was surprised and thrilled and beside herself, to the left and right, with pleasure to find that one of the three friends already in her abode was Alex. The other two were Enzo and Hector but, as fond as she was of them, right now they were only doubling the number of now-extraneous people preventing her from seizing the moment to make crazy, passionate, and exhilarating love to the woman of all her wildest dreams.

Alex unfurled her denim-clad legs from the couch and, without disturbing The Cat in her arms, stood up and came to welcome home the grinning-like-an-idiot Katherine O'Malley, as if it were an everyday occurrence.

Had they been alone, Kit sighed, their kiss would've been more deeply personal and erotic; but there was nothing wrong with Alex's toe-curling offering of lips and tongue tip; especially as the sensation was enhanced by her hand sliding under Kit's jacket to the small of her back. Admit it O'Malley, Kit quivered as all her senses started humming, Alex's hand anywhere on your body is breathtaking.

"Ooh, you're home," Kit sighed, trying those words on for size.

"I am," Alex smiled broadly and then stepped back, but only a little. And she didn't let go of Kit when she did, and she obviously only moved at all because they weren't alone, and there were a few people in the room who didn't know each other yet.

"Everyone, this is Carrie," Kit said. And even though her mother had told her it was rude, and she always believed Lillian, Kit began pointing because sometimes courtesy just had to lose out to efficiency. "Alex, Enzo, and Hector. And you all know Erin, and this is Thistle."

"Hurglert?"

"Hurglert indeed, Thistle. Now, who wants a drink of any description?"

"We're fine, Kit," Enzo said, waving a champagne glass.

"I'll have whatever's going," Carrie said, standing on someone else's ceremony.

"Yak shake for you, then," Kit said, nudging Alex towards the kitchen.

"I'll join you in a Jim Beam and ice, if you have any left," said Erin. "I've gone off the yak shakes ever since I read they put earwigs in the fermentation process."

Carrie was frowning, but not entirely fooled.

"Are you being mean to your new friend?" Enzo asked.

"Yes," Kit and Erin said in unison.

"It's okay, I'm getting used to it," Carrie smiled.

Kit poured two Jims and an Andrew Garret, then handed the bourbon to Erin and the champagne to Carrie who, despite "getting used to it," was obviously relieved she recognized what was in her glass.

Kit took a swig of her drink and leaned back against Alex, accidentally squashing The Cat, who so *didn't* complain that Kit turned to make sure it was her cat and that she was conscious. Thistle blinked at her and returned to her quiet adoration of Alex.

"I didn't think you were a cat person," Kit noted, reveling in her own bit of adoration.

Alex shrugged. "I'm not really; but as you can see, Thistle is an Alex cat."

For some reason, that made Kit exceptionally happy.

"Earth to O'Malley!"

"Yes, Hector. What?"

He was standing on the other side of the kitchen bench, as was everyone now, but he was looking pleased with himself while also wearing a sense of urgency like it was a coat. "I have to tell you the cool news now, because I have to go soon."

"Really? Well that explains why you're here," Kit said, taking stock. "And I hope I know why Alex is here, and Erin and Carrie came to gossip with me about secret police business, so that just leaves you Enzo-my-darling."

Enzo clasped his hands to his chest. "I came to deliver Alex-your-darling, and I was hoping to lose the Dumbling Duo somewhere en route between our place, here, and Dorothy's Caviar Bar where I'm due to tinkle the ivories and have steamy sex with my Ricardo in the upstairs black-and-blue room."

"You can make-out with Rick at home or his place," Alex noted. "Why do it at Dot's?"

"Because we can, Alex love. And don't ever call it Dot's, or you'll be banned from the chorus line. Also, if we do the grand hoochibiz there ..."

"Too much information, Enzo," Kit noted.

"Possibly," Enzo agreed, "but you'll only know for sure if you let me finish. As I was saying, if we make with the fandangalado at Dorothy's, then we possibly won't later on; which means I'll get enough sleep to not mind getting up at six in the a.m. when my brother rings to tell me he's on a flight from Wellington, or not."

"You have a brother?"

"Yes, Kit," Enzo nodded. "Do you find that strange?"

"Yes, no," Kit said thoughtfully. "It's just that I thought you were unique."

"Darling, I *am*," Enzo reassured her. "Believe me, Nigel and I are nothing alike."

Alex nodded to reinforce his statement. "Nigel McAllister suffers from A-grade anal retention," she said. "He's stitched-up something shocking."

"And he's a computer head," Enzo added.

"And he lives in New Zealand?" Kit queried.

"No, he lives in California," Enzo explained, "but was waylaid in Wellington on his way to ... some place, I've forgotten where. But also via Melbourne so he can give me yet another big-brotherly lecture about all that I could be if I wasn't who I am."

"Well, you're a daft bastard for meeting him at the airport so that he can do that to you," Erin scoffed.

"Possibly," Enzo agreed. "But the alternative is Duncan McAllister."

"That sound ominous," Carrie said.

"Och aye," Enzo said, all Scottish. "See, if I was to avoid Nigel, then my parents will think something is awry, and they'll dispatch Uncle Duncan from Scotland to make things right."

"Are you a grown man?" Erin asked. "Or are you just big for your age."

"I'm fully grown, as you can see, but I was sired by lunatics descended from mad bastards. And a visit from that uncle is a scary prospect indeed, because Duncan's a ben of a man who wears his kilt *all the time* because he believes it makes mortal men, as in non-Scotsmen, fairly tremble in their socks. And that dear lassies, and Hector, is truly embarrassing."

"I'm glad you mentioned me," Hector said, "because I still have to go soon."

"Speak, then," Kit prompted. "Oh, I remember, you went to the library for me today."

"Crikey," Erin exclaimed, "have you got the poor boy returning your books for you now?"

"No, Judgmental One," Kit raised her eyebrows.

"I went to the Supreme Court Library to look up a law report," Hector said. "It was cool."

"No accounting for taste," Alex noted.

"And what did you find there, Hector?" Kit asked.

"Page 379 of volume three of that *Victorian Report* makes reference to two people of your recent re-acquaintance, but in circumstances unrelated to anything you may think you know about them or their relationship."

"Hector," Kit snapped.

He curled his lip in response. "In October of that year, one Gerald Ian Anders appeared before the court charged with the attempted murder, by motor vehicle, of a Bruce Paxton; a man who was one minute a pedestrian, and the next a quadriplegic."

"God, that Gerry sure had trouble with his car," Carrie noted.

"Very interesting, Hector," Kit said, and then frowned. "But you implied I knew them both, and I don't think I know a Bruce Paxton; in fact, I believe my life is completely Bruceless."

Hector held up a "just wait for it" finger. "That's coz he's not the one you know, O'Malley. Bruce Paxton is, however, the husband of Maria Stano, sister of Mickey. He's also co-owner of Swiggers Nightclub; and therefore arch-enemy or business rival, by marriage, of the Anders and the Rileys and the Barkers."

Kit felt a tremor of anticipation, but tried not to smile too soon in case she jinxed the chance that Hector's report might contain actual valuable information. "I sense, young Hector, that there is even more to this story," she prompted.

"Oh yes," Hector agreed. "The main point leading up to page 379 was the alibi that got Gerry Anders off willy-free, despite an apparently objective, unbiased, and unthreatened eyewitness, who swore that he, Gerry, was not only in the car at the scene of the hit and run, but at the very wheel of the offending vehicle."

Kit and Erin both turned to give Carrie the "see, what did we tell you about witnesses" look; then Kit queried, "What kind of alibi could a known criminal have, that could beat a brave and miraculously still-living eyewitness?"

"The 'it couldn't have been me, Your Honor, coz I was having a drink with an officer of the Victorian Police at the time of the alleged offense' kind of alibi," Hector grinned.

"And yes, O'Malley, the report includes the statement by that policeman supporting Gerry's alibi and therefore blowing a car-sized hole in the Department of Public Prosecution's attempted-murder-by-panel-van case."

Kit sighed. Please let this be an actual pointer to ... something, she shrugged mentally—like a clue to who killed Gerry, or a light on Toad's interest in Gerry's death, or his allegation of a cop hiring him for henchbloke duties.

"Hector, mate, who gave Gerry this long-winded alibi?" As the question left her lips, she realized she already knew what the answer would be, because in that moment she remembered who had set them on this course of research in the first place. Or rather, *why* he had.

Hector grinned. "It was Detective Senior Sergeant Graham Charles ..."

"... bloody Parker," Kit finished.

Bloody obvious really, she thought.

Chapter 16

Kit pulled up outside the Riley residence, switched off the engine, and turned to her passenger.

"I'd prefer you didn't come in with me. I don't want Queenie knowing who you are, Alex. It's bad enough that I suspect she plans to adopt Hector and me, but ..."

Alex placed her fingers gently on Kit's lips. "If that woman is going to throw you into her cellar again, I want to be there with you," she stated, with what appeared to be genuine love and concern—until she grinned, "if only to share one of the more valuable bottles of Grange."

"Charming," Kit laughed in surrender. "Come on, then; the sooner I wangle this favor from Grandma Riley, and check Sasha's well-being, the sooner we can go somewhere for dinner."

As they walked up the front path, Kit recalled the first front door they'd approached together in the course of an investigation, only a couple of months ago. Kit had been awash with lust then too, but figured it would be forever unrequited as she thought Alex didn't like her. There'd also been the matter of Alex's impending marriage to Enzo, which Kit thought was genuine—until she met Enzo. Her thoughts were halted by the opening of this door.

Will Thumpya, wearing a gold tracksuit, a red beanie, and black eye, said not a word.

"Will," Kit nodded. "Queenie is expecting me, so stand aside or lose a limb."

"I know that, O'Malley. She's in the kitchen," Will pointed down the hall. "Now lemme out, I've gotta go to work." He made quite a performance of getting out the door between Kit and Alex, without touching either of them.

"Hey," Kit called after him, "who gave you the shiner?"

"Who do you bloody think?" he said over his shoulder. "And shut the door after youse."

Following her nose, or the deliciously spicy aroma that was leading it, Kit led Alex in search of Ms. Riley's kitchen, while reluctantly pondering the "who did you think." The only candidate she could come up with, that Will would know she knew, was the last person Kit wanted it to be. Because if Toad had got a punch in while Will and whoever were … Uh-uh, don't go there, O'Malley.

She and Alex found the lady of the house leaning over a huge timber table and surrounded by cookbooks, vegetables, and jars of everything.

"Ah, Kit," Queenie exclaimed, "come taste this for me."

"Queenie, this is my friend Alex," Kit said.

"Welcome, Alex," Queenie said enthusiastically, as if she were an ordinary everyday septuagenarian grandma cooking up a storm.

Kit approached the boss cook and crook of the Riley family and her could-be-anything concoction simmering in a huge pan.

"Yum," she said, after allowing Queenie to handle the tasting spoon all the way to her mouth. "It's even better than it smells. What is it?"

"An unpronounceable Thai dish. I've been taking Thai cooking classes, but I'm beginning to think I should also take the language course. Do you think I'm too old?"

"Never," Kit said. Cut to the chase, she thought. "How's Sasha?"

"Honestly, that child!" Queenie scoffed. "If she wasn't my own flesh and blood once-removed I'd wonder what strange world she'd come from."

"Don't tell me she's giving you a hard time, even with a broken arm and messed up face?"

"I wish she was, but she's not even home. She went to the pictures with her friend Tina. I had to send a Moshun Club bouncer to watch over her, because you," Queenie dismissed what she was about to say, with a wave. "For the record, Kit, I don't blame you for not wanting to continue with her; and I'm profoundly sorry if her reckless behavior put you in danger."

"You've already apologized, Queenie; besides, that was my job

205

last night," Kit said. "And, it's not that I didn't want to continue, it's just that our deal was for last night alone."

"Kit shouldn't do bodyguarding anyway," Alex noted. "She can't look after herself."

Well, that's a nice backhand support, Kit smiled. Now go on, O'Malley; you *need* to know, so you *have* to ask her. "Queenie, while we're on the topic of recklessness," she said, "who gave Will that lovely and most-deserved black eye?"

Queenie raised and clenched her left fist.

"You're joking," Kit laughed, her relief coupled with an invocation that it was true.

"What?" Queenie mocked. "Don't you think I've got it in me, Kit?"

"It's not that," Kit smiled.

"I doubt I need to tell you that Will's not the brightest worm in the can. A left hook was the only way he'd learn not to throw my visitors into the cellar," Queenie said picking up the coffee pot. "At the very least," she smiled, "he'll check with me first next time."

Kit feigned disappointment. "You could have let me do it."

"Yes, I could. But then it would have been payback, not discipline. Now, why have you called in?" Queenie sat at the table, and gestured Kit and Alex to the empty chairs opposite.

"It's about last night, Queenie," Kit said. "I need a favor."

"You need a favor from me?" Queenie smiled broadly. "I am intrigued."

Alex accepted a cup of coffee. "Thank you, Mrs. Riley,"

"Alex, honey," Kit said, leaping into the fray. "Don't call her Mrs. Riley, coz she isn't. She's Miss, Ms., Queenie, even Honeybunch I imagine, but never *Mrs.* Riley."

"Thank you, Kit," Queenie smiled. "It's a long story, Alex, that your friend can bore you with later if you're interested."

"As an addendum to that story, I did mean to ask you," Kit said curiously, "how come you raised Sasha? Where is, or what happened to her mother? And her father, for that matter."

Queenie Riley's upbeat demeanor took a nose-dive straight for the black-and-white lino. Just as well she was sitting, Kit thought. "Sorry, I didn't mean to upset you."

"It's all right, Kit, it's hardly your fault. It was an unexpected question, that's all; and one that few people ask. Helen never told me the father's name; she was happy to raise her child as a single mother. Sasha was five weeks' prem and incredibly tiny, so she had to stay on in hospital for a couple of weeks. Helen was ..." Queenie sighed. "My only child was killed, instantly, in a car accident on the drive home from visiting her only child in hospital."

"I'm so sorry," Kit said. And you could have found that out another way, O'Malley.

Queenie took a restorative breath and smiled a sad smile. "That's life. It goes on for some and not for others. It's a bitch really."

"Speaking of life's little idiosyncrasies," Kit said softly, "the guy who attacked Sasha ..."

"Sidney Gordon Peter Ralph," Queenie snarled.

"You know he's dead?"

"Oh yes," Queenie said suggestively, offering the milk jug to Alex. "It's okay, Kit, it was on the midday news."

"Oh," Kit tried to cover her look of high suspicion by turning it into a deadly serious one, as she delivered her half-truth: "The thing is, Queenie, the cops think I killed Toad."

"What would possess them to think that?"

"Coz it was my job to protect Sasha, and I *did* rough him up and leave him in the alley."

Queenie frowned. "But you did that because he attacked Sasha. There's no question you saved her from being very badly injured, or even killed, Kit. What's wrong with those idiots?"

"Oh the cops know all that. It's just that because he's now dead, and I was the last known person to lay a hand on him, they've kinda put me in the frame for it."

"Frame being the operative word," Alex said helpfully.

"But that's too ridiculous for any words," Queenie stated.

True, Kit thought, but how do *you* know that, Marjorie Riley? It's not like I *couldn't* have killed him. Accidentally at least, if not on purpose.

"Besides," Queenie was saying, "Barbara said Toad was gone. She saw him drive off."

"And that," Kit tapped the table, "is where my problem collides with one that you may end up getting as well. And by you I mean the family, as in Sean's or Tom's or Gerry's cousin, or ..."

Queenie sat there expectantly.

"The cops think I killed Toad and that Sean's bouncers disposed of the body to protect me because I was working for you. Or that they did it simply to protect your family interests in general, not the least of which would be your personal interest in payback—and I mean payback, not discipline—because of Sasha."

Queenie raised her coffee cup to her mouth, but otherwise remained thoughtfully silent.

"Is any of that too ridiculous for words?" Alex asked.

Queenie looked at her. "No," she admitted. "Not at all. Doesn't mean it's true, though."

"Is it true?" Kit asked.

"What? That you killed him or that we disposed of him?"

"Well, I don't *think* I killed him, Queenie, but what about the rest?"

Queenie shook her head. "I do not know who killed Sidney Ralph. Nor do I know who threw him, dead or alive, into the Yarra." She *looked* like she was telling the truth but, as Kit herself had said, Marjorie Riley had been conning people her whole life.

"Can you find out who did?" Kit asked.

"Is that the favor you're asking of me?"

"Yes," Kit smiled. "I figured you could use your connections to put some feelers out for me. I realize you probably don't give a damn who killed Toad, given what he did to Sasha, and I have it on good authority that the cops don't care much that he's no longer their problem either; but they still have to solve the murder and I don't wish to be their convenient bunny."

Queenie gazed at Kit as if she was sizing her up for ...

Long-term membership in the clan, no doubt, Kit worried. Hope it comes with private health cover and a good superannuation plan.

"It would be my pleasure to try to find out," Queenie said magnanimously, "for you, Kit. Do you have any clues to go on, that might help?"

"Nothing at all," Kit admitted. "Unless ... Did they say on the news how he died?"

"I don't think so. They just said his useless corpse was pulled from the river. Why?"

"It's a long shot," Kit said, "But I'm wondering whether a contributing factor to Toad's death might be, like, a trademark of someone who does things like that. Kills people, I mean."

Queenie waited several seconds before asking, "Are you going to tell me what it is?"

Toss up, O'Malley, Kit thought. The crook versus the crime. Divulge info you shouldn't; or hinder the favor you're asking of her. Idiot! You started this game, so play it.

"I shouldn't tell you this," she confessed, "but it might help you help me. Whoever killed or disposed of Toad also half severed his arms and legs."

"Oh that's horrible," Alex muttered.

"You don't have to feel sorry for him, Alex," Queenie said, shaking her head. "Sidney Ralph did many a thing worse than that, to more people than you'd care to know about." She looked at Kit. "This limb thing is not a trademark I've ever heard of, however."

"It's not hard to guess one or two possible causes of death, though, is it?" Alex said, her face still wearing disgust. "Because if he didn't bleed to death, he certainly wouldn't have been able to swim for the shore. And I can't believe I just said that."

Queenie laughed. "Humor in the face of death and taxes is the only way to remain sane and sensible in this crazy affair we call life."

"Hear, hear," Kit agreed. "As for finding the culprit who ended Toad's share of life, I'd be inclined to start with the door bitch, sorry female security person, at the Blaazt who responded to Sasha's call for help. She might be more inclined to give you or Sean, or whoever, more detail about Toad's getaway than she gave the police."

"Door bitch?" Queenie chuckled. "Haven't heard that one before. But Barbara Cluney is not a door anything. She is manager of Gerry's other club."

"Why was she doing the bouncer thing last night, then? Oh," Kit snapped her fingers, "I know; Tom had to fire a dickhead."

"Really?" Queenie shrugged. "I don't know about that, but Barbara's practically family. I assumed she was just there."

"Queenie, would you give me Tom's phone number, so I can check something?"

Queenie waved a finger at the bench behind Alex. "The phone's just there, dear."

Alex reached back, picked up the portable handset, and handed it to Queenie, who punched one of the autodial buttons, asked to speak to Tom, and then handed the phone to Kit.

"Hey, Auntie Queenie," Tom said a moment later.

"Hey, Tom, but it's Kit O'Malley. Remember me from last night?"

"Yeah, hi Kit. Good save, regarding Sash, but why are you impersonating my old aunty?"

"Thanks, and I'm not. I'm at Queenie's and we called because I need some info. When you and I were chatting last night you suddenly had a major reason to call out your troops. I think you needed an unwanted someone escorted from the premises."

"You mean I had three large blokes throw Toad Ralph out on his arse."

Yes! Kit cheered. "And you were going to fire the door-dickhead who let him in?"

"True."

"Would you tell me the name of that now-unemployed person?"

"Of course, why not?"

How about because you're the son of a crook descended from a long line of crooks and I'm one of the good guys? Kit thought.

"His name's Trevor Wagstaff," Tom was saying. "Sean's glad to be rid of him, I think. He always was a useless prick."

"How long had he worked for you?"

"Six years. You know, Kit, we've got security staff with degrees in all sorts of things from accounting to medieval history to cordon bleu cooking, but Trevor was our nuff-nuff champ. The only thing that moron was interested in was how to put more muscles on his muscles.

"Like most clubs, we have a photo gallery of folks not allowed into our premises. Toad's ugly mug has been in our top ten for years, so it's not like Trevor didn't know who he was."

210

"Did you wait until the end of the night to dismiss him?"

"Sean fired him on the spot, at the door. Wouldn't even let him back inside to get his coat."

When Kit hung up the phone, she noticed that Queenie was spoon-feeding Alex with the unpronounceable curry.

"Tom's going to be an architect," Queenie was saying proudly. "Did he help, Kit?"

"Yes. Last night he and Sean fired a bouncer, of six-years' service, for letting Toad Ralph into the Metro Blaazt a few hours before the miserable bastard beat Sasha up."

"Name?" Queenie's scowl was altogether ungrandmotherly.

"Trevor Wagstaff."

"Don't know him," Queenie stated. "Were you just curious about our employment practices, or do you have a theory to go with this name?"

"Me?" Kit pulled a face. "My theories are usually out of kilter with the natural world. But, let's try variations on the disgruntled staff member theme. Maybe Trevor was pissed off with his employers for some *small* reason, so he thought 'bugger it, I'll let The Toad in and see what kind of shit happens'. Or, maybe Trevor was *really* pissed off with his employers, so he actually hired Toad to attack Sasha; and he also let him into the club."

The plop-plop of the simmering curry was the only sound in the kitchen as they pondered Kit's words; until Alex finally said, "Color him truly disgruntled, and Trevor could be in a line-up for the big one."

"Oh yeah," Kit agreed. "He might have been so pissed off with his employers that his first act of bouncer-rage was, in fact, Gerry's murder."

"You have quite a vivid imagination, don't you, Kit?" Queenie noted.

"I did warn you. The problem with those theories, except the first one, is that according to your great-nephew, Trevor Wagstaff is several weights short of a decent bar bell."

"He could be working for ..." Queenie hesitated.

"For who?" Kit asked. "Are you holding out on me?"

Queenie gave Kit a look that said: "certainly not" and "yes, of course I am" but either way you can "trust me." What she actually said was, "For someone else. For whoever is assaulting my family from all sides at the moment."

"Are you sure Gerry's murder and the attack on Sasha are connected?" Alex asked.

"No, I'm not," Queenie admitted, with frustration. "And, to be perfectly honest, no one out there," she waved in the general direction of Melbourne's mean streets, "seems to know a bloody thing. Which means there's either an elaborate conspiracy going on, in which no one *will* talk to us, or the hoodlums responsible for this shit are clever."

"And you scoffed at *my* imagination. How many clever hoodlums do you know, Queenie?"

"Good point, but something strange *is* going on." Queenie stood to tend to her curry.

"As I've only just boarded this mystery train," Alex said, "can I ask whether the phone threat that prompted you to hire Kit to protect Sasha last night was specific in its intent?"

Queenie narrowed her eyes at Alex for a moment, then turned to Kit. "Is she a cop?"

Alex laughed and answered for herself, "No, she's a lawyer. And what I meant was, did the person specifically threaten your granddaughter?"

"No," Queenie stated, carrying the wooden spoon over to Alex for another tasting. Kit figured it was the matriarch's way of apologizing for the cop insult.

"He said, and I quote, 'keep an eye on your nearest and dearest because they could all go the way of Gerry, one by one.' His words, disguised by one of those voice devices, do seem to imply a connection between what happened to Gerry and Sasha, but ..." Queenie shrugged.

"Or," Kit proposed, "this hoodlum might have just used Gerry's murder to ramp-up your anxiety levels and put the fear of Thanatos into you, so he could follow up with an attack on *anyone* in the family who got within Toad's reach at the grand opening last night."

"Thanatos?" Alex queried.

"Death," Kit explained. "What's your gut feeling, Queenie? Are they connected or not?"

Queenie sighed. "I believe they are, but I don't know why. For that reason I'm going to ask you to reconsider, Kit. Please take on the case of finding out who murdered my nephew."

Kit shook her head. "I really can't, Queenie."

"Why not?" Alex asked, not helpfully.

Kit widened her eyes meaningfully—at the lawyer, not the crook. "Because I'm not allowed to investigate murders, Alex, you know that."

The lawyer apparently missed the point. "But Queenie could put you on a retainer to look into where Gerry was and what he was doing right up to when he wasn't alive any more."

"Are you mad?" Kit asked. Ooh, maybe Queenie's curry was a magic "trust her" potion.

"Alex," Queenie said softly, offering her another now highly suspect taste treat, "I don't think Kit wants to take my money. It's a good guy, bad guy thing."

"Oh." Alex offered Kit her infuriating cryptic look. "But you two seem to get on so well."

What is *that* supposed to mean? And stop feeding my woman, you evil crime queen!, Kit thought, suddenly feeling slightly to the left of Bolivia, and wondering whether she'd been hijacked to the criminal underworld. And speaking of scary netherworlds, what the hell was Alex on about?

"We do, don't we?" Queenie was nodding. "But we dance to different beats."

Kit shook her head in disbelief. "If I found out who killed Gerry *and* I told you who it was, Queenie, what would you do with the information?"

Queenie raised her eyebrows. "I can't answer that, Kit."

"Why not? Because you might pre-incriminate yourself?"

"That is a possibility, but it's not the reason I can't answer you," Queenie said. "I simply don't know the answer. I won't predict my actions on any matter until I know what I'm acting on, or reacting to. It may depend on who the culprit is and whether they had a reason."

213

Kit laughed. "You are kidding, right? You really think there's someone out there who might have a valid reason for murdering your nephew, draining him of his blood, and putting him on naked display in a gay women's bar?"

Queenie frowned. "Not when you put it like that, no. But I can't deny that Gerry was not a well-liked or well-behaved bad guy in a world of bad, bad men. If his murder was retribution for something beyond my reach, as in *not* family business, then that is where it will stay. I'm an old woman, Kit. I don't need any new enemies."

"And if it turns out to be a Barker or a Stano?"

Queenie shrugged. "There still could be reason enough to let it rest. None of this means, of course, that I don't want to know who is responsible."

Kit had to admit she was baffled. "I'm baffled," she said. "It is totally beyond me, Queenie Riley, how this feud or whatever it is between your families has persisted as long as it has, when *you* at least appear to be reasonable in your judgement."

Queenie laughed heartily. "One day, Kit O'Malley, I may tell you the long story of how this feud came to be; but for now let me say, god help the streets of Melbourne when Leo Barker, Paul Stano, and I shuffle off this mortal coil. Although, now that Gerry's met his unmaker things might settle down," Queenie sighed. "Unless that *has* to make things worse."

"Have you ever thought of retiring and taking a long cruise?" Alex asked.

Queenie was about to speak when she noticed Kit's attention-seeking finger. "Yes?"

"Speaking of Leo Barker, did you hear that he had a stroke? He's in the Alfred Hospital."

"Oh my God, really?" Queenie said, as if she gave a damn about what happened to old Papa Leo. "How terrible. That's such an awful way to go."

"He hasn't gone yet. And I've no idea whether it was even a big enough stroke to take him out," Kit said. "And on that sour note, Alex and I have a dinner engagement, so we'll leave you to your cooking."

"Oh, of course." Queenie flustered to her feet. "I'll show you out."

As they made their way to the front door, Kit said, "Can I run a few names by you?"

"If you like," Queenie agreed. "But is this part of the favor I'm doing for you, or the investigation you're not doing for me?"

"Both," Kit grinned. "I'll give them all to you at once so you can pick and choose the ones you want to own up to. Neil Porter, Nathan Pittock, Graham Parker, Nino Piantoni, Charlie Parker, Bruce Paxton, or Nigel Pippineetal."

Queenie's *who are you trying to fool* smile probably said a lot more than she was about to. "Neil Porter, Neil, Neil, that rings a bell—can't place him, though. Oh, Hector asked me about him, and the Nino person. Still don't know. And I've never known a Nathan. Who else?"

"Graham or Charlie Parker?"

"Charlie Parker was a saxophonist, wasn't he?" Queenie said with amusement.

You can't get out of knowing Chucky's name that easily, Kit thought.

"But," Queenie continued, "I think Gerry might have had a run-in or two with a copper called Graham Parker."

Okay, Kit amended, you're not trying to deny him.

"Bruce Paxton is Paul Stano's son-in-law. Oh, that's where I know the cop's name from."

"How come he gave Gerry an alibi?" Kit pounced, astounded that Grandma Riley was being so forthcoming.

"Because he's an officer of the law, Kit, and they always tell the truth," Queenie declared.

"I've seen those flying pigs too," Kit grinned. "Come on, Queenie, it's not like Gerry will be adversely affected if you tell me."

Queenie cocked her head and made like she was trying to read Kit's mind. "Is Graham Parker the cop you don't like?"

Blimey, Kit thought, the woman's got a memory like a steel trap. "Yes, but that's not why I'm asking about him. I'd just like to know *why* he gave Gerry an alibi."

"I actually don't have any idea," Queenie said. "Would you like me to find that out for you too?" Kit looked hopeful, so Queenie shrugged, "Why not? Now, was there another name, before I throw you both out for the night?"

"Nigel Pippi ..."

"Ah yes," Queenie raised finger. "That silly name's familiar too. I think, maybe, that Gerry or was it his cousin, Adrian ... No, it was Gerry; he played cricket as a teenager with a Nigel Pippineetal."

Crikey, Kit thought. *That's* his real name.

Chapter 17

It was the clock radio that provided the incentive to return from a trek through vine-strangled and crimson Inca ruins, but when Kit woke she found that her legs and arms, and her heart and slowly rousing mind, were completely entangled in the warmth of Alex's body. As Kit nuzzled closer still, pressing her lips against Alex's neck, her whole being smiled with blissful fulfillment and … The phone rang.

Thistle raised her head from the pillow behind Alex, who stirred in her sleep. The phone kept ringing because Kit was pinned to the bed.

"Noise," Alex complained.

"Arms," Kit requested. Alex rolled onto her back, the Cat slid off the pillow, and Kit reached for the phone and croaked, "Hello."

"Kit?" said someone.

"Yes. That's a name I call myself."

"Far, a long long way to run," Alex mumbled.

Kit sat up in surprise and stared at her movie-challenged woman. Alex the Gorgeous offered a sleepy, gray-eyed grin in return.

"But, but you don't know stuff like that," Kit remarked.

"I have many skills, Gabrielle," Alex confessed.

"Yes!" Kit cheered. She would have tried a Xena-ululation to celebrate Alex's confession, but her voice wasn't up to it yet. "Pop culture, one; feral religions, zero," she said instead. "We'll make a twenty-first century gal of you yet!"

"Yoo hoo!" It was the phone.

"Yes, Rabbit?"

"Um, I need to see you. I think I might know something."

"About what, Rabbit?"

"About something I shouldn't."

Kit pinched the bridge of her nose. "Where are you?"

"Outside your office, waiting for you to come to work."

"I'm at work wherever I am, Rabbit. Go to the top of the stairs at the end of the hall and I'll let you in for coffee."

Ten minutes later, Kit, Alex, and Rabbit settled around the dining table with coffee and toast. Kit had threatened Rabbit with bodily harm if she even tried to talk about anything serious before she'd had her first caffeine fix for the day.

Having made two false starts, Rabbit now waited, poised on the blocks, for Kit to take one mouthful, then she was off: "I think I witnessed a murder. Or the lead up to a murder. Or something that happened before a murder, which means he could've just been a witness to a murder too. All of which might be six of one, and the same. But, whatever, I'm freaking out; coz this is not like my normal life, you know."

Kit's personal well-being flipped automatically into self-defense mode with her visitor's first sentence. She concentrated her gaze on Rabbit's thumbs, hooked as they were in the straps of her black overalls, as she thought: no more murders; no more bodies; no more crimes; no more criminals. Enough already! From today O'Malley, you're confining yourself to jobs that involve just watching—like insurance fraud or extra-marital transgressions. You should even consider fidelity testing …

"Are you with us yet, Kit?" Alex asked.

"Yes. Worse luck," Kit widened her eyes.

"Whose murder do you think you witnessed?" Alex asked, to get the ball rolling.

"Dunno," Rabbit shrugged. "Some woman's. And I didn't, like, *see* the murder, but I saw her with the guy."

"What guy?"

"The guy she was with."

"Rabbit," Kit begged. "What *did* you see?"

"Okay. It was about two in the morning. Scooter, me, Booty, Sal, Ben, and Elvira were coming out of Three Faces when Scooter goes all excited and distracted-like, coz she's just spotted her secret ah-more on the street. Imagine this spectacle, right? Scooter's all *ooh*

218

coz the woman of her lust is there, but also agimitated coz so is the husband. And this is the first time Scoot's ever laid eyes on him. Well, she assumed it was him; and that's when my life went all dead-body again." Rabbit stopped to drink her coffee in four gulps, while checking her hair to make sure it was still nice and spiky.

Kit refilled all the cups and went back to sitting and waiting. She, for one, was not in a rush to learn about yet another deceased person.

"Anyway," Rabbit wound herself up again, "Scooter was all on for following them, to see what they did, how they *were* together, where they live, 'cetera. But ...'"

"Doesn't Scooter know where the woman she's having an affair with lives?" Alex asked.

Rabbit shrugged. "Apparently not. She talked me into her plan, coz you know I always wanted to be a detective, and we were going that way anyway. So, we start tailing them up the street, pretending to look in windows and shit. You know what I mean, O'Malley." Rabbit gave Kit a knowing nod.

"Next thing, the woman—her name's Chrissie by the way, I managed to get that out of Scooter before she pissed off and left me there. Where was I? Oh yeah, *she* hops into a car and gets ready to drives off—alone. Scoot's got two minds then. But she's smart, coz she recalls she's also got Muggins here." Rabbit indicated herself by slapping her palms over her jolly big Partons and wiggling them. "So Scooter says she'll follow Chrissie, like *der*, and I should stick with His Nobs."

Alex's auburn hair fell gracefully forward to shield her face, as she rested her elbow on the table and hid her mouth with her fingertips. Kit noticed this about Alex because she was still aware of every single move—*oh yes*—her woman made; but also because she wished she too had camouflage. As her hair never fell anywhere, and was currently doing its morning best to appear vertical, there was going to be no help there. She'd just have to keep a straight face.

Rabbit had barely drawn breath. "Scooter dashes over the road to her car and hoons off after Chrissie, and I turn and follow the husband." Rabbit helpfully raised her hands and tweaked fingers to quote-unquote *the husband.* "Back down the street we go and all of a sudden the bastard is trying to pick up chicks, or one anyway.

"I think to myself, what a bastard. Then I think, maybe this dick *isn't* Chrissie's husband; coz he's a pig after all. Maybe this dick had already tried to pick Chrissie up and she'd just told him to rack off. Or maybe *she'd* picked him up and they'd already done the shimmy in one of the clubs. I mean, you know, if she's cheatin' on hubby with Scooter, maybe she cheats on both with anyone who comes along. These are all my thoughts as I keep following; both of them now, coz this tarted-up chick looked like she was into whatever he was offering. He's got his arm round her, she's kinda leaning on him, 'cetera.

"Next, they turn a corner and head up a side street, then down a smaller side street. And now I'm thinking, yuk. Serious, I do not wanna see any weird hetero stuff, not even for Scooter's sake. That's when me mobile rings and it's Lady Muck herself, saying she'd just got a call from Chrissie asking her to meet at their usual hotel; so of course she's gunna. Scoot tells me not to bother with the hubby, that I should go home. Or whatever. I chose whatever, and went back to Three Faces to hang out with the real people."

That appeared to end the story of how Rabbit was eyewitness to a murder; *not.* Kit and Alex glanced at each other, realized that would only lead to laughing, and returned their attention to the Bard of the Half-told Tale.

"Correct me if I'm wrong, Rab, but didn't you say you saw a murder?" Kit said.

"Yeah."

"Well, who?" Alex asked.

"The chick," Rabbit emphasized, as if it should be obvious.

Kit and Alex in unison: "What chick?"

"The one the guy, the probably-not husband, picked up and took walkies," she explained, fishing around for something in the bib-pocket of her overalls.

Kit shook her head. "But you went back to Three Faces. How did you see anything else?"

"I didn't, Kit. I saw this." Rabbit offered a page of *The Herald Sun.* "That's today's, mate."

Kit had a feeling. It should have been a slap in the face feeling, but then she'd assumed Rabbit's adventure had been *last* night—Monday night—so this was more of a slow-burning sick in the pit of her stomach kind of feeling.

"Rabbit? When did all this happen, exactly?" she asked.

"Sunday night, like two in the morning. Oh, I guess that makes it Monday."

Kit unfolded the page to face—as she now knew she would—the photo of Sheryl Mapp, unnamed by the paper in the headline, story, or caption because "the police were looking for clues to the murdered woman's identity."

"You okay, Kit?" Alex asked, reaching for the page.

"Yeah, this is, um," Kit gave Alex a hush-hush look, "nasty by the sound of it."

"Do you think maybe I saw something then?" Rabbit asked.

"Well yeah, Rabbit. I'll ring my mate Marek, you know the guy from Homicide you met last Thursday, and see if he'd like you to pop into the Police Complex and give a statement."

Rabbit grinned broadly. "I could do an identikit."

"You probably could," Kit smiled. "Have you talked to Scooter about this?"

"No, she's gone AWOL. I saw this in the paper on the tram, and came straight here."

"Good," Kit nodded approvingly. "Could you not mention it to Scooter, or anyone else? This should probably stay between us and between you and the cops."

"Sure thing, mate. Why, though?"

Careful, O'Malley. "Having been a cop, in Homicide, I know that when a newspaper story gets written a certain way it can mean the police know more than they're saying, *or* the media has agreed to withhold certain things to help, or at least not hinder, an investigation."

"Of course!" Rabbit nodded. "Like not giving all the details of a serial killer's modus op?"

"Yep," Kit agreed.

"Whadda ya think they're not saying about *my* case?" Rabbit queried, staking a claim.

Kit looked thoughtful. "Maybe they have a possible suspect, but need other witnesses."

"Right. That's sensible," Rabbit said. "But mate, if they do that with this, what the hell kinda stuff do you think they're withholding from us about that sicko creep the Rental Killer. I mean, we know a fuckin' lot about *his* modus; so what pukey things aren't they telling us?"

"You probably don't want to know," Kit said.

Detective Martin came down from the ninth floor in person to escort Kit, Rabbit, and Alex up to the Homicide Squad rooms. The moment the lift door shut them in, and four uniformed cops out, it was obvious that Cathy also had news.

"Charlie brought Macklin in for serious questioning over the Mapp thing," she announced.

"Errg," Kit growled. "Chucky is such a …"

"That's what we said," Cathy interjected. "But he's been grilling him for an hour already. Marek's been taking bets on how long it takes for Boxer to get up and just walk out, with or without decking Charlie, *and* on whether any of the rest of us will stop him." As the lift opened, she turned to Rabbit. "You think you can give us a suspect or witness?"

"Yes, Detective. My guess, however, is that the male in question is a suspect."

Cathy glanced at Kit, who shrugged, and then they all went and found a quiet corner with a desk, so Rabbit MacArthur could give her eyewitness statement.

"Do you know what her surname is?" Cathy asked, after the Bard finished her story.

"No, I don't," Rabbit said. "I only found out her first name coz Scooter let it slip. And Scoot's done a bunk again, so I can't ask her; and I don't know which hotel she and *Chrissie*," Rabbit waggled her head, "do the extra-marriageable thing in."

"I gather you don't know the husband's name at all, then?" Cathy sighed, as if half the facts were about as useful as none at all.

"Nope. Remember, though, I'm not so sure he was her husband. But, if he's one of ya known criminals, then when I do you an iden-

222

tikit," Rabbit raised her eyebrows, "*you* guys might recognize him. Or, 'ternatively, if he really *was* her husband, then ditto; coz like I told O'Malley, Chrissie's bloke is a policeman, so you lot should know ..."

"What?" Kit said. "You didn't tell me that, Rabbit."

Rabbit squinted as she juggled her thoughts in her hands. "Pretty sure I did, mate. Remember? I was wondering whether he was Chrissie's husband or just some bloke. I told you Scooter had never seen him before, and that the jerk wasn't acting like a cop or a spouse."

Kit looked dubious, but Alex laughed and said, "Pig."

"What?" everyone else said in unison.

Kit's spine began to tingle.

"That's what you said, Rabbit," Alex grinned. "You said he was a pig, in the same sentence you'd called him a dick. We thought you meant a pig pig, not a ..."

The inside of Kit's skull was crawling with annoying ant-sized possibilities.

"Yeah, well," Rabbit said, coming over all mortified and not wanting to look at Cathy. "I meant that if he was a cop he was being a pig."

"It's okay, Rabbit," Cathy smiled. "How about we go see Maggie, our expert face artist."

"I'm with you on that," Rabbit nodded.

Cathy glanced at Kit with a "yes I'm shuffling the jigsaw pieces, too" look; then said to Rabbit, "Meanwhile, if you give Scooter's number to O'Malley, she could try calling her."

"Okey-doke," Rabbit said, pulling her mobile from a pocket, "but she's had her phone turned off forever." She pressed a button and handed it to Kit, then followed Cathy.

"Engaged," Kit said. "I s'pose that's better than not answering."

"Why did you and Cathy find Rabbit's last little revelation so significant?" Alex asked.

Kit leaned in conspiratorially. "If you recall, well-dead Toad implied that a cop hired him to attack Sasha. Cathy and I had already tossed and discarded the idea that, on hearing that, one of the Anders or their thugs then saw *and* recognized Sheryl and thought

223

she was *it*; coz that would've made her seriously unlucky, as she had *nothing* to do with the Rileys.

"But," Kit held up a finger, "if the guy that Rabbit followed was a cop, then maybe *he's* Toad's cop. In which case, being a cop, he'd be more likely to recognize Sheryl. He may have assumed because she was so close to the Blaazt that she was surveilling the Riley–Anders mob, one of whom he'd just sicked Toad on, rather than being undercover with a drug lord's mob."

Alex frowned. "But if he *did* kill her, I take it because Sheryl could've linked him to Toad and the attack on Sasha, wouldn't that also beg the question: Who the hell is Chrissie?"

"Possibly," Kit agreed. "So it's not likely, especially if we go with Rabbit's assumption that he wasn't Chrissie's hubby at all. Which means, cop or not, if that bloke did kill Sheryl, then the reason could be anything. Like," Kit searched her mind, "he has, or wants to have, a connection to Mr. Big Bloke, the drug guy. He might have blown Sheryl's cover and then offered to take her out to prove he'd be useful." Kit hit the redial button.

"You worked all that out, just like that?" Alex said, in amazement.

"I wish," Kit grinned. "I mean, if it made any sense, I wish I was that quick. But I've had this shit, in various permutations, running round my warped cerebrum since last Thursday. Each new fact or fiction just oozes in and makes a bigger stew. It might *sound* logical, but it's just as likely to be nonsense." She hit the redial again.

Ringing. "Yo?"

"Scooter. It's about bloody time."

"Who's that?"

"It's Kit O'Malley. Listen, I just bumped into Rabbit and she told me that you asked her to follow your girlfriend's husband on Sunday night."

"Oh, what the hell did she tell you that for?"

"To impress me. She wants to be a detective, Scooter, you know that."

"So I gave her a reason to show off to the real PI," Scooter said. "So what?"

"So what? What's wrong with you, Scoot? What do you know about *Chrissie's* husband?"

Scooter groaned. "Nothing much."

Alex raised a shushing finger to remind Kit to keep her voice low. "Have you checked up on Rabbit? Did you, for instance, make sure that your friend *did* stop tailing him when you told her to; while you went off to screw your brains out with the guy's wife?"

"Stuff you, Kit! I don't have to listen to this," Scooter shouted.

"Yes, you do. Otherwise that nice detective will have to drag you in for questioning."

Four heart beats of silence. "Why? Where is Rabbit? Is she all right?"

"Ah, better late than never," Kit said patronizingly. "You send your best mate after some bloke she's says *you've* never seen before, and *now* you ask if she's okay."

"Well, is she?"

"She's fine. But *I* need to know how sure you are that the guy was your girl's husband."

"Why?"

"Scooter."

"I'm *not* sure. I just assumed he was."

Kit sighed. "What's the husband's name?"

"I dunno."

Kit shrugged at Alex, to let her know that hearing Scooter Farrell's answers didn't make the conversation any more sensible. "What do you mean, you don't know?"

"I have no idea what his name is," Scooter enunciated. "Don't know; don't care."

"Well, what's Chrissie's surname?"

"Why?" One breath, two breaths. "I don't know that either."

"It's quite a meaningful relationship, then," Kit noted.

"It's bloody good sex, is what it is. Not that it's any of your business, Kit."

"Is her no-name husband a cop?"

"No. He's a mechanic. I think."

"Scooter? Why does Rabbit think he's a cop?"

"Um, because Chrissie's *ex*-husband was a cop."

"Is a cop, or was a cop?"

"No idea, Kit. I'm not interested in the current jockstrap, let alone Mr. Previous. I believe she met guy two through guy one, but that's *all* I know."

"Can you find out if he's still a cop?" Kit asked. "Actually, coz this'd be more relevant, can you find out *who* the guy on Sunday night was."

"Why?"

"Because you don't want a visit from Detective Martin about you and Chrissie and her husband and Suzie and Tom."

"All right, for Christ's sake! It will be difficult, but I'll try."

"Thank you, Scooter. I expect to hear from you, one way or the other, within twenty-four hours." Kit hung up and filled Alex in on the Scooter side of the conversation.

"A lot of cops, of one sort or another, seem to be involved in these two cases," Alex noted.

"Yeah, strange isn't it?" Kit agreed. "And spooky because half of them are looming up out of my past, like *I'm* the connection to everything. It's starting to make me a little paranoid."

"I thought you were always paranoid, darling."

Kit smiled affectionately. "I am, you're right. But this is like having actual people going through my rubbish bins, rather than imaginary ones."

"Kit, I don't think ..."

"Speak of the devils," Kit interrupted, "there be two: Andrew Boxer Macklin in the lead, and Chucky Parker sniffing along behind." Kit nodded towards the blond, moustached, denim-dressed, and not in the least intimidated murder suspect, who was crossing the squad room towards them, and the noxious weed who pursued him. Kit sniggered as she noticed every cop in sight was checking the time, to calculate who'd won Marek's bet.

"Oh, and merde!" Kit groaned, as if she'd just remembered where she'd left her memory. "Speaking of *all* the devils, there's a couple I haven't given any thought to at all."

"Who?" Alex asked; but the moment was overtaken by Boxer throwing himself into the chair opposite them.

"Hey, Kit."

"Hey, Box. What are you doing here?" she smiled.

"The Chuck thinks I'm a cold-blooded killer. Can you imagine that?"

"I can imagine that he thinks exactly that," Kit said. "Morning, Charlie," she added, as Parker caught up with the sheer nerve of his prime suspect.

"O'Malley," he acknowledged, then snarled, "Macklin, you can't wander around here. You're not one of us any more, remember?"

"Do not push *that* button, Charlie," Boxer warned. "And bugger off, I want to talk to Kit."

"She doesn't work here any more, either."

"Parker!" bellowed Detective Inspector Marek from his office around the corner.

Parker squinted. "Don't you move without an escort, Macklin. Or I'll have you."

"I don't swing that way, Chuckles," Boxer smirked. "And if I did, you would not be my choice of stud muffin."

"Walk away, Charlie." It was Marek again.

"That bloke is prime-cut deadshit," Boxer muttered as Parker heeded his boss's call.

"Did you really want to talk to me?" Kit asked him.

"No, I just wanted to get away from the prick." Boxer grinned, then glanced at Alex and raised an eyebrow.

"Andrew Macklin, this is my friend, Alex Cazenove, and likewise in reverse."

"Your friend friend?"

"Yes, Boxer, my friend friend. Now, before I flay you with loud questions about a certain cop giving a certain crim an alibi ..."

"Not here, O'Malley," Boxer growled.

Kit flung an *as if* look at him. "As I said, before I do that some-where else, you can answer these curly ones: are you now or have you ever been married to or in a defacto with someone called Chrissie; and if not, do you know anyone by that name?"

"Why?" When Kit didn't respond he said, "In a word, that answers all of the above, no."

Phew, Kit thought, strangely relieved. That's if he was telling the truth, of course. "Okay," she continued, "how do I get in touch with Doghouse Dixon and Deon Mason?"

"No clue about Mason," Boxer shook his head. "Like I told you the other day, he went bush to go opal mining. Ask the Police Association, they might know.

"Doghouse lives on his big fishing cruiser down the Mornington Peninsula. Last I heard, from a mate who saw him moored at Brighton about a month ago, he's berthed and mostly works out of Western Port Marina, at Hastings. Why do you want to know this?"

"Because they're the only two people from the old days, connected to all that crap from those old days, who haven't turned up on my doorstep yet. So I'm beginning to worry."

"Why?"

"Why not?"

Chapter 18

In Kit's life so far, the main route out of Melbourne in the general direction of Gippsland or the Mornington Peninsula had been named the South-Eastern Arterial or Freeway—or carpark depending on the traffic—and more recently the Monash Freeway or M1. Kit wasn't entirely sure, but she thought it still connected to the Princes Highway, aka federal Highway One—the major road that connected Queensland with the Northern Territory by the long way via New South Wales, Victoria, South Australia, and Western Australia.

Travel on the now-M1, in or out of the city, was fast and efficient as long as it wasn't peak hour; which was an inaccurate label for what it measured because the traffic congestion it referred to lasted at least three hours at both ends of the day. Longer if it was Friday arvo, when morning and afternoon peak hour ran smack into each other, making it more of a peak day.

Where it bypassed Dandenong and offered—yes, there it was, Kit thought—an exit to the Princes Highway and on through Gippsland (and eventually to Cairns nearly 3000 kilometers to the north), the M1 Monash South-Eastern Arterial Freeway became the Dandenong-Hastings Road.

Entertained on the journey by Enigma and Queen, Kit and Alex traveled southeast towards Western Port through mostly open countryside and farmland, except where the hint of new housing developments augured that the urban sprawl would some day infect the entire eastern side of the Mornington Peninsula with concrete driveways and paling fences.

Kit drove while Alex finally confessed that Enzo, to his delight, had been tutoring her on movie musicals, to complement the lessons Kit had been giving on film and TV pop culture.

"My dear woman," Alex said, in an Enzo voice, "Mrs. Peel and Xena are all well and good but a baby-buff, trying to catch up on a youth not misspent in the flickering darkness, needs a rounded education. That simply must include Dorothy, Fraulein Maria, Mrs. Anna, and Sally."

"Sally who?" Kit asked.

Alex turned in her seat and shrugged. "No idea. But so far we've followed a brick road, doe-a-deered, and got to know a king, etcetera—at least twice each, just to make sure. Enzo's threatening me with *Kiss Me Kate* and, um, *Life is a Cabaret* for our next session."

Kit laughed. "Just *Cabaret*, Alex honey, which means it's Sally Bowles as played by Judy's daughter, who ..."

"Oh no," Alex cried. "There's a lineage? Do I have to care whose daughter Sally is?"

"It's not Sally, it's Liza," Kit smiled. "And not really, but don't tell Enzo I said that."

"I think I'm too old to be starting from scratch," Alex admitted. "If I'd known that I'd have to make up for thirty-seven years of my life, in the year that I actually turn thirty-seven, just because I met you ..."

Kit's stomach turned over. "Are you sorry you met me?"

"Don't be silly, darling. And if you'd ever let me finish a sentence before you go all Ms. Tragic and Bereft on me, you'd be less inclined to do so. I was saying, had I known what was in store for me, wait," Alex raised a qualifying finger, "in this, the significant year, that we came together, then I would have planned ahead and left home as soon as I could crawl."

Kit glanced at Alex, still amazed at how remarkably sane her woman was, given that her entire youth and childhood had been devoid of make-believe—no fiction, no fantasy, no vicarious thrills or adventures, no entertainment, and no frivolity of any kind.

"Without being too rude about people I've never met, especially as some of them are your actual blood relatives," Kit said, "I feel I must say that your mother has a lot to answer for."

"That is an understatement," Alex agreed, pushing her hair behind her ear.

Kit took a mental whip to Alex's de facto stepfather, and the other small-time religious wackos of the world who imposed their nonsense on unsuspecting children, and gave them all a darn good thrashing; until a little bell started tinkling in the corridors of her own obsessive mind. "Alex," she said, "you don't have to get into all this stuff just because *I* like it."

"I know that," Alex smiled. "And in the abstract it's true, but in reality I don't *get* half of what you talk about, so I'm opting for crash course in O'Malley. Besides I enjoy most of it."

"You do?"

"I do. But pay attention to the road, there's a roundabout coming up."

Twenty minutes and five roundabouts later they drove into the coastal township of Hastings, population pushing 6500, and cruised along Marine Parade with its car yards, petrol station, motel, churches, and houses.

Kit pulled up beside an expansive waterfront reserve opposite the local council offices and near the T-junction of the shop-lined High Street. She reached for the Melways to check their position in the grand scheme of all things cartographic, and then took a look at the view of the place her map detailed. "Looks like a swim is out of the question," she said, observing that there was no actual "water" to go with the "front," as the tide was so far out of the Hastings Bight that there was nothing but mud flats and the impression that no amount of water could ever return to fill the space.

"It's twelve degrees and drizzling," Alex pointed out.

"That's another good reason," Kit said, peering across the bight to the monster storage tanks of either the Whitemark Petrol Storage and Distribution facility and/or the Esso-BHP Gas Fractionation Plant—whatever the hell that was. She assumed the sky-high flaring-flame-topped chimney belonged to BHP's Western Port steelworks, and that the humungous ocean-going tanker in the channel near the opposite shore was visiting one or all of them.

Kit pulled out again and they cruised along the mudfront looking for a marina. They found some actual seawater lapping the pylons of a pedestrian and fishing jetty, but there were only a few small yachts moored to the adjacent dock. In fact, there seemed to be more pelicans than boats—verified by Alex, who

231

made a silly-beak-count of eighteen bobbing birds all, oddly, facing north—and no vessels big enough to fit Boxer's description of a large fishing cruiser.

Kit wound down her window to ask directions from a kid with a fishing rod. He gave her a suspicious look as if "where is the marina" might be a trick question before pointing at a so incredibly obvious collection of masts. Oh, apparently it was a *stupid* question not a trick one, so Kit decided that squinting as if she were half-blind was better than being thought of as an idiot by a ten year old. As it turned out, the masts belonged to the local yacht club, and the main Western Port Marina was even farther around the bay.

Ten minutes later, having left the car in the enormous carpark of the elaborate waterfront complex, they received directions to Dixon's boat from a tall rotund man wearing an actual captain's hat, who pointed towards the end of a narrow berthing jetty between opposite rows of very big yachts, cruisers, and flashy speed boats. Kit thanked him, but then stopped for a moment to consider why she was even here.

"Why *are* we here?" Alex asked.

"Not really sure," Kit replied. "But so far, and in less than a week, everyone connected with Chucky's biggest internal affairs triumph has re-surfaced in my life. No, hang on, I am *not* laying claim to this. They've simply all turned up in this investigation, in one form or other. Everyone that is, except Mark Dixon and Deon Mason. So, I believe we're here to find out what those two don't have in common with Boxer and poor Sheryl and, who knows, even Chucky himself."

"But what about Gerry?" Alex reminded her. "How does he figure in this? And is he even connected to all these ex-cops at all?"

Kit blew a raspberry. "If I knew that, I'd probably know everything. I could *guess* that he helped the bad boys, as in the bad boy cops, with the burglary scam that eventually got them in the deepest of shit all those years ago. But I don't remember his name in connection with that whole debacle. So I'm rather hoping that Gerry *was* got by a gay vampire or that Mr. Big Bloke. The latter, however, doesn't explain the choice of Angie's as an interim morgue, because despite the fact that they *are* now the bad guys, I am ever hopeful that my ex-colleagues are not in cahoots with a major drug dealer."

"Why do you care?" Alex queried. "About your ex-bad-cops I mean?"

"Because there's bad, and there's *bad*. And drugs far outweigh burglaries in which no one got hurt. Except insurance companies."

"And because you like Boxer Macklin."

"And, because I like Boxer," Kit nodded. "Um, are we moving, or am I having a turn?"

Alex laughed and took Kit by the elbow as they walked. "It's a floating dock."

"How disconcerting," Kit remarked, and then exclaimed, "Good grief and bugger my bank manager! Look at that boat. They want $230,000 for it. Mum's house is not worth that much."

"But her house won't take you to the Whitsundays," said someone. Oh, it was the Skipper from Gilligan's Island again, and gosh darn it if he didn't step onto the for-sale *Argenta Spirit*.

"She's lovely," Kit grinned.

"She is that," he agreed. "You'll find Mark's boat another six along."

And they did, although Kit found nothing she expected. The disheveled character winding a rope around the thing a rope gets wound around, looked quite out of place on the splendid cruiser named *Gemini*, which was a good forty-feet-huge and probably also worth more than a house. Nor did he match Kit's memory of Boxer Macklin's partner in crime and punishment. Okay, so it's a side view, O'Malley, she thought. And maybe this is not even him.

"Doghouse?" she said.

The man jerked his head but continued with his important rope-coiling task.

"Dixon," Kit said a little more loudly.

The man—oh dear, it was Doghouse all right—turned and peered at Kit, then Alex, then left and right to see if there was anyone he knew who was using his name. It had been at least five years since they'd laid eyes on each other, and Kit knew she'd changed to the point of not being recognized by people she'd only rarely worked with; but blimey, she thought, Dixon had seriously gone to the dogs.

His torn grease-filthy jeans, flannel shirt, footy beanie, and a sleeveless parka, zipped to the throat, *almost* suited the fact that he was working on a boat in inclement weather—if this had been a dilapidated trawler in a storm—but his look only enhanced Kit's impression that a once super-fit, snappy-dressing cop had gone so far undercover with a bunch of homeless blokes that he'd forgotten how to get home.

She'd never liked Mark Dixon and agreed with Boxer that he was a signpost waiting for directions, but Kit wanted, for but a moment, to put a positive spin on his apparent situation: the "poor bloke" was suffering conjunctivitis or the monster flu; his five o'clock shadow, at just after noon, was a homage to Chuck Norris; and he was somehow three months pregnant. Nah, Kit thought. Dirty, messy, and bleary-eyed, Mark Dixon looked like he'd been on a two-year beer and burger bender, and it was not a pretty sight.

"You talking to me?" he said, then snorted with laughter and repeated himself.

"De Niro you ain't, Doghouse," Kit half smiled. "It's Kit O'Malley, remember?"

"Fuckenell! Whadda *you* want?" His was not a welcoming tone.

Nothing at all, Kit thought. "Just passing, saw your light on," she said.

"Sure. You wanna shit in me other boot now?" he asked and then hoicked-up something nasty and spat it into the bay.

Kit had visions of an entire ecosystem being polluted by the gunk from Dixon's lungs.

"It's my guess you want somethink, O'Malley."

Ever the bright boy. "You got me there, Doghouse. You been up to the city lately?"

"Why?" he asked, glancing back towards the cabin.

Kit shrugged. "There's a few of our old friends in town; in fact, they're popping up all over the place like bad memories."

He sniffed. "I do not recall us havin' communal friends."

"True," Kit agreed. "How about mutual acquaintances?"

"Is there, like, a reason I'm s'posed to care about whoever the fuck you're talkin' about?"

Kit shrugged again. "Depends whether you care that some of them aren't alive any more."

Dixon clambered to his feet, pulled his woollen beanie farther down over his eyebrows, and adopted a couldn't-give-a-shit slouch.

Ee-yew, Kit thought, as Alex also made a strange gurgling noise. Dixon the deadbeat now looked like an overweight white rapper. Scary.

"Well? Like who?" he asked.

"Pauly-J," she said.

"Jesus, O'Malley! He's been dead forever. If he's turnin' up uninvited you should be callin' an exorcist or somethink."

"He hasn't turned up. But Chucky Parker, Gerry Anders, and Boxer Macklin have."

Dixon looked like he was gearing up for something, then stalled. "Is the Box dead?"

"No."

"Oh. Well why'd ya mention him in the same breath with Anders, who I know *is* dead, his demise being in the paper and all. S'pose that means that scumbag Parker's not dead either. You know …"

"Mark? Who are you talking to?" came a woman's questioning voice.

"She's sort of an old colleague from the force," he said over his shoulder, before nodding at Kit. "You're a private dick now, though, aren't you, O'Malley?"

"Oh yeah, that's me," Kit nodded agreeably, while wondering why Doghouse didn't mention Sheryl Mapp. Was it coz *she* hadn't, or because he hadn't read today's paper yet?

Meanwhile, "Don't you dare let anyone on the boat, Mark, I'm not dressed for company," warned the owner of a tousle of red hair and a pair of mascara-smudged eyes, which was all that was visible through the hatchway. "What does she want anyway?"

"Dunno yet."

"Well, I don't mean to be rude, whoever you are, but Mark doesn't want to have anything to do with the old days on the job.

235

He's not big on reunions with a bunch of wankers who left him out to dry, but he's probably too polite to say so."

Doghouse, polite? Kit thought. "Who did that to him?" she asked.

"It's okay Ellie," Dixon said. "O'Malley wasn't one of them."

"It's not okay; but if you want to be a masochist, go ahead. But you won't sleep tonight."

Dixon shuffled his feet. "Ellie's right. I'll have a sleepless night if I talk to you too long."

"Is he for real?" Alex muttered.

"Why?" Kit asked him.

"Sh-i-t," Dixon said, using three syllables to do so. "Bad memories, mate. You know."

"Why? Because Gerry Anders is dead?"

"As if," Dixon snorted.

"Mark, honey, we have to go up the street to do that thing soon, remember?"

"We do? Oh yeah, we do. Gotta go, O'Malley, duty calls." Dixon began to retreat below.

"Doghouse?"

"Don't call him that."

"Sorry, Ellie," Kit said to the formless voice. "Mark, you don't happen to have any idea who killed Anders do you?"

He turned slowly and, possibly, thoughtfully. "From memory, such as mine is, I'd say start with Stuart Barker and work through every second crook in town. Then take a look, no, take a lie detector to about half the guys on the job."

"A cop did it?"

"I didn't say that. Did I say that?" Dixon glanced at Alex, for the first time.

"Not exactly," Alex said.

"Not exactly," Dixon repeated scornfully. "Man, you see how your shit gets taken out of context? Story of my bloody life."

"Well, stop talking to them, Mark," Ellie stated the obvious.

"Look, I don't know nuthin'," Dixon said, not heeding his woman's advice. "I don't care about any of those arseholes any more, and I got no interest in whatever crap is turnin' up, or turnin' you on, O'Malley. Okay? Me and Ellie, we just keep to ourselves and our boat in this nice little place where no one knows me. So don't you go spreading any stories around here."

"I wouldn't, Dog ... Mark," Kit smiled. "Okay, I'll leave you to it. Catch you another time."

"Don't rush back on my account," he said and disappeared below.

"Did we learn anything from that?" Alex asked as they bounced back along the dock.

"Not that I can figure," Kit said, stopping casually in front of the *Argenta Spirit* to cast a glance back at Dixon's boat. Yes, they were being watched. "Except that he's not the man he used to be, which in general terms is not saying a lot. But he did used to dress well."

"So what now?" Alex asked.

"... my love," Kit sang, and then pulled a face. "Now we return to the car and wait in plain view, so whether they were planning to or not, they'll feel impelled to leave the *Gemini* soon because she *said* they were going to. Then you, my darling, will follow them, close enough that they *know* you are; while I sneak back and take a look below."

"Why? He seemed harmless enough."

"He did, didn't he?" Kit agreed. "But after that whole True Blue thing earlier this year, I take to harmless with a sledge hammer. In fact, god is more likely to exist than a harmless human, and you know my opinion of omnipotent beings. So while we're here, I intend to make sure that Doghouse is not keeping Gerry's or Sheryl's left toes as trophies."

"What?" Alex was appalled. "Did the killer take their toes?"

"No, Alex darling, it was a figure of speech."

"That's not a figure of speech, O'Malley. That's a very strange thing to say."

"I do hope you ladies are arguing over whether to buy my boat," said the Skipper, emerging from his stateroom or galley or ball-room or whatever was worth so much money.

"As a matter of fact," Kit said thinking on her feet, "I was just going back to the car to get my camera to take a photo of Mark's boat so my husband could decide whether to hire it for some over-seas clients next month. Oh," Kit pressed her fingers to her lips, "but please don't tell Mark that my Wayne's decision will come down to that. Anyway, I do believe my brother might be interested in your beautiful *Argenta Spirit*. He's due back from Honolulu on Friday, so if I take a couple of snaps of your boat too, you might be in luck."

"My dear, you're most welcome and I'd be delighted to show you around."

There was nothing on board the *Gemini* above or below decks that would have interested anyone but a scientist on a quest for strange amoebae. There was certainly nothing that would invite anyone to hire either the vessel or its owners for a cruise of any duration. Cleanliness, in the galley at least, was obviously not next to anything that resembled Doghouse or Ellie. Plates encrusted with strangeness, and growing something that waved, had been laid to rest under several pizza boxes on the sink. Almost-empty beer bottles, complete with soggy cigarette butts, covered the table; and several newspapers—ah! including today's *Herald Sun*—were scattered over the bench seats but didn't appear to be hiding anything more suspect than some rips in the vinyl. And a dead blowfly.

Kit opened cupboards, looked in bags, checked under the two single bunks strewn with clothes, gagged at the mustiness of the tiny shower and toilet cubicle, and wished she had a gas mask to enter the only separate cabin, which was mostly a messy double bed. She found one thing of vaguely nostalgic interest buried under a pile of fishing magazines, so she stole it and made good her escape onto the deck, just before the deluded Skipper of the all-but-sold floating house waved at her as he motored off, bound for Phillip Island.

Having wasted valuable minutes on the *Argenta Spirit* to secure his confidence by lying like a snake, Kit only had ten on the *Gemini*, before the agreed burgle time ran out. She made it back to the marina carpark just as Alex returned from following Ellie and Doghouse.

"So, where did they go?" Kit asked, leaping into her passenger seat.

"A petrol station, a milk bar, a hardware shop, then the pub. I think I made them go to places they weren't planning to by making it so obvious I was tailing them."

"Good," Kit said. "That was the idea."

"Did you find any toes?" Alex queried.

"Not unless they're being used to grow cultures in the sink. It was disgusting down there, which explains why Ellie didn't want anyone to come on board. I really can't reconcile the Doghouse I remember with that sad bastard; yet the Dixon we just met fits perfectly with the squalor lurking on that once very nice boat."

"Were there clues to any of the mysteries you're investigating?"

"Nope. I did find this, though," Kit said reaching into her jacket pocket.

"It's a photo," Alex said.

"Very good, Watson."

"Don't be patronizing," Alex said, "and tell me why you removed this personal article from Mr. Dixon's boat. Who are all these people?"

Kit leaned closer and peered at the photo, while slipping her hand between Alex's thighs.

"Is that going to help with your explanation?" Alex asked sweetly.

"No, but it feels good," Kit grinned.

"Hmm. Perhaps we should call into that motel down the road for a while," Alex suggested.

"I love the way you think," Kit said admiringly.

"I'm renowned for it," Alex nodded. "The photo?" she added.

"Oh yeah. It was taken at a barbecue about six months before Chucky Parker's merde hit the spinning thing, and half the people pictured were hauled before IA, either as suspects or witnesses, or just for questioning. I know this because I was there along with about thirty cops and their partners or, in some cases, their entire families. It was a big farewell do for this guy, Doug Campbell, who was retiring," Kit indicated a bald man holding a yard glass.

"From the back," Kit began pointing, "Boxer, Pauly-J, Deon Mason, Doghouse, Jim um Thing; middle row is Boxer's then-girlfriend Carla and her two rugrats, Deon's sister, me, Sheryl Mapp's fiancé, who I think ran off with the wife of this guy, Paul Vickery. Don't know those three; but front row is Jill Porter, her husband, Sheryl herself, Barry Park, and Jonno."

"And you nicked it, why?"

"I don't know," Kit admitted. "But you never know."

"You never know what?"

"I don't know. That's the problem."

Kit's phone started ringing. Alex's phone started ringing.

They looked at each other and sighed; and Kit had the sinking feeling that a few hours R&R in a motel bed with the love of her life was not going to be on the afternoon cards.

Chapter 19

Precisely one hour later Kit pulled her RAV up within walking distance of the St. Kilda Road Police Complex, and she and Alex made a dash through the now pelting rain. Kit had called Cathy a moment before they parked, to announce their imminent arrival and request an escort to the ninth floor. Again it was DSC Martin herself who met them and made sure they rode up alone. Before they got to the squad rooms, however, she stopped the lift on a lower floor and held her finger on the door-shut button.

"There's something up with Charlie," Cathy said. "He's acting very strange today."

"There's always been something strange up him," Kit noted.

"No, O'Malley, I'm serious. I think he's losing his grip on reality."

"That too was always strange. And tenuous, Cathy."

Cathy tugged on her fringe as she peered at Kit and Alex. "Why are you here exactly? I don't mind that you are—and in your case, Alex, it's a good thing—but how did you find out?"

"Carrie McDermid rang me from Angie's in a fit of verbal high dudgeon over, I think she called it, police thuggery," Kit said.

"And Angie rang me, at the same time, and requested our services," Alex added.

"According to Carrie," Kit said, her tone implying a big grain of salt, "Chucky swooped in with a veritable SWAT team, armed to the teeth with Starsky-only knows what, and arrested Angie in front of a capacity crowd, who then caused a riot. What really happened?"

Cathy tried not to smile. "Senior Sergeant Parker and the three detectives he specifically requested to accompany him, which included me sadly, entered The Terpsichore at precisely 1:30 p.m. and arrested the owner, Angela Nichols, on suspicion of the murder of Gerald Anders. There was a small lunch-time crowd, all of whom objected strongly, but the suspect came quietly and no firearms of any description were drawn or even revealed."

"And *why* did you arrest Angie?" Alex asked.

"I didn't," Cathy said emphatically. "Charlie did. Apparently because he unearthed an old restraining order filed *against* Gerry by your mate Angie."

"What on earth for?" Kit asked.

"I don't know. I've yet to lay eyes on the paperwork." Cathy gritted her teeth. "Charlie was about to start the interview when Marek put a stop to it, until Angie's lawyer got here, before rushing upstairs for a meeting. I assume that's you, Alex, although I didn't realize she'd even made her call yet. Marek also stipulated to Charlie that I sit in on the interview."

Kit was puzzled. Lawyers or solicitors holding the hands of suspects during interviews was not standard practice in Victoria, because it meant that they could later be called as witnesses in court against their own client over what was said during that interview. "Why do you suppose Marek did that?" she asked. "Alex can only observe from afar."

"I guess he wanted Gung-ho Charlie to cool down a little," Cathy said, releasing the lift button, "and figured Alex's presence may contain his enthusiasm."

"You mean his witch hunt," Kit said.

"That too," Cathy smiled. "Marek added that when—not if, you'll note O'Malley—but *when* you turned up, that you could also watch from the ob-room."

Which means, Kit thought, that Jonno thinks Chucky's murder charge against Angie is as likely as the one he tried on Boxer that morning.

"Can you get me a copy of the restraining order?" Alex requested.

"I'll try. If she's officially charged with anything, you'll get the lot of course, but ..." Cathy trailed off as the doors opened.

Chucky Parker was in his element. And watching, as she was, through the two-way mirror Kit could imagine that element in all its glory:

this was *his* reptile cage, with its glass front and its artificial habitat; and Angie was his prey, that he'd cornered.

"What *is* he doing?" Alex asked.

"Playing with his food," Kit said.

Parker's oily accusatory voice was getting nowhere with Angie, however. "Miz Nichols," he oozed, "this will be easier on everyone, you included, if you just come clean about your prior association with the late Gerald Anders."

"No, Detective, it would be a damned sight easier if you'd listen to what I'm saying," Angie responded. "Until I discovered his dead body in my bar last Thursday, I had never in my life so much as laid eyes on the late Gerald Anders."

Parker made a show of caressing the stapled pages of what he obviously considered to be proof positive of the guilt of the woman before him. "I have something here that makes a mockery of that statement," he said.

"Really?" Angie said, not in the least bit threatened by the desperate policeman and his bits of paper. "So now I'm supposed to be a murderer *and* a liar?"

"She's not at all worried. Do you think he's just stirring?" Alex whispered.

"I'm sure he's stirring her," Kit nodded, "but he seems to think he's on to something."

Angie Nichols, however, was not a woman, person, or citizen to be toyed with. "Detective Parker, will you stop fondling whatever that is," she challenged, pointing at the paper, "and tell me what you're rabbiting on about."

Detective Martin leaned back in the chair she occupied next to Parker's, wiped her face straight, and glanced at the approximate position of Kit and Alex behind the mirror.

"If you insist, Miz Nichols," Parker smiled, "but don't say I never gave you the chance to reveal this information yourself."

Angie gave an expansive shrug. "For goodness sake, man, get on with it."

Parker slammed the pages down on the table, swiveled them round, and pushed them towards her. "I have here a sworn complaint made by you, Angela Audrey Nichols, about a man you claimed had been harassing you and the *lesbian* patrons of your nightclub for over a month two years ago."

"What?" Angie demanded, taking a closer look at the pages in front of her.

"Of course, as you know full well, that man was Gerald Anders. A person you claim never to have met, but against whom you also took out a restraining order," Parker smirked. "You'll find your reminder of that fact on the second page there," he pointed.

"Oh shit," Alex swore.

"Understatement," Kit added.

"You're kidding," Angie laughed. "What kind of nonsense set-up is this?"

"You're not going to deny this evidence are you, *Miz* ..."

"Of course I bloody am, you stupid little git," Angie snapped.

"Uh-oh," Kit said.

"Oh dear," Alex added.

Cathy cleared her throat. "Can you explain this at all?"

"There's nothing *to* explain," Angie insisted. "I have never made a complaint of any kind to the police about anyone. I've certainly never had the need to take out a restraining order against Anders, or any other man. Although I am considering one now." She glared at Parker.

Cathy reached for the documents of alleged incrimination. She frowned as she read, did a double take, looked from Angie to the magic mirror, then excused herself from the interview. Parker, meanwhile, was oblivious as he stabbed the table with his index finger, repeated his accusations, and demanded a confession of some kind to something.

Cathy opened the door to the observation room and joined Kit and Alex. "See what I mean about Charlie. I've seen his one-track mind at work before, but not like this. He's demented."

"But isn't this one of those good cop–bad cop deals?" Alex asked.

"If it is, I wasn't clued-in about it," Cathy stated.

Kit pointed to Cathy's hand. "What's with the thing?"

"*This* is weird. Take a look," Cathy said, standing so they could all read the police report.

"Hmm," Kit said. "Apart from Angie denying that this happened, the report appears to be kosher."

"I gather you don't remember this incident, either," Alex noted.

"As Angie said, she's never had a reason to call the cops. Nothing ever happened at the bar that we couldn't handle," Kit explained, noticing Cathy's strange expression. "What is it?"

"Take a look at the name of the investigating officer," Cathy said.

"Whoa!" Kit exclaimed.

"Ah," Alex raised an eyebrow, "now *that* seems odd."

"I'm going to find Marek and sort this out," Cathy said, and left the room.

Kit and Alex returned, without comment, to their observation of Parker's unique interrogation skills. A uniformed officer, following usual protocol, had stepped into the room when Cathy left, but that hadn't curtailed the Senior Sergeant's peculiar attempts to get Angie to admit to something she quite clearly knew nothing about.

Moments later the door to the interview room was opened by Detective Inspector Marek, who ushered Cathy in and called Parker out.

"He is *so* in for it," Kit said with pleasure.

"What do you suppose he was thinking?" Alex queried.

"I don't think he does," Kit stated.

Cathy addressed the mirror wall. "O'Malley, Alex? Could you join us please."

"Kitty, Alex," Marek nodded, poker-faced, as they passed him and Parker in the hallway.

"O'Malley," Parker drawled, wearing way too much smug and apparently unaware that his little ball of string was about to unravel. "I *did* ask you for an insight into your dyke friends."

"So you did," Kit smiled, opening the door to his now-vacated reptile enclosure. "No hard feelings, though, *Chuck*, and don't hesitate to give me a call if you need my services for anything else I can ignore."

"Thank the goddess," Angie exclaimed, as they entered the interview room.

"And you're free to leave any time you like, Ms. Nichols," Cathy was saying.

"Oh yeah?" Angie sneered. "I want to know what the bloody hell is going on first. That lunatic was accusing me of all sorts of rubbish. Is that how you normally do business?"

"I apologize on behalf of anybody I can apologize for," Cathy began.

"Hey, you are only responsible for yourself," Angie stated.

"And for what you have tamed," Kit added, then shrugged when everyone except Angie looked at her askance. "Irrelevant, sorry."

"In that case," Cathy smiled, "I'm sorry for allowing the situation to proceed as far as it did. It seems the documents that were thrust under your nose as proof of I don't really know what, are in themselves slightly suspect."

"Really?" Angie's tone said it all. "Just slightly?"

"The police report of your alleged official complaint about Gerry Anders two years ago was signed by a Detective Sergeant Charles Parker," Kit chipped in.

Angie shook her head. "What? But I'd never met *him* before last week, either," she insisted.

"I'm guessing Cathy worked that one out herself," Alex said.

"Oh yeah," Cathy smiled. "I really am sorry, Ms. Nichols, we would greatly appreciate it if you didn't take ongoing offense over this mess. I mean, we hope you will accept that mistakes like this will be dealt with internally, and efficiently and …"

Everyone looked around to see whose mobile was ringing.

"It's mine," Kit said, taking a few steps away to answer it.

"Apology accepted, on one condition," Angie said.

"What's that?" Cathy asked cautiously.

"That you stop calling me Ms. Nichols."

"O'Malley," Kit said.

"Ah, Kit, it's Queenie here."

"Hello," Kit said cheerily. "What can I do for you?"

"Is this not a good time to talk?" Queenie asked intuitively.

"It's a bit awkward, but fire away."

"I have secured a name and two places for you. Can you write them down?"

Kit pulled a notepad and pen from her bumbag and wrote down the addresses of a café in Carlton and a hotel in Collingwood.

"At the café at 12:30 p.m. tomorrow you will find a bloke by the name of Morley, who will explain to you why *your* friend said he was with *my* nephew that time."

"How will I know him?"

"He's got a face like a rat and dresses like a bookie," Queenie explained. "In room nine of that hotel, or behind the bar, you'll find a chap called Santo, who claims to know about that creature who couldn't swim the Yarra the other night. He will talk *a lot* if you tell him you work for me; and that we, as in you and I, were very impressed with his recent service."

Oh no, Kit thought, that's how rumors start. "Can you elaborate?" she asked.

"I'd rather not. Besides, I'm sure you can wing it."

"Okay. Thank you, I think."

"Kit?" Queenie said hurriedly, before she could hang up. "Would you call in tomorrow for morning tea, say around ten-thirty?"

"Um, yeah, sure," Kit sighed, thinking even the barter system should have its limits.

"Excellent. I'll make scones." Queenie hung up.

Dr. Jekyll and Grandma Hyde, Kit thought. "Do you need a lift home, Angie?" she asked.

"Yes, please. Unless Cathy wants to haul me home in a cop car."

"O'Malley can take you," Cathy smiled with relief; and then caught the expectant look on Kit's face. "You want something."

"A small favor," Kit grinned. "Do you know Rob Preston? He's probably a detective."

Cathy shook her head thoughtfully. "Doesn't ring a bell. Why?"

"He was Deon Mason's partner a few years back."

"Deon Mason?" Cathy said questioningly.

"One of Chucky's targets during his toe-cutter stint. Deon and Sheryl Mapp were wrongly charged, along with Pauly-J and the others. But, according to Boxer, Deon voluntarily left the force afterwards. I was wondering where he was."

"Why?" Cathy asked.

"Just curious," Kit shrugged. "I'm getting all these blasts from my past, and he was always one of the nicer ones." She frowned. "Why? Do you know something?"

"No," Cathy said, eyeing Kit suspiciously in return. "Should I?"

Kit wondered if there was such a thing as an honest lie. "I don't think so," she said.

"So what's the favor exactly?"

"Rob Preston?" Kit smiled.

"Oh right. I'll see what I can do." Cathy told them to sit and wait while she went elsewhere to make calls. As the other officer remained in the room with them, no one felt inclined to chat about what had transpired in the last few hours, so a lot of gazing blankly around the room was followed by very small talk about Kit's and Alex's no-reason trip to the beach.

Cathy returned ten minutes later wearing a sad frown, apparently for Kit's benefit. "Good and bad news, I'm afraid," she said. "I have a number for Detective Sergeant Rob Preston, who works in Warrnambool now; but you may not need it. I'm sorry, Kit, but Deon Mason was killed about two years after he left the force. It was a hunting accident in South Australia."

Kit's stomach dropped a few feet. "Oh man," she groaned. "That poor bastard. He never had any luck."

"Were you friends?" Alex asked.

"Not really," Kit shrugged. "We worked together a few times, socialized occasionally. He was young, likeable, funny, and dead now." She sighed. "That does weird things to your place in the universe when you don't find out until years after the event."

The journey home was circuitous and full of phone calls—both incoming and outgoing. Alex drove because she claimed that Kit was too distracted; Angie rang ahead to tell Julia she'd been released on a technicality; Carrie called in to find out what was happening, and to say she was at Kit's place for some reason with Erin and Lillian; Kit rang Hector to ask him to find out if Doghouse actually owned the *Gemini*; Enzo called in to arrange a Tereshenko case-progress lunch with Sarah; and Cathy Martin called to say that Marek had taken Chucky Parker off the Anders' case completely, pending an internal investigation.

Yes! Kit cheered.

As Hector had also informed her he'd scored the necessary data in the Boyes-Lang affair, Kit suggested to Enzo that they meet to close the case at Toto's the next day—*before* the appointment she already had there at twelve-thirty with Morley the rodent-faced informant.

After depositing Angie at Angie's, Kit rang her mother and asked her to order pizzas for anyone who was still going to be there when they got home; whereon, half an hour later, she and Alex met the delivery boy coming down her stairs on their way up. Lillian had ordered five family-sized pizzas—two Hawaiians, an Aussie, a capricciosa, and a marinara—and four rolls of garlic bread, so it was handy that Hector and Brigit arrived ten minutes later to help with the eating.

"You don't really think Detective Parker is actually trying to frame Angie?" Carrie asked.

"It looks like it," Kit said. "But he had to know he wouldn't get much farther than he did. It's possible he was just hoping she'd admit to something he had yet to discover, by implying he already had. If that *wasn't* the case, though, then arresting her on such a flimsy fabrication or, rather, fabricating such a flimsy reason to arrest her in the hope that real evidence would turn up, borders on the desperate and truly vindictive."

"Not to mention stupid," Alex said.

"Yeah," Erin said. "Angie could sue for defamation, slander, and aspersion-casting."

"Don't forget libel," Alex added. "He did write those fictitious charges to support his argument."

"Bastard cops," Brigit stated.

"Don't be too hard on them, dear," Lillian said, reaching for another piece of the Hawaiian. "If he's had anything to do with trying to catch that serial killer, then he's probably frustrated and just wants to arrest someone for something."

"Lillian," Erin said seriously, "that is hardly a good reason to fabricate evidence. I mean, it's not like Angie is a known criminal who needs putting away."

"She's not even an unknown criminal," Brigit noted. "Hey, unless she's *really* good at it."

"I didn't say it was a good reason," Lillian said. "But just imagine how the police feel. There's an awful lot of murdering going on in this town lately, and very little solving. What with that lot Katherine found last month, and dead people being hoicked out of the Yarra or found in dumpsters, and men with no clothes being found at Angela's …"

"*And* no blood," Brigit reminded her.

Lillian threw a "see she agrees with me" gesture at Brigit. "And through all of that there's been the annoying Rental Killing person, who's up to number five now."

"Six," Brigit and Hector said.

"Mum."

"Yes, dear?"

"The Rental Killer is a sadistic and brutal degenerate who is defying all attempts to apprehend or stop him."

"I'm aware of that, Katherine," Lillian said. "In fact, that is my point."

Kit frowned at her mother. "Don't you think all that makes him a bit more than annoying, then?"

"I meant annoying for the police, darling," Lillian stressed. "It's terrifying for the likes of me and Connie, and no doubt even young Brigit here. That's why I choose not to dwell on the specifics, thank you very much. You professionals, however, are used to it."

"I'm not," Erin and Alex said in unison.

"Me neither," Carrie raised her hand.

Kit shook her head in disbelief. "Neither are the cops, Mum. Nor, I might add, is *this* ex-cop now private-eye," Kit said, slapping her own chest. "And it's Jonno who's in charge of finding this creep, and it's doing *his* head in."

"He has nightmares," Erin added sadly, and then curled her lip. "Just the thought of Bubble … the Rental Killer makes my skin scrawl."

"You could change the subject and not talk about it, then," Hector suggested.

Brigit patted the back of his hand. "That's all very well for you to say, Hector. But the scary-arse serial killer is not after you."

"He's not after you, either."

"Yes he is," insisted the six women in the room.

Hector cowered apologetically, then looked baffled. "Why do you *think* like that? Doesn't it create more fear? It's like a collective self-induced psycho-trauma, especially when *thinking* you'll be got by an unknown-to-you killer is like being afraid of a lightning strike or alien abduction."

"Please don't go there," Kit warned, hoping someone would speak up before Lillian did.

"The thing is," Brigit raised a finger, "we can't know for sure we don't know him, until we know who he is. Which adds to the scary."

Phew! Kit thought.

"My friend Mimi Burrage was abducted last year," Lillian said, brushing her hair back with one pizza-sticky hand, while reaching for her wine glass with the other. "Which makes me only one decree of separation from *that* breed of serious unpleasantness."

Merde! Kit amended.

"Isn't it a degree?" asked Carrie who, as she'd only known Lillian for two hours, didn't know any better. "Abducted?" she added, when the other words sank in.

"Yes, by an explorer alien on the road to Ballarat," Kit elaborated, reaching over to pluck mozzarella from her mother's otherwise immaculate hair.

"Okay, forget the aliens," said Hector, who did know better than to question or encourage Lillian. "So you're all afraid of this sicko ..."

"Which is exactly what he wants," Erin said.

"Of course it is," Hector agreed. "But you're paddling in his warped psyche by allowing him to do that to you. Granted, right now he's a faceless and nameless monster, but he is just *some guy*. He'll turn out to be a nothing, who's no more likely to get you than ..."

"The six women he's already taken and killed?" Carrie interjected.

"I know that, I get that," Hector said with frustration. "But your fear makes him more like the bogeyman; you know, scary in concept."

"Yes and no," Brigit nodded. "Except he's not *like* the bogeyman— he *is* the bogeyman, incarnate. He's real and he's out there, trawling the streets for women of no particular kind. So we are—*all* of us—

potential targets, because he has no obvious preferred type of victim."

"But ..."

"But nothing, boyo," Kit proclaimed. "Imagine if the Rental Killer had a thing against male computer experts, or was only after twenty-something, blue-eyed boys with brown hair who lived in St. Kilda? Would *you* feel safe?"

Hector thrust his shoulders back and his chin out, in a fair impersonation of macho posturing. "Okay, no I wouldn't. I'd die my hair blue and move to Warrandyte."

"You see our dilemma, then," Lillian pointed out. "We don't know what color to put in our hair or which suburb to hide in."

"Or whether it makes a difference that we're sixteen or sixty, Irish or Asian," Erin added.

"Getting back on the other track," Alex said, "no matter how scary and elusive the Rental Killer is, his noncapture does not justify what that cop did to Angie."

"Especially as that cop is not even *on* the Barleycorn Task Force," Kit said.

"He was in the beginning," Carrie said. When all eyes turned to her, she shrugged and added, "He told me he was on the case *before* it was a task force."

"Big-noting no doubt," Kit scoffed. "Did he tell you that at the same time he told you about Gerry's nonexistent interest in Angie's bar?"

"Yes, as a matter of fact," Carrie said petulantly.

"Fact does not seem part of that dude's credentials," Hector said.

"Bugger it," Kit said, leaning back in her chair. "I think I have to talk to him."

"Who?" Lillian asked.

"Chucky Parker," Kit snarled.

"What? Voluntarily?" Alex asked.

Kit sighed. "Yeah. It's time to surrender to the inevitable and go ask the bastard some curly questions."

"But why?" Carrie asked. "You said he's been suspended, virtually; so he's not going to cause Angie any more trouble. Surely he's out of the loop?"

"What do you care?" Kit frowned. "And why are you defending him?"

"I'm not."

Kit squinted at her. "He is not a reliable source on any subject, Carrie."

"I realize that, O'Malley."

It was Erin's turn to study her closely. "Do you two have some kind of thing going?"

"No! Don't be ridiculous," Carrie said.

Kit stood up dramatically. "Chucky Parker is fairly stinking with motives and actions bred in the No Good Department. It's time I sussed out what the hell he's up to. So," she pushed her chair back, "who wants coffee before I venture out into those wretched streets?"

Chapter 20

As far as anyone knew, away from the job Graham Charles Parker lived a quiet life in a quiet cul de sac in Fitzroy; just a zig and a zag off Johnston Street, not too far from The Peel Hotel. Actually, according to Cathy, few of his colleagues even knew that much. The seven members of his homicide crew knew, of course, because they sometimes had to pick him up for a job; but that was about it. Detective Martin—the officer now effectively in charge of not only the Anders' case but, for the duration, the remainder of Chucky's crew—had been only a little reluctant to divulge her boss's address. She'd also told Kit what she knew of Parker's personal, home and social life: nothing.

It was thought unlikely that Chucky ever dropped into The Peel for a drink, as he didn't—drink that is; and he wasn't gay. He wasn't anything, as far as anyone knew. That he was acquainted with Bubblewrap Man's sixth victim revealed two previously unknown things about him—that he was an unlikely gym bunny, and that he went to church.

Kit had discovered something his colleagues couldn't be sure of: that he had at least one friend, or just someone who drove him around. But because of that friend, or chauffeur, she also knew that Chucky was into fishing of some kind, on weekdays, at night, badly dressed.

Oh, damn it! she thought. It's night now, he might not even be home. She parked five Victorian (era, not state, although technically both applied) workers' cottages away from the one inhabited by G.C. Parker, the Unknown Quantity. She allowed herself to wonder, for a brief and nauseous moment, how she could have such strong feelings for someone about whom she knew so little. When they'd worked together ...

Hey, O'Malley! Let's not get carried away. Kit mentally cleared her throat. When they'd worked for the same organization, she'd hated his guts. Now, as she tried to find any reason to continue avoiding him, she realized the sensation that Chucky currently aroused in her was more like that caused by a festering, irritated boil.

But who is he? she asked herself.

Hello! she shouted to herself. Who cares? Not to mention too much time already wasted pondering his existence. Kit shook her head and then took a moment to consider what that whole thought process said about *her*, but was rescued from delving too deeply by Hector.

"Which one is his?" he asked, looking up from his laptop, which he'd connected to his mobile phone so he could connect to the Internet, and thus the entire world, all while riding as a passenger in Kit's car. She feigned lack of interest by pretending not to notice what he was doing—as if a mobile connection to cyberspace was as normal as flatulence.

"The house second from the end on the left with the huge number seven," she said.

"So why are we parked all the way back here?"

"Um, let's see. It's sensible PI practice not to park right on someone's doorstep; I'm still trying to decide whether I really have to visit this person *anywhere*, let alone in the privacy of his own home; and, there's already someone carrying out surveillance on the same residence."

"What? Where?" Hector sat up and paid attention. "Who?"

Kit pointed to the combi-van two cars down on the same side of the narrow street.

"Is it the cops?" Hector asked. "I mean other cops. Would IA dudes be on him that quick?"

"Sure, if there's a good reason," Kit said. "But I believe that vehicle, so well-camouflaged with stickers of cowboy hats and bulls, contains a newspaper photographer."

"O'Malley," Hector chided, "you didn't blow the whistle on Parker out of spite did you?"

"Hector," Kit echoed his tone, "we just ate dinner with two journos."

"Oh, so we did. Sorry."

"So you should be," Kit said, "coz spiteful me would've called *The Age*, whereas that guy is from the *North Star*. I saw him and his van with Carrie at Angie's last Friday."

"So now what? I assume you don't want to be photographed sneaking into Parker's place."

"I didn't plan to sneak, Hector. It was my intention to boldly walk, while splitting infinitives, up to his front door and demand entry and answers. *You* were the one who was going to sneak."

"Oh. And why was that again?" Hector said, obviously hoping to be filled in on Kit's plan sometime before dawn.

"Because I want to drop your little bug inside somewhere, while you find an unobtrusive spot outside to leave the recording doo-dad."

"Leave it? Are you mad? This thing is worth five hundred bucks."

"Money well spent if you let me … if you actually use it. Otherwise it's just a toy."

Hector pouted. His computer jingled at him. "Incoming," he said. "Oh, and it's for you."

"What?" Kit said. "Who the hell knows I'm here?"

Hector looked at her, long and hard, as if one of them was incredibly stupid and the other didn't know which.

"Well?" Kit finally said.

"I asked a mate to run a check on that boat," he explained.

"Oh mate," Kit groaned. "You're not supposed to get other people to do stuff for me."

Hector shrugged. "O'Malley, you've got people; I've got people. My people do things for me, not you. They don't know you exist. Actually I can't vouch for that, as they may have seen you in the paper, or found your name in the phone book, or …"

"Hector."

He pulled a face. "They don't know I work for you. That's what we agreed, you and I, because you wanted me to, remember?"

"Right," Kit gave him a dubious look. "So what did your person find out, then?"

Hector consulted his email. "The *Gemini* is owned by one Ellie Jones."

"Ah, so it doesn't belong to Doghouse," Kit nodded thoughtfully, wondering what significance that info had to anything at all. Then she whimpered, "Oh, but Jones? That's as bad as Smith or Nguyen. Can you, or your person, run a check on Ellie Jones to see if that's her real name?"

"Yeah. But you know, there's something you might find intriguing about the Smiths and Nguyens and that is, one possible reason for them being among the most common surnames on the planet is that there's a bloody lot of them out there who actually are them."

"Really, Hector?" Kit ran her hand back through her hair. "What are you trying to say?"

"That her name might be Ellie Jones."

Kit snorted. "Might be Ellie Smith-Nguyen too."

Hector pointed to Parker's house. "Are you going in there or not?"

"Eventually," Kit nodded. "I'm working out how to get rid of that photographer."

Hector raised a finger. "What if there are lurking toerags too?"

"Toe-cutters, mate, not toerags. Although the latter is apt." Kit opened the door. "There's no reason for IA to be here, so I'm off to dispense with camera guy."

She didn't wait for him, as she knew he'd have to switch off all his World-Wide-Wait gear and hide it under the blanket on the back seat, and then get his Right-Here-Now gear and his act together. She strolled down to the combi and drummed her fingers along the full length of it so as not to completely startle the shutterbug inside. Wasted consideration, as it turned out, because when she rapped on the window she frightened the wits right out of him because the guy had been sound asleep. He wound down the window, but before he could abuse her for anything he felt like, Kit smiled and said, "Isn't your mobile working?"

"Yeah, why?" he asked testily.

"Because Carrie's been trying to get you for the last hour," Kit lied. Well, she hoped it was a lie, and that Carrie hadn't called to warn him about her imminent arrival—in between Kit leaving home and him falling asleep, of course.

"Why?" he asked, picking up his phone to check for missed calls. "And who are you?" he queried, looking as if he almost recognized her, or should.

"Kit O'Malley, private investigator. We weren't introduced outside The Terpsichore on Friday," she explained. "And now, I was on my way to … nearby, so Carrie asked me to tell you to meet her ASAP in the Savoy Tavern opposite Spencer Street Station. She's got a lead on this guy's," Kit waved at Parker's house, "um, partner."

"He's got a partner?" he asked, starting his engine.

"Apparently," Kit shrugged. "Anything been happening here?"

The guy pulled a face. "Nada," he said. "He's got a visitor at the moment, but it's just the bloke from next door. Been in there about fifteen … ah, there he is now."

Kit peered at Parker's front door, knowing neither she nor the photographer could be seen from there because the street was badly lit. Chucky's front light had come on, however, bathing his driving-fishing buddy—the already sickly-pale Guy the guy—in a bug-discouraging, hepatitis-yellow glow.

"He's a neighbor?" Kit asked quietly.

"Yeah. From number nine at the end." They watched Guy the neighbor go home, which was more than Parker had done. He'd already retreated inside.

"Well, better go. Thanks for the message."

"No worries, mate," Kit smiled, stepping away from the van so he could leave by reversing out of his parking spot and back up the street. No worries at all, she thought, heading back to her car to see if Hector had found his plot yet. "Come on dufus, you're as slow as a wet week."

Hector poked out his tongue, then slid out of the car and locked the door. Between his thumb and index finger he held up his teeny microphone, placed it carefully in the palm of Kit's hand, and closed her fingers around it. "It's magnetic," he said.

Kit stashed it in her jacket pocket, and gestured down the street. As they drew level with house number five, Kit's mobile rang. Hector jumped.

"What's with you?" Kit asked, yanking the phone out of her pocket.

He screwed up his face in disbelief. "You're the movie buff, O'Malley. You know that's how you get got by the bad guys; they know you're coming."

"Yeah, right," Kit smiled. "Hello?" she answered.

"O'Malley?" said the caller.

Hector reacted to Kit's reaction by mirroring her startled expression, so for his benefit she pointed at Parker's place and said, "Chucky? How'd you get my number?"

"I asked your new friend, Cathy."

"Really?" she laughed. "Okay, what can I do for you?"

"I need to talk to you."

"You *need* to talk to me?" Kit repeated. "Well go ahead, I'm right here." Literally.

"No. In person. I want to hire you."

Kit pinched herself to see if she was awake. "Me? You want ... What the hell for?"

"I think I'm being set up."

"*You're* being set up? That's funny, Charlie," Kit remarked, opening his front gate.

"Please don't be patronizing, O'Malley. I'll pay your going rate, whatever it is."

"Well *that* goes without saying." Kit drew Hector's attention to the narrow, shoulder-high gate that provided access to the path down the left side of the house. The right side shared a common wall with Guy the guy's abode.

Hector reached over and unlatched the gate and slipped into the dark. Kit hoped there was a place for him to leave the receiver in range of wherever she could leave the mike.

"Can we meet, then, and discuss this?" Parker asked, as Kit rang his doorbell. "Damn," he interrupted himself. "Hang on, O'Malley, there's someone at my door."

Graham Chucky Parker, slightly suspended policeman, looked disarmingly like a mullet of the stunned kind when he opened his front door.

"My new friend Cathy gave me your address," Kit said. "I expect coffee."

Although definitely miffed, or confused, by this turn of events

Parker was obviously not going to complain too loudly. He ushered Kit down a short narrow hall into his commodious but crowded lounge; a room that looked as if it hadn't seen so much as a magazine from the modern world since being furnished by his grandmother in the 1930s. The oak and tapestry decor was heavy and funereal. Thick velvet drapes drawn tightly against the outside world, which right now included Hector, formed a backdrop to a large dining table very neatly half-covered in stuff. Jacobean-style antique dining chairs, upholstered and carved armchairs with antimacassars, sideboards with curled legs, and bookshelves with very old books filled the space, while the blanched wallpaper was populated by framed sepia family photos and prints of fading English hunting scenes.

The odd thing—ha! Kit thought—one of the odd things, was that the aged and musty smell that usually lived in lodgings like this was only a background. The aroma here was fruity-sweet, with a hint of cinnamon.

"Take a seat," Parker said, waving at a dining chair before leaving the room through the other door. Kit did as she was told, noting the clear demarcation line between the clutter on the window side of the table, and the empty and spotless side where Kit now sat. And it wasn't that Chucky's stuff had been temporarily pushed back out of the way either; no, it had obviously been trained from a young age never to cross the line.

Parker returned with a trivet on which he placed a hot coffee pot, then went to the drawer in the sideboard and came back with …

Oh shit no! … doilies.

He scuttled back to the kitchen, returning a moment later with china cups and saucers, and then off he went again—and all without a word.

Kit wanted to leave. *Right now, O'Malley!* There was something rising in her stomach—or mind—that was not at all pleasant. It wasn't just the possibility that Norman Bates Parker might have his dear old mummy stashed in a back room; no—there were the doilies to consider. Katy Frances O'Malley shivered and wondered if her dislike of lace placemats was a diagnosable phobia.

She tried to distract herself by checking out the paraphernalia on the other side of the table's DMZ. There was a bowl of corks and another of fine copper wire; a shoebox-sized metal chest of plastic drawers filled with lots of small silver and brassy things; a large magnifying glass on a swivel arm; a metal gadget designed to hold something small firmly in place, probably under the mag-glass which had its own light; plastic boxes with colored things in separate compartments; an elegantly carved wooden box; and a large set of small tools folded in a suede swag.

There was also an old black bakelite telephone. Kit lifted the heavy handset to see if it was connected or just part of ye olde decor. The dial tone said it all, so she hung up, hefted the whole phone upside down, and snapped the magnetic bug into place on the underside.

Parker's voice preceded his next return. "Do you take milk or sugar, O'Malley?"

"No. Thanks."

Sitting opposite Kit, he placed a plate of cake on the table, finally covering—and not before time—the largest of those terrible crocheted-crimes against twenty-first century sensibility.

Fruit cake, yum, Kit sighed. That explains the cinnamon smell.

"Why were you on my doorstep?" Parker asked, playing mother with the coffee pot.

"I wanted to find out why you were trying to set up my friend for a murder rap."

Parker cricked his neck and peered at Kit. "I didn't. And that is precisely why I wanted to talk to you. Someone is setting *me* up to think your friend is a murderer."

"Oh *please*," Kit scowled at him. "You and your prejudice thought Angie was the killer from the get-go; you both made that quite clear."

"Yes, well, I'm sorry about that O'Malley, I truly am. And I know I can be ..."

"A complete prick," Kit interrupted.

"I was going to say prone to rash judgements, which make me speak before I should."

"That's called foot-in-mouth disease," Kit said. "And you should've outgrown it by now."

261

"I'm aware of that. But do you think you could wind your aggro down a few notches, O'Malley? I may well be a prick, but you always come at me like a bitch on lighter fuel."

"Lighter fuel?" Kit laughed, reaching for cake. Ooh, it was warm. "Did you make this?"

"Yes."

"Blimey! Chucky Parker: domestic man of mystery." Kit surrendered with her empty hand. "Sorry. I'll try and remember not to call you that."

"Look, O'Malley, you don't have to like me in order to work for me, do you?"

"Not at all."

"Good. So perhaps you also don't have to like me to believe me."

Kit pursed her lips. "Don't know about that logic," she said. "But *if* I take you on as a client I will, at least, try to remain objective. What I don't get, is why you want to hire *me* at all. I mean you don't like me, either."

"That's not exactly true," Parker said, scratching his head without ruffling his thinning thatch. "I find you obnoxious, O'Malley, but I neither like nor dislike you. And I wish to employ your services partly because we know each other, but mostly because you are already *au fait* with this case. You being in on it should help me sort this out more easily."

"Hey, I'm not in on anything. Especially if you're now accusing me of being a murderer."

Parker shook his head. "That's not what I meant."

Kit sniffed. "Okay. But before we get down to business, I need to know about your place."

"Why?"

"I like to get a landscape fix on my, possible, clients," Kit lied. "Did you inherit all this?"

"Yes," Parker frowned.

"So you grew up here or something? Is this your childhood home?"

"No. I bought this house six years ago. I inherited all the furniture and artwork from my parents in the early nineties."

Artwork? Kit cringed. That means this is *his* idea of interior

262

decorating. "And you bake cakes, and you …?" Kit waved a questioning hand at the boxes and contrivances on the far side of the table.

Parker stood and reached for the carved box, lifted the lid, and turned it to show her the contents: twenty colorful and delicate flies. Fishing flies. Handmade fly-fishing flies.

Ee-yew, anal retentive, Kit thought. "They're gorgeous," she said, and actually meant it.

"I'm still learning. This is my favorite so far," Parker said, pointing to an exotic black insect-like thing. "It's a Woolly Bugger. And this one's a Nymph, and …"

"They really do look like insects," Kit said in amazement.

"That *is* the general idea." Parker actually smiled, and then reached for two of the plastic boxes, lifted the lids, and began pointing out the contents. "I used these black marabou feathers for the Woolly Bugger. The slender ones here are hackle, from the necks of poultry and the like, used for making legs. Flies are often dressed with herl, which are the barbs of feathers; um, these ones are black ostrich. I've also got turkey and quail feathers and pheasant tippets. Sometimes I might use this fine copper wire, or the red floss there for winding onto the hook to make bodies for certain fly patterns.

"In this box," Parker was way off in a little fly-tying world of his own, "there's elk hair, which we use because it's hollow, so it floats. With that grasshopper," he pointed to an elegant critter in the wooden box, "I spun the deer hair onto the hook, and then trimmed it into shape, so it flairs."

Parker suddenly glanced up at Kit in surprise—with himself apparently. "Sorry. This is probably boring as bat shit for you, but I've only just got into the tying, and the fishing, in the last month or so. When my new neighbor came over and introduced himself, and later his hobby, I discovered a whole new recreational world. It's so relaxing."

Kit smiled, politely. "But you don't go fly-fishing at night, do you?"

"At night? Oh. No, we were going out on the bay for whiting that time. Usually we go up the Goulburn River near Thornton, or to the

263

Upper Yarra out the back of Launching Place, where Guy has a weekend shack." Parker cocked his head. "O'Malley? What possible ..."

"Charlie, I know diddly about you. In order for me to work out who might be involved in a so-unlikely attempt to frame you, I need to know why he, she, or they would even want to."

"Obviously to discredit me," he said.

Kit presented her doubtful face. "Given your rep, this conspiracy is more likely designed to embarrass you."

"Why?"

"Because Charlie, it'd be bloody easy *and* tempting. I don't mean to be rude—sorry, yes I do—but you've been so vociferous about your prime suspect being a version of the archetypal pulp-fiction evil and murderous lesbian, that you are ripe for any number of practical jokes."

"I don't think the forgery of a police report bearing my name to cast doubt on your friend, O'Malley, is in any way a practical joke—on me or her. What's more, I object to you diminishing my predicament by implying this is being done in fun. Besides, who would?"

"Who would what? Set you up for fun?"

"Yes. Who would frame me? Who would think it's funny?" Parker was beside himself with frustration; and no doubt also questioning his sanity in turning to Kit for help.

"Did you think it was funny when *you* did it? Or was it clever or perhaps strategic then?"

"I just told you, O'Malley, I didn't set your friend up. I swear."

Wasn't talking about Angie, you dickhead. "Well, I think it's funny you reckon someone is framing you. But I'll humor you, Charlie. Let's see. For deadly serious fun, how about the entire Anders and Riley clans who probably think you're taking the easy way out of this murder case by proclaiming the lesbian bar owner *with no known motive* killed their precious Gerry. Or, for just plain old-fashioned fun, how about your colleagues, the gay community, the women's movement, the Reasonable Citizens Brigade, the RSPCA, you name it."

Parker swallowed, rearranged his shoulders, and tried not to glare at her.

Strange, she thought. He *really* wants to hire me. Why? *Der.* He's probably tried every other PI in town and they laughed in his face.

"I got a phone call," Parker explained calmly, "suggesting I take a look at the dealings Ms. Nichols had two years ago with the Fitzroy CIB. Her so-called complaint about Anders led us to the restraining order."

"Us? Who's us? You're not using the police force equivalent of the royal We, are you, Charlie, coz I already know the rest of your crew didn't know about this info until the arrest."

Parker cricked his neck again to help his little self stay calm. "*Us,* as in an admin person who collected the report for me, and Constable, um, Hadley from Fitzroy who gave it to her."

Kit refused to even look apologetic. "Have you considered that this has nothing to do with you; except in the sense that someone is trying to frame Angie by using *your* willingness to believe her guilt?"

"If that's the case why use my name on the forged documents and then give me the info?"

"Did you know your name was on those documents?"

"Of course not, O'Malley," Parker stressed, "*that's* what I'm trying to tell you."

"Charlie, I'm over the fact that you forged them, okay; but it's pretty fucking obvious you didn't look at them properly either, did you? And why? Coz you didn't want to; coz you didn't need to; coz you thought you had proof that *your* suspect was it. Am I right?"

"Yes."

"And *that* is probably what the mystery person behind this little hoax was banking on," Kit said, regarding Parker with the same incomprehension she gave the giant mutant moths that stupidly rammed their heads into her patio windows to get to the light inside. She took a breath. "You have a brutally and melodramatically over-murdered known criminal whose *already-dead* body was, according to the forensic pathologist, moved from somewhere completely else to the place you first saw it ..."

Whoa, and hang on! The officer of suspicion in Kit's mind threw a pebble onto the track in front of her train of thought: Parker and Anders—Chuck and Gerry. No. Wait for the facts.

265

"And yet," she continued, "because of the nature of the place in which he was found—and again I say, *not* the primary crime scene—your natural, prejudice-inspired notion is that the woman who called the police, about the dead person who'd been *left* on her premises, must be the killer because ..." Kit shrugged. "Why?"

"Because, O'Malley, your friend is a homo, a gay, a dyke, a lezzo. You know, a pervert."

"Oh, that's why," Kit remarked, demonstrating incredible self-control. Strangling would be the way to go with this, she thought.

"Yeah, but no offense, you know."

"What do you mean, no offense?" Yep, the full hands-on approach.

"I mean, I didn't mean to offend *you*, I was just explaining my thought process at the time. Although I am entitled to think what I like."

"That *is* true," Kit nodded. "And we could make a fortune bottling your thoughts and selling them to the neo-Nazis and other tiny minds of this world. But what's your real beef, Charlie? Did you try a bit of poofter bashing once, and come off second best or something?"

Parker looked defiant.

Kit squinted at him. "You're really telling me that your alleged mind went from witness to woman to lesbian to pervert to murderer?"

Parker shrugged an affirmative.

"Think about it, Charlie," Kit said, in a tone that suggested his reasoning was merely flawed, and not begging to be hit with a cricket bat, "that doesn't necessarily follow, because *you* being an unenlightened bigoted wanker doesn't make *you* a serial killer."

Parker raised an eyebrow. "Will you take my case or not?"

Kit glared at him and his audacity. "Yes," she said.

But, she thought, I'm going to charge you like a bitch on lighter fuel, find the hero who's framing you, and help them finish the job.

"Excellent," Parker said.

You're telling me, Kit thought. "I require a two hundred dollar cash deposit on signing of my contract," she decided. "After that, it's a hundred bucks an hour, plus expenses."

"What? You've got to be kidding!"

Kit shrugged. "I've got three other jobs on the go, Charlie. You won't get a daily rate coz there's only so many hours in the day. This way, you pay for exactly what I do."

It was Parker's turn to glare at her damn cheek. "Fine," he agreed.

"Meet me here," Kit pulled out a business card, "at my office at 9 a.m. tomorrow. I need names—of cops, crooks, friends, enemies, relatives, or anyone you can think of who might be behind this. I also want the names and contact numbers of any cops, admin staff, or gofers who helped secure those now-discredited documents for you; and think about anything else that's been weird or out of the ordinary lately. Okay?"

"Okay," Parker agreed.

Chapter 21

Kit followed Will Thumpya down the hallway, trying to figure out whether her gremliny grumpiness was the result of: a) not having spent the night with Alex; b) being idiotic enough to make a 9 a.m. appointment with anyone, especially Chucky Parker; or c) unrelenting and vicious PMT. Realizing it could be a fiendish mix of all three, she told herself that now would be a good time to turn around and go home *before* Queenie Riley called in a favor for a favor, for a debt for a job, for a … Shit! This really was how people got into beholden-to-the Mob-type situations.

The silent Mr. Thumpya left Kit at the door of the kitchen, where old Ms. Riley awaited her like a spider in a web. Granted, she was a homely granny spider, dressed in a crimson silk track suit and lurking in a scone-scented web; but Kit refused to be completely hoodwinked.

"Good morning, Kit."

"Morning, Queenie. They smell perfect." Kit deliberately chose a different chair from her last visit, so there was no chance of a recognizable routine happening here in the familiar kitchen of the now-friendly Riley home.

"Thank you, dear," Queenie smiled, looking even more Anne Bancroft than usual. "I may be a novice with the Asian cuisine, but I'm a dab hand at scones. Now pour a coffee, while I tend to the jam and cream and ask you why you didn't think to tell me you used to be a cop."

Whoa! Incoming curly from way out in left field.

Queenie was getting important scone condiments from the fridge but obviously required an answer, because when she turned back her face was as expectant as Kit's was puzzled.

"Um, because my status as an ex-anything wasn't relevant?" Kit shrugged.

"I would have thought that your past as a police officer would enhance your credentials for your line of work," Queenie noted, sitting opposite Kit.

"Usually," Kit nodded. "But, given your relationship with the force, I doubt you'd have been impressed. Also you didn't ask for my CV or references, and I wasn't offering you my services. You just wangled them out of me."

"Is that what I did?" Queenie laughed. "And what are my chances of doing that again?"

"Just like last time, it depends what you want," Kit stated, wishing she'd stayed home in bed, even without Alex.

"I wish to visit a friend," Queenie smiled, "and was hoping you'd take me to see him."

"Me? Why?" Do *not* fall for this one, Kit thought. "I don't think so," she said.

"Why not?" Queenie asked in surprise.

Because I'm not a bloody idiot, she thought. "Because I'm not a driver for hire," she said.

Queenie chuckled. "I'm not asking you to drive the getaway car while I rob the TAB."

"No, but that'll be next," Kit predicted.

"No, dear. I only take volunteers for armed robberies," she said deadpan, while offering the scones.

Ha ha! Do not go where *she* wants you to with this. Kit chose the biggest scone. Are you listening, O'Malley?

Oh obviously not, she realized, as she heard herself taking the "give me more info before I decide" route. "*Why* is a better question than why not, Queenie. Followed by *who*—as in, who do you want to visit. So, why me when you have a Sasha and a Will and nephews and staff and whatnots?"

"The reason 'why you,' is actually because of the 'who.'"

Kit's mind whimpered: you do not want to know this, O'Malley. Don't ask. If you ask, then you're a bloody fool. "Who is the who?" the fool asked, reaching for the strawberry jam.

"Leo Barker."

"Papa Leo?" Kit said. "Blimey! Now the answer really is no, Queenie. For starters, you said you wanted to visit a friend."

"Leo is a friend," Queenie said. "Or he was. And I'd like to visit him in hospital, in case he never makes it out. I can't ask anyone in the family because they'd never understand."

"Stack me with the family, Queenie, because I don't understand, either. I don't get it, or you, or this whole feud thing or …"

"But Kit, dear, that's the point. You don't have to, or need to; that's why you're perfect."

Kit was shaking her head. "Nope. Am not. No way," she said emphatically. And please stop calling me dear!

"Gra-an!" It was Sasha a-hollering.

Queenie rolled her eyes. "That child is always yelling."

Kit noted that Queenie did not respond; she simply waited for the child to find them.

"Here you are," Sasha exclaimed cheerily on entering the kitchen. "Oh, hello, Kit."

Now *there* was an attitude shift. Apparently, saving Missy Riley from the clutches of the wicked Toad was worth something. Coming so close to possible death had not, however, knocked any clothes sense into Sasha; but hey, she was still young, and breathing, and might yet grow out of the slave to the five-minute fashion re-trend.

"How's the arm?" Kit asked, jumping as her jeans pocket began to vibrate. Bloody Hector!

Sasha waved the plastered appendage, but frowned. "I can't feel a thing, but are you okay?"

"Yeah. Hector put my mobile on silent but silly mode. Excuse me a sec." Kit wriggled to get at her phone. "O'Malley," she said.

"Um."

"Oh no," Kit groaned, "what now?"

"I thought I should apologize before you start thinking bad things about me."

"I already do; but why do *you* think I would?"

"Because I gave Doghouse the heads up."

Kit pinched the bridge of her nose. "About what?"

"About you planning a visit to his boat."

"Why?" Kit shook her head, then remembered he couldn't see her. "Boxer, why did you do that, and why are you now telling me that you did?"

"Oh."

"Oh?" she repeated. "What the hell does that mean?"

"It means, oh you obviously haven't seen today's paper yet. Ring me when you have. I'm at the bar."

"Boxer," Kit said to a non-responsive dial tone. She smiled at Queenie. "Do you get a daily paper delivered?"

"The *Sun* is probably still in the front garden." Queenie indicated to Sasha with a nod that she should run and take a look. "What's up?" she asked.

"Don't know yet. But I doubt I'm going to like it." Kit drank her coffee, refilled the cup, and prepared another scone, with lots of jam and double cream, so she could enjoy something about today-so-far before it went the rest of the way to hell in its bent little hand-basket.

Sasha returned with the newspaper through which she was rifling, an action she continued on the table for Kit, who was still busy with the scone eating.

"Stop, go back," Kit mumbled round her mouthful. "Oh bugger."

There, on page three, in all his black-white and grayish identikit glory, was Mark Dixon. Adding to the surprise—as if it wasn't *enough* that Doghouse was Rabbit's prime suspect in the not-quite-witnessed murder of Sheryl Mapp, or "Jane Doe" as the paper was still calling her—was the very odd fact that he looked almost how Kit remembered him; and not at all how he'd appeared to her yesterday.

So maybe it's *not* him, Kit frowned. Maybe it's a brother or a doppelganger. Or maybe you've been well and truly had, O'Malley.

"What, what, what?" Queenie was saying. "In fact, both of you, what?"

As Queenie headed for their side of the table, Kit realized Sasha was doing her own version of "I can't process what I'm seeing."

"Oh, him," Queenie noted. "What's he done? Oh, he's killed someone. For the record, that is not why I know him."

"You know him?" Kit *and* Sasha exclaimed.

271

"I know a lot of people," Queenie declared. "His name's Mark Docker. He did a little job for me about twelve months ago."

"Nuh," Sasha said. "His name's Marco."

"Marco?" Kit repeated.

"Yeah, he's Tina's boyfriend. Remember? You saw him on Sunday night at the Blaazt."

Kit cast her already-reeling mind back, then yanked it in again. "I saw the rear view of a muscle-bound, blue-haired bimbo," Kit said.

"Yeah, Marco, the old yob. That's what his front looks like."

Kit looked seriously at Queenie. "What kind of job? And yes, I really want to know."

"He brought something back from Sydney for me," Queenie said hesitantly. "It was a unique and valuable collection of necklaces."

Kit sighed. "Let me guess. Not paid for, by you or him?"

"Not exactly," Queenie admitted. "Nor by Gerry, who organized it for me."

Kit tapped the identikit picture. "Let's get this straight. You, Queenie, know this suspected murderer as an 'acquirer' named Mark Docker; and you, Sasha, know him as Marco, the boyfriend of your friend Tina. I take it that neither of you knew the other knew what you knew about him. Or even that you both knew him at all."

Queenie and Sasha looked at each other, then back at Kit and nodded.

"I have the feeling you are also acquainted with him," Queenie noted.

"Oh yes. This here is Mark Dixon, aka Doghouse; previously, just like me, also a member of the Victoria Police ..."

Queenie thumped the table. "I swear if it wasn't too late, I'd kill that nephew of mine."

"... unlike me, however," Kit continued, "Doghouse was drummed unceremoniously out of the force several years back for conduct unbecoming."

"Meaning?" Queenie queried.

"Meaning the bastard was bent and stupid."

"You mean he got caught," Queenie smiled.

"That explains his connection to Uncle Gerry," Sasha stated.

Queenie returned to her chair and fiddled with her hair while gazing thoughtfully at Kit. "What do you think this has to do with Gerry's death?" she finally asked.

Kit threw her arms out. "I don't know whether it does. *You* said they knew each other. All *I* know, is that Doghouse is wanted in connection with this other murder on Sunday night."

"I'm going to ring Tina and ask her," Sasha proclaimed.

Kit shook her head, as Queenie pronounced, "You'll do no such thing."

"I'm with your grandmother on that one," Kit said.

"But," Sasha began.

"No buts," Queenie said sternly. She turned to Kit. "Are you thinking what I'm thinking?"

Let's see, Kit thought, I'm thinking: Mark Dixon is a murdering bastard; home now and no horse sparing; Boxer Macklin is setting you up for something so incredibly convoluted it can't possibly be likely; maybe Alex would like to visit New Zealand too; Doghouse was expecting you at his boat yesterday so he was—what?—in disguise; bent Boxer is possibly stupid too, coz he warned Dixon; a bourbon would be nice, no it's too early; Doghouse Dixon cut Sheryl's throat; Doghou ... shit, I feel sick; Doghouse knew Gerry— a fact, now; Doghouse *killed* Gerry—unlikely; Doghouse was Toad's bent cop—possibly; Doghouse killed Toad—also possible; Doghouse has girls in every port—obviously, coz he has an Ellie in Hastings and a Tina in Melbourne; Boxer Macklin is so going to pay for this, whatever it is; and, whatever it is, Mark Doghouse Dixon is not smart enough to be organizing any of it. So, the big question is, who the hell is he working for? You idiot, Kit scowled. Doghouse Dixon and Boxer Macklin are mates.

"Kit?"

"I don't know. I'm thinking so many things at once, that not one of them is making sense."

"Do you think this man killed my nephew?"

"I doubt it," Kit said honestly. Whether it was true or not, was another matter. "He might be the hoodlum we talked about taking advantage of Gerry's murder to get at you for some reason. It's remotely possible he hired Toad."

"But why?" Queenie asked.

"You're asking me?" It was Kit's turn to study Marjorie Riley, because for an otherwise intelligent person she was being remarkably obtuse. "Queenie, there must be a hundred reasons why this city's largest crime family is being targeted by secret forces in the community. It's my guess there's more than a few crooks, bent ex-cops, and maybe even some good guys, who have an ongoing interest in you and yours."

"I meant why him, Kit," Queenie pointed to the newspaper.

"No idea," Kit said. "He's not terribly bright, so I'd say he's a hireling. But for what or for whom, no clue. He may have nothing to do with anything that's happened to you. As I said, all I know is *this*," she tapped the paper, "that he's wanted for questioning over a murder."

"*And* he's my friend's boyfriend," Sasha reminded them.

"That is Tina's problem, not yours," Kit said. "She's the one dating a possible murderer."

"And you are to stay right away from her. Until we know what's what." Queenie ignored Sasha's pout, but looked like she was gearing up for the obvious.

Kit shook her head. "Uh-uh. I may be the PI, Queenie, but you're in a much better position to find out who Dixon might be working for, and whether it's connected to you or not."

"I suppose so," Queenie sighed, obviously amused that Kit had technically refused her again, before she'd even asked.

"And when you find that out, you can fill me in on what the hell is going on," Kit smiled, deciding in that moment that she had to go visit Boxer Macklin, and beat him to a pulp and then ...

Crikey and be damned! Doghouse Dixon also knows Scooter's girlfriend Chrissie Whatever. Well, *der*, that's how all this is known; because Rabbit saw him with Chrissie, then Sheryl.

Get out of here now, O'Malley. "I have to go now," she said.

"Just like that?" Sasha said.

Kit nodded. "Yes. All of this," she waved her hand at the newspaper, "and just like that."

◆◆◆

On the drive from Queenie's house to Boxer's bar Kit mulled over the possibility that Tina's Marco, aka Doghouse, *was* also the ex-cop, ex-husband of Scooter's girlfriend, Chrissie.

Don't be silly, O'Malley. That is too stupid and far-fetched for words. They might know each other, though, Doghouse and the ex-cop-husband.

And, she argued, what was it that she and Enzo had touched on last week about finding someone to rat on, or sell out, the city's major crime family? That it would take months of undercover work to find the right someone to squeal—*if* you were the good guys, and the idea was to rack up some convictions.

But what if you were the bad guys? What if you were trying to deal the Rileys *and* the Barkers out of the game? In that case, if your objective was to bring down both houses by inciting a bigger war between them, then standing on the sideline while operating spies or unwitting accomplices in *each* camp, would be the way to go.

Wouldn't it, Boxer?

And if you were on the side of the sideline, letting your mate Doghouse work his girlie agents—Tina with the Rileys through Sasha, and Chrissie with the Barkers through Scooter—then it would appear to all and sundry that you, and *your* employer (head of the city's *other* criminal clan), were completely unconnected to this devious plot.

What's more, O'Malley, if you think for even a moment that any of this is vaguely possible, then you're in dire need of help and a good dose of something you're sorely lacking—reality.

Kit rang Scooter to find out if *she'd* discovered the identity of the guy she and Rabbit had seen with Chrissie on Sunday night or, failing that, the name and current serving-status of the ex-husband. When, as per usual, Ms. Farrell did not answer her phone, Kit rang Rabbit.

"Yo."

"Rabbit, it's Kit. Can you do me a favor?"

"No worries."

"Can you find Scooter, in person, and tie her to a chair somewhere so I can talk to her."

"Okay," Rabbit said agreeably. "I'll ring you when she's contained."

Contained? "Thanks mate."

Kit parked her car right out the front of Swiggers in Prahran and strode inside, looking for Andrew Boxer Macklin who—if he knew what was good for him—better not turn out to be a criminal master-mind. He was sitting at the bar going through a stack of receipts.

"Hey, O'Malley," he said, warily cheerful. "I'm sorry, I really am. If I'd known what that stupid prick had been up to I'd never have called him."

Kit punched Boxer in the mouth and knocked him clean off his stool.

"What the hell was that for?" he asked from the floor, waving off Mr. Muscle the barman.

Kit held her hand out to help him up. "If I find out that you're behind any of this crap, so help me Boxer, I'll offer you up as a sacri-fice to the city's blood-feuding crime families—the two you don't already work for, that is."

"I swear I'm not behind anything," Boxer insisted, rubbing his mouth. "Man, that's a mean right hook you've got; no wonder you got the jump on Toad."

"Don't mention him either," Kit snapped. "Just tell me why you told Doghouse I was looking for him."

"Coz he was a mate." Boxer looked suitably contrite.

"*Was* a mate," Kit repeated, her hands indicating bafflement and the need to strangle. "Was! You blokes are amazing. No, you're unfathomable. I can't begin to work out how men have held the balance of power in this world for as long as you have. Actually, the bigger mystery is why *we* women haven't risen up and poisoned you all like weeds."

"Are you having a bad day, Kit?" Boxer asked.

"You really don't want to know. Ask your biffo-boy there to pour me a bourbon and I might reconsider my original plan to call Marek and dob you in for Toad's untimely demise."

"Why me?"

"Why not?"

"Because I had nothing to do with it?" Boxer shrugged.

"Like I care," Kit shrugged back. "Was Doghouse ever married?"

"No. At least, not that I know of."

"Did he ever live with or have a thing with someone called Chrissie?"

"Again, not that I know of. But who's this Chrissie? Yesterday you asked me if *I* was married to her."

"I don't know who she is. It's possible Doghouse does, though."

"So?"

"So nothing," Kit lied. "Why did Chucky give Gerry Anders that alibi?"

"I don't know."

Kit glared at him, then nodded her thanks to the barman.

"I really don't know why," Boxer stated. "That's why I gave the lead to you, Kit. I have my suspicions about stuff in general, but not that in particular; even though I think the particular thing, the reason for the alibi, is what led to the general shit I'm suspicious about."

Kit peered at the usually coherent Andrew Macklin. "Are you on drugs?"

"Don't be cute," he said. "I don't know what Gerry had on that bastard, but whatever it was, it made Charlie Parker bend right over and take it up the clacker."

"Charming; I don't think. Was Gerry involved in the scams you guys were running?"

"Nope."

Kit waited for any kind of elaboration, then gave up and jabbed Boxer once, but firmly, on his forehead with her index finger. "*You* got me this far into this, Box, so hand over your suspicions or I'm gone, never to return. What connection did Chuck and Gerry have?"

"Apart from the curious alibi," Boxer said, "I think Gerry was one of Chuck's snitches."

Kit ran her hand through her hair. "Gerry Anders? A police informer? Are you mental?"

Boxer squinted. "I think he gave Chucky info, to exact revenge on people he didn't like. He may even have pulled jobs to set people up. Chuck would then 'solve the crime.'"

Kit's open mouth said more than any words. She reached for her bourbon and drank it.

Boxer waved at his barman to leave the bourbon bottle on the bar. "I think those fires in Willy and Geelong were part of it."

"You think," Kit sighed. "Boxer, that was an insurance scam which involved all the Melbourne crime families *except* the Rileys."

"Yeah," he nodded. "But I believe Gerry was the torch. That man loved a fire."

"This is all speculation, isn't it, Box?"

"It's more like an informed guess."

"Who informed you?"

"An insurance broker named Neil Porter."

"You mean Nathan-Nino-Nigel."

"I do?"

"Yeah. They're all really a bloke named Nigel Pippineetal."

"That's a really stupid name," Boxer said. "So now what?"

"Are you playing me?"

"No."

"Why are you doing this, then?"

"Because Graham Charles Parker deserves to be got."

Kit laughed. "But he got *you* fair and square, Boxer."

"That's not the issue, Kit."

"Is he bent?"

"Not in the usual sense."

Kit sniffed. "There shouldn't be a usual sense," she said, drumming her fingers on the bar. "So Chucky's not *bent* bent, but you're implying he knew what Gerry was doing. Do you think he knew he was arresting the wrong people?"

Boxer inspected his thumbnail for a year. "Don't know. But you and I do know that Charlie *bends* the rules he's such a stickler for, to make sure they don't get broken. He needs taking down a peg or two."

Kit regarded Andrew Macklin, the good bad cop, thoughtfully. "I found out yesterday that Deon Mason was killed in a hunting accident not long after he went opal mining," she said.

Boxer frowned, then reached for the bourbon bottle.

Chapter 22

Life as we know it, Jim! Kit smiled and cradled her macciato as she contemplated the historical significance of the alfresco table she'd chosen. Living—being, going-on, whatever—would simply not be worth much without the Lygon Street legacy. Toto's Pizzeria, for instance, where she sat waiting for Enzo and their client, was an institution in a Melbourne street that was itself a national cultural and culinary landmark. Although it was doubtful that last century's local Italian migrants could have foreseen the impact of importing the city's first espresso machine, Carlton's Lygon Street was indisputably the birthplace of Melbourne's café culture. And, despite the influx of other international cuisines into the dining and shopping precinct, the area would forever be Little Italy.

And not just, Kit noted, because of the number of Italian restaurants, cafés, and businesses that still existed in among the Thai, Spanish, Vietnamese, and so-called modern Australian eateries (which as far as Kit was concerned *was* Thai, Spanish, and Vietnamese); nor because of the still mostly Italian-themed annual Lygon Street Festival. No it was because, like the upper reaches of a river that siren-called the return of spawning salmon, Lygon Street was the place to which a breed of fans, of Italian descent, returned in times of … soccer. And here they would celebrate and litter or riot and wreck, depending on whether a particular foreign team on the other side of the bloody world had succeeded or failed in a stupid ball-kicking contest.

Kit felt a vexatious need to rant about this incomprehensible phenomenon but, as she was alone, hailed a waiter instead and ordered another coffee. She rejected the thought that a cup of camomile hippy piss would be more calming.

She scanned the restaurant interior again, verifying that Toto's was still crowded with early lunchers, many of whom were probably students from Melbourne Uni; checked the outdoor tables for signs of an early appearance by her ratty informant; and then became so intrigued by the strange auricle hair of the person at the next table that her four remaining wits were easily relieved of duty when someone gripped her shoulders from behind.

Kit swore, then smiled up at the handsomely attired Enzo McAllister, and the pink-swathed horror that was Sarah Boyes-Lang on a Wednesday. Kit held her breath until her lunch companions sat down because, thank the sea turtles or someone, the table hid most of what her client was wearing. While shocked by the whole pinkness of the woman, Kit did make the positive observation that Sarah had at least left her cat's-bum face at home today. She had instead, and sadly for all who had to see it, brought her Mick Jagger mouth out for an airing. Kit couldn't decide, however, if those lips had been attacked by a collagen-wielding nutter or several large wasps.

One thing Kit did know was that lunch as she knew it, was not going to be easy. Thankfully, though, the cosmetically enhanced future mother-in-law of a Russian-American almost royal, had managed to kick nearly all thoughts of soccer hoolis into the next World Cup.

"Sorry we're late," Enzo smiled.

"It's nice to see you, Katherine," Sarah said, rearranging her lips over her teeth.

Kit smiled. "And I do enjoy closing a case with a positive outcome, and in person, Sarah."

"Lorenzo tells me you have good news."

"Yes," Kit smiled. Good for Gregor and Vanessa, she thought. She paused while the waiter took their drink orders, then she proceeded to ruin her client's week. "My associate carried out a thorough background investigation on Gregor Tereshenko," she said. "He is the son of two New York doctors. Gregor Senior is a psychiatrist, and Junior's mother, Irina, is a paediatric surgeon. His maternal grandfather was also a doctor; and his paternal grandparents were concert musicians.

"Gregor has a PhD in Linguistics, a Masters in Sociology, and a few little degrees in things like Russian and French. He spent the last six years studying Linguistics in Russian in Moscow. His passport and hotel itinerary indicates that his travel route from Russia through several European countries to Greece, where he met Vanessa, was typical of the kind of first-class world tour taken by those who can afford it. In a nutshell, Gregor Tereshenko is exactly who and what he claims to be."

As Kit spoke, Sarah Boyes-Lang's eyes had widened, but not in pleasure. And yet, "Excellent, I'm so pleased," she said, without a skerrick of honesty.

"Didn't I say you had nothing to worry about, Sarah," Enzo said, squeezing Kit's knee.

"So you did," Sarah agreed. "But you are sure, Katherine?"

"Quite sure," Kit said cheerily.

Sarah nodded thoughtfully. "Lorenzo's genealogical investigation proved Gregor's royal Russian lineage to be valid; so I'm glad your investigation indicates that he is also an upright citizen in all respects." If her face had been a tea strainer, not one drop of sincerity would have made it through the lie-clogged mesh. Her truth was stuck in there somewhere.

The waiter reappeared with Sarah's complicated lowfat, decaffeinated, what's-the-point coffee and Enzo's Heineken, which gave them each a chance to look elsewhere and regroup. Kit dragged her attention from Mrs. Pufferlips to gaze vacantly at her fellow Melburnians who were pretending, like she, that the sun being out meant that thirteen degrees was warm enough to be sitting outside. She zipped up her jacket and ... Okay, forget the vacant staring, she thought, as she caught sight of the Fairy-Following Feds, lurking at the café next door.

Memory flash! Ah, she must remember to ask Hector if he'd found out anything about the two not-so-secret agents from the photo he'd taken last Friday.

"Are you aware that Nip and Tuck are at yon table?" she asked Enzo quietly.

"Mm," he nodded, "couldn't shake them without frightening the hoojahs out of the harridan. Also, I wasn't driving."

Sarah finished fussing with her calorie-free sweetener and turned to Kit. "With Gregor being so rich and clever, are you sure there's nothing else there? Like a wife perhaps?" The poor dear so wanted there to be a spouse or rent boy, or a criminal record, or pending bankruptcy.

"There's no wife," Kit reassured her, *not*. "You're putting on a brave face; but you're not as happy as you're making out, are you Sarah?" Kit's tone was full of understanding, while her hand held Enzo's in a physical demonstration of mirth.

Sarah Boyes-Lang looked sheepish, although Kit knew there'd never be a sheep with lips like hers. "I admit I was hoping there'd be a skeleton in his closet," Sarah said. "But only because I don't wish to lose my darling Nessa to marriage *so soon* ..."

So soon? She's twenty-four for ewe's sake, Kit thought.

"... especially when she may spend part of her future ..."

Not to mention your money.

"... in a foreign land."

"New York is hardly a foreign land, Sarah," Enzo pointed out. "It only takes a few long hours to fly there. And they do speak English, of a sort."

"Yes, I know all that. Perhaps it's the age difference that still worries me." Straw-clutching was a serious sport in some Melbourne suburbs.

"Oh Sarah," Enzo berated her in as friendly a tone as one could muster for a selfish, not-very-old, but complete and utter bitch. "It's only thirteen years."

"And, correct me if I'm wrong, Sarah," Kit said sweetly, "but wasn't your second husband eighteen years your senior?"

Sarah's eyebrows shot up—perhaps in surprise that the private investigator knew stuff about *her*—but she covered well by tilting her head and redirecting her gaze to where Kit's cleavage would have been if she had one. "No, you're not wrong, Katherine. Maurice *was* older, but then so was I when we married." She met Kit's gaze. "Older than Vanessa, I mean. I was in my thirties, and wiser than my daughter; yet look how that union turned out. Disaster!"

Diddums, Kit thought. And then, *struth!* her mind alerted her, as another walking tragedy caught her attention. She ran a mental

ID check on the bloke who'd just entered Toto's: long nose, beady eyes, comb-treads in the thin Brylcreamed hair, scrag of bum-fluff under the little mouth—definitely homo-rodentus. Morley, Queenie's contact and hopefully the only man in town wearing a red and yellow plaid jacket with brown flecked trousers and white loafers, chose a small window table inside. White loafers! Kit cringed, wondering whether there was a bad-taste convention happening at the nearby Royal Exhibition Building.

"Would you two mind if I excused myself from lunch?" Kit asked. "I actually have another appointment and because you were running a little late ..." Kit left the sentence hanging.

"That's fine, Katherine," Sarah jumped in first. "In fact I might beg off too. It seems my case is definitely closed, for which I thank you both. I might pop off home."

Enzo looked from Kit to Sarah and smiled accommodatingly. "Suits me."

"I can give you a lift home if you like, Enzo," Kit offered.

"Wonderful," he nodded.

Sarah Boyes-Lang, unsatisfied client, took her leave and her lips and left them to it.

"Thank Judy and the chorus line!" Enzo exclaimed. "And thank you for coming up with a way to end that torture."

"My pleasure, sweetie," Kit grinned. "Although it's true. I do have a meeting. See that gentleman on his lonesome in the window there."

"Och, you're kidding," Enzo exclaimed. "Quick, let's catch Sarah and introduce them. With his dramatic dress sense he could have made hubby number four."

Kit left Enzo with his beer, and sauntered inside to talk to the hopefully informative bookie. "Are you Morley?" she asked, just to be sure.

"O'Malley?" His tone was hushed, but flabbergasted.

Kit sat opposite him and cut right to the chase. "Our mutual friend says you might be able to fill me in on her late nephew's possible connection to a certain officer of the law."

He sniffed, twice. "She's actually a *friend* of yours?" Now his tone mixed awe and fear.

"Oh yeah," Kit assured him. You fool, she thought.

Morley nodded and leaned forward. "About ten years back, a certain *Mr.* Parker thought he had Gerry over a barrel for some shit he'd done. Turns out *having*, but doing nothing about that shit when he should've, kinda re-versed the pecking order."

Speak English, Kit begged silently. "Can you elaborate?"

"Mr. Parker caught Gerry red-handed in the act of almost possibly setting a fire."

"How?"

Morley smiled with self satisfaction. "Someone tipped him off."

"You?"

"No."

"But you know who," Kit said.

"Gerry."

"What?"

"Yes. Gerry a-nonymously tipped Mr. Parker off about a job that he, Gerry, was not really about to do; so he could pre-*tend* to ask for a break by proposing a contra deal. Gerry offered Mr. Parker ongoing information in ex-*change* for being let off a crime that was actually bogus."

"Did Chu, Mr. Parker know it was fake?" Kit asked, worried she'd lose the thread because of the distracting emphasis Morley placed on his words. It was as if he had verbal hiccups.

"No, not till years later."

"When Gerry asked for the alibi for the hit and run?" Kit prompted.

"No, before that," Morley said. "Gerry worked Parker like a puppet for a few years, while the mis-*guided* cop thought he had the arson a-*ttempt* to dangle over Gerry forever. When Mr. Parker changed squads, Gerry's info changed too, from fires and insurance to burgs and armed robs. Plus, there was one or two jobs that Mr. Parker over-*looked* Gerry for, in ex-*change* for him dobbing in bigger fish. The thing was, Gerry was always the biggest fish."

"Should I be inferring that Gerry pulled or organized jobs," Kit said shrewdly, as if she were working this part out for herself (thank you, Boxer), "but fingered innocent people to keep Parker happy and off his back?"

284

Morley raised his eyebrows. "You're pretty smart."

For a girl, Kit added. "But why Parker?"

"Have you ever met him?"

"Yes," Kit nodded.

Morley's expansive shrug declared "enough said." "You got Gerry's reason as-*kew*, but."

As-kew? Where's this guy from? Kit wondered. "I did? Which part?" she asked.

"There was way more to it than keeping that bloody copper's nose out of his real business. 'Specially as the Rileys, by which I mean Queenie and not the Anders branch, don't mix with the filth. She's got class, that lady. Wouldn't touch a bent copper with a rubber glove."

Oh, that's class all right, Kit agreed. "But Mr. Parker wasn't bent. Technically," she noted.

"Pre-*cisely*," Morley said. "Gerry set out to cultivate a good cop. He didn't want to pay, and therefore be beholden to, a corrupt *de*-tective, coz he figured no way could they be trusted. But a manip-ulated straight cop was a different kind of animal, 'specially if he could be fooled into doing wrong."

Kit snorted. "Except he wouldn't know he'd done anything wrong—until Gerry needed him for something important, that is."

"Bingo! That's why some of the guys Gerry gave Parker on a platter were volunteers."

"You're kidding!" Kit exclaimed.

"Nope, little lady. Gerry handsomely paid anyone who'd take a minor rap just to help set Mr. Parker on the road to Stupidville. Sometimes the crims *were* actually *in*-volved—coz it was easier—but oftentimes they had no connection and just needed some dosh. And every now and then, Gerry would also set up someone he just plain didn't like."

Little lady! Kit narrowed her eyes. "You were one of the volun-teers?"

"I was indeed. Fall guy number one, that's me. Took a short sentence for a warehouse fire that Gerry set and I watched burn. Mind you, he paid me twenty grand up front just to sit around in jail for seven months and another five and a job when I got out."

"Did any of these crimes include a set of fires in the western suburbs?" Kit asked.

"That was a profitable en-*deav*or," Morley grinned, "but no one got caught that time."

Kit shook her head in disbelief. "Apart from being a crook, an arsonist, and whatever else, what was Gerry like? Was he a nice guy?"

"Shit no," Morley laughed. "Gerry was a prick. You wouldn't ever wanna get on his bad side; but if he said he'd do something, he would do it—whatever it was. You could re-*ly* on that. If you were on his team, he'd do anything for you: medical care, child support while you were in-*side*—whatever. If you played by his code, hell, he'd even kill for you. Flipside: if you let him down or broke his rules, then it was best to leave town or wake up dead."

What a way to live—or die—Kit thought. "Did he kill the Sherwoods?"

"What do you reckon?"

Kit raised an eyebrow and nodded. She wished Hector's superbug was in her hand instead of lying on Chucky's windowsill. "What about Alan Shipper?"

Morley raised his small hands and shook his head. "Better ask *your* friend about that one."

My friend? Bloody Queenie, Kit thought. She *had* asked her about Shipper, but that cagey old tart had evaded the question by deflecting Kit's attention towards the Barkers.

Kit frowned. "Okay. Mister Parker unwittingly put all these wrong people away, until such time as Gerry needed him for something big. Was that the alibi three years ago?"

Morley shrugged. "First there was a clincher. About two months before that alibi became necessary, Gerry orchestrated a meeting at which Parker, accidentally on purpose, was a witness to Gerry beating a bloke to death."

"Oh, man!" Kit moaned.

Morley actually reached out and gave Kit's hand a there-there pat. "It's okay," he said. "I mean it's not right, but this man really wasn't a very nice person."

I don't want to know, Kit's mind wailed. "What did Ch ... Mr. Parker do?"

"He went hys-*ter*ical, pulled his gun, and was threatening every-one with arrest and bodily harm, until he got knocked unconscious. Whack, boom, down he went." Morley looked left and right, then leaned even closer. "I did that part. When Parker came to, Gerry explained to him just what his famous arrest record—and there-fore his reputation, not to mention his ob-noxious ego—were built on."

Kit shook her head in amazement. "Lies and deceit on a grand scale," she said. "So Parker *couldn't* do anything about the dead guy because of everything else; and because he didn't, Gerry really had him dangling when he needed an alibi."

"You catch on real fast."

"Do you know who killed Gerry?"

Morley shook his head. "Wish I did. *Your* friend, his aunt, would no doubt look favorably on anyone who could answer that ques-tion."

"You must have your suspicions," Kit prompted.

He laughed. "Mr. Parker springs to mind as having the most to gain; but I doubt he'd have the balls. There's a number of folks out there who are not *mour*-ning his passing, his wife included, no doubt. Strongest rumor I've heard, though, is that it's payback for the *Sher*-woods. And I ain't speaking no names in that regard. Sorry."

In an attempt to round up her thoughts, Kit glanced out the window—straight into the eyes of the overly curious secret agent Snick. Or was it Snack? He dropped his gaze immediately while his surveilling partner grabbed a menu to hide behind. Crikey! They are the world's worst spies, Kit thought.

She returned her attention to Morley. "Do you know anything about Parker's internal affairs case against some cops a few years back?"

"If you're talking about that mad son of a bitch, Pauly-J, then yes but not much."

Kit raised an eyebrow.

Morley sniffed. "I know that Gerry had a hand in the setup."

Whoa! Wasn't expecting that. "But it wasn't a setup," Kit said. "They *were* on the take."

"Yeah, but Gerry, like a-nonymous phantom-man, helped Mr. Parker set up the sting that got them caught."

Boxer, you bastard! Kit thought. "Did they ever find out about Gerry? The cops I mean."

Morley pulled a face, an even stranger one, and shook his head. "Doubt it. Pauly-J would have done Gerry without hesitation if *he'd* known."

"But *you* know," Kit said. "For sure?"

"Yep. Gerry told me."

Kit took a deep breath. "Do you know any of the other cops involved in that deal?"

"Nope. I was in-*side* when all that went down. Gerry told me about it, but not who, later. Then later still, like maybe in the last year before he got sick and carked it, Pauly-J and I had a few, um, things in common. He didn't talk much, but I knew he used to be filth, and that he hated that nice Mr. Parker something chronic. I just figured he must have been one of 'em."

"And you can't tell me about Alan Shipper," Kit tried again.

"Nuh-uh. That wasn't all down to Gerry, so I'm not dealing with you on that one. As I said, ask the lady who knows."

Chapter 23

"Do you come to charming places like this often?" Enzo's question was dressed in irony and topped with a very butch hat.

"What's with the macho voice?" Kit grinned. She glanced at the bellied, bald, and tattooed boofhead sitting three stools away in front of his very own jug of ale, before widening her eyes at her companion who'd kindly volunteered to sit with her to await the return of Santo from the laundromat. Queenie's second informant lived upstairs in the Hoppers Arms and worked as a barman, but was off-duty for another fifteen minutes. "You do realize that this is an endangered habitat," Kit noted, trying to sound learned. "There aren't many pubs of this kind left in the country, and this is a fine example."

"Of what?" Enzo inhaled his Scotch to smother the pub's ambient aroma. "No, don't tell me."

Kit took him at his word, but smiled nostalgically because in a world infested by family or up-market hotel-bistros and pokies venues, the Hoppers Arms was indeed a dying institution. Her maternal grandfather and his mates spent every Thursday night playing darts in a pub like this; except, of course, his local wasn't old-fashioned then. The public bars were mostly all like this one, though: stinking of beer with just a hint of the urinal, and a bar-top dented by decades of leaning blokes. The Hoppers was a time capsule of early twentieth-century hotel decor, complete with green wall tiles and a serviceable floor so the puke and spilt booze could be hosed out after closing time.

Enzo looked like he was in pain, so Kit tried to distract him with a different kind of torture. "How was your brother yesterday?" she asked. "Did he lecture you on your wicked ways?"

"No. He rang at six in the cold dark of morning to say he hadn't made the flight. So we're doing the sibling rivalry thing for an hour at four this afternoon. I'm actually going out to the airport with Comrade-Duke Tereshenko, who has to pick up a suitcase that has finally tracked him down after taking a wee trip on its own via Istanbul and Delhi."

"Lucky suitcase," Kit noted. "Lucky for you too. Gregor can provide backup should your brother, um," she squinted.

"Nigel," Enzo reminded her.

"Should Nigel's interrogation or rebuking get too rough for you. I still can't believe there's another you out there."

"I told you, Kit, he's not another me," Enzo insisted. "Even my mother maintains she got Nigel from a gypsy in exchange for a dirty pickle jar. Personally, I think the gypsy came out in front."

Kit laughed. "My Dad used to say he found Michael in a Kashmiri spice shop."

"Ah, there's a ditto. I've yet to meet *your* brother, and a male *you* is," Enzo waved his empty hand around, "unimaginable. You and your wonderful mother are nothing alike, so it's anyone's guess what mold your bro has broken."

"All of them," Kit stated. "Michael is ... Well, he's actually deranged. He was born on a houseboat on Dal Lake in Kashmir. The family theory is he was either deprived of oxygen prior to birth—coz Mum spent the last months of the pregnancy even higher up the Himalayas—or he's had too much of the big O ever since returning to sea level. He believes his sub-space link with far-away galactic beings began *in utero*, and that those voices now inspire his art."

Enzo raised an eyebrow. "I see. And is he actually an artist?"

"Oh yes. And a very good one—especially if you like cosmic landscapes, which I do, and abstracts, which I don't."

"Are you close?" Enzo asked, drawing the barman's attention to his empty glass.

Kit shook her head. "Never have been. I love him coz he's my little brother; but Michael and I have nothing in common, except Mum. Lillian understands him even less than she does me; and Michael just doesn't get that he's incomprehensible to his own mother.

"I at least offer Mum a translation service, for both of us

sometimes. And, as you've seen, Mum and I can even socialize with each other's best friends. We also get on quite well, when she's not cracking me up by demonstrating her *idea* of understanding me and my friends, or the whole gay thing, or me being a PI, or how answering machines work, or why her best friend Connie is an accomplished golfer but is no good at cards—don't ask—or just about anything that goes on in the world really."

The barman cleared his throat to indicate the entrance of a guy in jeans and a denim shirt, and carrying a laundry basket, who'd just used his bum to open the front door.

As Santo passed them on his way through, and no doubt upstairs to his room, Kit raised her eyebrows at Enzo. "You want to come with, or wait here?"

"With," Enzo jumped to his feet. "In fact, not waiting at all," he added, following right behind the unsuspecting Santo as he went through the door labeled "Ladies Lounge this way."

"Wait up, Enzo," Kit called after him. While she assumed he'd slow down, she didn't expect him to stop dead on the other side of the door for her to run into.

And then she saw it too. "Oh hell. And we're in it," she groaned, as her senses were assaulted by the red and white floral carpet that *was* the hallway. The carpet was down the corridor, up the stairs, and halfway up the walls where—ye gods—it met the differently patterned gold with black flock wallpaper.

Enzo was transfixed.

"Do you guys need help?" Santo was saying.

"Ah, yeah," Kit replied, jabbing Enzo in the ribs. "Are you Santo?"

"Who wants to know?"

Catwoman, Kit thought. "Name's O'Malley," she said. "Queenie Riley sent me along for a chat. She's heard you might have some info for her."

Santo squinted, as if that would help him evaluate the situation. "You work for Queenie?"

"Yeah. She also wanted me to pass on how pleased she," Kit flipped her palms up, "*we* were with your recent service."

Now you've done it, O'Malley! You could've left the job-approval solely in *her* hands.

"Yeah? She is? You were? Come on up, then. Who's your mate?"

"This is my colleague," Kit rolled her shoulders, "Larry."

This time Enzo jabbed her in the ribs as they followed Santo up to the first floor and along the hall to another corner pocket of Melbourne's underworld. This bloke didn't know them from Victor/Victoria, but room nine at the Hoppers Arms was opened up for Kit and her mate Larry just at the mention of Queenie's name.

Santo's bedsit was large but cluttered, with two long windows that opened onto the hotel's front balcony. The man of the space moved books and clothing from an overstuffed and crooked couch and told them to have a seat.

"We believe," Kit began, hoping Enzo the Fastidious wouldn't suffer an attack of the screaming vapors in this fast food-studded environment, "that you have some news about the recent death of one Sidney Ralph—whom you may know as Toad."

Santo settled in the armchair opposite and nodded. "I heard a, well, it's more than rumor."

"*I've* heard rumors," Kit said. "So what's the more?"

"A confession," Santo nodded. He liked nodding. It was irritating.

"Are we gunna have to drag it out of you, laddie?" Enzo asked—all Scottish brute-like. He was either trying to be helpful or was desperate to get out.

"'Course not," Santo insisted. He glanced at Kit. "What'd you say you do for Queenie?"

"I didn't," Kit stated. "But since you ask, I do personal security. The Toad attacked Queenie's grandkid a few hours before he got dumped in the Yarra. Queenie wants to know why he did that, and I wanna know who saved us from having to deal with the little prick ourselves."

Kit ignored the surprised look that Enzo flashed in her direction; while Santo took to grinning and nodding as if he knew something really special.

"Oh, like wow!" he exclaimed in a dude-voice. "Are you? You are! You're the chick what beat the crap out of him, aren't you? I mean person and, um, no disrespect, at all."

And oh, like this is *too* weird, O'Malley, Kit's mind wailed. You now have a rep with Melbourne's criminal element. This can't be good.

She put on her flinty-eyed "I'm waiting, but not patiently" face, realizing it wasn't all bad either, coz some time today this weed was going to tell her everything. You tough gal, you.

Santo obliged. "One of our regulars was in here late Monday, real pissed and big-noting to anyone who'd listen—which was only me, as it happened—that he'd taken care of The Toad."

"'Taken care' as in looked after, or knocked off?" Kit asked.

Santo nodded and grinned. "Both. First, he reckons he helped Toad get away from you—that is *so* cool—and then he whacked him."

"Details?" Kit asked.

"He said Toad had paid him extra to wait there in the alley; but when he saw *what* Toad done to that girl, and then what you done, he figured he'd get in sweet with the Anders' mob, or maybe Queenie herself, by dealing with him—for them. For you too, I guess."

For me? Oh shit oh merde oh shit! "Paid him extra?" Kit repeated.

"Yeah. The Toad had already paid him to let him into that swanky new nightclub."

Kit laughed a hearty internal laugh. Mr. Disgruntle, the bloody bouncer! So it wasn't Doghouse after all. "He got the sack for that, yeah?"

Santo nodded. "You know who he is, then."

"You tell *me*, Santo. And I need details of the details. Otherwise you're both just wankers."

Nod, nod. "His name's Trevor Wagstaff. Reckons he dragged Toad into his car, then took him down the river and chucked him in." When Kit raised an eyebrow, Santo continued. "Oh yeah, *and* he hit him some more, then hacked at his arms and legs with a machete so the poor dickhead wouldn't be able to swim to shore."

Bingo, and yuk!

Enzo took a sharp breath of the totally unprepared kind, but remained, otherwise, perfectly still.

"Do you know where Trevor lives?" Kit asked.

Santo unearthed a piece of paper from the crap on the coffee table and scrawled an address.

"Thanks," Kit said, getting to her feet. Enzo and Santo followed suit. "Is that all?"

"Yeah." Santo's head was going to noddle right off if he wasn't careful.

"Queenie will be grateful, indeed," Kit said. "We'll be in touch."

"Anytime," Santo offered, hesitating before extending his hand to her, and not to Enzo.

Unaccustomed as she was to getting blokey respect from a bloke, especially when there was another, well, man present, Kit tried not to look too amused.

"I believe," Enzo said, when they'd safely reached the street, "that you have a new fan."

"You think so?" Kit unlocked her car.

"Young Santo is obviously smitten with you, either as a—and I mean no disrespect—*chick* or as *the* chick who beat up a frog."

Kit laughed. "It *was* pretty impressive," she boasted, showing him her fists. "I'll have you know Enzo, that Toad Ralph was a prison prize fighter."

"Really? Well, Ms. Kostya Tzu, I'd love it if you'd rush me home so I can shower that place right out of my hair."

An hour later, Kit rode up in the mirror-walled lift, ignoring herself to the left and right, while wondering whether this was such a good idea. Of course it is, she insisted. You need a fix, O'Malley, and this is the only place to get it. She pulled out her phone and dialed just as the lift doors opened; and her call was answered as she proceeded in through the glass doors.

"Are you in your office?" Kit asked, relieved there was no one in sight.

"Yes."

"Are you alone?" Kit headed down the plush purple hallway.

"Yes."

"Good," Kit said, opening the last door on the right. She stepped in, closed the door, and leaned her back against it.

Alex Cazenove—drop-dead delicious and approvingly surprised—uncurled her long dressed-as-a-lawyer-in-a-skirt legs, stood, and walked casually across the room towards her.

Oh yes, Kit's body cheered, then sighed, then cheered again. The prelude to any Alex-fix was always worth not having seen her for too many hours.

And it wasn't just the afternoon light, casting a halo around her whole body, that augured a divine experience and made Alex so breathtakingly desirable; it was simply that Kit always forgot to breathe around her—well that, and the fact that Alex Cazenove was Kit's own personal revelation.

"Hmm, I know you," Alex smiled, standing close so she could trail her finger from Kit's earlobe, down her throat, and into the cleavage that she still didn't have.

"I missed you," Kit whispered.

"Why are you whispering?" Alex asked, unbuttoning Kit's white shirt.

"Voice just fell into my crotch," Kit croaked, with a huge smile.

"Really, my darling? Should I look for it?"

"Lips first," Kit requested, lacing her fingers through Alex's hair. She kissed her woman—in itself a spine-tingling notion—gently, then passionately, using her tongue, then not; then Alex used hers, then didn't, then ...

"O'Malley?"

"Yes, Alex?"

"I do believe you are seriously aroused." Alex bent her head to take Kit's tinglingly out-there right nipple gently in her lips, then firmly in her teeth.

"Uh-huh," Kit breathed. "You don't say?" She bent a little, to reach under Alex's skirt, clasp her cheeks, and pull her closer. She ran her hand around Alex's thigh, between her legs and felt, hmm, expectation. Alex's breathing and the look in her eyes declared she was a woman working up to something serious and ...

... then she stepped back and shook her head.

Okay, Kit thought. It wasn't an and, it was a but.

No. Not that either, because Alex was still smiling. Seductively.

Yeah, right. Alex just *being* is seductive.

"Is all of you here with me?" Alex asked, her shining gray eyes expressing amusement at Kit's expense, as usual.

Kit nodded. "The parts of me that aren't spinning, are completely in your hands."

Alex laughed and kissed Kit's mouth and her throat, as one hand held Kit's face and the other teased her breasts.

Helpless, Kit thought. I am helpless. And I love it.

Alex was now holding herself infuriatingly out of reach while she caressed Kit's *everything*, and Kit was utterly at Alex's mercy as her lips traveled down over breasts and stomach while she undid Kit's jeans, which Kit helped push down and out of the way. Then Alex was on her knees and her mouth was between Kit's legs and all over her *incredibly* sensitive and meaningful bits, and Kit thought she was going to become one with the actual door, and couldn't tell whose breathing was faster, but knew her own was very loud, and then a cold heatwave rose upwards from Alex's mouth through Kit's groin, flooding everything on its way to her brain where … where … where … white noise, spangles, tremors, and … *Whoa!* A barely contained gasp accompanied Kit's shudder of sheer indescribable pleasure.

And then she went completely limp and Alex tried to catch her before she slid all the way to the floor—which Alex didn't quite manage so they both ended up in a laughing heap, especially Alex who also looked very pleased with herself.

"Wow," she said.

"Wow yourself," Kit grinned, trying to pin Alex to the floor.

Alex pushed back, and ran a finger along Kit's bottom lip. "No, darling, I can't."

"What do you mean, you can't?"

"I mean, when you came," she shook her head, "when you rang and arrived I *was* on my own, but I actually have a client."

Kit sat bolt upright and clasped her shirt to cover herself as she looked around.

Alex snorted with laughter. "You fool. He's in with Douglas at the moment."

"You mean you had your way with me and I can't get you back?"

Alex smiled. "Are you complaining?"

Kit nodded. "A bit. I want *you*," she growled. "Now."

"Can't have me now."

"Later?"

"Oh yes."

Alex helped Kit up off the floor and kissed her gently.

"Don't you start that again," Kit warned her, hauling her jeans up. "And it's best you get yourself sheveled or there'll be an embarrassing moment or two when your client returns."

Alex pulled her skirt back down and then helped Kit button her shirt.

"Did you just come for the sex, Miss O'Malley?"

"I came for a dose of you, Alex. Didn't care how much," Kit grinned. "I needed the look."

"Which look?" Alex asked curiously, while pretending to ignore her phone.

"Your look. Any of them," Kit confessed, then screwed her face up in disbelief as her phone started ringing too. Surrendering to the outside world, which seemed determined to end their brief encounter, Alex headed for her desk and Kit picked her mobile up off the floor. The display told her it was Rabbit.

"Sit down and shut up," Rabbit was saying.

"Hey, Rabbit," Kit said.

"Oh, hey, Kit. I have located and contained Scooter, but she's bein' a right pain. And the language that's comin' outta her mouth is shockin'. *Sit, girlfriend!*"

"Where are you?"

"We're at Scoot's place in Willy. Can you come here? You know where?"

"Yes and yes. I'm in the city, so it should take me about … hang on," Kit hesitated. Alex who'd just got off her own phone, was waving at her.

"If you can wait ten minutes, I'll come with you," Alex said.

Kit nodded. "About half an hour, Rabbit. Please do not let Scooter out of your sight."

Twenty minutes later Kit was driving over the West Gate Bridge. Her attention—or, at least those bits of it that weren't in charge of the car or still doing the post-wow vibration thing—was impressed, as always, by the splendid view out across the docklands on one side and down to the Scienceworks Museum in the historic riverside pumping station on the other.

It struck her as amazing, just how many things a human mind and body could do at the one time. For instance there was everything she'd just thought, while also driving and trying to find a radio station that wasn't playing rap. Plus she *felt* like she was grinning like an idiot, but apparently *looked* like something else because Alex had a different take on where she was at.

"At the risk of getting a serve like that taxi driver who cut you off back there, O'Malley," Alex began, slipping her hand affectionately between Kit's thighs, "are you in a bad mood?"

Kit glanced at Alex. "I was," she smiled, "but you fixed that. As for the taxi driver? I swear at them all the time, often before they do something stupid, just in case they do."

"Do you have high blood pressure, my love?"

"No. And that's *because* I let off steam."

Alex shook her head in amusement. "You were *wildly* tense when you arrived at my office," she said. "You looked like a beautiful thunderstorm."

Kit thrilled-up, gave an embarrassed laugh, and then sighed deeply. "I hit someone."

"A different someone from the now dead one?"

"Yes, and the one this morning was unprovoked. Technically."

"Did he—I assume it was a he—deserve it?"

"Yes. No. Maybe." Kit took the Melbourne Road exit off the bridge, heading south to Williamstown, and filled Alex in on the "who" of Rabbit's identikit pic; the odd connections between Doghouse and Sasha's friend Tina, Queenie, Sheryl, and Chrissie; and finally what she'd done to Boxer.

Alex stroked Kit's face. "Sounds fair to me."

"Nuh-huh. You're humoring me. Why?"

"Because, my love, you need it. And I reckon Boxer had it coming; so it's okay."

"Thank you, Alex, but no it isn't. I've managed not to hit lots of people who deserved it much more than Boxer. Like Chucky, for instance." Kit slowed for the traffic lights in Newport, which turned green before she had to stop.

"Speaking of the rogue detective, what happened with him last night?" Alex queried.

Kit replayed the highlights of her visit to Parker's, then divulged the info Morley and Santo had given her, before asking, "Wanna hear my latest wacky theory?"

"Always, Kit. I love your theories."

"I think Doghouse or, more likely his employer, is trying to destabilize the tenuous sort-of truce that exists in the tedious quarrel between the Rileys and the Barkers. I believe Doghouse has spies in both families, who keep him abreast of the Riley/Barker reactions to the bad deeds that Doghouse and/or his employer are doing to put pressure on the city's major crime clans."

Alex stared at Kit thoughtfully. "That's pretty wacky," she agreed. "Who's the employer?"

"No idea. Not a clue," Kit replied. "Probably the Stanos. I thought it might've been Boxer, but he swears it isn't. It could be the Prime Minister."

"You think?"

"Why not," Kit shrugged. She turned right at the Williamstown waterfront to cruise the café and gallery strip of Nelson Place. It was renowned for its bay views, at least where they weren't interrupted by Gem Pier's imposing maritime museum, which included a retired mine-sweeper, the HMAS *Castlemaine*, and a curious little black submarine called *Vampire*.

Alex smiled. "Let's assume, O'Malley, that the culprit in this elegant plot of yours is closer to home than our nation's capital. What would be the point of so much subterfuge? Surely it can't be too hard to spark an all out war between two already-feuding families."

"True, except that Queenie and Leo have a strange pact to hold tightly to the reigns of quasi-peace. They deal in retribution only when there's no question of responsibility."

"What do you mean?"

"That any sleight on either family would have to be *absolutely* the fault of the other before Ma Riley or Pa Barker would sanction payback. So, any attacks on the clans made by someone else, would have to be subtle, accumulating, and of ambiguous origin. For instance, if the Barkers *never* find out who ran Stuart down, just back there on The Strand," Kit pointed behind them, "or the cops never catch Gerry's murderer, then—even though right now they don't think the other is responsible—the suspicion will forever be a-simmering. This way, when the criminal mastermind finally makes his big move … well *kablooey!*, that's all I can say."

Alex was laughing even before Kit had blown the Rileys and Barkers out of the equation. "Darling, even 'far-fetched' does not do justice to that theory."

Kit laughed at herself while tending to a right, then left turn. "I did say wacky theory. I'm just suss about coincidences, Alex. And right now, either our mean streets are littered with them, *or* there's a devious plot afoot. Personally, I vote for the plot coz I reckon I'm starring in my own B-grade mystery movie." She lowered her voice, "While investigating a gay vampire murder, private eye Kit O'Malley finds herself caught in a web of intriguing clichés."

Alex laughed. "Are you unraveling, my love?"

"I do believe I am, my darling," Kit replied, peering at the street signs. "I'm losing my thread, my seams are coming undone, and I feel like a flounder, floundering; you know, in the bottom of a boat, flapping around trying to figure out why it can't bloody breathe."

"Interesting concept, that: a seamless flounder," Alex kept a straight face. "Why?"

Kit parked the car, turned to Alex, and took a deep breath. "Because I'm half working several semi-connected cases, but I don't feel like I'm actually investigating anything. People just keep telling me stuff, and quite frankly I don't want to know most of it.

"But they ring me up and tell me shit; they invite me over and report rubbish; they call me into offices and give me ears-only info; and they make proxy appointments so other people can fill me in. And I don't know why they're all being so generous."

"Because you care, so you listen?" Alex suggested, her shoulders rising as she searched for a sensible answer. "And all these people know that about you; and, oh, it's your job; and …"

"And coz I can't say no," Kit declared, running her hands through her hair.

"Yes, that too."

"Well shit, and double it, because I think I'm going to say yes to Queenie bloody Riley *again*. And you know why?"

"Why?"

"Coz I want to know—even though I'm aware how dangerous the knowledge might be—why she wants me to take her to visit Leo Barker in hospital, when she says her own family wouldn't understand her reasons.

"That's not quite right; I know why she wants *me* to take her. It's so she doesn't have to ask them, and coz then she'd really have her hooks in me. But damn it, Alex, I want to know *why* she wants to see him. So, I'll probably take her. And you know why?"

"Apart from the reasons you just gave?" Alex said.

"Yes, apart from all that babbling, I'll do it, because I want to understand *her*."

"Why?"

"I don't know," Kit snarled.

"She *is* likeable," Alex admitted.

Kit blew a raspberry. "Yeah. The likeable matriarch of a vicious crime family. And, being a regular employer of such things, she's also one step back from being a killer; and she's a money launderer, and a thief, and a ..."

Alex shrugged. "She reminds me of my grandmother."

"Yeah, that too," Kit agreed.

Chapter 24

The lounge room of Scooter Farrell's upstairs flat was number six in a set of fourteen identicals that formed a white-brick block on a corner with no sea view despite the street name's proclamation. She'd decorated it in kd lang and Bluehouse posters and furnished it with a red vinyl couch, a bean bag, fish tank, TV, and stereo.

Scooter herself, dressed all in black including her mood, was ensconced in the bag, pretending to be engrossed in a Playstation game. Rabbit, who'd very carefully let Kit and Alex inside, had returned to her post by the only exit from the room.

Kit squatted down in front of Scooter and peered at her. "Scooter, mate, apart from one brief interlude this arvo, I'm having a *really bad* Wednesday. So if I have to wrench that thing from your hands to get your attention, I will. But I'd rather you'd just co-operate."

"Co-operate?" Scooter snarled. "Who the hell do you think you are, Kit?"

Dunno, but I *don't* need attitude. "How about, any second, I'll be your worst nightmare?"

"Oh ha, like I'm quaking in my boots."

Kit cocked her head. "Rabbit followed a perfectly strange man on Sunday night, because *you* asked her to. That man, who at the time was allegedly your secret girlfriend's husband, may have murdered a woman in cold blood only moments after you told Rabbit to stop following him because your girlfriend, his possible wife, had invited you over for sex."

"What?" Scooter's face registered confusion and disbelief. "Who got murdered?"

"A woman he met on the street shortly after you left to follow Chrissie," Kit explained.

302

"Bloody hell, Rabbit. Why didn't you tell me?" Scooter demanded.

"Like you're easy to find when you're chasing skirt," Rabbit waggled her head.

When Kit indicated that Rabbit could now show Scooter the articles that had brought her attention to the crime in the first place, Rabbit pulled the pages from her bib-pocket. "This is the woman who got killed," she explained, handing Scooter the clipping with Sheryl's *Jane Doe* picture. "And this is my identikit, that the cops did, of the bloke we saw with Chrissie."

"The police asked her not to tell anyone what she'd seen. Especially you," Kit explained, to help head off any recriminations between long-time friends.

"Me? Why?" Scooter got to her feet.

"Because if this man is Chrissie's husband, then your relationship with her places you under suspicion, not to mention one degree of separation from two murders."

"Two murders," Rabbit noted. "Scooter girl, you oughta choose your women better."

"Don't be ridiculous, Rabbit," Scooter snapped. "As for you, Kit O'Malley, I didn't know about any woman being murdered until now. And as I was following, and then was *with* Chrissie on Sunday night, when you say this guy may have killed someone, then she can't be involved either. So cut this degrees bullshit. I'm more likely to be close to half the killers in town because I know *you*, than coz Chrissie might know this guy."

Oh, that's way too true, Kit thought.

"You did know the naked man at Angie's, before he was dead," Rabbit reminded her.

"Shut up, Rabbit."

"And you did see this guy and Chrissie together," Kit said. "It's because of *your* assumption about their relationship that we know any of this. It's how Rabbit came to ID a possible suspect in the murder of that woman."

Scooter looked unconvinced. "But—and in a big way—*so what?* And tell me again why it's your business to be in mine, Kit. After all, me seeing an alleged killer, pre-crime, and recognizing a dead man, post-murder, just means that I've had a bad week."

"Very bad," Kit agreed. "Let's see, why am I here? Oh. There's a guilt-by-association chance that this same guy, as in your girlfriend's murdering husband, may also have had something to do with the bloodless Gerry Anders."

"You're kidding," Scooter said.

"Why would I?" Kit asked ingenuously. To stretch a weak link to breaking point, that's why, she thought.

"Oh, far out!" Rabbit was exclaiming. "You mean I was there to find the dead dude and then followed his murderer just before he killed someone else? Shit." For a big, tough-talking dyke Rabbit suddenly looked like she'd rather raise alpacas than be a private eye.

Scooter meanwhile had screwed her face into bewilderment. "How can you possibly make that flying leap, Kit? Unless ..." she smirked. "You know who this guy is, don't you?"

Kit widened her eyes. "But I didn't say he killed Gerry. I merely implied he knew him."

"You know who he is?" Rabbit said. "How come you didn't clue me in, Kit?"

"Coz I didn't see your identikit pic until this morning, Rabbit."

"So who the hell is he?" Scooter demanded.

"I'm not at liberty to divulge that, as he's now an official suspect," Kit stated. "But I will tell you, and only because it might save your life Scooter, that he *is* an ex-cop—a very nasty ex-cop. So you might have been almost right about his connection to Chrissie."

Scooter looked puzzled. "Almost?"

"He could be her *ex*-husband," Kit stated.

"I really wish I'd kept my mouth shut." Scooter flopped morosely onto the couch next to Alex, and then raised a point-making finger. "By that same token, Chrissie might—well, obviously she did know him—but it might have been *through* her ex-husband, the cop. That guy, your alleged killer, may simply have been an acquaintance, or ex-acquaintance, from her ex-marriage; and they just bumped into each other on the street that night."

"Did you ask her who he was?" Kit queried. "Did you find out your girlfriend's surname or anything about any of her husbands?"

"Yes and fucking-no," Scooter snarled. "I carried out your orders,

Kit. And the 'who was he' question was one of the last things I got to ask her before she broke up with me."

"Oh. Really? When did she do that?"

"This morning. Thanks to you."

"I find that unlikely."

"You think? You blackmailed me into asking her questions that we'd agreed we wouldn't ask each other. She freaked out, said her husband would kill *me* if he ever found out about us. She told me that's why she'd wanted our relationship to be a secret. To protect me."

Kit couldn't help herself: she started laughing. "I'm sorry Scooter," she said. "But that's the biggest load of cods I've ever heard. You honestly believe she wouldn't tell you her surname or who that guy was, in order to keep *you* safe from *her husband*. That's crazy."

"Says you!"

Alex placed a comforting hand on Scooter's knee. "It's more likely she wanted to protect herself, her straight life, and her hetero-marriage from you."

"Yeah," Rabbit nodded sagely from the doorway. "Those damn day-tripping dykes always keep us career lesbians on the side plate, under the serviette."

Kit and Alex offered straight-faced nods, but they couldn't quite look at Rabbit.

Scooter, however, looked huffy. "So Chrissie did things arse about. So what? When we first met, she told me that he could be violent. I thought she meant with her, not in general."

"When *did* you meet?" Alex asked. "And where?"

"The end of last month at the Girly Bar."

"Did you go out on the scene together often?" Kit asked.

"No. Not at all."

"Never even brought her to Angie's," Rabbit remarked.

"Why not?" Alex queried.

Scooter shrugged. "Too busy having sex. We hadn't got to the going out and socializing part of the relationship yet. In fact, *hello guys*, it wasn't even a relationship. We were having an affair which, by its very nature, is not a thing to be aired in public."

"Angie's is hardly public, Scooter," Rabbit pointed out. "Her hubby wasn't likely to see youse together there. You know, him bein' a man and all."

Scooter gave her friend a snarly look.

Kit sighed. "Are you in love with her?"

Scooter frowned and pursed her lips. "No, but ..."

"But you were on your way," Alex finished.

"Yeah," Scooter's voice was small. "Probably. Until this morning anyway. She turned, mate; you know, she became nasty. But it was like everything was my fault; that I was bad and stupid for ruining a good *casual* thing by breaking a promise and asking questions."

"If it's any consolation," Kit said softly, "I suspect it was headed that way from the start."

"Oh, and what would you bloody know?" Scooter demanded.

"Kit is worried that you might have been used," Alex explained.

Scooter looked incredulous. "You mean by someone other than *her?*"

Alex smiled. "Yes. And for something more sinister than wanting to find out someone's name."

While Scooter snorted derisively, Rabbit wondered aloud, "How come women don't use me for sinister sex?"

"Alex didn't mean the sex was sinister, Rabbit," Kit said.

"O'Malley, you should tell Scooter about your infiltration theory," Alex suggested.

Kit sighed. "There's a chance that Chrissie might have been using you to get inside info on your family for someone else. And by your family, I mean the Barkers not the Farrells."

"Are you mad?"

"Quite possibly," Kit nodded.

"Information like what?"

"I don't know, Scooter," Kit admitted. "Maybe just their reactions to current events, like your uncle being hit by a car, or your grandfather having a stroke. Vows of secrecy aside, I bet *you* mentioned your family, at least in passing, which would have given her an innocent reason to ask you any questions she cared to."

"Again I say, like what?"

"I dunno," Kit shrugged, "Like who's running things while they're incapacitated; or, how on earth would your sweet old grandpa cope with a hit and run on his son?"

Scooter glared at Kit as if everything was now *her* fault. "Okay, so maybe I mentioned things, without naming names, of course; and maybe she asked questions. But it was just conversation. As a conspiracy, your theory is way out there in preposterous land."

"I know," Kit nodded. "But that guy on Sunday—whatever his connection with your mistress—probably killed that woman in Prahran. He *is* an ex-cop and he *is* known to have had crooked dealings with Gerry Anders. Oh, he also has at least two girlfriends, one of whom just happens to be a friend of Queenie Riley's grand-daughter."

"Oh, fucking hell," Scooter moaned.

"Couldn't have said it better myself," Kit agreed.

"Are you saying the Rileys are spying on the Barkers through me?" Scooter demanded, leaping to her feet. She looked like she was ready to defend her once-removed family from all-comers even though, by her own admission, she didn't much like them.

"No, I'm not, Scooter. Settle. I think someone else is spying on both families. And if they're not actually responsible for your uncle's accident, Sasha Riley's attack, and maybe even Gerry's murder, then they are making the most of those things."

"What on earth for?"

"Any number of reasons," Kit said, inventing a few on the spot. "To generate suspicion between two families already at each other's throats, either for gain or fun. To sidetrack them, and probably the cops, while they—whoever they are—mastermind a plot to rob all the banks in town at once, and then frame your families. Or, perhaps, they're doing it to destabilize the power base between the city's two biggest warring criminal clans in order to deal them out and orchestrate a takeover of Melbourne's under-world."

"Or," Alex smiled, "they don't exist at all, and they're not in fact doing anything."

"You read too many comics when you were a kid, didn't you?" Scooter remarked.

Kit shrugged. "Hey, I figure if I can dream it up, then someone with something to gain must already be way ahead of me in the actually-doing-it stakes."

"Let's get the reality of this straight," Alex suggested. "Scooter, are you saying that you met Chrissie in a crowded gay bar, after which you never went to places like that together; not even your regular haunt which, from my own observation, seems to be your second home."

"That about sums it up, your worship," Scooter pouted.

Alex raised an eyebrow. "Was it full-on *mutual* lust that kept you indoors, or was it only Chrissie who didn't want to go out-out?"

Scooter's frown and pursed lips answered that question.

"Who picked who up, in the first place?" Kit asked.

"She picked me," Scooter admitted.

Alex looked thoughtful. "When did she offer the sometimes-violent husband as her reason for the 'ask-no-questions' policy? Was it right from the start? Or was this morning, when she freaked out about your questions, the first time she claimed *you* might be the one in danger? That he'd kill *you* if he found out?"

"God, you guys are mean. You sure know how to pick at a wound, don't you?" Scooter complained, before tuning her tone to the ultra-patronizing. "Oh, I just remembered, you're a lawyer, aren't you, Alex. Well, you may *think* you've hammered your point beyond reasonable doubt, but it doesn't make it true. It's still a way stupid and crazy theory."

"We didn't intend to be mean, Scooter," Kit said, "we just need answers. And my theory may be silly and implausible—I hope it is—but that doesn't change the fact that Chrissie knows or knew this guy. You, yourself, and your good mate Rabbit are witness to that reality."

Scooter slouched farther into the couch. "In the beginning, Chrissie said it made the affair even sexier and more exciting if we didn't know the boring details about each other's lives. Today *was* the first time she implied I might get hurt. And you're right; that doesn't make sense, because how would he find out about us, just from me asking her questions about him?"

"Given the great veil of secrecy, I don't suppose you have a photo of her?" Kit asked.

Scooter looked torn, or guilty, or pissed off; or torn between guilt and pissed-offedness. "Yeah, I do actually. A bad polaroid I took late one night when she'd unintentionally fallen asleep."

Scooter was allowed to leave the room only after Rabbit verified she wasn't going to do a runner for the front door. She returned, moments later, with a bad polaroid indeed. "There wasn't much light in the room."

The image of Chrissie's face, and just her face, was up close and altogether too personal. It was the sort of crappy photo that Scooter no doubt fondled as a true representation of her *objet d'amour*, but which, in reality, made Chrissie look like a smudged, sleeping "anyone." In fact, Kit thought, the pic was so bad that Chrissie could even be a vaguely familiar someone, and they'd never know. "You sure she's never been to Angie's?"

"No. I'm only sure she's never been there with me," Scooter said.

Kit showed the photo to Rabbit, who glanced at her friend as if she was questioning her taste or her photographic skills, and then shrugged.

It was Alex who actually said, "This could be anyone. What's her hair like? And her eyes?"

Scooter sighed heavily. "Brown eyes. Her hair is longish at the back and two-tone, blonde with dark bits. She's slim, so high," Scooter indicated about five-foot-five, "and if she hadn't broken up with me eight hours ago I wouldn't be telling you any of this."

"Thank you, Scooter," Kit said. "Can I hang on to this for a while. I won't lose it."

"You can burn it for all I care."

Punt Road, South Yarra-ish, a few blocks from the Alfred Hospital, 6:30 p.m. It was still Wednesday, as it had been for too much of the day, and Kit was getting mighty sick of it. En route to pick up Melbourne's crime queen, she'd dropped Alex at home, grabbed a souvlaki and a chocolate milkshake from a takeaway in Hawthorn, and organized a rendezvous with Cathy and Marek for nine-thirty. There was still a third of Wednesday to go, as she made a right turn onto Commercial Road, fluked a parking spot, then turned to face Marjorie Riley.

"Before we do this, or you do this, I need to know about Alan Shipper."

Queenie's eyebrow's could only have gone higher if she'd intended them to. "Where's this coming from, Kit? And why now?"

"Because, I don't know why I'm here. By nature I'm what you'd call a cynical optimist, but right now I'm riddled with nought but suspicion as to why you really wanted me to bring you here. Why, for instance, couldn't you drive yourself or take a taxi?"

Queenie squinted. "Which has what to do with Alan Shipper?"

"I'm getting there," Kit said. "First, I'm saying I don't know why I agreed to this."

"Because you're curious," Queenie smiled, too-knowingly. "As for me, I don't drive anywhere, as I never learned how; and taxis would neither be safe nor sensible."

Kit shrugged. "The prevailing theory regarding your nephew's death is that it's connected to the earlier murders of Mike and Julie Sherwood; that it's drug-related revenge. The cops think that and so does that strange Morley chap."

"Is that what you think?" Queenie asked.

Kit nodded grudgingly. "Problem is, I can't find a reason why his body was left at The Terpsichore. Maybe there was no reason; but until I know for sure, I'm not ruling anyone out. Not your rival drug dealers, not the Barkers, not drowned thugs, not his wife, not ex-cops who bring you jewelry, not even you," she said. Not even Chucky Parker, she thought.

"For the record, Kit, I don't have any rivals in the drug trade," Queenie stated categorically. "That was Gerry's own little sideline, one of several I not only didn't approve of, but which I had long ago banned from the regular family business.

"And don't pull faces, Kit; I understand why you wouldn't believe me. Yes, historically, opium, marijuana, and speed were great little earners for us, but things got nasty. The drugs got nasty. I wanted nothing to do with the waste, with that level of human desperation. No amount of money is worth that kind of misery." Queenie looked sincere enough, but …

Oh, she's avoiding the question again! Kit rolled her eyes. "Tell me about Alan Shipper, coz he's still on my list, too."

"But he's dead, Kit."

"I'm aware of that, Queenie. But why is he dead? Why did Gerry kidnap him? Why did he let him go?"

Still hedging, Queenie shook her head. "What does it matter? He died long before Gerry."

"Yes," Kit nodded. "And maybe there's someone else out there, besides me, who gives a damn about how and why he died. Maybe Gerry's murder is that simple."

Queenie considered the possibility, briefly. "Well, I can tell you his wife wouldn't give two hoots. She ran off to Spain with the bloke she'd been screwing for years, the moment Shipper's will made her a very rich woman. And her daughter, apart from being a teenager at the time, wasn't his child; so I doubt she'd give a damn either."

"Queenie Riley, you still haven't answered my question."

"Alan Shipper's wife, unbeknownst to him, owed me a great deal of money."

Kit shook her head. "His wife did? The one who went to Spain?"

"Yes."

"What for? I mean the money, why did she owe it to you?"

"Sandy ran a brothel I used to own, from which she embezzled half a million dollars. She went to ground just before I found out and resurfaced years later as Mrs. Alan Shipper."

"So why did you kidnap Mr. Alan Shipper?"

"Because Sandy didn't want him to find out about her past, and therefore couldn't just hand over a cool million to me."

"You said half a million," Kit pointed out.

"Interest," Queenie smiled. "She suggested the kidnapping as a cover, and as a way not only to pay me back, but to double my original *investment* as she called it. Plus interest."

"And Alan Shipper knew nothing about this?"

"About the reason for the *four* million ransom? No. He genuinely thought he'd been kidnapped for his own worth—which is why he wanted to testify against my idiot nephew, who'd not been nearly careful enough during the three days that Shipper was in his care."

Kit absolutely did *not* want to know the answer to her next question; but she asked it anyway: "Was Alan Shipper murdered so he couldn't testify?"

"Was he murdered, Kit?" Queenie asked, with a perfect poker face. "Interesting theory. If he *was*, it's just as likely to have been Sandy's doing."

"Just as likely as who?" Kit pounced.

"As anyone else," Queenie shrugged.

"Who did she run off to Spain with?" Kit asked. With whom, she corrected herself. Pedant, herself said!

"My goodness child, you expect me to remember that?" Queenie frowned. "Oh, no wait. The other day, you rattled off a few names. Remember, I thought one was familiar. That might be why." She seemed to be searching her memory, both the short- and long-term banks.

Well, I know it's not Charlie Parker, Kit thought. "Nino Piantoni?" she suggested.

"No, it wasn't an ethnic-type name. It was …"

"Nathan Pittock? Neil Porter?"

"That's it!" Queenie smiled. "Neil Porter."

"Um …" Kit couldn't believe that Queenie really didn't know this man and all his aliases.

"What is it?"

"Neil Porter *is* Nathan Pittock *and* Nino Piantoni. Collectively, and individually, they were helping Gerry run his fire insurance scam."

Queenie was gobsmacked. "How do you know this? Oh, color me thick, *you're* the PI."

I so wish I wasn't, Kit whimpered. Get your head around that one, O'Malley. The late Alan Shipper's thieving conniving wife ran off with his kidnapper's money man, the multi-named broker, with whom she'd been bonking even *before* Queenie tracked her down and Gerry abducted her hubby.

"Are you telling me, honestly, that you don't know who Porter is?"

"Yes, I am. I didn't approve of that scam, as you call it. It was, therefore, not Riley family business. So what did this Neil character do?"

What *is* Riley family business, then, Kit wondered, if it's not drugs or insurance fraud? "Porter was the insurance broker. He was also, and perhaps originally, Nigel Pippineetal."

Queenie thumped the dashboard. "As I said this very morning, Kit, if that nephew of mine hadn't already come to a dreadful end, I'd kill him myself."

Kit smiled and shook her head. "You are a strange one, Queenie Riley. You want to go visit Papa Leo now?"

Chapter 25

Vegemite, Kylie, Skippy, Elvis, Xena, Germaine, Phar Lap, Phryne, Uhura, Mr. Squiggle ... Real or fictitious, person or thing, it makes no difference. If you recognize the name, that's all you need. A name alone is the trigger for all you know about it or them. So what's really in a name? Kit wondered. What would Dame Edna say? Ah, her side-tracked mind commented, it depends whether you mean Edna the woman, or the ego that goes with the alter. And a name certainly isn't just a specific label or identifier, because it can also support an association—pleasant or un—or spur the imagination.

Case one: If you were school-bullied by a Wendy, professionally betrayed by a Graham, or stabbed by a Carla, then you'd, quite illogically, be wary of every Wendy, Graham, or Carla who came within cooee for the rest of your life. Flipside—the names of friends or lovers would make you recklessly accepting of any Del, Hector, or Alex in the world. Not to mention all those Thistles out there.

Case two: Knowing as she did that he headed a family of crooks, the name Leo Barker conjured the image of an arrogant, swarthy, meat-ax of a man, with tattoos, steely eyes, and a crew cut. The name Papa Leo, however, evoked the impression of a commanding yet charismatic, slightly flabby, octogenarian patriarch, with a droopy moustache, steely eyes, and wavy-gray hair.

Looking at him now, for the first time, Kit realized that at different times in his life he might well have fitted both of her mental pictures; but right now Papa Leo Barker was merely an old old man ravaged by a stroke that had all but killed him. Reduced to a dribbling crumpled shell with watery eyes, he was still with-it and could speak with great difficulty, but he couldn't move anything on his left side.

Queenie Riley, neatly dressed in black slacks and a blue twinset sans pearls, was holding Leo's right hand with more than a little tenderness. She was smiling, talking softly, and, every now and then, stroking his head. Papa Leo, as much as his condition would allow him to show it, was unquestionably pleased to see her.

This is not going unexplained, Kit swore, half-watching from the doorway where she was also playing lookout for any *other* members of the Barker clan. As she and Queenie had arrived during feeding time, though, there was no general rush of caring civilians yet, and the action in the corridor was mostly the patients' waddle of pink chenille or tartan robes, and flashing bums in hospital gowns.

Kit returned her attention to this most peculiar Old Crims Reunion and decided there was no way that these two were mortal enemies. They were more like an old married couple, or a long lost brother and sister. Not wanting to be too intrusive in her coat of blatant curiosity, Kit kept glancing at the floor, or down the hall, or across to the nurses' station. She decided to fill in her mental time by running over the events of the last seven days, starting with Angie's phone-delivered panic about a naked dead man in her bar and finishing with today's revelations about Chuck's and Gerry's long-standing relationship.

Kit glanced at Queenie and Leo, who were still deep in the meaningful somethings, then tried putting Charlie Parker in her frame for Gerry's murder, but couldn't quite focus the picture. Mind you, she reminded herself, he *was* very late to the crime scene that first day. Perhaps he didn't want to be the one to ID a body that he'd put there.

No, she recalled, Chucky had been truly surprised when Marek revealed the deceased's identity. Although, and putting the not-bloody-likely scenario of Charlie as a killer to one side, if there was truth in Morley's story, then Detective Parker would have oodles to gain from Gerry being dead. *And* he'd later tried to frame Angie. Or someone had.

Sure. Even Morley didn't think Chucky had a murderer's knackers. Besides why on earth would *he* have left the body at Angie's? Then there's his claim that *he's* the one being framed.

Kit gazed down the corridor as a nurse, of the harassed variety, rushed by and collided with a doctor, of the oblivious kind, who stepped into her path just because he could. The crash of bedpan to floor coincided with the arrival in Kit's mind of a possibly important point. Whoever it was who'd deposited Gerry in The Terpsichore—whether it was Chucky, Toad, Mr. Big the drug bloke, a Barker, an Alan Shipper fan, or a complete un-bloody-known—they had to be a certain size. *Or* they had to have a smallish accomplice who could fit in the window.

Queenie waved to indicate she was ready to leave, so Kit left instructions with herself: make a note, O'Malley, find out why the nice detective was late on the first day of this case; and go check for yourself how the bad guys got in. She then watched in wonder as Queenie Riley bent and kissed Leo Barker on the forehead, placed something in his right hand, and closed his fingers around it.

Forty minutes later, the private eye and the lady crime lord stood side by side in the dark and cobbled laneway behind an infamous lesbian bar, shining torchlight up at the repaired, and now barred pantry window.

"What do you think?"

"I think, my dear, that if there was one louver broken and only one removed, then the person who gained access to this place was indeed a bastard of limited stature and girth."

Kit laughed. "In other words, a skinny short-arse."

"Precisely," Queenie agreed.

"I therefore reckon," Kit proposed, "given the condition in which Gerry and his, um, contents were found, coupled with the forensic evidence that this was the point of entry, that whoever killed your nephew had help—at least after the actual fact."

Queenie nodded. "That would make sense anyway if, as you suggest, he was killed by drug dealers, ex-cops, or Toad. I'm sure even Poppy could've gotten help from her aerobics man."

"It also means Gerry probably wasn't done in by an as yet unidentified psycho killer, coz they tend to work alone," Kit noted, then frowned. "Unless he's a very small, lone psycho."

"And one of them in the city at a time is one too many," Queenie proclaimed, hanging onto Kit's elbow as they made their way back down the dark lane. "That Rental Killer on the loose is another reason why I'd never take taxis anywhere."

"Why? Have you heard something about taxi drivers?" Kit asked, alert to the sound of careful footfalls behind them.

"No," Queenie was saying. "But I'm a firm believer in the stranger-danger code."

Indeed! Kit thought, with half her mind on the creep creeping behind. She was just about to turn and do the confrontation thing, when her wits deserted her at warp speed because of the bigger threat that stepped abruptly out of the dark ahead yelling at them.

"Aaggh," Queenie and Kit screamed together. "Shit!" they both added.

"I said, what do think you're doin' there!" the big scary person demanded again.

"For fuck's sake, Rabbit!" Kit shouted. "Are you trying to frighten us to death?"

"Kit? Gawd, sorry mate. I *was* tryin' to scare you. Only I didn't know it was *you.*"

"Obviously," Kit said, spinning around, hoping to at least catch sight of their pursuer, who'd no doubt fled in screaming confusion.

Wrong. There was Angie Nichols, sand-wedge slowly wilting from the danger-position at the top of her swing, looking a lot like Lucy when Ricky came home wanting some 'splaining.

"What *are* you doing?" Kit asked.

"Ditto," Angie insisted.

"We were strolling down this public laneway," Kit explained, "figuring out how to get a body into your nightclub. You?"

Angie planted her hands on her hips. "We were making sure the two noisy pervs hanging around this public laneway weren't trying to break in and leave *another* body in my club."

"Well, you oughta be more careful, coz we could've been dangerous crims." Kit glanced at Queenie, who raised an eyebrow. "Correction. We could *both* have been dangerous crims."

Angie dangled her golf club. "Ha, you're damn lucky. That's all I can say."

"Really?" Kit laughed. "Well, all I can say is: Queenie, these are my friends—Angie, as in Angie's Bar, and Rabbit. *Guys*, I'd like you to meet Queenie Riley."

Angie's wedge actually fell from her hand; Rabbit simply exclaimed "Way cool," then added with a nod of seriousness, "Your majesty."

Kit felt Queenie flinch, so she whispered, "It's a compliment."

"You coming in for a drink?" Angie asked, using the retrieval of her weapon as a cover for selecting her best unfazed expression.

"No thanks," Kit replied, before Queenie could. She doubted Grandma Riley would have said yes; but Kit wasn't taking chances on the old tart stealing any more of her time tonight, either out of politeness or curiosity. "I'm taking Queenie home, then I'm meeting Marek."

The hulking figure peering through the gap in the curtains as they pulled up in front of Chez Riley did not go unnoticed, but nor did his surveillance deter Kit from locking the car doors from the inside to detain her passenger.

"Sorry," she said, "but I'm not letting you out until you tell me the Queenie and Leo story. What was all that about tonight?"

Queenie smiled. "You're not worried about Will charging out to secure my release?"

"He'd have to pry you out with a can opener. Now speak ... Please."

Queenie sighed deeply. "Leo Barker was my first love. My only, and my one true love."

"Oh, um," Kit stammered. "That's not at all what I expected you to say."

"I bet," Queenie laughed, sadly. "In the beginning, the rivalry between our two families was plain healthy business competition. And before you make a smart remark, I'm aware that 'healthy' is not a word that you or the law would apply to our business; but, nevertheless, in those days it was a simple, honest," she shrugged, "contest. The turf war, the feud, the stupid ongoing state of affairs—call it what you will—came about because of a car and a woman."

"A car?"

"Yes a motor vehicle and, actually, it was two women. Remember,

Kit, we're talking about men, grown men, and the things they do. You mightn't have much experience of it, my dear, but I've been cleaning up their mess my entire life."

"The women bit I understand, Queenie. But a car?"

Queenie released her seat belt and turned a little to lean her back against the door. "My father, Sean Riley, and Leo's father, Ray Barker, played football together and ran brothels separately, imported opium together and supplied it separately, mostly from their brothels. They had joint deals, scams, *jobs*, and then they had fights over who did what.

"I was sixteen when they had their first long-term falling out, when Ray Barker won the heart of my father's mistress, Grace Beckinsdale. They reconciled a year later when Ray married Grace, thereby making an honest woman of her. That meant my father could be big about everything and attend their wedding—as did my mother, who I think was even bigger about the whole affair than my father ever was. I went along to give her moral support.

"It was at the reception that Leo, who was twenty-one, and I began our courtship which lasted seventeen exhilarating months—until the car happened.

"I choose not to remember *what* kind of car it was, as that would endow it with more importance than it ever deserved. But it was apparently beautiful and one of a kind. And they both wanted it, our fathers, but only one could possess this thing that ultimately held more value to them than a woman. Ray Barker won again; and that time, there was no forgiving.

"My bastard father banned Leo from our hearth and home and, of course, my life. I was sent away to country cousins for two years, and the Riley–Barker rivalry became all out war.

"I'd been gone eleven months when Leo married Joy Prentice, because he had to, because she was pregnant—with Stuart. A few years later, and mostly out of spite because I'd always hoped Leo would defy our fathers, leave his wife, and take me away, I married mad Jim Puig."

"But you and Leo, I mean you looked like you still," Kit circled her hands. "And you've had this keep-the-peace understanding all these years."

Queenie smiled. "Yes. We made that pact, eighteen years later, on the day his father died. Which strangely, as if they were a squabbling but inseparable old married couple, happened within a week of *my* father going to god or, more likely the devil.

"Despite our best efforts, trouble raised its ugliness on occasion, long after those two old bastards were dead and buried, because we couldn't completely erase the interim years of hate and mistrust bred into the rest of our respective broods. For the most part, though, things settled into a game of keeping out of each other's territory."

Queenie fiddled thoughtfully with her hair. "And then, as it's wont to do, history went and bloody repeated itself when my sister's son, Gerry, and Leo's son, Stuart, had a to-do over a woman. Sadly for us, and me in particular, on that occasion the Riley clan came out on top when Gerry won the heart and oh-so-vacant mind of Poppy Barton."

Kit laughed. "You don't like her much do you?"

Queenie demonstrated a need to strangle. "She's a selfish, vacuous clothes horse with no taste. It's truly beyond me how she managed to help produce those wonderful boys."

Uh-oh, speaking of History Channel repeats, Kit thought, as she unlocked the doors, stay tuned for the Tom and Suzie Show.

"Last question," she said. "What did you give Leo before we left the hospital?"

Queenie's dark expression indicated that Kit might have just overstepped the mark. "A choice," she said, opening the door. "And, really, *none* of your business. Now, Kitty-Kitty, is the rest of your curiosity satisfied?"

"Yes. Thank you," Kit said sweetly. "I wasn't just curious, though, Queenie," she insisted, despite the dying cat suggestion/reference/threat. "You asked something of me that, given who Leo is, didn't make sense. Not to mention—although obviously I'm about to—given who *you* are, the more info I have the safer I feel."

"Well, I'm glad you feel that way, Kit," Queenie said, clambering out of the car. "Because there'd be nothing worse than still being in the dark when your time is up."

Queenie looked deadly serious, so Kit tried to look neither shaken nor stirred.

Whereon Marjorie bloody Riley laughed, raucously, all the way up the path to her front door, which opened just like sesame.

A rowdy singerless blues band was playing something Kit recognized but couldn't name and hindering her attempts to ascertain from the off-duty cop at the bar where Marek might be lurking. He finally pointed towards the rear of the pub before returning to his VB and cheese Twisties.

Kit eventually found Marek and Cathy in a slightly quieter back room with a jug of beer and three glasses, one of which they filled for her as she joined them.

"You're late," Marek stated.

"Sorry, but I've had a weird night," Kit said.

"Spit it out; why are we here?" he demanded.

Kit narrowed her eyes. "I only invited *you*, Inspector Snitty, to see if I could get you out of the office and away from your case," she said. "And to pass on a message from Erin; she'd like a photo of you, coz she can't remember what you look like."

"Oh ha. If you weren't so funny I'd squash you like a bug. And, FYI, we had lunch today."

"I get out a lot," Cathy smiled, "so why am *I* here?"

Kit placed a folded piece of paper on the table between them. "This is the name and address of the fool who killed The Toad. Which one of you wants it?"

The two detectives looked at each other, then Cathy said: "That's Sally's case."

"Ah," Kit pronounced, "but I don't know Detective Evans like I know you two. And besides, she thought *I* killed that creepy little prick."

"You could've," Marek said encouragingly.

"Yes, that's true," Kit said appreciatively, "but I didn't."

"I gather, then, that we get this coz you want something," Cathy said.

"She's quick. You should keep a promotional eye on her," Kit said to Marek. "Tell me, either of you, is Detective Senior Sergeant Parker being investigated by Internal Affairs?"

"Why?" Marek asked. "Should he be?"

"Of course, Jonno. And I've been saying it for years," Kit said, with-holding because she wasn't ready to share Morley's allegations until she'd personally questioned the Chuckster—her client. Crap! How *did* that happen?, she wondered. "Don't you listen to me?" she asked.

"Never, you know that. But is that the only reason?" Marek asked suspiciously.

"Ah, yeah," Kit rolled her eyes. "You might remember he tried to set up my good mate Angie. I'm kind of hoping he's in really deep doo-doo for that at least."

"Well he is; but what else is there?"

Sometimes Kit hated it that Marek knew her as well as he did. She shrugged and tried leading him astray. "Ever find out why he was late to the crime scene on Thursday?"

"Said he was on his way back from a fishing trip," Marek said.

"Yeah?" Cathy looked puzzled. "He told me he'd been staying with a *friend*."

Kit, knowing both answers could be true if he'd gone fishing with the pale Guy, was as amused as Marek at Cathy's assumption that Charlie Parker had a *friend* friend.

"Kitty, is there something you're not telling us?"

"Of course there is, Jonno," she smiled, "always. But what do *you* think it is?"

He snorted. "Speaking of shit you don't know …"

That's better. He thinks you're bluffing, or digging. Kit looked expectant.

"Why didn't you tell us it was Dixon who your mate Rabbit saw with Sheryl?"

"Coz I didn't know until I saw his ugly mug in the paper, that's why. Have you picked him up yet? Hang on. *Why* was it in the paper? How come none of you recognized him?"

Cathy was about to speak when Marek gave a dismissive wave. "Don't ask, and we won't have to tell you how or why it was released to the media without approval from anyone who had a clue. But because that unnecessary photo is out in the wild, we've lost any advantage we might have had. Doghouse probably left town at dawn with a rocket up his arse."

"Doesn't live in town. He lives on a boat at Hastings," Kit said.

She pulled her phone and a business card from her pouch, and keyed in the number for the *Argenta Spirit*'s skipper.

"How do you know?" Marek was asking.

"Boxer told me," she explained. "And I saw him, Doghouse, there yesterday."

Marek's glass accidentally made a slamming sound as he put it down.

Kit threw him a *what* look? "That would have been *before* I knew about Rabbit's ID, Inspector Marek," she stipulated, as the ringing in her ear finally stopped.

"Hello. Over."

"Mr. Fellows? This is Kit O'Malley. We met yesterday when you showed me your boat."

"Yes, yes," he said. "Have you heard from your brother yet?"

"Not expecting to until the weekend. In the meantime, are you docked at Hastings?"

"Yes, dear."

"Is the *Gemini* there too? It's just that I've been trying to get in touch with Mark and Ellie, but their phone seems to be off."

"They took off this morning, so it's probably out of range. Ellie said they were going to Paynesville to take a tour group out fishing."

Yeah right. "Thanks Mr. Fellows. I'll call you when my brother gets over his jetlag." She hung up and passed the bad news on to Marek. "Mind you, if *they* said they were boatering to Paynesville, I'd be looking everywhere but there."

"Jeez, Kitty," Marek complained. "You could have told us this hours ago."

"Jeez yourself, Jonno. You're the guys with all the resources. I assumed you'd have the sense to ask Boxer." Kit grabbed her phone to stop it vibrating all over the table. It was Alex.

"Yes, my love," Kit said by way of hello.

"O'Malley, I need you," Alex said. Which was such a lovely thing to say. "Enzo is missing." Which wasn't.

"What do you mean, Enzo is missing?"

"Just that, Kit. He can't be found. We don't know where he is. Rick is beside himself. We're at my place."

"I'm on my way."

323

Chapter 26

It took Kit thirteen high-speed minutes to get to the apartment shared by Mr. and Mrs. McAllister/Cazenove, where Enzo's wife and boyfriend were generously sharing their anxiety over their man's disappearance. Alex was the calmer of the two, though obviously concerned, while Rick was well on his way to mild hysteria. Given that Enzo had been "missing"—and even then only supposedly—for only a few hours, Kit figured Alex's response was the more sensible. But then she *was* only the spouse, friend, and housemate, not the partner and lover.

"Calm down, Rick," Kit begged. "Where have you checked so far?"

"My place, here, Dorothy's, the Thai Thai café. I checked all his, and our, usual haunts and every friend I could think of. I even rang Rosie to see if he'd been in her bookshop tonight."

"Did you try the airport?"

"Yes, but they wouldn't page him. Besides he wouldn't still be there, Kit. His brother was only on a stopover."

Kit shrugged. "Maybe Nigel's connecting flight was delayed."

Rick clasped his hands. "We had extra special tickets for the Turandotty Cabaret, so he would've called me. And he's not answering his phone, which must be on because it rings."

Alex handed Kit a mug of coffee. "Enzo is nothing if not reliable, dependable, and every other 'able' there is," she said.

"Granted," Kit agreed. "What about Tereshenko? Have you tried calling him?"

"Why?" Alex frowned.

"Because he was going to the airport with Enzo to collect something," Kit explained.

"But I've no idea how to contact him," Rick moaned, starting to flap again.

"You would if you thought about it, Rick," Kit said soothingly. "Make yourself useful and find me a phone book." She pulled out her mobile and hit the speed dial.

"Hector the Humble."

"In your dreams," Kit remarked. "Where are you?"

"Hello to you, too, O'Malley. And why?"

Kit closed her eyes. "Are you near a computer?"

"Always. You sound stressed. What's up?"

"I am stressed, and therefore apologize in advance for being snappy. Enzo is missing."

"What do ..."

"Please don't ask what I mean by that, Hector. Do you know of any way to check Tullamarine Airport to see if he's there, with or without Comrade Tereshenko; or, failing that, whether his brother Nigel McAllister was on a flight from New Zealand to here at about 5 p.m., and/or whether he later left for, hang on ... Alex, where was Nigel going?"

"London—for a software convention."

"London, Hector," Kit said. "No idea about airlines or exact times, except that he had about an hour between flights."

"I'll see what I can do, O'Malley," Hector said. "I'll call you back."

Rick labored back into the kitchen with every phone book known to Telstra. He dumped them on the island bench, then ran into the adjoining lounge to answer the phone before Alex even had the chance to react to the ringing. Judging by his body language, it wasn't Enzo.

Kit pushed the Yellow Pages, the Melbourne Big, and a Perth directory out of the way and opened the A–K White Pages to look for Boyes-Lang. As Rick still had the landline engaged, she used her mobile again.

"Therah Boyth-Lung."

Blimey, Kit winced. The woman's new lips must have taken over her face. Either that or she's pithed. "Hi Sarah, it's Katherine O'Malley. Sorry to bother you so late, but have you seen Lorenzo tonight?"

"No, dear. Not thinth lunch."

"How about Gregor? Is he there?"

"Why?"

"Gregor and Enzo went to the airport this arvo. I thought they and Vanessa may have gone out somewhere after."

"Haven't theen a thoul thinth I got home. Give me your number and I'll call Netha and thee where they are."

"That was Loretta," Rick explained moments later. "Enzo's not with them either."

Kit drummed her fingers on the A–K. "Whose car did they take to Tullamarine?"

"Enzo's Renault, I assume," Rick said. "I don't think the Russian has a car."

"Where does he normally park when he's home? Have you checked there?"

"Basement car park," Alex replied. "I didn't notice it, but I wasn't really looking. Rick?"

Rick shook his head while turning on his heel and rushing towards the hall. Then he stopped dead in the doorway. "No, you two go look. I'll wait here in case he rings."

"Rick, mobile, come," Kit said. "Enzo's not going to ring you on his own home phone."

As they waited for their lift to come from the first to the eighth floor, Kit gazed at the three of them in the hideous gilt-framed mirror opposite the lift doors. She was still dressed in the blue jeans and shirt she'd left home in twelve hours before; Alex had changed from her lawyerly suit into black jeans and a pale gray jumper; and Rick was wearing tails and a green-sequined waistcoat. He looked like a suave and demented symphony conductor; Alex looked exquisite, of course, but worried; and she, herself, looked tired beyond words.

When they got into the lift, about three days later, Alex pressed the B button while Rick kept redialing Enzo and swearing all the way down. The underground car park was large enough to accommodate forty-six vehicles, which apparently allowed for 1.5 cars per apartment. Alex's red Celica, parked in its usual spot close to the front security gate, was not keeping company with Enzo's Renault, which was also not anywhere else to be seen.

326

"Now what?" Alex asked.

Kit sighed. "We wait for Hector to call back and if he has no news, then I'll call ..."

"Ooh! Wait. Listen!" Rick exclaimed. He was spinning in circles with an empty hand to his ear, as if he was trying to tune in to a new frequency.

"Sounds like?" Alex raised her hands questioningly.

"Valkyries," Kit said in surprise.

"Alex, Alex, open the gate, please," Rick said urgently. "It's coming from out there."

The Valkyries continued their ride, in the oodle-doodle tones of a ringing phone, as they all scrambled out into the street the moment the gate was high enough to get under.

"There." Alex pointed beyond a giant skip being used by building renovators next door.

On the other side of the bin, parked right up against the overflow of plaster chunks and scrap metal, and with one wheel up on the footpath, was Enzo's car. The passenger door was ajar, the interior light was on, and they could see the uncharacteristic mess of papers and audio cassettes strewn across the back seat.

There was no Enzo in sight, but they could still hear his phone. Kit dashed around to the driver's side, hesitating for a nanosecond in case there was something there on the road that she wouldn't want to see. There was—phew—nothing. Well, half a phew. She got down on her hands and knees to retrieve the not-very mobile from the ground underneath his car.

"Oh my God; oh my Lord," Rick wailed. "Jesus H. Christ and all the bleeding saints—what the hell is going on?"

"I don't know, Rick," Kit said, "but this is no time to get religion."

Rick glared at her and then looked apologetic. "But where is he?"

"We'll find him," Alex said reassuringly, while giving Kit another *what now?* look.

Kit shrugged and answered her mobile, but then asked her side-kick to hang on while she motioned for Rick's phone. She keyed in Marek's number and handed it to Alex. "Fill Jonno in, and ask him to send a divvy van." She took a deep breath before acknowledging Hector.

"Nigel came in by Air New Zealand just before five," he informed her. "He left, on time, on a Qantas flight for London, via Dubai, at 8 p.m., having cleared customs at seven.

"So Enzo's not at the airport, O'Malley, unless he's loitering for fun. And the bastards won't page anyone unless they're overdue for a flight that their luggage is already on."

"Thanks, Hector. We've just found his car, unlocked, in the street outside his and Alex's place. His phone was on the ground underneath it."

"That does not sound good," Hector said, then repeated Kit's news to someone wherever he was. "O'Malley? If his car is there, maybe he didn't get to the airport at all."

"That's possible," Kit agreed. "Where did you say you were?"

"You know I didn't. But I'm in a car outside Charlie Parker's place. I figured it was time to check and change the disk."

"Good thinking," Kit said. "Hang on. You said a car. Whose car, who are you with?"

"Um. Carrie."

"Oh really. And what is *um*-Carrie doing there?"

"Same thing as us, O'Malley. Spying on the lying cop. What? Oh. Quick, get down!"

"Hector?"

"O'Malley," he whispered. "The woman's leaving. We don't want to be seen."

Kit groaned. "That idiot Carrie isn't parked right out front is she?"

"Not since I got here; no," Hector replied, a definite smile in his voice.

Woman, Kit registered. "What woman?" she asked him.

"The chick who's been visiting him. Ow! Don't snatch."

A chick? That's unlikely. "Do you or Carrie happen to know who she is?" Kit asked.

"She's a police staff person," came a whispered voice that was neither Hector nor Carrie.

"Erin?" Kit said in surprise. "Oh *man*, now I'm really worried."

"Hey, you should be pleased. I'm doing quality control here."

Kit blew a raspberry. "What do you mean, police staff?"

"You know, an admin person. What? Oh right. Carrie reminded me you were there too. Remember that woman who came into Jon's office the other day? Liz something? It's her."

Kit screwed up her face. "Hang on a sec, Erin." She put her phone on the bonnet of Enzo's car, and rummaged through her pouch, then all of her pockets before finding the page that Chucky had given her, so many hours ago now that this morning felt like last week. She checked his possible hate list, marveling again at how narrow his sense of reality was. In fact, even his imagination didn't run to much, as his list of all and sundry who might have it in for him was only eight names long and didn't even include Boxer Macklin. Or her.

Mind you, Chucky didn't know that she *now* knew that he had an entire career of suss collars to cover up; so it was unlikely he'd have given her the name of *everyone* who'd like to see him burn in hell, in case he came across as paranoid.

The names of associates who'd helped in the acquisition of the false documents on Angie, was also short: a Constable Mick Hadley from the Fitzroy cop shop, and—there she was—Liz Nash, who'd collected them on Chucky's behalf.

"Liz Nash," Kit said to Erin. "Small and mousey, yeah?"

"Yep, that's her. Couldn't see all those tats you'd imagined from here, though."

"How long was she there?"

"About an hour. Why?"

"Coz it's very strange," Kit remarked, noticing that Alex was no longer on the phone.

"Should we have followed her?" Erin asked urgently. "We might still be able to catch her."

"No, but it might be worth hanging there for a while." Out of trouble, she thought. "You can all take turns getting donuts and coffee. Bye now, cherub." Kit hung up and joined Alex and Rick on the footpath.

"Jon has dispatched a unit to check Enzo's car and take our statements," Alex said. "He asked if we'd checked the hospitals yet."

Kit glanced questioningly at Rick, who reacted by launching into another attack of the flails. Alex reached out to calm him, then apparently changed her mind. She turned instead to Kit with an expression that mixed a frown with "why didn't we think of *this* before?"

"What?" Kit asked.

"The Typhoid Twins," she said. "Where are those damn Feral Feds when we need them? They must have seen what happened. Or ..."

The possible implications left hanging by that "or" were enough to render them all silent and motionless for a year-long five seconds.

Alex got in first. "Maybe they took him into Immigration for questioning."

"Maybe they deported him," said Rick, ever the optimist.

"They wouldn't do that without talking to his wife. Would they, Alex?"

"They better not have, because this wife is a lawyer."

"Maybe they didn't take him, but saw what happened. Let's ring their office," Rick said.

"At ten-thirty at night?" Kit said. "Which would also be an odd time to take him in. I doubt there'd be anyone there to ask, wherever there is. Besides, if Riff and Raff saw a crime ..."

Rick looked horrified, or like he was ready to appeal to a whole new set of deities.

"Or whatever," Kit added, "they'd have reported it to the ordinary cops. And unless they're watching us right now coz they've also lost Enzo, I'd say we're out of luck until tomorrow."

They all frowned at each other, nodded simultaneously, and traipsed out into the cul de sac to check the few parked cars for any signs of life. They were still standing in the middle of the street when Kit's mobile rang again and a police divisional van cruised around the corner.

"O'Malley," Hector said. "Erin just told me the name of that chick—*ow!*—woman person. I don't know what it means, but you remember you asked me to follow up on Ellie Jones?"

"Yes," Kit said cautiously, as her skin took to crawling.

"Well, she's not a Nguyen or a Smith, but you were right—as per—and she's not a Jones either. Her real name is Ellen Nash."

Shit, what does *that* mean? Kit's mind cried. Process—come on, O'Malley. What the hell does it mean? Right now, I mean. Is it relevant to anything right now?

"You there, O'Malley?"

"Yes, Hector. Just give me a sec, I'm letting that sink into the quag of my mind."

Okay, she prodded. Ellen Nash is Ellie Jones is Doghouse Dixon's girlfriend. *Liz* Nash is what? Chucky's friend, colleague, lackey? His partner in crime? Which crime? And what were they—Liz and Ellie-Ellen—to each other, if anything? Were they sisters, sisters-in-law, cousins, or just a ridiculous coincidence?

"Do you need a rescue rope yet?" Hector queried softly.

"Nuh," Kit said. "Don't think I can be dealing with this now, though. Can you do me another fave? Can you trace, track, check, uncover, whatever, anything you can on the Feral Feds, from the photos you took at Leo's on Friday?"

"Sure. I started on that on Sunday. You think they might have arrested him or something?"

"It's doubtful, but they might have seen what happened here tonight. Oh, and let me know if there's anything interesting on the disk when you get it."

"If I can. The next door zombie-dude just went visiting the Chuckster with a big box."

An hour later the uniforms had taken Enzo's vital stats, his last known whereabouts and had secured his car; Loretta Lorikeet, the draggest queen in town, had arrived to take Rick home to his own place to wait for Enzo, or word of or from him; Kit had phoned to ask Marek if he could suss out the Immigration Department and/or the feds on her behalf; and, after a return call from Sarah, backgrounded by a shrieking daughter, Kit and Alex were almost all the way to the Boyes-Lang's heart-of-the-city apartment overlooking the Yarra River.

As the lift began its trip to the penthouse, Alex suddenly, and surprisingly, relaxed her trademark unflappable and self-contained composure and took a moment to unravel. A bit.

331

"O'Malley?" she said softly. "What if something awful, I mean, what if Enzo …?"

"Alex, honey," Kit wrapped her woman in her arms and held her tight. "It's okay. We'll find him, I promise. There's probably a really simple or silly explanation for this."

"He's my best friend," Alex whispered.

"I know," Kit said, kissing her gently. "But it's way too soon to think the worst."

Kit knew that wasn't so, at all; but for both their sakes she figured that positive thinking was the only way to proceed and remain focused. And to deal with their next appointment.

As the doors opened into a tiny lobby, Kit witnessed a fair dinkum girding of the loins. Alex stepped out of the lift, inhaled deeply, and then took charge of the last of too many levels of security by pressing the "front door" bell. They stood waiting for what sounded like all-hell approaching, but a moment before they found out what that might look like, Alex surprised Kit again by turning to kiss her passionately with an about-to-be-caught urgency.

Holy hijack! Kit swooned, and then had to pretend all was normal as the door was flung open. Oh, it's not hell, she thought. It's just another hysterical person with a missing lover.

Vanessa, stomping and red-eyed, headed back into the spacious lounge where Sarah and her wasp-lips were standing in mid-rant. The moment she caught sight of Kit and Alex, and without drawing breath, she changed the direction of her tirade. "I knew it, Katherine; I jutht knew there wath thumthing about that man. He'th a bloody terroritht. Or a fortune hunter."

Like *they're* in the same basket, Kit thought. "What's going on?"

"What's going on?" Vanessa exclaimed, with a wiggle that made her dark hair flounce around like the star of its own shampoo ad.

Two things occurred to Kit in the moment that it took Vanessa to take a breath: people always echo each other in times of stress; and maybe Enzo's unknown-to-them position and condition had something to do with Tereshenko, and not Enzo. Not that she thought Gregor was the cause, but he might be the reason.

"My fiancé is missing," Vanessa was wailing. "My mother thinks

332

he's the reincarnation of Rasputin; *you* apparently are the private eye she hired to spy on him; I've no idea who that is," Vanessa pointed at Alex, "and if you don't hold me back I'm going to throw *her*," she pointed at her mother, "off the fucking balcony."

"Bloody typical that ith," Sarah screeched. "I'm only contherned with your well-being and happineth. I employed Katherine and Lorentho to check out Gregor, for your *own* good, Netha, out of love and the goodneth of my heart. I didn't want you conned by a thleazy money-grubbing old foreigner. But look at the thankth I get: bad language and the threat of murder. While he," she hoiked her thumb, "he'th off kidnapping people."

"Mother! Gregor being missing doesn't make him a kidnapper, you stupid old bitch."

"Oh you ungrateful little thit. I ought to ..."

The language and accusations continued to fly, so Kit and Alex sauntered over to check out the view from the window beside the aforementioned balcony—like they had nothing better to do with themselves at nearly midnight. With Alex holding her arm, and the glass safely between her and the dizzying view, Kit could almost appreciate the sight of Crown Casino off to the left, and the Yarra far far below. Given that her nervy ends were already stretched to screaming, a wee dose of vertigo didn't seem to have much impact at all.

"Ooh look, that's the first time I've seen them go off," Alex commented, as they watched Crown's huge riverside gas burners go through their explosive spectacle. While Alex was impressed by the special effects, Kit hoped no passing bats or night birds had just been incinerated.

Speaking of bad language, murder threats, and big bangs, Kit *really* wished, and not for the first time, that she was allowed to carry a gun. Or a cannon. Yeah, that'd be perfect, she thought, just a smallish big gun to fire at the ceiling to get their hosts' attention.

Use what you've got, O'Malley, she told herself; and then told Alex to cover her ears. She stuck her fingers in her mouth and blew a screeching whistle.

"Enough," she pronounced. "The two of you, sit down and shut up. Please. Or Alex and I will chuck you both out the window."

The bickering Boyes-Langs did as they were told, and looked quite surprised as they did so. Probably *because* they did so.

"Thank you," Kit said. "Okay, you first, Va …"

"Well, after you rang," Sarah began.

"Your daughter first, please," Kit interjected, while calculating the best trajectory from balcony to river. She turned to Vanessa, registered belatedly and with shock what the girl was wearing—a green leopard-patterned, skin-tight tube of fabric—and said, "Um, when did you last see Gregor and why do you think *he's* missing?"

"Because he's not here," Vanessa said, as if it was the stupidest question she'd ever heard. When Kit merely raised an eyebrow, she elaborated. "Enzo picked him up from my place just after three to go to Tullamarine. He, they, were due back about six-thirty at which time we, as in not Enzo, were going to a friend's birthday dinner. Gregor is not here, he's not there, he's not anywhere."

"You mark my wordth. Words," Sarah declared, trying to regain control of her lips and her S's. "He's kidnapped Lorentho."

"Why would he do that?" Kit asked, her tone implying that that notion was also fairly stupid.

Sarah threw her hands up. "How do I know? Maybe he knew he was under invethtigation and had no choith. Choice."

"You're completely mental, Mother."

I'm with you, Vanessa, Kit thought. "Hear, hear," Alex muttered.

"Sarah, you know I found nothing about Gregor to cause any concern," Kit said. "He really *is* a wealthy traveling linguist who happens to be in love with your daughter, so …"

"See," Vanessa stressed to her mother, while giving Kit a back-hand wave. "Even the hired help knows the truth."

I'll help you, *Nessa*, Kit's thoughts snarled. Right off the roof. "So, there's no reason," she continued, "why Gregor Tereshenko would abduct Enzo, even if it was Enzo himself who told him about the investigation."

Sarah chuckled dubiously, knowingly, or insanely—it was hard to tell which. "Will you be thaying that when he comes after you? Next."

"Why would he do that?" Alex asked.

"She ith the private detective. And he, well he's a Ruthan."

"For the hundredth time, Mother, he's not Russian. He's an American."

"Yeth, well, we all know about American communists, don't we, what with Macarthy shooting John Lennon and all."

Kit nearly choked. "On that wacky note, I think we'll be on our way," she said getting up.

"But you can't go," Vanessa pleaded. "You're the detective. You have to find him. Them."

"I intend to find *our* him; which might mean I also find them," Kit smiled. "But unless they're hiding in your mother's closet, I can't do anything *here*." She handed a business card, a piece of paper, and a pen to Vanessa. "Call me, please, if Gregor turns up with or without Enzo. And if you give me your home and mobile numbers I will do the same. Okay?"

Vanessa nodded, but Sarah said, "What if we get a ransom demand?"

"Who for?" Alex asked.

"For Lorenzo, of course."

Kit squinted at Sarah. "I think *we* would get a demand for Enzo. You'd get one for Gregor. Which is actually more likely given that you and he are the ones with all the money."

"Oh my God! Are you saying that Enzo might have kidnapped Gregor?" Vanessa demanded.

"No, Vanessa," Kit said slowly. "I'm saying it's just as likely as Gregor having abducted Enzo, which means *not at all*. Personally, I suspect Bajoran Buddhists, or the local podiatrist's club."

Chapter 27

Conscious or un, that is the question. Whether 'tis possible even to tell the difference or, after so little sleep, whether one gives a shit at such an uncivilized hour. Kit sighed. At least it wasn't Wednesday any more.

A shiver crawled its way up her back, only to get lost in the cold clammys she still had from her rude awakening ten minutes before. She'd been standing in front of the bathroom mirror, making sure the various parts of her face were still where they should be— mad hair, check; two tired green eyes, check; left cheekbone still smudged by the remains of the cellar-induced bruise, check; one mouth—when something too-many-legged scuttled into view on the wall behind her. Expecting the worst, she whirled around to confront the huntsman spider from a safe screaming distance, only to be loomed at by human eyes—dead human eyes, floating in their dead human face in a giant green test tube. Bloodless Gerry Anders, it was. No, it was Papa Leo's wasted form. *Oh my very soul*, Kit's mind had wailed … it's Hector.

The ringing phone had mercifully ripped her back from a hell she recognized too vividly—to her own bed, the one she'd been sharing with Alex. *Enough* with the re-runs already! Kit grabbed the edge of the kitchen bench so she could shake herself like a dog, to be rid of the nightmare dregs.

"Fnertle?"

"I don't think so, Thistle," Kit mumbled. "It's a tad more complicated than that."

"What is?" Alex queried, emerging from the hallway, wearing just knickers and Kit's shirt, not yet done up.

"Existence," she replied, grinning broadly as reality took charge of her day and the dream dissipated into this better-looking version of life. Kit loved it that Alex put on the closest thing to hand when she got out of bed, because more and more often it was something of hers.

"That, my darling, is an understatement." Alex slid her arms around Kit from behind and nuzzled the back of her neck.

Oh yeah. The "my darling" was another thing Kit loved. That, and the neck kissing and …

"Please tell me that was Enzo on the phone, or Rick about Enzo," Alex said.

"Wish I could," Kit shook her head. "And I just spoke to Loretta, at Rick's place, and Enzo still hasn't turned up. They tried every hospital on the hour, every hour, all night."

"Fuckit," Alex whispered, closing her eyes for a moment. "So who rang? It's only eight."

"Hector. He's on his way here with pictures."

"Pictures of what?"

"Liz Nash going in and out of Chucky's place; Guy the guy going in and out of Chucky's place; and Chucky ditto."

"But you know what they all look like, darling. Why do you need photos?"

"Interest; and to see if *you* think this Liz Nash looks anything like Ellie/Ellen Nash/Jones. You got a much better look at Doghouse's boat bimbo than I did the other day."

"Do you really think they're related?"

Kit flipped her palms up. "Frankly, my love, I stopped thinking anything at about noon on Monday."

A nanosecond before the doorbell rang, Kit knew it was about to, because The Watchcat went all tippy-toe and startled—as a prelude to fleeing, if necessary. Alex glanced down at her bare legs, pointed over her shoulder, and returned to the bedroom for more clothes, so Kit went to open the front door and let …

"You're not Hector," she said.

"Aren't I?" said Cathy Martin. "Who's Hector?"

"I am," came a voice halfway up the stairs.

"I'm not," said Carrie, bringing up the rear.

"Oh, by all means," Kit ushered, "come on in. Everyone."

Whereon Thistle made an executive decision to flee, because everyone traipsed towards her bench, all talking at once. She returned a moment later, however, in a stroll of cool cat-wanting-breakfast bravery, and escorting a now fully clad Alex.

Kit lined up the cups and began pouring coffee. "Righto. I know why *you're* here, Hector; I can guess why Carrie is," Kit began, "so that just leaves you, Cathy."

"And I have three reasons," Cathy smiled. "First, Marek asked me to pass on that he has no news about your friend Enzo, but that he's still trying to wake up the Feds. Second, Sally needs you to call in this morning and make a statement regarding that bloke you told us about last night. And the third is just gossip really, but I thought you might be interested to know that Papa Leo Barker died last night ..."

Whoa! Kit was surprised—no, suddenly affected—by the kind of shock one feels when, having just met a bloke, he then goes and dies, like almost immediately. At the same time, she was also thinking: well, that's no surprise really, coz he hadn't exactly looked the best.

"... of a drug overdose," Cathy finished.

"What?" That woke her up.

"Self-induced," Cathy added.

Oh. Okay. Hmm. Kit's mind surged with the kind of vertiginous confusion that usually accompanied those sideshow rides that fling people halfway to a low-slung cloud and then leave them hanging there, waiting for gravity to take control again.

No doubt about the state of consciousness now, though, O'Malley. "But isn't, wasn't he ..."

"In hospital? Yeah, in the Alfred," Cathy nodded. "It happened, I mean *he did it* during visiting hours last night. It was damned lucky for the family, given their rep, that a doctor and nurse were present in the room at the time. As it was, Prahran CIB had to question two of Leo's sons, a wife, and several rug rats who also saw what happened."

"And what did happen?" Alex asked.

"According to the unbiased witnesses, Stuart and Brian Barker were busy arguing with each other when Leo suddenly said, 'Bullshit, yah useless bastards. Not takin' no more of your crap.' Then he plunged a syringe into the cannula in the back of his hand and dosed himself with potassium chloride. The old bastard was dead in no time at all."

"Bloody hell," Hector exclaimed.

"Amazing," said Alex.

Nothing said Kit, for she was speechless. She was also seething.

"Wonder what they were arguing about?" Carrie said.

Kit gave a pondering, clueless kind of shrug. She couldn't let anyone know that she was seething, because then she'd have to explain to the nice lady cop how it was she *possibly* knew how Papa Leo had achieved his end; or, rather, from whom he'd gotten his choice. Fucking Queenie, she thought. I'm going to have words with her after I throttle her. Kit blinked. No, that *is* the right order, coz that way around she won't be able to deny anything.

"Kit? You okay?" Alex was apparently repeating her question.

"Yes darling, I'm fine." Kit then looked at Cathy who, instead of giving her a suspicious look, gave her one that implied that there was more to her visit than the delivery of bad news.

Cathy downed her coffee and said, "Well, I'm off to the fray for another day."

Kit walked her to the door. "Why are you really here?" she asked quietly.

"Just as I said. But while I'm here," Cathy grinned, "last night I got the feeling that you know something more about Charlie. Can you tell me?"

"Yes I do, and no I can't right now; but I will."

"Is it bad? I mean, is it detrimental? Can you at least tell me that much?"

Kit raised an eyebrow. "It's seriously bad, and it's mean and detrimental," she said. "I'm not sure yet if it's entirely his doing or his fault. But what are you really up to, Detective Martin?" she squinted. "Why have you come here out of your way to ask me that?"

Cathy seemed to be tossing up whether to be more forthcoming than Kit. Cramming one hand into the pocket of her green trousers, she said, "I had a strange, anonymous of course, call about Charlie this morning. I wanted to see if you could enlighten me before I deal with it."

"It wasn't me," Kit shook her head. "I didn't call you."

"That much I do know," Cathy nodded. "It was a woman, though."

"Can you tell me what she said?" Kit looked hopeful.

"No," Cathy said with an as-if laugh. "Sorry."

"Could you squeeze me in a favor, then—for when I come in especially to see Sally."

"Depends how much time you're giving me to do whatever it is," Cathy said.

Kit checked her watch. "About two hours. It's about the false report on Angie. Supposedly, a Constable Mick Hadley from Fitzroy handed the documents to Liz Nash, one of your office admin staff, who gave them to Chucky. Would you be able find out if Hadley offered them, or was asked to find them; and anything you can about Nash. Like, if she has a sister called Ellen or Ellie either Nash or Jones."

"Why? Who's she?"

"Ellie Jones, aka Ellen Nash, is Dixon's girlfriend. The one he's done a runner with."

"And you think her sister works with us? I don't like the sound of that connection. I shall therefore do my best," Cathy said agreeably. "And we'll see *you* about ten-thirty then."

Kit returned to the kitchen where Hector, who'd already loaded the digital photos from his camera onto his laptop, was putting on a picture show.

"I suppose they could be related," Alex said reluctantly as everyone, including The Cat, peered at the image of Liz Nash emerging from Parker's house. She was ram-rod straight and watchful, but nondescript; the sort of person you wouldn't really notice. And she was still all brown and mousey in hair and complexion and clothes—just like she'd been on Monday.

"There's a similarity there," Alex continued, "but it's hard to tell, because Ellie was a slouchy redhead. Of course, her hair could have been a dye job. "

Kit laughed "Are you kidding? That bogan hairdo had to be natural, Alex. No one in their right mind would do that to their head on purpose."

"I'm a redhead," Carrie said, pointing at her red hair.

"Are you really?" Kit asked, in astonishment.

"Perpetual rudeness is quite unbecoming, O'Malley," Carrie the Miffed noted seriously.

"Sorry, but the morning grump in me is easily vexed by statements of the obvious."

"My point, O'Malley, is that hair color is not a clue to anything. My stepsister, as in unrelated to me, is exactly the same natural red as me; but my real sister is a blonde."

"That's curiously interesting," Kit said. She reached out and used her fingers to frame the face of Liz Nash so her hair could not be seen at all. "Now what do you think, Alex?"

"Yeah, maybe. There's something familiar but ..." she trailed off.

"Oh bloody hell," Kit moaned, as her mind yoo-hood at possibly the same "something familiar but." She ran across the landing into her office space, rummaged around in the mess on her desk, then skidded back across the polished boards. Squeezing in between Alex and Hector, she propped Scooter's bad-indeed polaroid on the screen next to the mousey mug of Liz Nash.

"Now *they* could be sisters," everyone said.

"Damn it! What are we dealing with here?" Kit demanded, of no one in particular. "This is like a Danielle Steel mystery movie—*The Nash Twins Revisited* or something."

"Triplets," Alex corrected. "Or a trio. We're not sure about Liz and Ellie, except for the shared surname; but Liz and Chrissie look similar-ish. If you're right about Doghouse trying to infiltrate the Rileys and Barkers, then it looks like he's got a whole bevy of spy girls."

"Yeah," Kit nodded. "And a family bevy at that."

"Is there another crime family in Melbourne?" Carrie asked.

"Several, but none called Nash," Kit said. "Unless they're moving in from interstate."

"That would better fit your theory of a plot to destabilize the two major clans," Alex noted.

"If you want," Hector offered, with a hint of glee that his expertise could again be utilized, "I can play with both faces to show you what they'd be like with different hair. Especially this chick, " Hector said, flicking the too-close photo of Chrissie.

Kit's eyes lit up appreciatively. "My techno-hero. You need to give both of them a curly red mullet thing. And, um, Alex, what did Scooter say about the mysterious Chrissie?"

"Blonde with dark stripes, long at the back, with a fringe. And brown eyes," Alex said.

"No wuckers," Hector grinned. "Give me a couple of hours."

"Excellent," Kit said. "I'm now going to shower and dress, so I can go give yet another statement to a short arm of the law." And then, O'Malley, she thought, we're going to go question the queen of this fair city's underworld about aiding and abetting a suicide.

Kit was almost out of the room when a thought struck her. She turned back to the kitchen. "Carrie? You mentioned a stepsister earlier. Does that mean you have a stepfather?"

"Stepmother. Why?"

"Do you get on with her?"

"Like a couple of peas in a pod. We love to shop, eat, and play tennis together. At least we did before I left WA."

"Did she raise you?"

"Since I was ten. Why?"

"Just curious. But not about you. And I did not mean that the way it sounded, either."

It took Kit ten minutes to give Detective Evans her statement about Trevor Wagstaff, the poor misguided ex-bouncer who'd been picked up at dawn. After starting sensibly, for his own well-being, with complete denial, he'd apparently devolved into his own worst enemy; a prize idiot of the kind who only opened his mouth to change feet.

Even though she knew Kit couldn't personally identify Wagstaff, Sally let her take a look at him from the observation room. Given what he'd done to Toad, Kit was very glad Trevor didn't know who *she* was; although right now, Sid Ralph's murderer was a sad looking bastard indeed. It was amazing how pathetic 120 kilos of steroid-induced muscle could look when facing a guaranteed twelve years in jail.

After performing her civic duty, Kit went looking for Marek or Cathy. No one was anywhere so, after getting the okay from someone she knew in the squad room, she wandered into Marek's office to wait. And wait. Alex had opted to do her waiting in the car, so she could make follow-up calls about Enzo and cancel the rest of her working week. Kit rang and filled her in on the situation so far. She then took the liberty of pouring a coffee from her ex-partner's always-on-the-go machine and sipped it as she strolled his space and tried out all his furniture. At the end of her Goldilocks routine she settled in Marek's own comfortable desk chair because there was the best place from which to read a list pinned to his notice board. Kit smiled, knowing without doubt that Marek would morph into the Big Bad Bear if he caught her doing what she was doing. But damnit, it was a list. People automatically read lists. That's what they're for. And if it *was* an eyes-only list it shouldn't be flapping around in plain view of any curious tart who happened upon it, and happened to lift the cover sheet that said 'BwM Inventory.'

Reading the forensic evidence list of everything that was found at the different crime scenes with the Rental Killer's six victims, was way less affecting than looking at a table covered with the actual items, as Kit had done on Monday, but this was still like peeking at a psycho's filthy laundry list.

The cross-referenced inventory, the one which applied to all six cases and listed items not belonging to the victims but found at one or more scenes, recorded a strange collection indeed. And, to Kit's mind, this multi-crime inventory was way more creepy than the case-by-case catalogs of each victim's personal items, like underwear, lipsticks, or jewelry. It took Kit a moment to reason that while the latter humanized the victims, and quite disturbingly so, there was *nothing* personal in or about the stuff in the cross-reference. The victims had names and sad reminders of their lives; but there was nothing personal about the things the killer left behind. Or might have left.

Kit rubbed her eyes and read the list again. Beetles—black; banksia nuts—small; blue tac—green; cuffs—toe and hand, spiked; feathers—magpie, quail, turkey; barbed fencing wire—9 cm lengths; fibers—2 cm, green and yellow; flints—cigarette lighter; floss—4-strand, blue and red; garlic—peeled cloves; fur/hair—calf, dog, and deer; hair—human, no match to victims; nails—6 cm, bullet head; teeth—4 × human molars, no match to victims; rice—uncooked grains; rubber strips—small, cut from occy strap; rust—1 mm flakes; thread—17 cm lengths, nylon invisible; tickets—bus and train; wire—5 cm lengths, fine copper.

It occurred to her that finding so much stuff in supposedly empty houses was strange in itself. Marek had told her last month that none of the residences were the primary crime scenes, so Kit assumed he and his Barleycorn Task Force had questioned just how much of this so-called evidence was actually related to the murders. Much of it could be just plain rubbish; while other stuff could be relevant; and some could've been deliberately left by the killer to confound and confuse.

"In a perfect world I'd arrest you for that." It was grouchy Papa Bear, but he looked too tired to really give a damn.

"Hi, honey," Kit smiled, swiveling on his chair.

"Don't 'hi, honey' me, O'Malley, unless your snooping has enlightened you to the point where you can give me fresh insight." Marek poured a coffee and slumped onto his couch.

"Well, young Jon," Kit said, all school teacherish, "if Bubblewrap Man's killing ground is somewhere else, how is it that you guys found so much stuff in those vacant houses?"

"We didn't find it in the houses, Kitty. We found all those items with the bodies. Wrapped with them, in different layers of the plastic. You know, like the charms and shit that ancient Egyptians used to place in amongst the wrappings of their mummies."

Kit pulled a face. "Really? So it's *all* either specifically relevant or …"

"Completely not," Marek finished. "There's been no attempt to disguise fingerprints, as in no obvious smudges where the killer might have used gloves to hold items handled by him or someone else. And although there are lots of different prints, none match any in our database; except those of the women, and only then because they're the victims. We've got evidence up to our ears, including DNA from what we assume is the bastard's own semen; but nothing to match it to. Until we catch him. And when we do that, we'll have him. No question about it."

344

"But this," Kit tapped the cross reference, "is such a peculiar assortment of bits and bobs that it's got to be bullshit."

"You think?" Marek asked.

"Yeah. We know, you and I, that Bubblewrap Man is more likely to be a deluded deadshit with a Bower Bird mentality, than a Lecterish genius with a definable but no doubt deeply damaged reason for: a) killing, and b) leaving this strange stuff. It's all suspiciously like herrings of the colored variety. Or rubbish. Either that or, and apart from serial murder, Bubblewrap Man has some weird-arse hobbies."

Kit's eyebrows raised themselves in surprise at her own freakish thought processes, while her mind quite clearly shouted: *Well, bugger me! And with a woolly one at that.* She turned her attention back to the cross reference while also recalling how she'd read recently that the human brain never forgets anything. Not one single thing. And that while she might never actually have cause to remember what she got for her third birthday, the info was in there somewhere.

"Jeez, I hate it when you do that, Kitty," Marek noted sullenly.

"Do what?" she asked absently.

"Look like you've seen the light, and then taken a trip to La-La Land alone. It's not fair."

"Sorry," Kit said, running her finger up and down the page, as she re-ordered items into her own mental list: quail feathers, colored fibres, and invisible thread; deer fur—that's got to be the same as elk hair; red floss, copper wire.

"O'Malley," Marek said impatiently.

"Flies," she announced.

"What?"

"Flies, Jonno," she repeated. "Fly-fishing flies. Has Chucky Parker seen this list? Has he seen the stuff you're hoarding in that room over there?"

"I don't know. He might have, but he's not on the task force. Why?"

"Coz I think half of these things can be used to make flies. If he hasn't seen this stuff, you should get him to take a look."

"I don't get it; why Charlie?"

"Because he's a fly fisherbloke."

"So? As I said he's not on Barleycorn; but the first murder *was* picked up by his crew." Marek looked thoughtful. "Come to think of it, so was the second. In which case, if he knew anything, wouldn't he have put the reliable old two and two together then?"

"One would think so, wouldn't one?" Kit said suggestively.

"Do not go there, Kitty," Marek laughed. "*That* is ridiculous."

"*That* might be," Kit smiled, "except you did tell me he knew victim number six. But that was not my point, Jonno. Someone who knows about angling-type things needs to have a look at the collection in there as parts of a whole; not as individual bits and pieces. Detective Parker has very recently taken up the sport of fly fishing and the hobby of fly-tying, so why not haul him back in here and make him useful?"

"He's here, in interview room four," Marek stated, while doing a double take on something Kit had just said. "How the hell do you know about Charlie's hobbies?" he asked; while she scowled and said, "He's back at work already?"

Kit was livid, and determined to avoid answering Marek's question. "You let him return to duty after what he did to Angie?"

"No, Kitty. But he is helping us with our inquiries into a related incident."

"What related incident?"

"He's being questioned in connection with the murder of Gerald Anders."

Chapter 28

Before Kit had a chance to ask Marek to run that by her again, for fun, frustration personified appeared in the doorway. "I think I'm the wrong person to be questioning him, boss."

"Why, Martin? Can't you be objective?"

"Hardly!" Cathy snorted. "I'd rather take him out the back and shoot him."

"Later; we can take turns," Marek smiled, rubbing his chin. He frowned at his hand, as if it was the source of the scratchy-whisker noise, then added, "I assume he's in denial."

"Denying everything, with a loud and thoroughly obnoxious 'how dare you ask me this' attitude. With emphasis on me being the you. He's also demanding a union rep, a lawyer, the Minister for Agriculture, you name it. Oh, hey, O'Malley."

"Hey, Cathy," Kit waved. "Can one of you fill me in? Or give me an outline, at least."

Cathy glanced at Marek who nodded, so she closed the door behind her. "The anonymous caller I told you about, said that if we searched Charlie's car we'd find evidence linking him to the recent murder of an underworld figure."

"Discounting Leo Barker's case as self-murder," Marek said, "that left good old Gerry."

No way, Kit thought, mostly because, apart from all that was logical, Chucky being Gerry's killer put the whammy on her elaborate theories. "Did you find anything in his car?"

"Blood," Cathy nodded. "I thought it was a small bottle of tomato juice at first."

"A bottle of blood?" Kit said incredulously. "In his car? Come on, guys. Anyone, including the person who made the call, could've planted that on Chucky; or something like it on any one of you. Do you know yet whether it's actually Gerry's blood? Or even human?"

"It's humanness was verified at nine-thirty this morning," Marek said with a curious frown. "And twenty minutes ago it was cross-matched as B-negative to the rather large and easy to access sample we have of the stuff that once flowed freely through Mr. Anders."

"Lovely imagery," Kit remarked. "But it's got to be a setup, yeah? I mean even if he did kill him, why on earth would Chucky keep a bottle of Gerry at all, let alone in his car?"

Jon Marek's highly-suspicious-of-Katherine-O'Malley face was slowly taking the place of his tired and questioning one. "Are you all right, Kitty? You're normally the first to wedge our Chuck firmly in the frame for anything from careless language to implying, not ten minutes ago, that he's the Rental Killer."

"You didn't?" Cathy laughed.

"I did no such thing," Kit denied. "Marek merely inferred that notion from a comment I made about Chucky's fly-tying hobby."

"Charlie has a hobby?" Cathy was astounded.

"It's a new thing for him," Kit confided. "He makes beautiful fake insects and uses them to catch poor wee fish."

"So he's a fish killer," Marek nodded sagely. "In which case, tell me again why you don't think he killed Anders? Or, more specifically, Kitty O'Malley, why are you defending the man that you—and this is a known-throughout-the-universe fact—have no positive feelings for, of any kind, at all, whatsoever?"

Cathy raised a finger. "If he *is* being set up, O'Malley could be the culprit."

"Oh ha! And you bite your tongue, Jonno," Kit scolded. "I am *not* defending Graham Charles Parker. I *am*, however, defending the virtue of using common bloody sense, because the notion that Chucky possesses the required amount of testosterone and intestinal fortitude to do to Gerry what was done to him is so beyond laughable it's no longer funny."

"What wouldn't he possess?"

"Man-juice and guts, Marek. Chucky wouldn't have the nerve, nor the balls, nor the brains, nor the wherewithal," Kit elaborated. Motive is another matter entirely, she thought.

348

"Anyone can kill."

"Not like *that* they can't, Jonno. But why are you so convinced he could, or did?"

"I'm not. But your reaction to the possibility is highly suss. So what gives?"

Kit turned her palms up. "Let's see. Someone needs to keep you lot in line coz you keep arresting the strangest people after jumping to conclusions based on anonymous phone calls and questionable evidence," she said, and then rolled her eyes. "And he's my client, so I had to ask and say all the right things. Right from his point of view, I mean."

Marek's expression skipped surprised completely and went straight to stony-faced stunned.

"Please do not ask me how it happened. And breathe, Jonno, before you turn blue."

Marek was spurred into motion only by his ringing phone, whereon he shooed Kit out of his chair so he could pretend to be the boss of the Homicide Squad for a moment.

Kit smiled sweetly at Cathy. "Any luck with that info I was after?"

Cathy gave a yes–no nod, leaned wearily against the filing cabinet, and said softly, "Liz Nash apparently has no sister going by any name. She's been working here on a part-time basis for about six months but, as of yesterday, is on extended sick leave."

"Sick leave?" Kit frowned. "How curious. How convenient."

"Yeah. I am checking on it, because it gets even more so." Cathy narrowed her eyes. "O'Malley, there is no Constable Mick Hadley at Fitzroy—not now, not then, not ever. And not anywhere else, as far as I can find."

Kit decided to keep her frowny face on until something positive arrived to replace it. "That requires answers from the weasel you've been interviewing. Can I beat them out of him?"

"You can talk all you like when we release him in about ten minutes."

"What?" Kit was appalled. "Why isn't he being locked up? On suspicion of something; or anything," she shrugged. "You could at least get him for impersonating a human."

Cathy laughed. "You want us to lock up your client?"

"That one—yes please. Why the hell aren't you keeping him?"

"Because it *is* more likely that someone planted that blood in his car."

"Um, Kit," Marek said thoughtfully, pointing at his phone. "I just got some very strange news, and I've no idea whether it's good or bad."

"Good for who?" she asked. "Or not?"

"You," he said. "Or rather, Enzo."

The worst! Kit thought, as all her internal organs dropped, and crammed themselves into her pelvis. Bloody hell! Why does human adrenaline always assume the worst? Because Jonno called you Kit, that's why. He rarely does that. "What news?"

"The Immigration Department is not investigating anyone by the name of Lorenzo, Enzo, or Lawrence McAllister."

"What, um, what?" As that had not been even remotely close to what Kit thought Marek was going to say, she had major trouble processing that strange-indeed strange news.

"There are no federal cops tailing your mate and/or his wife. Never have been."

"But I've seen them," Kit insisted. "Hell, you saw them, remember, at the wedding."

"Maybe," Marek shrugged. "I don't remember anyone pointing them out to me."

Kit planted her hands on her hips. "Are you saying I'm making it up?"

"Course not. I know you're not the only one who's seen them. What I am saying is that they're not cops. Well," Marek hesitated, "they're not Immigration agents."

"Too weird," Kit scowled, then stamped her foot. "Well, damnit! Who the fuck are they?"

"Not a clue," Marek said. "I don't suppose you've been a sensible little PI and …"

"Yes, as it happens," Kit interjected. "I'll get Hector to e-mail the pics to you. But Jonno, if they saw what happened to Enzo and they're *not* cops, they may have done a runner. We may never find them to ask them what they know."

"Kitty, think about it! If they're not cops, maybe *they* are what happened to Enzo."

Kit stewed on that possibility for about five seconds. "No," she cast her hands out. "Coz why? Ding and Bat have been following Enzo since January; so why do ... whatever, now? *And* do it to Gregor too. It makes no sense."

"Only because we don't know what the whatever is," Marek pointed out. "But the new big question is: if they're not cops, *why* have they been following Enzo at all?"

"Perhaps they were after this Gregor fellow, not Enzo," Cathy suggested.

Kit shook her head. "Enzo didn't know Gregor back in January. He didn't even know of him then. They only met about three weeks ago."

"And why did they?" Marek queried. "Is he, the Russian guy, is he gay too? Are they like an item?"

"No, Gregor's as straight as," Kit said. "And Enzo has Rick; you know that, Marek."

"So what's their deal?" Marek ignored her reprimand for a question that had to be asked.

"Enzo was doing a genealogical thing on Gregor for his, Gregor's, girlfriend's mother. You know, to prove Gregor's lineage was the real deal. But they, Enzo and Gregor, were only going to the airport together yesterday because it was convenient."

"So, it all gets stranger of its own accord," Marek noted. "Call Hector and get me the photos, and I'll ring around to see if those guys belong to a different department."

"This is so not good," Kit muttered as she made her call.

"Hey, O'Malley," Hector answered. "I was just about to ring you."

"ESP," Kit said absently. "Could you e-mail the photos you took of Snick and Snack on Friday to, hang on ..." She reached for the card Marek was offering and read the e-mail address.

"The Snick-Knacker Twins were why I was going to call you," Hector said. "They're not with the Immigration Department, O'Malley. And unless they're undercover, badly, for some other reason they're not Federal cops at all."

"Tell me about it," Kit complained. "Marek's gunna try to find out who they are."

"Maybe they're with ASIO," Hector speculated. "They might be spooks who think Enzo's a spy. Woo, maybe Enzo *is* a spy. "

"And maybe you're not as smart as you occasionally look."

"Why thank you, O'Malley. Anything else I can do for you while I'm still doing the other thing?"

"No, but thanks." Kit turned back to Marek. "The pics are on the next wave in. And now, if you don't need me for anything else, I have to get out of here and strangle a few people."

"Fine," Marek said, grabbing his phone. "And we'll vice versa on the Enzo thing."

"I'll walk you out," Cathy offered. She waited until they'd passed through the squad room before catching hold of Kit's arm. "*Now* can you give me the goss on my temporarily-ex but otherwise immediate superior?"

Kit shook her head. "Not until I've spoken to him, Cathy. Sorry. But first I have to verify, or discard, a few way-inflammatory bits of info I've been given. Can I wait here for him?"

"Sure," Cathy growled in friendly frustration.

"Oh, one more thing, Cathy."

"Isn't there always?"

"Alan Shipper's stepdaughter. Can you find out her name and where she might be?"

"I guess. Why?"

"Coz I've been thinking about step-families. How some work and some don't. Like, my Alex would like to see her narrow-minded fundamentalist Bible-preaching stepfather boiled in oil—holy oil, or the dark satanic variety if there is such a thing. But Carrie McDermid gets on famously with her stepmum. So, I was just wondering how Shipper's stepkid might have reacted to his untimely demise in an alleged accident."

Cathy looked at her curiously. "You think *she* might be behind Gerry's death?"

"Yes. No." Kit sighed. "There's actually not a lot of thinking going on up here," she tapped her head, "just random bits of info colliding in my weary brain."

"It must be contagious," Cathy remarked as she headed up the corridor.

While Kit waited for Chucky to be released she decided to phone and make sure that the Angel of Death was going to be in for her to call on—and tell off—in no uncertain terms.

"Queenie, hi, this is Kit."

"Good morning, dear."

Don't you good morning me, you old witch. "May I drop in on you in about an hour?"

"Certainly."

"Good. I'm at police headquarters at the moment," Kit said, with a tone vaguely suggestive of trouble, or its making. "I have to talk to someone about, oh, that doesn't really matter; but then I'll pop over and see you."

"Whenever you like, Kit. I'm not going anywhere." Queenie's tone suggested amusement.

"Good. Oh, have you heard about Leo?"

"Yes, Kit. I have."

"Queenie? Do I know something I shouldn't?"

"I'm sure you know lots of things, dear. Whether you should, or not, is debatable."

"Should I be worried?"

"That's entirely up to you, Kit," Queenie said. "What's the worst that can happen?"

"I have a vivid imagination."

"I bet you have," Queenie laughed. "Let me see, what can I say to help? Just consider how far one should be prepared to go for one's dearest friends. See you soon." She hung up.

She bloody hung up, Kit's mind shouted. And what does that mean? Whose friends? Queenie's friends. My friends? Oh crap!

Kit tossed the possibilities. Was it an abstract reference to mates in general, as in anyone's friends, anywhere? Or was it a loose reference to any or all of Queenie's friends, including Leo? Ooh, and a hex on that ooh, she thought, coz that group could now include her. Was it a pointed, but not-exactly-threatening, reference to her friends? To Katherine Frances O'Malley's friends? Uh-oh.

Kit came over all queer and clammy because that thought naturally led to a much worse, and rather bleeding obvious, one. Queenie Riley had just made a specific reference, but with an inaccurate plural, to Kit's actual and particular friend: Enzo. And Gregor.

Don't be ridiculous, O'Malley!

Oh yeah? she argued. Rat-faced Morley and strange-boy Santo, both Queenie's own handpicked contacts, saw you with Enzo McAllister yesterday arvo; prior to Enzo picking up Gregor Tereshenko and them both subsequently disappearing.

Get real! And stop with the gun jumping, O'Malley. You know bloody well that's the problem with cryptic conversations: they're suggestive of everything, and nothing and …

"O'Malley?"

"Yes? Me. What?" Kit whipped around to face the Chuck monster.

"Why are you pacing? I'm the one who's been locked up in there for hours."

Kit whacked the down button on the wall next to them. "Do not give me any attitude, Charlie, because I've got a skeleton of bones to pick with you." The lift made a perfectly punctuated arrival. "Get in," she finished.

Parker did just that, but barked "Attitude? Those bastards, my so-called colleagues, have been grilling me—*me*—for the murder of the prize prick of all time, and you talk about …"

"Chuck!" Kit faced him and waved her accusing finger. "Given what I now know about you and that particular prize prick, it's my guess you *really* don't want to have our chat in this confined space. So, do me a favor, and shut up."

A supercharged silence accompanied them to the ground floor, out into the leading edge of a nasty little wind storm, and over to the footpath beside Kit's car, in which Alex remained, with the window down. Parker then exploded with gesticulations and, "What friggin' bones? What is it that you think you know?" He didn't call her "girlie," but he may as well have.

Glaring at him as if he were an absurd cockerel with his fists planted on his skinny-arse hips and his chest all bantamed-out, Kit began: "I know, *Detective Senior Sergeant Parker*, about all the crooks that Gerry Anders helped you catch and put away. I know,

Charlie, that some of them were innocent. That some, *Chuck*, were volunteers involved in Gerry's setup of you; while others were framed, by your mate Gerry, for his own benefit."

The face of Graham Charles Parker turned the color of the footpath.

Yes! Kit cheered, and marveled that even the whipping wind was on her side, as it slapped soggy leaves into Parker's legs and chest and pricked at his eyes.

She smiled. "I know, *Chucky*, that you witnessed a murder carried out by Gerry and about which you could do fuck all, because of the concurrent discovery that your wonderful arrest record was a work of fiction. That your reputation, courtesy of the sweet little deal you thought you'd made with the prince of the Melbourne underworld, was mostly bogus.

"And I know—you stupid, arrogant, homophobic, sexist, self-righteous, pitiful excuse for a police officer—that because Gerry had you over that stinking barrel, you lied under oath to give him an alibi for the attempted murder charge brought against him for the hit and run that paralyzed Bruce Paxton."

Whatever the opposite of hyperventilating was called, DSS Charlie Parker was doing it: exhaling the short sharp, last breaths of his life as he'd previously known it.

"I *know* all this, Charlie," Kit continued. "It's not speculation, rumor, or guesswork. And I will have to do the right and proper thing with this information, *but*," she hesitated, to let as much as possible sink into the man who was shrinking before her verbal assault as if she were physically beating him, "I also believe, despite your criminal association with Gerald Ian Anders, that you are probably not his murderer."

Parker was surprised, but as he was still speechless, Kit continued. "I reckon you have the best of all reasons for being elated that Gerry is very dead, but I think you *are* being framed."

"You do? Thank God."

"God has nothing to do with it," Kit said, shoving her hands in her jacket pockets. "And I said, I *think*. I don't know it for sure. Not like the other stuff, which I do know—for sure—and which I trust you're not going to try to deny, are you, Charlie?"

He pursed his lips. "Seems pointless."

"Was that a yes or a no?" Alex threw in.

Parker cricked his neck and ignored her. "Does that mean you'll keep working my case?"

"Only if there's no more bullshit, Charlie," Kit warned. "I expect only the truth from now on; otherwise I walk and you can sink in your own crap. If I ask you about Anders, or Paxton, or anyone else, you tell me everything. Deal?"

"Deal," Parker nodded, offering his hand. Kit ignored it. "I promise," he insisted. "Look, before it was just fraudulent paperwork, but now it's murder. And I swear, O'Malley, I did not kill Anders."

She shrugged. "So what does Liz Nash have to do with any of this?"

"Liz Nash? Why? I mean, what do you mean?"

"Charlie," Kit growled at him.

"Sorry," he surrendered, "but I don't understand why you're asking. She's no one. She's just a secretary. You know, a general office gofer."

"Yeah?" Kit said dubiously. "But she got that fraudulent paperwork for you. True?"

"Yes," he nodded.

"And she collected it for you from a cop who doesn't exist."

"What?"

"Am I not speaking English?" Kit asked Alex, who indicated that she understood.

"O'Malley," Parker waved his hands in frustration. "I've no idea what you're on about."

"The connie at Fitzroy, remember?" Kit prodded. "Constable Mick Hadley, who allegedly gave *your* secretary the documents you were so keenly waving under my friend's nose in your characteristic zeal to arrest any old pervert. *He* doesn't exist."

Parker looked naively baffled. "Well, how would I know that?"

"Why the hell wouldn't you?" Kit demanded.

"Because someone else placed the call to him for me," he said, snidely. Then, "Oh."

"Oh in-*bloody*-deed," Kit retorted.

"Liz Nash, perchance?" Alex suggested.

"I don't get it," Parker said. "It's not like *she* came to me with the info on your friend."

"But I bet she just happened to be there when you got the call about it," Alex said.

"Yeah," Parker squinted as if trying to recall the event. "And she offered to call Fitzroy and to go pick it up for me."

"Ah, Charlie, you really are a fabulous fuckwit, aren't you?" Kit noted, with pleasure. "So, if Liz is not batting for your team, why was she was at your place last night?"

Parker frowned; he looked puzzled; he looked outraged. "Are you spying on me?"

"No, Charlie," Kit lied. "I'm *working* for you. What was Liz Nash doing there?"

"Dropping off my briefcase with my phone and shit in it. I left the office in kind of a hurry on Tuesday."

"You mean they threw you out in a rush," Alex muttered.

"Who *are* you?" Parker finally asked her.

"She's the family lawyer," Kit explained. "Angie's in particular at the moment. But let's stick with your mess, shall we. Had you asked Ms. Nash to provide this service?"

"No. She rang and offered. Said she'd be passing."

"She was there for an hour, Charlie," Kit pointed out. "What were you doing all that time? Oh no," she held up her hands. "Please don't tell me that you, um, know her in the biblical sense." The world's stupidest euphemism was necessary to protect Kit's delicate sensibilities from the thought of Chucky doing it with anything more animate than a vacuum nozzle.

"No, of course not." Parker was aghast, as if the idea was as scary as hell for him too. "We were talking about flies."

"How very strange," Alex noted.

"Not buzzing flies, Alex," Kit explained. She turned back to Parker. "And that's it? She doesn't go to your gym or your church or your Klan meetings?"

"No, O'Malley," Parker sneered, then obviously remembered he was giving attitude to the only person who was on his side. "Liz was just doing me a favor. At least, that's what I thought." He crossed his arms to hold onto the lapels of his suit jacket, which the wind

357

was trying to rip right off his body. "Do you really think she's involved in this mess?"

"The few signposts we have are pointing that way," Kit said. "It's possible she's part of a plot to cause more trouble than usual between the Rileys and the Barkers."

"But what's that got to do with me?" Parker asked, apparently forgetting that the whole world, present company in particular, no longer believed in his squeaky cleanliness.

Kit didn't even deign to humor him. "What about the name Nash? Do you know if there's a new player or organization in town with that name?" When Parker looked blank, she continued, "What about an up-and-coming family or an interstate connection?"

"No," Parker said. "I didn't even know what Liz's surname was until I had to find out for the list you wanted. And the only Nashes I know, as in a family, are on the job."

"They are?" Kit said.

"Yeah. You must remember Superintendent Nash from the Academy, O'Malley. The guy with the famous 'put the spoon down now' story."

"Oh yeah," Kit smiled. "He was a sweetheart."

"Whatever," Parker said. "If you recall, everyone called him Super-Stud because he sired seven or eight sons, when all he'd ever wanted was a girl. Anyway, Jim's retired now, but all, bar one, of his sprogs joined the force."

"What did the one do?" Kit queried.

"Ballet dancing. Ha! Guess he got his girl in the en ..." Parker snapped his mouth shut.

Kit squinted at him. "Did you do anything to any of the Nash boys?" .

"Anything like what?"

"Like," Kit waved her hands around, "investigate them for any reason while you were in IA; or set them up, with Gerry's help, for any old bust?" she suggested. Her mobile beeped.

"No. And most certainly not."

Kit yanked her phone from her pocket and retrieved the text message from the ether, whereon her amusement that Parker was still trying to fit into his tired old righteous suit was swamped by another *oh, shit no* adrenaline surge. There, on the screen, was confirmation of her worst-case suspicion of what had happened to one of her dearest friends. She thrust the phone through the window to Alex and rushed around to the driver's side.

"What are you doing?" Parker demanded.

"Gotta go, Charlie. I'll ring you later," she yelled into the wind as she leaped up into the driver's seat. With barely a glimpse to make sure it was safe to pull out into the St. Kilda Road traffic, Kit floored the accelerator, switched lanes so she could swing right, and then ... Waited and waited ...

"Bloody, bloody, bloody hell!" Alex swore. "They *have* been kidnapped."

Waiting ... "Come *on* you bastard!" Kit shouted at the slowest tram in Melbourne. The moment it was out of her way, she chucked a U-ey across several lanes and headed back towards the city.

Alex, gripping the dashboard to save herself from being flung all over the place, read the message aloud: *"Remain silent or your friends get it. Voice contact at noon."*

"What's the time now?" Kit asked, trying to calculate the quickest route.

"Eleven-twenty," Alex replied. "But this is crazy. Who would kidnap Enzo and why, and where the hell are we going?"

"We're going to Hawthorn to visit the Queen. I reckon Ma Riley is responsible for Enzo and Gregor not being where they should be."

Chapter 29

"All right, for God's sake. I'm here," Will said, as he yanked open the door on which Kit had been banging for nearly a minute. He glared down at her, "You've got an appointment this time, girl. So untwist your knickers, or I'll throw ..."

That was as far as he got. Kit kicked him the balls, then stepped over him.

"You've got to stop doing that, darling," Alex noted as she scooted around Will's writhing body and followed Kit up the hall.

Will grunted, groaned, and managed to bellow, "Queenie."

Marjorie Riley came rushing out of her kitchen, but stopped dead when she caught sight of her fallen first line of defense, and a very unhappy Kit striding down the hall.

"What on earth's going on? Wouldn't he let you in again?" the Queen of Innocence asked. "You idiot, Will. I told you she was expected."

"He was in my way," Kit snarled.

"Oh dear," Queenie said, in a tone that acknowledged the probability that she was the target of Kit's anger, the cause of her mood, the reason for her still-clenched fists. "Please, come and sit down, Kit. You too, Alex." Queenie Riley, demonstrating just how agile seventy-six years could be, made haste to put the kitchen table between her and her guests. Just in case.

Kit planted her hands on her hips and demanded, "Where is Enzo?"

Queenie looked surprised, almost as if she was expecting Kit to say something else. "Enzo," she repeated. "Who is Enzo?"

"One of my *dearest friends*—remember?"

"No, dear," Queenie said.

"What do you mean, 'no, dear'?" Alex demanded.

Queenie reacted as if Alex had slapped her. "I mean, Alex, that I don't know who your friend Enzo is. I've honestly no idea why you're both so upset."

Kit scowled. "Less than an hour ago, Queenie, in response to me asking how safe I should feel knowing you had a hand in Leo's departure from this world, you told me that I should consider how far one should go for one's dearest friends."

Queenie narrowed her eyes. "Yes, I may have said that," she agreed, reluctantly. "And?"

"*And?*" Kit echoed. "And our *best friend* Enzo, and his friend Gregor, have been missing since last night. Since just after our," Kit waved her hand between herself and Queenie, "little trip to euthanasia-ville."

Queenie looked genuinely puzzled. "I'm sorry, Kit, but I don't think my mind works as quickly or—and by your own admission— as imaginatively as yours."

Kit stamped her foot. "Damn it, Queenie, you asked *me* what was the worst that could happen because of what I knew; then you suggested I consider my friends. Two of my friends have been missing— as in nowhere to be found—for about eighteen hours now."

"I do believe you misunderstood me," Queenie said, shaking her head slowly. "I didn't mean *your* friends. I was talking about me and Leo, hoping you'd understand."

"Oh yeah? So how do you explain this?" Kit held out her phone. "I received this ten minutes after our chat in which you *weren't* referring to my friends."

Queenie lifted her reading glasses from where they dangled around her neck, peered at the message on the screen, then snapped her gaze between Kit and Alex. "You really think I've kidnapped your friends. Why?"

"To make sure I don't tell the cops what I know about you and Leo."

"For goodness sake, child," Queenie exclaimed. "What do you take me for?"

Kit snorted. "A ruthless fucking criminal—what the hell do you *think* I take you for?"

Queenie Riley either had a perverse sense of humor or wanted to add insult to abduction, because she roared with laughter. "Really? And yet you're not afraid of me, are you?"

"No," Kit declared. "Although it's quite possible I'm in the middle of a psychotic episode and don't have a sense of my own mortality."

Will Thumpya launched himself into the kitchen doorway. "You all right, Queenie?"

"*Now* you ask! When I'm laughing, Will," Queenie managed to say. "A minute ago they could've killed me with my own kitchen knife. Where were you then?"

"Nursing his brains," Kit said, trying not to give in to Queenie yet. Besides, the laugh welling up inside her felt more like hysteria than funny because, given the old tart's reaction to her accusation, Kit surmised she'd just pointed her wavy stick at the wrong conclusion.

"You aren't holding Enzo and Gregor captive, are you?" Alex verified.

"No, Alex," Queenie smiled. "And Kit, I wasn't concerned with what you might do about Leo. I trusted your understanding of the situation last night; and I have faith in our friendship, or at least our friendly relationship."

Merde, Kit thought. Shit and poo, she added dropping her head for a moment before meeting Queenie's gaze. "I wasn't wanting a relationship of any kind with you, Queenie."

"Ah, so that's the problem," Queenie smiled, sadly. "But if you think so little of me ..."

"It's not that," Kit said. "I quite like *you*, Queenie. It's what you *do* that's outside my box."

"Each to their own," Queenie shrugged expansively. She glanced at the wall clock, waved at the kitchen chairs, then smiled warmly. "We have ten minutes before they call, whoever they are. So sit, have some cake and coffee, and tell me about your friends. Then we'll see if there's anything this ruthless fucking criminal can do to help you."

Despite their clock watching and counting down to midday, when Kit's mobile rang at two minutes past the hour all three women jumped.

"Yes?" Kit answered.

"Ve have your friends. They vill not be urt; if you do as ve ask." The voice was slow, deep, male, and thickly coated with such a bullshit accent that Kit almost laughed. The bloke sounded like Hollywood's idea of an Eastern-European villain on Valium.

"What do you want?" Kit asked.

"Ve vant ze disk."

Ze disk? Good grief, we're trapped in a bad Cold War movie. "What disk?" Kit asked.

"Ze disk your friend's brodder brought into ze country yesterday," he explained, this time in kind of a Swedish-flavored Italian.

"Does my friend know what you're talking about? Because I don't have a clue," Kit said, although it was a fair assumption that unless Gregor had smuggled a sibling through customs in his lost suitcase, the kidnapper was talking about Enzo's brodder Nigel.

Alex flashed her a "don't taunt the kidnapper" look.

"Of course he do. Your friend vill now instruct on its retrieval and delivery to us."

There was a click, then a scraping sound, then, "Yes, fine, I *get* it. Hello, Kit?"

Kit clasped Alex's hand and nodded with relief. "Enzo," she said.

"Hang on. Ouch. Okay, I'll be careful. Stop twisting my arm, you brute."

Not insulting him would also be sensible, Kit thought. "Enzo, have they hurt you?"

"We're fine. They," he grunted, "want a disk that Nigel gave me at the airport yesterday."

"But if they've got you, why haven't they got the disk?" Kit asked.

"Good question. Ow, oh for goodness sake I am not talkin' in code," Enzo said, his own accent getting more Scottish by the word. "I have to tell her what it is and where to find it, don't I? Can I talk now? Thank you. Kit?"

"I'm here. Can they hear *me*, Enzo?"

"No. The disk is in my apartment, where we went after the airport. These gentlemen picked us up on our way out again, and didn't bother to tell us what they wanted until we got here."

"And what is this disk exactly?" she asked.

363

"As you know, Nigel is a software designer. The disk contains a revolutionary new computer game program that these guys want. Today."

"A computer game? Enzo, why did your brother give it to you?"

"It's a MacGuffin game, Kit," Enzo said pointedly, "a bit like *The Maltese Falcon*."

Now *that's* what I call a code, Kit thought, grinning at Alex. "Should I assume, Enzo, that the thing they're after is not real."

"Aye, kind of," Enzo agreed. "And they want it by one-thirty."

"Kind of," Kit repeated, making a note to brush up on her cryptic. Her record so far today was not in their favor. "Um, do you mean it *is* real, but you don't have it?"

"Aye. And you've got ninety minutes to get it from my place. I hid it under the fish tank."

"You hid what you don't have under your fish tank," Kit said. Alex squeezed her hand and shook her head. "I'm guessing we don't really need to go there. Right?"

"Aye lassie. And if you could feed Ying and Yang while you're there, I'd appreciate it."

Ying and Yang? Oh, you're kidding! Kit then heard: "*Give* me *ze* phone," and "It's not code, you git, I'm Scottish."

"You still there, Miss PI lady?"

"Of course," Kit said. "I'll get the disk. Just tell me where you want it."

"Bring it to me in ze Monaro Bar in South Melbourne at half-past one."

"Will my friends be there?"

"Yes. Bring me the CD, you will get your friends back. And no police. If I see police, your friends won't get out alive."

The line went all dead air, so Kit placed her phone thoughtfully on Queenie's table.

"Darling," Alex said, "we don't have a fish tank."

"I'm betting you don't have a couple of fish called Ying and Yang, either," Kit smiled. "I do believe Enzo just asked me to feed the Typhoon Twins; you know, Nip and Tuck, Bill and Ben, Stupid and Fool—the dumbling duo of not Immigration agents."

"You are joking!" Alex exclaimed.

"So the men who've been watching you are not cops of any kind?" Queenie said.

Kit smiled. "I think they're just thieves; albeit with international connections, coz they knew about Enzo's brother, Nigel. Whatever they are, they're misinformed and not very bright. Which doesn't mean they're not dangerous."

"There are actually few things more dangerous than stupid kidnappers," Queenie noted.

"Should we call Marek now, then?" Alex asked.

Kit shook her head. "Enzo doesn't have what they want. So I figure the best way to rescue him, is to play along with this little charade and hope that Wing and Wang are as incompetent at abduction as they are at undercover surveillance."

"But without backup?" Alex asked, as if she were used to having cops at her beck and call.

"Not exactly." Kit raised a suggestive brow at Queenie. It was her turn to do a favor.

Queenie pursed her lips. "What do you need, Kit?" she asked.

"Two or three of your biggest boofheads will do nicely," Kit grinned. "Preferably guys you'd never mistake for cops."

Half an hour later—en route to possible mayhem with her girlfriend and three burly blokes—Kit finished the call she'd placed to an old friend at the South Melbourne cop shop. Sandy had described The Monaro Bar as a toxic little dive, with a lane beside and behind, and set between a couple of small but deserted warehouses. Kit was warned not to go anywhere near it without leathers, chains, and a two-day growth.

Sounds perfectly suited to *my* mood, Kit thought, turning to brief her posse of biffo boys while Alex practiced her rally driving in, out, and around the traffic over the Swan Street Bridge, under the overpass near the Art Centre tower, and on up City Road.

Will, on the condition of obeying without question anything that Kit said, had been made third in charge—after Alex—should it come down to it. Queenie had also enlisted the aid of a polite but toothless professional bouncer called Jacko; and the most-tattooed human Kit had ever seen in the actual flesh.

365

And there's that name thing again, Kit thought, marveling at their fully illustrated fifth team member. Big, bald, middle-aged, and multi-colored from his crown to his fingertips, and everywhere else apparently, this man couldn't possibly be anyone's idea of a "Julian."

Kit gave a mental shrug, realizing that there was something else about the name thing—not to mention the madly tattooed thing—and that was the judging biffo-blokes by their appearance thing. Julian the bodyguard was also eloquent, thoughtful, and charming. He also had PhDs in literature and philosophy—just what they'd need if push came to shove.

Kit's mobile rang again and, suddenly feeling very Dana Scully, she wondered how she'd ever operated without her handy little connection to Mulder-only knew who; until she recalled that more often than not she wanted to defenestrate the stupid thing.

"O'Malley?"

"Yeah. Hi, Cathy."

"Alan Shipper's stepdaughter works as a computer tech whiz in Singapore."

Kit blew a raspberry. "There goes that theory, then."

Cathy cleared her throat suggestively. "Her name is Christine."

Kit felt a tingle in all the right places. "Christine, you say. And are you sure, Detective Martin, that this possible Chrissie is actually *in* Singapore at the moment?"

"Checking as we speak. Will keep you informed. Bye. Oh, any news on your friend?"

"Just a small rumor I'm chasing down," Kit fibbed.

Ten minutes later the newly formed O'Malley Gang were parked in sight of, but just around the corner from, The Monaro Bar.

"Would you all agree that a lot of thought and attention to detail went into the design of that establishment's façade?" Julian asked.

"Looks like a car drove off a bridge and in through the upstairs window," Alex said.

"Yes," Julian nodded, "that too. But which do you suppose came first, the Monaro car in the window, or the name of the watering hole itself."

"Do we care?" Will asked.

"You should always take time to look around and wonder," Kit said instructively.

"Whatever you say, Kit."

"As it should be," Kit smiled. "Righto you lot; you all have an idea of what our friends and their kidnappers look like and it's nearly ten past one, so let's do this. Julian, you head in first, suss out the joint, and then call and let us know whether they're in there yet, or not.

"Will, I'd like you and Jacko to check the alleys, side and back. Then make like you're drug dealers and keep any exits covered. I'll ring you when Alex and I are about to go in."

The testosterone trio clambered out of Kit's car and flexed-up for their mission.

"Do you find this a bit surreal?" Alex queried, as she and Kit watched Julian, then a moment later Jacko and Will, saunter up the street towards the bar where the bum of a red car, wedged in the front wall, provided shade for the tables on the footpath out the front.

"What I don't believe," Kit said, as Julian blended chameleon-like into the clutch of bikers and knuckle-draggers out the front before disappearing inside, "is that I, Katherine O'Malley, have actually resorted to using hired man-muscle to get a job done."

Alex laughed. "Don't lose any sleep over it, darling. They were lent to you. It's not like you actually hired them, and after today you'll never have to see them again."

Kit gave Alex an all-knowing look. "You've obviously never heard of the curse that binds you forever to the people, or things, that you never want or need to see ever again, but that you always run into at precisely the worst possible moment."

Alex smiled. "Oh well, Julian seems quite nice. Even Lillian might like him."

"Quite," Kit agreed, then flinched when her phone vibrated in her hand.

"Hello, boss," Julian said. "There's about twenty blokes in here, plus the weedy members of the opposing team who have your mates squashed into a booth at the rear. Judging by their general furtiveness they are more than a little nervous in this environment.

367

However, given the anxious expressions worn by your good buddies, I'd guess that the bad guys are armed."

"Bugger," Kit said.

"Perfect response, given the circs," Julian said.

"Can you get near or behind them?" Kit asked.

"Only by lurking in the toilet. The door to the men's is about five feet from their booth."

"Can they see the front door from where they are?"

"No. But I can see it, and them, from where I am."

"Righto," Kit said. "We're coming now. Head for the loo as soon as we enter, but keep an eye on us through the door. Is that possible?"

"Yes."

"Good. See you soon." She hung up and rang Will. Five, six, seven rings and counting later, Kit was one breath away from Will-inspired crabbiness when, instead, she suddenly felt light and breezy, as a delightful realization visited her. She leaned over and kissed Alex.

"What was that for?" Alex smiled.

"I love you," Kit grinned. "And it just hit me that we can kiss each other anywhere and anytime we like, because whatever else those two wankers might be, including armed and stupidly dangerous, they are *not* Immigration agents spying on us."

Alex's gray eyes lit up. "Let's celebrate," she smiled, kissing Kit's free hand. "We could make wild and passionate love right here in the car. Oh, damn, we have to ..."

"I know," Kit grinned. Fourteen, fifteen rings. "We have to go rescue your husband."

"I adore you, Katherine O'Malley."

Seventeen. "Is that you?" Will's whisper finally replaced the ringing in her ear.

"Yes, Will, it's me." Kit rolled her eyes. "How many exits are there?"

"Just the one, Kit, so I'd like to be inside, to watch your back. For Queenie."

Oh goody! "Okay, but ask Jacko to man that back door with his, um, body. You go in now, ahead of us, get a drink, and stand as near to that exit as you can without being too obvious. I need you to ignore us, do not talk to Julian, and don't even glance at the kidnappers."

"No worries." Will hung up.

Kit sighed and wondered what the outcome looked like at the mid-point between successful mission and unmitigated disaster. Grabbing their own Maltese Falcon, she and Alex got out of the car and headed towards The Monaro Bar. Only then did it occur to her that if Ning and Nong looked out of place inside this joint, then Enzo and Gregor certainly would. But, and more to the immediate point, what kind of impression would she and Alex make?

Oh *that* kind, she thought, as they were blessed with a range of virile male-hetero grunts and one very special wolf whistle. "Isn't that lovely," she remarked.

"If even one of them mentions our tits I'm going to kick their bikes over," Alex promised.

Inside The Monaro Bar, ignoring strangers seemed to be the done thing, even when those strangers were the only girlies in the place. Staring at *anyone* was obviously considered bad manners, or just ill-advised; because, by the looks of most of the clientele, a sideways glance at someone you didn't know would be tantamount to a challenge, of the pre-brawl "what are *you* looking at?" kind.

"Over there," Alex said, and Kit was close enough to feel her woman tense up, as if *she* was the one who was about to cause big trouble in a biker bar.

"Can I beat them up. Can I? Huh?" Alex begged.

"Steady, darling, let's just wander over and make with the smiles," Kit said. She glanced at Will, who was doing a lovely brood over a beer near the pool table by the rear exit; and hoped that Julian was in fact watching them from the slightly ajar door labeled—oh dear—"Pistons."

With Alex right behind her, Kit approached the back booth, nodded at Nit and/or Wit, and said, "I believe you're expecting us." Before either man could speak, she sat down on the bench seat, invading the Wit's personal space and crowding Gregor farther into the corner.

"Hi Kit, Alex," Enzo said. "I don't think either of you have met Gregor. Gregor this is ..."

"Shut up," the Nit opposite her hissed. "This is not happy vucking vamilies."

That's what you think, Kit thought, noticing that the Wit beside her was indeed holding a gun, or something, on Comrade Tereshenko. "Let's get this over with, then," she said. Kit handed the talkative Nit a DVD case containing an illegally imported, high quality, pirated Hong Kong action movie, which Queenie had kindly re-labeled with an important-looking yellow sticker. Not quite what the Nuff-Nuff Twins were expecting but …

"This is it, then?" Nit-Nuff asked, his accent slipping as he checked the contents.

"No, it's a Kung Fu movie," Kit said, pulling a face. "Of course it's it."

"Amusing. We *will*, of course, have to verify its actuality." Accent going.

"Of course," Kit agreed. "But how? Or when?" she asked, looking around for the verifier.

"My colleague will take the disk to our vehicle, while we wait here." Accent gone.

"Ah, no," Alex said. "That disk does not leave our sight until our friends are released."

"Good point," Kit nodded. "So, how about we all go to your vehicle, and when you've verified the kosherness of the thing, we can all go our separate ways."

Nit Knack Idiwhack telepathically consulted his apparently mute colleague and then nodded. "We'll use the back door," he said, pointing at the exit about thirty feet away.

"Shall we go, then?" Kit stood up beside Alex, blocking the route to the bar, so that the only way out was to the right of the pool table where Will was loitering with veiled intent.

The silent Wit led the way, guiding Gregor and prodding at him with his prodding thing. He was followed by Enzo, then Alex, then the majorly unaware Nit. Kit brought up the rear, although she could sense a large someone following at a distance. As they came abreast of the door marked—of course, "Valves"—she mouthed *stay* to Will, who obediently continued his terrific impersonation of a thick wooden post.

There was a moment's gathering at the exit, then silent Wit pushed the door open and shoved Gregor out into the back lane. Alex took that as her cue to do the same to Enzo, who in turn knocked into Wit; while Kit rushed at Nit's back, forcing everyone outside and into a confused and complaining muddle. Toothless Jacko bounced on Wit and disarmed him a second after Alex pointed him out; whereon Enzo took delight in kicking the bad guy when he was down. Once. Lightly.

Nit, suddenly smart enough to recognize a trap—when he was in it—made a valiant attempt to escape by trying to shove Kit out of his way so he could get back inside. Kit smacked him in the face. He punched her in the chin. She kicked him in the leg. He grabbed her arm, yanked her off the step, and threw her to the ground.

He then flung the door open only to find the way completely filled with a huge tattooed gentleman who flicked him, with his middle finger, right between the eyes. The city's worst undercover operative and most incompetent kidnapper blinked in shock, then dropped to his knees and scuttled between Julian's legs. The big man shrugged and stepped casually outside. Seconds later a backwards-flying Nit joined Kit, bum first, on the uneven bluestones.

"That'll learn you," Will declared, dusting off his hands as he rejoined the O'Malley Gang.

"You tell him, Will," Kit nodded, noticing that Enzo and Alex were laughing and hugging, and Comrade Tereshenko was grinning but asking, "Who are all you folks?"

When Nit made like he was going to roll to his feet and make another escape bid, Kit lurched from her cross-legged position on the ground next to him and woman-handled the fool onto his back. She leaned on him, her elbow digging impolitely into his breast-bone.

"Get off me, you bitch," he shouted.

"Oh do shut up," Kit requested. "If you had *any* idea of the inconvenience you've caused me in the last few months you'd be amazed at how restrained I'm being with you right now."

"Would you like a hand up, Kit?" Julian smiled. "I'll watch the super moron for you."

"Why thank you, sir," Kit said, accepting his offer. "Did that bastard bruise my chin?"

Julian peered at her face with concern, while casually standing on Nit-Wang's foot. "No dear. Though I'd be more worried about the one you'll have on your arse, if I were you."

Kit chuckled and pulled out her phone. Again. She rang Marek, told him what she'd—yes, stupidly—just done, and asked what she should now do with the Idiot Twins.

Chapter 30

The kidnappers, Stuart Palmer and David Wincott, were handcuffed to their chairs in separate but adjacent interview rooms, each with a detective who took statements of their version of the events that led to them being charged with the unlawful abduction and incarceration of Messrs McAllister and Tereshenko. The previously talkative Stu was refusing to speak until he'd conferred with his legal representative; but silent Dave, on discovering that Enzo never had, or was ever likely to have, the thing they'd kidnapped him for, was talking his head off and putting his partner-in-crime right in it—mostly for being such a complete dickhead. Both men could be viewed from the same two-way mirrored observation room where Kit, Cath, and Marek stood drinking coffee and listening to Mr. Wincott's ridiculous story.

According to Dave, he and Stu were "freelance consultants" who *acquired* new software, then sold it to the highest bidder. Back in December, according to Dave, Stu had heard that Nigel McAllister, fed up with being a second-string director of the California software company Arincorp, had gone underground to sell not-yet-released products.

According to Dave, Stu decided they could piggy-back on Nigel's already illicit dealings by stealing directly from him, blackmailing him for the software they wanted, or kidnapping one or more of his international contacts and ransoming them.

According to Dave, Stu—for some reason known only to Stu— decided that Enzo was Nigel's main broker; perhaps because of meetings Enzo had had in London, New York, and Honolulu with his brother in December. While lowly paid lackeys in the UK, US, and New Zealand kept an eye on Nigel and his other "contacts," Stu and Dave had been watching Enzo.

"I gather," said Cathy, who'd arrived halfway through Dave's full and pissed-off confession, "that there was a fundamental flaw in their operation."

"Oh yeah," Kit laughed. "Like, not only is Nigel second to no one, but Enzo says he makes more money from legit clients over a single lunch than he ever would selling his own programs on the black market. The other doozey of a defect in their plan, of course, is that Enzo McAllister wouldn't know a software program from a Harley-Davidson."

Cathy turned from the window. "Speaking of software—Christine Shipper. Oh, and Liz."

Kit grinned and waited expectantly.

"Ms. Shipper's been home on holidays from Singapore for six weeks. She's supposedly tripping around Queensland and the Territory somewhere, but I haven't located her. Yet."

"Interesting," Kit remarked, catching Marek's curious look. "She might, by a long stretch of all that's vaguely possible, be the Chrissie of one of our equations," she explained. "And, as such, might be responsible for Gerry's fatal blood loss."

"Oh good," Marek noted, "another suspect on a list which already includes drug dealers, the deceased's wife, half the crooks in town, and at least one cop—who shall remain nameless. But, I suppose Shipper's widow is as logical a candidate as any of the others."

"She's his stepdaughter, not his wife," Cathy corrected. "And while we're on the subject of nameless cops, can you tell me anything yet, O'Malley?"

"Sorry. But, as a matter of interest, how come Charlie isn't on the Barleycorn Task Force? I'd have thought it was a given, considering your team picked up the first two murders."

Cathy pulled a disgruntled face while Marek said dryly, "Chuck does not give good PR."

Cathy snorted. "He, who needs his tongue stapled to his lips, described the killer of the woman who turned out to be Bubblewrap Man's second victim, as 'an attention-seeking loser with a severe sexual dysfunction.' Apart from having no actual basis on which to make that kind of judgement—especially about a *classic* attention-seeking loser with a severe sexual dysfunction, who also turned out to be a serial killer—Charlie made his declaration to a national TV news reporter. His words, of course, became front-page headlines the next day.

"His excuse," Cathy's tone was mocking, "was that he was exhausted, and mentally distracted by the worry that he was going to miss his plane for a long overdue holiday."

"Not a good idea to insult a multiple murderer's *raison d'être* at the start of his career," Kit noted. "Point-proving escalation being one possible consequence that comes to mind."

"My thoughts exactly," Marek said. "So when we realized we did have a serial killer on our hands, we used Chuck's week in Sydney to shuffle the teams and set up the task force."

"And where Charlie went after that, so did his faithful crew," Cathy sneered.

"Just be thankful you don't have to follow him at the moment," Marek noted, as a bald detective poked his head around the half open door. "Gotta go," Marek said, and did just that.

Cathy sighed. "I'd better get back to my own stuff too."

"But you mentioned Liz, too. What about her?" Kit asked.

"Thin air," Cathy explained. "Took leave for knee surgery, but seems to have vanished. I did find out that she was married briefly to one of us. It ended about two years ago."

"Which one of you?" Kit queried.

"A Senior Constable from Northcote, name of Colin Nash," Cathy stated.

No doubt one of Jim SuperStud Nash's progeny, Kit thought. "Have you ..."

"No," Cathy interjected. "Because he, of course, is on leave and in Fiji for another week. So I can't find out if he knows what Liz's agenda might be."

"If Christine Shipper *is* involved in this, maybe Liz is simply working as her inside man," Kit suggested. Her phone began vibrating, so she glanced at the caller ID.

"Possibly. I'll get someone to look for a link between them." Cathy headed for the door.

"Boxer?" Kit said, answering her phone.

"Yes. And you need to come visit," he said.

"And why would that be?"

"Got two of your mates facing off in my bar and you might want to deal with them."

Kit contemplated chucking her phone in a bin and hiding in a closet, but instead she asked, "Who?"

"An idiot dogbreath by the name of Mark Dixon."

"Boxer, sweetie, did you locate your social conscience and catch him for us?"

"No, Kit. Your other mate who's here, one Rabbit MacArthur, caught him. Or rather, she hauled him off me and is now sitting on him."

"Rabbit? What's she doing there?"

"Dunno, O'Malley, but kinda glad she is. Perhaps you can ask her when you bring the troops to scrape Doghouse off my floor."

"On my way." Kit gave a victory fist, and then went in search of Cathy and what was left of her own gang.

Ten minutes later Kit was en route to Prahran, in her own car following a cop car, and wondering how her posse had been reduced to one unlikely sidekick. Toothless Jacko, who'd done his bit for Queenie's friend *at* The Monaro Bar, had chosen not to visit the police at all, so Kit had found only Alex and two of her commandoes in the waiting area. As Enzo and Gregor were still giving statements, Julian had offered to make sure they and Alex got home safely. That left good old Will Thumpya, whose surname she'd discovered was really Curtis and who, until Queenie told him otherwise, was still on *her* body guard-duty; so Kit put him to work in the passenger seat answering her still ringing phone.

"It's Hector," Will told her; then he said, "Whadda ya want, dude? It's Will. You know, from the cellar. Yeah-yeah, I'm still sorry. I'm talkin', she's drivin'. Come on dude, she might be waiting for an important call."

"Will," Kit said softly, making the turn into Commercial Road at the Punt Road lights.

Will cricked his neck. "Sorry dude. I guess *you're* important. Yeah, okay. Dunno. I'll ask." He turned to Kit. "Hector says he's done the pictures and you won't believe your eyes and he wants to know where we are so youse two can meet up quick."

376

"Ask him to meet us at Swiggers Bar in Prahran. And tell him *not* to bring Carrie."

Will relayed the instructions, then dropped the mobile in his lap. "He said okay and that Carrie went with, um, someone to go parking?"

Kit frowned. "Do you mean she went with Erin to go to Parker's?"

"Um, possibly. Oh cool," he pointed, "there's a parking spot. Ha, the pigs missed it."

Kit parked in front of Swiggers. The pigs double parked next door coz, ha, they could.

"So this doof that they're gonna cart, he might have done Gerry too?" Will asked, as they entered Boxer Macklin's bar without waiting for the three detectives.

"Maybe," Kit shrugged. "We're not sure yet. But he *might* know who did."

"About bloody time," Boxer called out. "This wanker is scaring away my customers."

"Now-now Boxer. That's no way to talk about your good mate," Kit remarked, grinning broadly at Rabbit, who was indeed sitting on Mark Doghouse Dixon.

"Hey, girl," Rabbit said, looking pleased with herself.

"Hey, yourself, Rab. Good catch," Kit said. She bent down to peer at Doghouse whose face was squished, right cheek down, between Ms. MacArthur's hand and the sticky lino floor next to the bar. "Lost a bit of weight since I saw you and your lady friend the other day, eh, *Mark*."

"I've got a hunch that his she-ain't-no-lady has dumped him," said Boxer.

"Yeah? Oh crikey!" Kit said, registering Boxer's messy face. A badly swollen eye was spreading blue tentacles across his cheek which, along with his moustache, was also smeared with nose blood. "You fall down, Box, or did Doghouse do that?"

"Funny. For some reason the stupid turd thinks I'm responsible for his woman deserting, and leaving him to take the rap for something," Boxer said. "She thought the cops were on to them, through you, via me. That's ..."

377

"Fuckin' shut up!" Dixon tried to squirm free, but his beanie merely slipped over his eyes.

Boxer gave him the finger. "Apparently, she also told him she'd been using him, and that he was a stupid useless prick; which, as it happens, is a description I'd be happy to verify."

"Lemme at him," Dixon demanded. "Gonna break your arms, Macklin."

Kit bent over again. "*Which* woman thinks you're a witless dick, Doghouse? Tina or Ellie?" She yanked his beanie off his blue hair. "Or is it something they agree on too?"

Dixon's laugh was a bugled grunt, then he snotted over his own face. "O'Malley," he said, "will ya get this bitch off me?"

Kit shook her head, "Nah, she looks comfortable."

"So that's the famous Doghouse," Cathy noted, peering over Kit's shoulder.

As Dixon's face was already forced into a sneer, his attempt to do so voluntarily was wasted. "Lemme guess, you're the dyke reporter," he spluttered.

"No, you dickhead; I'm the police officer who's going to arrest you," Cathy stated.

Kit helped Rabbit up off one of Melbourne's most wanted, so the other two detectives could cuff Dixon's hands behind him and drag him to his feet.

"What the hell?" Dixon demanded. "It was just a fight between old mates."

"Fancy that; he *is* a stupid prick," Cathy observed. "Mark Dixon, I am arresting you for the murder of Detective Senior Constable Sheryl Mapp. Anything you … Oh bugger it, blah-blah."

"Ask him about Gerry," Kit suggested.

Dixon curled his lip. "Ask what ya like, ya scumbags. I'm not sayin nothin', about nothin'; and what's more," he crossed his legs, "I refuse to go anywhere until I've been to the dunny. The incredible hulk's been sittin' on me bladder and I need to piss."

Cathy nodded to her offsiders to accompany Dixon to where Boxer was pointing beyond the end of the bar; then she, Kit, and Rabbit sat down at the nearest table.

"How come you happen to be here, Rabbit?" Kit asked.

"Well now, imagine this coincidental," Rabbit grinned. "I was walking by, on my way to buy a book from Hares & Hyenas, when I heard a commotion in here and who should I find laying into this nice gentlemen, but him," she hoicked her thumb towards the men's, "the bastard I saw walking off with that poor woman on Sunday night."

Kit gave her the curious stare. "You just happened to be walking by?"

"Ooh! I just realized what you said," Rabbit turned to Cathy. "Was she a police officer?"

"Yes, Rabbit. Sheryl was working undercover," Cathy nodded.

"Rabbit," Kit growled.

Ms. MacArthur studied the room for a week, then surrendered. "Okay." She rolled her head with so much oh-gosh that her boobs went along for the ride. "Scooter told me which motel she and her chick had been shagging in. So I went there to, like, check the register for her name. Didn't get a chance coz *he* turned up same time as me. So I staked out the joint, all night, then tailed him here. And, I know, I shoulda called you guys."

"Was Chrissie there with him? Or a redhead. Or a plain woman with brown hair?"

"Nuh. Just him," Rabbit said.

"Yo!" someone yelled from the front door. "Is this a private party or can anyone join?"

Oh crap! Kit did not want to face *that* familiar voice, coz it was too far removed from its right context in space and time to make sense. "What are you doing here?" she finally asked.

"Don't know," Sasha Riley said. Which was odd. As was her outfit, but that, at least, was not unusual. "Your sidekick rang and asked me to meet you both here."

"Curious," said Kit. "He's not here yet."

"Right behind you," Hector announced.

They both sat down at the table, while Kit made the necessary introductions.

"So where are Will and Julian?" Sasha asked. "I thought Gran's finest were watching your back today."

"Julian's taking Alex home, and Will is ..." Kit looked around for her suddenly nowhere-in-sight bodyguard. Fat lot of good he is, then, she thought, before amending that to: uh-oh.

"Cathy," she said, "Doghouse and your guys seem to be taking a very long piss."

Cathy scraped her chair back and, with Kit right behind her, made a dash for the toilets. Rabbit crowded them into the short corridor which usually featured only four doors, but which now included two groggy detectives propping open the men's room door, and a nice view of freedom through the wide open fire exit. There was no Mark Doghouse Dixon, and no sign of Will Thumpya Curtis.

"Fuckit! What the hell happened, Mick?" Cathy demanded.

"That other guy king-hit Crosby, then Dixon belted me over the back of the head. With the hand dryer." Mick kicked at the broken appliance.

"You took his cuffs off?" Cathy shouted.

"Hey! We weren't gunna take his wang out for him. Didn't get to re-cuff him in front."

Cathy turned slowly. "O'Malley?" she said sweetly. "Who was that guy? Exactly."

"Exactly?" Kit looked sheepish. "He works for Queenie Riley."

"Oh bloody great!"

"They can't have got far, Cathy," Kit insisted. "Will came in my car, remember."

"Yeah?" Cathy snarled impatiently. "How did Dixon get here, O'Malley?"

"A blue Subaru," Rabbit grinned. "It's parked in the street at the end of the back lane."

Cathy dispatched Mick to collect their car and delegated Kit to look after Crosby, then sprinted for the lane with Rabbit hot on her tail shouting out the rego number. Kit helped Crosby into a chair and filled the others in on the latest goings-on and running-offs.

"Oh boy, I bet *you're* going to be in for it," Sasha noted.

"Me?" Kit cried. "Just wait till I get a stranglehold on Will. As for your grandmother!"

"You leave Gran out of anything that that cretin does of his own volition."

"Stop bickering you two, and look at these," Hector said commandingly, as he slapped laser-printed color pictures down on the table.

The first two images were blown-up copies of the photos of Liz Nash, and Chrissie who might be Christine Shipper. The quality of the Chrissie picture was still awful, although being larger hadn't diminished the vague similarity between the two women. Kit was already disappointed, though, because she knew Christine Shipper was an only child; which meant either their resemblance was coincidental or Scooter's Chrissie wasn't Alan Shipper's stepdaughter.

Hector meanwhile was setting out his variations on a theme. First was Liz Nash, but with the red bogan hairdo of the boat bimbo whose surname she shared. Then it was the photo of Chrissie with the same red Ellie Nash do; then her again, but with Liz's mousey hair.

Lo and *bloody* behold! Kit's mind exclaimed. Liz and Chrissie still looked vaguely similar; but Liz in particular matched her memory of Ellie Nash.

"Are they sisters?" Boxer asked, not having a clue what the photo line-up was about.

"No idea," Kit said. "But if Liz 'the redhead' doesn't share genes with Dixon's ex-Ellie, then I'll spend the night on his filthy boat."

"O'Malley," Hector whispered, drawing her attention to Sasha's perplexed face. "Watch this," he added, laying out another set of faces. The doctored images this time showed Liz and Chrissie with the long dark-tipped blonde hair that Scooter assigned her mistress. Hector then laid out his last set which, for some reason, showed both women with short blonde hair.

Sasha's expression tripped right through surprise and on to disbelief. "That's Tina."

"What? *Which* one's Tina?" Kit asked.

Sasha tapped the short-blonde Liz. Then she tapped the long-blonde Liz, Liz the redhead, and Liz the original, pictured outside Parker's. "All of them. They're *all* Tina," she said.

Okay, I'm confused, Kit thought, while her sidekick grinned like a certain smartarse cat.

"They are one and the same person, O'Malley," Hector said. "I realized Liz was Tina the moment I gave her photo the long blonde hair. If you think she also looks like Ellie from the boat, then maybe they *are* sisters. Like hello, the Nash sisters.

"Or sisters-in-law," Kit said thoughtfully.

"Or, all three—Liz, Tina, and Ellie—might be the same chick; which, given Dixon in the middle, makes more sense," Hector stated.

"But who's the other one?" Sasha asked, indicating Chrissie.

"Buggered if I know," Kit admitted, relieved this time when her phone rang because it saved her from having to elaborate on what she couldn't explain.

"O'Malley, it's Erin."

"Hi, honey. My day keeps getting screwier, how's yours so far?" Kit asked.

"Frigging cold and boring as earwax. Until the fisticuffs a minute ago."

"Whose fisties?"

"That Liz Nash just turned up here. When Parker started to do his nana at her, she went all postal herself and shoved him backwards—and I'm talking clean out of his slippers and onto his bum in his own hallway. Then she stomped inside and slammed the front door."

"Damn. I should be there," Kit said. "Though I should probably wait for Cathy. Shit. Um, I'll send Hector to you, and I'll join you all as soon as I can."

"You don't have to, cherub," Erin said. "I'm just giving you an update. We have the situation under control here."

"Erin, the situation has changed and you don't know the half of it. I'll be there, asap. Take photos of anything that moves." She hung up and turned to Hector, who was packing his gear.

"I'm already not here," he said, handing Kit the pile of photos.

"Good Boy Wonder," Kit patted his arm. "Did you get your itty-disk back from Chucky's windowsill?"

"No, but I'll try again. And yes, I'll call when I get there. Bye."

Chapter 31

Four-thirty post meridian, and counting, on the second-longest day of Katherine O'Malley's forever was being spent in traffic, the kind engineered by morons, en route to Fitzroy. The closer Kit and her latest phone-handler got to their surveillance mates at Parker's house, the stranger the situation at their destination became. Layered, as it was, onto the multi-faceted adventures she'd already had more than enough of today, Kit was sorely tempted to ignore the latest unfolding drama and just head for them thar hills.

When Rabbit had returned to Swiggers with the news that detectives Cathy and Mick had continued their pursuit of Doghouse and Will by car *with* siren through peak hour mayhem, Kit decided it was time to get the hell out of Dodge. She'd left Sasha to her own devices, with a stern "hand Dixon back" message to give her dear old Gran; abandoned the wounded Boxer and Crosby to each other; and seconded Ms. MacArthur as her latest sidekick.

By the time they were halfway to Parker's, Rabbit had relayed two messages from Erin and one from Hector. Erin's first, informed them that Guy the Pale had come home and, but a moment later, gone next door to visit his buddy, Chuck. He'd walked straight in without so much as a knock, so Erin figured that the door was unlocked and that Guy was expected.

Erin's next call, six minutes later, detailed the curious relocation of Parker, Guy, and Liz to Guy's place, with a certain degree of urgency and seemingly at Ms. Nash's insistence. That event had prompted Kit to wonder just who had been expecting Guy—Chucky or Liz—until she told herself that not everything in the world could possibly be part of the same conspiracy.

Shortly after Hector's call, to say he'd joined Erin and Carrie and retrieved his disk, Kit finally turned left from Hoddle Street into Langridge. In crow-flying terms she was only five blocks from Parker's, but traffic and gravity-based reality would probably turn that into a fifteen minute drive. Rabbit, therefore, had time to get things straight.

"So Scooter's ex-secret-girlie wasn't necessarily having it off with the lady-cop killer, unless he turns out to be her ex-husband, but they do know each other."

"As witnessed by you," Kit nodded. "Which means Chrissie might be in cahoots with Dixon's suddenly ex-girlfriend Ellie who, in turn, might *be* his other girlfriend Tina. Unless they're sisters. And she, Tina, who is definitely Liz Nash, has been in the administrative employ of Victoria Police for the last six months."

"To frame this cop that none of you like," Rabbit nodded, as if it all made perfect sense. "It's not very sensible though, mate," she said. "Is that really what this is all about?"

Kit took a deep breath. "Yes. I think. That and Gerry Anders."

"Him? Why him?"

"Because Charlie Parker and Gerry Anders *have* been cahootsing. So this could be a two birds, one stone kinda deal."

"Are you saying that bastard Doghouse killed the lady cop *and* Gerry?"

"Possibly, but not necessarily. They could just be using Gerry's murder. Oh," Kit hesitated when a fact popped into her equation. "Except that whoever *is* trying to frame Chucky, does have access to Gerry's blood. Or blood type."

"Can you laborate again, Kit, on what any of this shit and caboodle has to do with Scooter's thing? You sure it's not just a coincidence."

"Pretty sure. It's way too flaky not to be premeditated," Kit said, slowing down, then taking off again as the Wellington Street lights turned green. "Consider this: a woman, who offers no surname, embarks on an affair with an inconsequential relative of the enemy clan of the man who once kidnapped and later, more than likely, murdered her stepfather."

Rabbit made a whimpering sound, so Kit said, "Okay, roses by other names. Chrissie, surname *possibly* Shipper, woos Scooter who belongs to the Barkers who hate Gerry Anders who, apart from possibly running Stuart Barker down with his car, probably killed Alan Shipper so he couldn't testify against him. Against Gerry, I mean, for kidnapping him, Alan."

Rabbit snorted. "If all that is the case, I ask again: Scooter? And hey, what happened to the gonzo theory about mysterious crooks setting the Rileys and Barkers against each other?"

"Um, that could be a red herring," Kit admitted grudgingly.

"But it was ..." Rabbit took a breath. "You made up your own red herring?"

"Yeah, well," Kit shrugged. "Scooter's ex-mistress might *not* be Christine Shipper; in which case my herrings could be ... whatever color they're s'posed to be."

Rabbit played thoughtfully with her hair spikes. "But what about this Tina/Liz bird? What's her beef with the rotten cop? And is she connected to the dead gangster?"

"Don't know," Kit said, stopping to wait for a small truck to complete a seventeen-point maneuver and *get out of her way*. "And won't know until we find out who actually killed Gerry; or what the link is between Chrissie maybe-Shipper and Tina/Liz-probably-Ellie Nash."

"Like der," Rabbit said. "The link would be the Doghouse man."

Kit laughed, and turned right into Smith Street. "Only if he recruited Tina/Liz into the plot to help Chrissie, or vice versa. Whatever else this might be, it isn't Dixon's plan; coz that man is not a facilitator's bootlace. Also Ellie and/or Tina-Liz, dumped Doghouse claiming she'd been *using* him. I reckon the link must be a direct one between the women."

"Maybe they're just best mates," Rabbit suggested. "Hey, or special girls. Have you factored in the possibility that they're a couple?"

"I *so* hope they're not; coz that'd give substance to the lesbian vampire cult rumors."

Rabbit drummed her fingers on her knees. "Another thing that bothers me about Scooter lies in your very own reference to her being an inconsensical relative."

"That would be a bother," Kit smiled. "But why?"

"Coz she avoids them Barkers. She's, like, out of her family loop. The bad part, anyway."

"But her mother *did* make her visit bad Uncle Stuart in hospital, and Scooter probably went to see her grandfather too. For insider gossip, that'd be enough for Chrissie to make use of."

"Depending on who Chrissie is, from one of your loopy subplots to the next," Rabbit noted. "You're just making this up as you go along, aren't you?"

"What can I say," Kit said. She stopped the car to avoid running into a reluctant pedestrian, who'd missed a tram and was now throwing his groceries, one by one, at the back end of it.

"Post-Checkout Syndrome," Rabbit noted casually, then returned to the subject. "Much as she hates them Barkers, you shoulda heard Scooter angsting about all the cats she might've let out of their bags. Not to mention her guilts about the dead guy being left at Angie's."

"Guilts. Why?" Kit asked.

"Paranoid, as she now is, about that bitch's ulteriors, Scooter recollected all the questions Chrissie asked about us lot finding the body that day. I suggested mere curiosity, given Scooter went straight from the dead body to the live shagging, and she obviously offered the news as a topic for conversing. But all *your* implying, has Scoot convinced that the corpse was put there at Angie's *because* of her. Coz she's a Barker cousin."

The ringing phone saved Kit from having to address that wacky notion.

"Hector wants you personally this time," Rabbit said, holding the mobile to her ear.

"Weird shit happening here, mate. Parker, Guy, and Liz came out of Guy's house, got into Guy's car, and all drove off together. And yes, we *are* following. East on Johnston."

"Guy's car? Bloody hell," Kit echoed and swore, while also trying to work out east from a Belgian waffle. "What's he got to do with this? With anything?"

"Clueless here," Hector admitted. "But Liz was in charge. She had a gun or something, and she made both guys sit in the front. The Guy guy is at the wheel."

"Hector, if you're not driving and are as usual umbilicaled to your laptop, could you ..."

"Check his car rego to identify him. Sure. We're now going north on Hoddle. You?"

Having located a compass in her mental landscape, Kit made the now called-for right turn down Peel Street. "Several blocks behind," she said confidently, figuring that with east taken care of she'd have no problem finding north. "I'm about to ring Cathy. Could you send your identipics to her at Marek's e-mail? Toodles." Kit pushed the ear piece into her ear while Rabbit plugged her in and scrolled for Cathy's mobile number.

"I really can't talk now, O'Malley."

"Cathy, I'm so sorry about Doghouse and that fool Will, but ..."

"O'Malley, I'm not angry. Well I am, but that's not why I can't talk. Mick and I lost those bastards in Windsor. I am now organizing a serious menhunt; starting at Queenie's. So, bye."

"Wait," Kit said urgently, "this is important, Cathy. You need to know that Liz Nash has been aliasing herself all round town."

"Why do I need to know this *now*, O'Malley?"

"Coz Sasha Riley knows Liz as Tina, and therefore as one or both of Dixon's girlfriends. Either that or he was her accomplice. Anyway, through Doghouse, she probably also knows Scooter's now-ex mistress Chrissie; the one who could be Christine Shipper."

There was silence for a moment. "That sounds a tad far-fetched, O'Malley."

"Hector is sending the photos-don't-lie evidence to Marek's e-mail."

"Back up; you said accomplice. Are you saying Liz Nash is involved in Sheryl's murder?"

"I mean, accomplice in whatever. It depends who's in charge, or what the big picture is. Liz and Dixon could both be working for Chrissie. But if they are all on some kind of revenge trip, then they wouldn't want to risk being recognized. So, if Sheryl Mapp saw Dixon and Chrissie, and maybe even Liz, together on the street on Sunday night, it might explain *why* Doghouse killed her—as a pre-emptive precaution."

"Well, that stinks," Cathy said. "Okay, I'll, um, process all that. Is that all?"

"Um, no," Kit said. "About half an hour ago, Liz fronted up at Charlie Parker's and decked him. She's now driven off with him and his neighbor."

"Driven off?"

"Yeah. No idea what part, if any, the neighbor plays in this; but I'd say the chances are slim that they've just gone fishing. I'm pretty sure Liz has abducted them both, possibly at gunpoint."

"Oh great. I'll send a car to check his house for," Cathy groaned, "for termites."

"Funny. Guy the neighbor lives in number nine," Kit said, joining the homeward peak-hour traffic heading towards Clifton Hill.

"O'Malley?" Cathy queried. "Are you recklessly and unofficially following them? I hope."

Kit laughed. "They're heading north on Hoddle in an old tan Holden. I'll keep you posted."

Rabbit disconnected Cathy, then Kit took another incoming from Hector.

"Take the Eastern Freeway ramp," he said. "The second exit, heading for the hills."

"Righto. Any info on Guy yet?"

"Yeah, sure, mate. It's Wonder Boy I am, not Miracle Man."

"I take it that means no. Bye now." Kit switched lanes, to be ready for the freeway exit.

"Been thinking I have," Rabbit admitted, "about premeditation and Scooter's paranoidals."

"And what have you come up with?" Kit asked.

"Doghouse Dixon. When I was squashing him, he asked that lovely Detective Cathy if she was *the* dyke reporter. Why would he ask that? I mean, how would he know about ..."

"Carrie," Kit finished. As she drove the loop onto the freeway bound for the eastern suburbs, and those hills she'd fancied earlier, she mulled over the implications of that notion.

"Well, I'll be buggered. And you, Rabbit, are a treasure. Carrie McDermid the reporter, not Scooter except indirectly, has to be *the reason* Gerry Anders' body was left at Angie's.

"Consider this. You guys all met Carrie for the first time last Wednesday night and arranged to meet for lunch on Thursday. When Scooter left Angie's later that night, she went to play tiddly-winks with Chrissie, during which she might have mentioned meeting a new dyke, who happened to be a journo, and with whom she was to do lunch the next day.

"Chrissie probably thought, Bingo! now *there's* a special place to leave Gerry's useless corpse: in a gay bar with the press already in attendance."

Kit was quite excited, until the second thoughts arrived. "Oh hell. That is crazy."

"Why?" Rabbit asked.

"Because it would mean that they're not just using the circumstance of Gerry's death to frame Charlie Parker. It means that one of them—Tina/Liz, Chrissie, or Doghouse—killed Gerry."

"So?" Rabbit noted eloquently. "The man's obviously not averse to knocking folks off."

"True. But the cops think Gerry's death was retribution for the murder of Mike and Julie Sherwood, who were killed back in January. Which is so much more likely."

Kit tapped the steering wheel. "Unless ... I s'pose Doghouse could also be working for Mr. Big Bloke, the drug lord. In which case, even if he only helped in Gerry's disposal, that would've been a fluky bonus for Chrissie's grand plan."

"But wouldn't her grand plan have been to kill the man who killed her father?"

"Stepfather," Kit said. "Only if she's out for revenge. Justice wouldn't require murder."

"Well, I'm bamboozed," Rabbit said. "And this PI work requires way too much thinking."

"And watching, questioning, sifting, sorting," Kit said, as they crawled with the rest of the traffic slowly towards the Bulleen Road overpass. They even had time to view the miles of golf courses; four separate courses so far, each connected by parkland to the one before and all straddling the winding Yarra River.

Lillian, she knew, would find strange comfort in so many roughs and greens and bunkers, but all they did for Kit was make her wonder how much of the planet's surface had been taken over by golfers, or used up by carparks and cemeteries.

"What other personal things does a PI need?" Rabbit queried, in an offhand manner.

Kit smiled. "Good analytical and people skills; the ability to act, lie, think laterally, and be unobtrusive. Comfy running-away shoes are a must; although, and you probably *don't* want to know this, Rabbit, most PIs never get out of their surveillance vehicles."

"Yeah right, Kit. How is it that you so often end up in the middle of bad action and trouble, then?" Rabbit snorted, reacting instantly to Kit's ringing mobile.

"Because, my dear Rabbit, I am a mess magnet," Kit declared. "Hello?"

"Hi, it's Carrie. First, Erin says we're nearly to Ringwood. But more importantly, you have to listen to this. It's the last conversation on Hector's disk. It's Parker and Liz, then Guy."

"Righto. Play it, Sam."

Liz: "You with me, Charlie?"

Parker: "Wha … what's going on?"

Liz: "We'll be leaving soon, but I'm just putting a liter of Gerry under the table here."

Parker: "Where'd you get that? God, what did you do, steal it from the morgue?"

Liz: "No, you tiny mind. I stole it from Gerry. When the pigs come looking for you—if they give a damn when you don't turn up anywhere—they'll find evidence up to their collective arseholes linking you to that creep's murder. Oh look, here's the knife. I'll just tidy it away."

Parker: "*You* killed Anders?"

Liz: "We did, yeah. Someone had to, Charlie. Don't you think?"

Parker: "I wish it *had* been me."

Liz: "But that's your problem, isn't it, Charlie. You're a gutless prick."

Parker: "What do you want?"

Liz: "Hmm. Your tiny balls in a vice. Your lying tongue on a toothpick. And a big fucking hole where your heart does not deserve to beat."

Parker: "Why, on earth? What did I ever do to you, Liz?"

Liz: "You helped kill one of the finest men that ever lived."

Parker: "What the fu ...? I've never killed anyone, you mad bitch."

Liz: "Shut up, you rat bastard."

A sharp smacking sound was followed by a thud.

Parker: "Ow. Shit, Liz. I didn't ..."

Liz: "What's that noise?"

Parker: "Front door. It's my friend."

Liz: "Friend? That's funny. Stop! Right there. Who are you?"

Guy: "Me? Who are *you?* Oh Christ, Charlie; you all right? Ah! Okay. Sorry. Not moving."

Parker: "The bitch hit me, Guy."

Guy: "She's got a gun, Charlie. I wouldn't be calling her names."

Liz: "Smart. I take it you're the neighbor with a fishing shack up the bush. Yeah?"

Guy: "How do you know that?"

Liz: "Because, you poor sorry wanker, you are probably Charlie's only friend. His conversations with the rest of the world are therefore boringly limited. But this is good; you and your shack in the backwoods. I think that's where we'll go. Uh-uh, don't be stupid. I don't know you or give a shit about you, so I *will* shoot if you make me."

"What do you think, O'Malley?" Carrie asked.

Liz Nash's voice had been calm and cold and unforgiving.

"I think," Kit said, "that Chucky and Guy are in deep shit. I think we now know who killed Gerry. And I know we're all heading for, um, it'll come to me. Liz was right about Charlie's limited chit-chat; he told me the same stuff. He said the Upper Yarra, out the back of Launching Place—that's it. I'll ring Cathy."

"Okay. Erin says we're way through Ringwood on the Maroondah Highway now. Bye."

"Wind the window down will you, Rab, so I can chuck another theory out," Kit said.

"Yeah, yeah, but tell me. Why are they in shit and who did Gerry?"

"Hector's bug recorded Liz Nash admitting to Charlie that she killed Gerry. And there's now no question that: a) she's trying to frame my deserving client; and b) she has abducted him and Guy." Kit filled her in on the details, then asked her to scroll for Marek's number.

"So do you reckon, then, that Liz's 'finest man ever' is the guy who got kidnapped, or the Sherwood you mentioned before?" Rabbit asked.

"I seriously doubt she meant Mike Sherwood. He and his wife were drug couriers and a nasty pair of slugs. My vote is for him being Alan Shipper, which makes it even more likely that Chrissie is his stepdaughter. And Liz did use the plural, as in 'we' killed him."

Neither Inspector Marek nor Detective Martin were answering their phones, so Kit left messages for them to ring back urgently, while marveling how her tag team's five-minute head start seemed to be exponentially stretching the distance between them, at a rate far greater than was indicated by any of the known laws of traffic flow. To prove the point, ten minutes later, just as Rabbit began rifling through Kit's CD collection for something to do, Hector rang with a directional change.

"We just went through Lilydale and are now veering onto the Warburton Highway."

"How is that possible, Hector?" Kit asked. "Don't you have any traffic where you are?"

"Not much, why?"

"Because, where we are, Rabbit could get out and paint a mural on the passenger door without having to jog to keep up."

"Just as well we're in front, then, O'Malley, if you're having work done on your car. And speaking of *Guy Ian Linden*," he boasted, "I'm still looking for a Launching Place address; but I can tell you that he's one of those franchised handyman gardeners. He's thirty-five, single, and only been renting next to Chuckles since March 19. Before that he lived in Beaumaris."

"Bet he's wishing he stayed by the beach," Kit noted. "Good job, Sparrow. Over and out." She rolled her shoulders. "Could you choose one of those CDs, please Rabbit, I'm starting to get the outer-suburban skin crawlies."

"The more time I spend with you, Kit, the stranger you get."

Kit smiled. "Well, I just don't get this strange endless sprawl that goes on and on and ..."

Rabbit's response was Vanessa Amorosi. Loud. A minute later, however, she had to turn it down, when Cathy finally rang back.

Kit filled her in on the whole Liz Nash being a murdering kidnapper situation, and then asked, "How come it's so hard to find out about someone who works in your own office?"

"Because until right now, O'Malley," Cathy sounded a wee bit exasperated, "investigating Liz Nash for anything, was kind of a low priority. Had we known that Gerry's killer was right here, running errands for us ..."

"Okay, sorry," Kit said. "What I meant was, how come no one *knows* her?"

"My guess? She didn't want anyone to know her. If what you say is true, then she was head down bum up, on a mission, not wanting to be noticed. I did put the word out, in case anyone remembers her from when she was married to Colin Nash; and now, of course, I'll organize a manhunt. Another one. I'll arrange for local cops from out Warburton way to meet up with you. And take over, O'Malley. Only until we get there. So please stay in touch."

"Of course, Detective Suddenly-Grumpy," Kit said to dead air.

Chapter 32

Kit, Rabbit, and Ms. Amorosi approached the turn off to the Warburton Highway fifteen minutes after the advance team, with whom Kit had lost contact in mid-conversation just as Carrie was telling her they'd reached Launching Place and were turning onto ...

Kit's psyche-clearing rant, about how reliable the mobile network was when it came to failing when you most needed it, was now being irrelevantly tempered by a mind trip to her past. Conceding the need to have her priorities checked once this case was over, she continued to note with pleasure that, while suburbia was creeping ever-outward, this part of the country looked no different from her memory of Sunday drives and school excursions.

It was tempting. We could *not* take this turn; we could just stay on this highway, enjoy the verdant pastures, and the rolling hills as we cruise by Dame Nellie's digs and head for the wonderful Healesville Wildlife ...

"Oh cripes," Rabbit growled, as Kit resisted temptation and took the right turn towards work not pleasure. "Just realized we're on the road to that creepy animal place."

"The Sanctuary?" Kit said. "I love that place. What's creepy about platypuses and koalas?"

"Nothing," Rabbit emphasized. "It's just that I had nightmares for years after I went there, about being chased around all them bushy paths by the letter S."

"That's very peculiar, Rabbit. And you think *I'm* strange. Could you try Carrie again," she requested, noticing how the now-twilight sky of dark-edged clouds was unnecessarily foreboding.

"Sure," Rabbit said, but jumped as the phone rang before she did anything.

"Kitty?" Marek's voice crackled in her ear. "I am at Charlie Parker's house," he said. And he didn't sound pleased.

"Really, Jonno? And why are you there? Don't you have more important things to do?"

"This has just become my more important thing. The first detectives on the scene here found some bad-arse evidence linking ..."

"Oh Jonno," Kit interrupted, "don't you guys talk to each other? Cathy already knows that stuff was planted there by Liz, before she abducted Chucky and Guy. *She* killed Gerry not ..."

"Kitty, will you shut up. I'm not talking about Anders. And the only thing I've heard from Cathy was a relayed message that *you* are following Charlie all over the city. Be careful, for God's sake. He is very dangerous. Don't do *anything* you'd usually do. In fact, go home."

"Dangerous?" Kit laughed. "I'm tailing Charlie and his friend coz they've been hijacked."

"Read my lips," Marek enunciated. "There's evidence con ... Charlie ... tot ... flert."

"You're dropping out," Kit said, as the world outside went dishwater dull and the sky began pissing on her windscreen.

"It ... Char ... arker is Bub ... man."

If Kit hadn't been driving she'd have closed her eyes and put her head down in sheer exasperation. "Marek, I'm pretty sure I told you about Chucky's fly fishing hobby."

"Yeah, but I'm not talking about flies ... en local Ds called us ... planted knife ... bottle blood. Even if we'd seen the fishing ... have ignored ... precisely coz you told me ... But Ds looking for leads on missing cop, not ... erial killer. But rerder ... ft ... herper can't ignore ... back room. By that, I mean evidence of the absol ... incrimina ..."

Kit's face screwed into an involuntary sneer. "*What* did you find?" she asked, recalling how Charlie's lounge had inspired thoughts of Norman Bates and his dear old mum.

"Lisa Benton's necklace, purse, as well as ... of women's under ... and shoes."

"Lisa Benton?" Kit repeated. "The latest victim? The one Charlie admitted he knew. Shit. You mean he ..."

"Yeah. Kitty, where are you now?"

"Woori Yallock en route to Launching Place. Marek, go next door to number nine, break in if you have to, and find out where Charlie's neighbor Guy Linden has a fishing shack. That's where we're going. Cathy's organizing a local team to meet me up here, as soon as I find …"

"O'Malley? Now you're starting to break up. Promise me you won't …"

"I promise, Jonno. But mate, if you're right about Chucky, how ironic is it that Liz has been trying to frame the Rental Killer for the murder of Gerry Anders."

"Who's this Liz you ke … rav … bout?"

Talk about a failure to communicate, Kit thought. "Liz Nash, your admin person. She, and probably Doghouse and Christine Shipper, killed Gerry Anders. Now she, Liz, has stolen Chucky and his only friend in the world and is making them drive to the back of woop-woop. Talk to Cathy, for goodness sake."

"Fuc … hell. What … Kitty … You know Liz Na …"

"Of course I do, Jonno. I've been following her for an hour."

"No, I mean uno … kdofis … shit …" The line went dead.

"Damn it. Can you ring him back please, Rab?"

"No mate. Signal's gone. Hang on, I'll try mine," she said, searching her pocket. "I have a different carrier. Oh, and wouldn't that piss you off. Battery's dead."

"Use my charger," Kit suggested.

"Did I hear you say the Rental Killer?" Rabbit asked.

"Yep. Marek says he found evidence that Charlie Parker is the Rental Killer."

Rabbit snorted. "The homicide cop that none of you like is a psycho killer? An actual cop, not even an ex-one, has been scari-fying the entire city?"

"Apparently. And how's this for a complete waste of our time, energy, well-being, and karma? Not only are we trying to rescue someone I despise from someone I don't know; but we are trying to rescue a vicious serial killer from a woman who murdered a gangster by draining his blood. If the others weren't way ahead of us, and incommunicado, I'd turn and go home."

396

"But there's the other bloke to consider, Kit," Rabbit reminded her. Kit sniffed. "Don't know him, either."

"But he needs our help. Unless, of course, Liz and the killer cop knock each other off; then Guy could just go fishing."

"That'd work for me. Oh look," Kit announced, "we're finally here. I hope Hector and his backing vocals left a trail of crumbs from Launching Place to Hellandback."

Rabbit pointed. "How about leaving a dyke reporter?"

Carrie McDermid was leaping about on the footpath outside a pub on the other side of the road. There was no traffic for a hundred meters in either direction, so Kit chucked a U-ey and splashed to a stop. Carrie darted from the cover of the verandah and leaped into the back seat.

"Bloody hell, you sure took your time. It's tit-freezing weather out there," she exclaimed.

Kit smiled. "Should I assume the others aren't inside the pub getting pissed?"

"Yeah. We were about to turn up there," she pointed to the road opposite, which met the highway at a T-intersection, "when we lost the phone coverage. We kept going for a few minutes before deciding one of us should walk back here, so you'd at least know where to turn."

"Hope the bad guys don't take too many more turns, then," Rabbit said. "Coz it's not like you had a pack of girl guides to leave one at every intersection."

"Well, this little Brownie is awfully glad your car is warm."

"Um," Kit pulled a face, "I need you to wait here for the police. Hopefully, it'll be Cathy; but I suggest you grab any cruising cops you see, coz they'll probably be looking for us."

"Why me?" Carrie said petulantly.

"Because you're experienced now." Kit tried not to smirk. "You have to tell them we're tailing a dangerous female murderer stroke kidnapper ..."

"O'Malley," Carrie snapped, "I know *exactly* who you are all following. Without me."

"*And*," Kit continued, "a police officer now suspected of being the Rental Killer."

"What?" Carrie squinted suspiciously. "You mean Parker?"

"Yep," Rabbit said. "And there's obviously been a subliminal reason why no one, it seems, has ever liked this Parker guy. He's a depraved serial killing whack-job, that's why."

"I'm getting out of the car now," Carrie said calmly, "against my wishes and all my so-called journalistic instincts, and *only* because Hector and Erin were a little gung-ho. They should be very interested in your news and will no doubt, by now, need your help." She opened the car door. "I'll follow asap with all the police who find me loitering on the street."

"Thanks, Carrie," Kit smiled. "Check over the back, there might be a jacket."

"Which you might need, O'Malley. Get going."

Kit did as she was told. Swinging back across the highway she headed northwards up Don Road, which, according to the road sign, would take them into the Don Valley.

"According to this," Rabbit said, checking their whereabouts in the Melways, "the Don Road and valley follow the Don River. Which kinda makes sense. And the Don joins the Yarra, somewhere over there to the left."

"What else is up here?" Kit asked.

"Not a lot," Rabbit said, flicking pages. "There's an intersection coming up, but this road keeps going past Mt Toole-be-Wong, which I'm guessing is not a very high mount, then up into the Great Dividing Range. We could get lost out here, Kit. This is like the serious bush, mate. Shoulda brought a compass and ration pack."

"We've got a map, Rabbit. We're not likely to get lost."

"That's what you ... woo! Is that one of your mates under that umbrella?"

"Oh yeah," Kit grinned, "that be Erin Carmody." Kit pulled up beside the woman who was sensibly swathed in hat, long coat, big boots, and gloves.

Erin jumped into the back seat. "Hello, cherub and someone I don't know."

"Erin, honey," Kit nodded. "This is Rabbit."

"Hi. Kit? Hector is driving my car. Does he drive okay? Because that's one of the few things of value I own. I wouldn't want to find it wrapped around a tree."

"He's a good driver, Erin. Which way did he go?" Kit waved at the choices: north on Don, west on Dalry Road, or east on the lesser Old Dalry Road.

"We have to stay on this one, Kit. I've just walked about a kilometer back from Burton Lane, which is a dirt road on the left."

Kit filled Erin in on why she had to wait for backup; then she and Rabbit continued north, before turning into the unsealed but wide, and therefore misnamed, Burton Lane. It soon narrowed to a width befitting its designation and began winding all over the place amongst the scrub and trees, before offering three choices: straight ahead, left, or more left.

Spotting something yellow way ahead, Kit bounced along the center choice to another divide in the not-quite road where she found Erin's parked car, but no Hector. She kept driving for a hundred twisting-turning meters, until the road ended at a magnificently huge gum tree beside a rusty old gate with a sign that said "trespassers will *really* be prosecuted."

"I guess we're here, then," she said, reaching across Rabbit to grab her binoculars from the glove box. She opened her door and stood up on the running board to get a better view across the darkening paddock beyond the gate.

"See anything?" Rabbit asked.

"A big rainwater tank attached to a weatherboard cottage, a tumbledown shed, and Guy's car." Kit climbed back into her seat and began reversing down the track. "I'm taking you back to Erin's car. She keeps a spare key in the wheel hub. I'd like you to drive it back to Erin, and her back to Carrie, or into the arms of the cops; whichever comes first. Take those pictures of Liz off the back seat and give them to the cops. That way, if the situation gets sticky they'll know to shoot her and not me. You could also use some of them to stick on tree branches, if you're worried about finding your way back in the dark."

"Shouldn't I stay with you, Kit?"

"I'll be fine. Hector's out there, somewhere. So I'll park about there," Kit waved to her right, "out of sight and then go find him.

I'd rather you went back and got Erin off the roadside before she catches cold or a Bunyip."

Five minutes later Kit had jumped the gate and, avoiding the beaten track, was taking the direct route across the hillocky paddock, run-stumbling towards the dash of light coming from the far side of Guy Linden's fishing shack. It was getting very dark and very cold, but at least it had stopped raining. Dressed in the jacket that Carrie had declined, Kit was armed with a small torch, a pocket knife, a can of pepper spray, and a useless phone.

Who knows, she thought, a handy satellite might pass between Jupiter and Mars and connect me to the Kremlin.

Reaching Guy's car, parked to the left of the house, Kit crouched behind it to listen and look for sights and sounds. The dilapidated verandah and the planks nailed over the windows implied that Guy's own home maintenance was less important to him than his fishing. Kit headed for the nearest and unlit side of the house, keeping close to the wall as she crept under the vine-covered tank stand. A quick look around the back corner told her it wasn't the back corner at all. She was surprised to find that the cottage was split-level and a good three times the size it looked from the front. The older section at the rear was built of red brick and timber and continued back and down, towards—what? Kit couldn't see farther than about twenty feet, so she kept going to find out what the what was.

Bugger! As she slipped, slid, rolled, and resisted screaming all the way to the gravelly wet bottom of a gently inclining *fifteen-foot bloody cliff*, she wished she was more sensible. In general. She picked herself up and checked for lights—back up there—that hadn't been on before, and then risked a quick flash around with her torch.

Oh, how lovely! A creek. That explains the wet. Turning to face the way she'd tumbled, she swept the light across the lower reaches of the rear brick wall, built into the embankment above her. She did another sweep higher up the wall, stopping at a barred window. The grimy window pane flung back her torch light and …

Aagh! Kit dropped the torch in fright. *Eyes.* Shit. A pair of eyes.

Not sure if she'd cried out that time, she threw herself onto the ground to cover the light.

Faarck, wanna go home now, she moaned silently, untangling her arms from the wet vegetation so she could sit up. There was still no noise from above, at least nothing she could hear over the super-excited thudding of her own pulse, so she stood and shone the torch on the window again.

Nothing, this time. What the hell *was* that then? A mutant redback or a damn possum? Looking around for the best route back to high ground, Kit headed for a worn path on the other side of the brick room. She began the easy climb, but stopped every other moment to separate and label the natural night sounds that were starting to make her jumpy.

It's damn noisy out here in the wild, she thought. Over there, a rustle of post-crepuscular creatures, hopefully escaping from her; up there, the tree-top jostling and chirping of ringtails or bats; up ahead, a grunting, possibly-koala but probably-human, as it seemed to be emanating from inside; and, ooh, also from inside, the ABC radio news jingle.

Kit crept along the side of the house towards the window where a tatty Holland blind, pulled almost all the way down, diffused the light oozing from what she assumed was the kitchen, given she could see the taps and faucet of a sink. Taking the requisite deep breath to face what, in the movies would be the murderous woods-man washing his bloody ax in the sink, but in real life would be three dead blowies on the sill or Mrs. Jones peeling spuds, Kit risked getting close enough to take a quick look inside. And yes, the kitchen it was, but ... *bloody hell!*

Kit shuddered like she'd been hit with a large wet towel. She was so sure her vital fluids were puddling around her feet that she wasn't game to look down. But she had to. No, not look down— *get down!*

Loud noise, O'Malley. Your arm whacked the wall, you fool. She dropped to her haunches and, realizing the underneath of the house was accessible, rolled in under the kitchen sink.

Oh shit oh shit oh shit, she swore silently, as running footsteps returning to the room overhead were followed by a couple of bangs and a muffled voice, that could've been anybody's, swearing about vermin.

Great! Kit thought, willing herself to stop shaking. Vermin now. On top of marsupials, bats, poisonous spiders, and … and crucified serial killers.

Stop bloody shaking, O'Malley, she begged. She screwed her eyes shut to escape, but the image was branded on her mind: Charlie Parker up on his toes, bare chest, Y-fronts, arms flung over his head, hands nailed to the kitchen wall. And it was seven o'clock.

Like *that* matters, O'Malley! Kit scolded herself. How, why do you even know that?

It was Parker; he was nailed to the wall under the kitchen clock. Even with that quick glance, Kit knew he was still alive because he was balancing on his toes, no doubt to prevent his own body weight from dragging the nails through his hands.

Kit began tossing all the ways she could solve, help, worsen, or run away from this situation. Obviously, the sensible thing to do would be to crawl out from under the house and run like hell back across the paddock to wait for reinforcements.

No, she couldn't do that, she reminded herself. Parker could die in that time.

You idiot! Who'd give a damn? Chucky is the Rental Killer; he deserves to die in agony at the hands of someone he wronged— even if she is a trifle misguided.

Kit rolled off her back and began crawling farther under the house, towards a dollar-sized shaft of light, which she calculated was only about four feet from the wall on which Charlie Parker was nailed. She could see nothing but the kitchen ceiling through the hole, but just by being farther under the room she could now hear what was being said up there.

Parker, in between groaning, seemed to be trying to talk sense into Liz Nash. She, however, didn't seem to care much for his sense.

"You still don't realize who I am, do you?"

"Right now, don't give a shit," Parker grunted, with a bravado that would have been admirable had he not deserved to be right where he was. "You got me. We're in deep trouble. All you can do is gloat. You completely mad?"

"Let me introduce myself," Liz said, dragging a chair on the floor-boards. "My name is Eliza Ellen Mason; and you killed my brother."

"Uh. Never killed anyone," Parker panted. "Still dunno what you're talking about."

Oh, bloody hell I do, Kit whimpered. She bowed her head into the dirt and debris and wished she could wail, at the top of her voice, *you've got to be kidding!*

"I repeat. My name is Eliza Mason. My precious Deon died in shame, by his own hand, because of you."

"Deon?" Charlie repeated, as if he couldn't get his head around anything.

By his own hand. Liz's words echoed in Kit's head. Oh, crap! Deon Mason didn't die in a hunting accident in South Australia.

"You ruined his life, you bastard!" Liz was shouting. "And you destroyed mine. Deon blew his brains out behind a pub in Coober Pedy, late one lonely night. And it's *all* your fault."

Kit shook her head in disbelief. In the room above her was Deon Mason's adoring younger sister—all grown-up and out for sweet revenge, served stone motherless cold.

What a waste. Kit remembered Eliza as a bright and funny teenager, who hero worshipped her big brother, and wanted to join the force to be just like him. She'd often gone to work barbecues and social functions with Deon, because they were each other's only family, after their parents' death in a light plane crash. Eliza Mason, it seems, had married Colin Nash—but not for long— and then teamed up with Chrissie and Doghouse Dixon, of all people, to exact revenge on Charlie Parker.

Kit covered the hole in the floor with her hand, so she could shine her torch around and find a way out. Making an executive decision, which didn't make it any less stupid, she reckoned it couldn't be too hard to overpower one woman who didn't know she was there. She could then find Guy and together they could get Charlie down off the wall—then tie him up again till the cops arrived.

Hang on, where the hell was Hector? Why hadn't she seen or tripped over him yet?

The torchlight revealed several planks hanging from the floor, so Kit began commando crawling the twelve or so feet across, she didn't ever want to know what, to a person-sized hole in the floor above. The loose floorboards were attached at one end only, by rust or habit, to a rotting joist, so Kit was very careful about pulling herself up on anything that might give way beneath her.

Although not completely trusting her bearings, she figured the room she carefully lifted herself into was one of the front ones overlooking the verandah. Keeping to the edge of the room along the interior wall, she moved quietly towards the half-open door. The only sound she could hear now was soft radio music. She glanced around the doorjamb and then pressed herself back against the wall.

Okay, she took stock: hallway going right about ten feet, meeting another which probably runs between front door and kitchen. No light this end, and no one in sight. Kit bent down and picked up a cricket-bat-sized piece of wood from the floor, then slipped out of the room. Keeping to the far wall, she edged her way towards the next corner, where another quick look told her she was correct about what lay in either direction. To the right was about ten feet of semi-darkness and then the front door; and to the left, a bare light bulb hung from the high ceiling between the closed doors of two rooms which opened off the hall before the kitchen at the end. All she could see in the latter was one end of a table, one chair, and the old wood-burning stove opposite the wide open door.

Reluctant to take a preparatory breath, after the ugly sight she'd encountered last time, Kit did cast a backwards glance to make sure no one was going to knock her out with a vase. She then crept down the hall with her fighting stick held up, but not too tightly, and her commonsense urging her to take notice of it and run in the other direction.

At about five feet from the kitchen door she could see half the red laminex table, two chairs, a fridge, and ... bound feet. Oh, please no, Kit begged. The presence of those particular feet was something she did not want to register as possible. She took another step, so she could bob down and look under the table at the body—no fucking way, O'Malley—at *the person* lying on the floor with his hands and ankles tied behind and then chained to the handle of the squat old fridge.

Damn it, Hector, she thought. You better be breathing, mate.

Fueled by the outrage that he'd been hurt and the cold fear that she was already too late, Kit barged headlong into the kitchen to confront a murdering kidnapper with the O'Malley version of the punishment Liz was inflicting on her captives.

The reality of the situation in the room threw that plan right out the window.

"What the hell?" she exclaimed.

Liz Nash, nee Eliza Mason, was bruised and bloody and tied quite firmly to a chair. The floor around her, and the box on which Parker was balancing, was covered in shards of glass. Liz looked totally bewildered by Kit's loud and sudden arrival, Parker looked relieved, and Hector—thank all that was worthy—groaned, and uttered her name. He also said "look out."

Aware of the looming shadow behind her, Kit was already diving to the floor in a roll towards Hector, and away from the broken glass. The only missing player in whatever bizarre game this had become, launched himself into the room.

Guy Ian Linden missed his target completely. His enraged momentum carried him, and the brick he held in his hand, forward and into the stove, by which time Kit was back on her feet and running for the door. Electing to leave the way she came rather than get trapped looking for an alternative, she dashed back into the front room, dropped down through the hole in the floor, and scrambled for the nearest wall. She was prepared to hide in a dark corner with the spiders until morning if she had to, but luckily the unlit side of the house was also high enough off the ground to crawl out of.

Kit found herself under the tank stand, but could hear Guy careering across the broken verandah after her, so she took off down towards the creek again. She'd almost reached the end of the house when she ran smack bang into a stationary object, both large and soft, that hadn't been there on her last trek in these parts. A big hand clamped over her mouth, and Rabbit MacArthur dragged her into the undergrowth on the embankment above the creek, between the back wall and the cliff edge.

They lay there, not daring to breathe, while Guy thrashed around in the bushes on the other side of the path. He gave up and ran back, possibly thinking Kit had emerged elsewhere.

"What are you doing here, Rabbit?' Kit whispered.

"Rescuing your arse."

"For which I thank you, but …"

"It's okay, I did like you asked. But Erin insisted on driving her own car, so I was looking at them photos of yours for the first time. And after my, like, *epiphany*, I used my recharged phone to ring Detective Cathy. I filled her in on where we all are, she reckoned they're all about ten minutes away, and then she gave me info, for you, which confirmed my new devout suspicions."

"What info and suspicions?" Kit asked, hearing the slam of a door at the front of the house.

"That Christine Shipper chick you've been talking about, is in hospital in Darwin. Been there two weeks with a broken pelvis from a climbing accident. So guess who she isn't."

Resisting the urge to dig a hole in which to hide from the ludicrous idea that Ms. Shipper was Scooter's Chrissie, Kit said, "Don't think I wanted to know that, Rabbit."

"Won't want to know the doozey either. Those photos were of Scooter's secret shag."

"Yeah. I know that."

"No, Kit. I mean they were *all* Chrissie. Every single photo was of Chrissie."

"No way."

"Yes way," Rabbit whispered. "That's why I got Erin to drive me halfway back here before she went into the little town. Chrissie is Liz *and* Tina. They're all the same person."

Kit pouted. "And they all used to be Eliza Mason, who is now the grown up little sister of a really fine human being," she explained. "Deon Mason was an all-round nice guy, devoted brother of Eliza-now-Liz, and her legal guardian. He was a good cop who left the force after he, and Sheryl Mapp, were framed by Chuck and Gerry. Then he shot himself."

"Bummer," Rabbit said, checking to see if the coast was clear. She gave the thumbs up.

"I suppose," Kit added, "despite the kibosh it puts on my theories, it *is* much better that there's only one angry woman hurtling along a path of self-destructive vengeance tonight. Especially seeing she's presently inside, tied to a chair."

"That's deep, O'Malley. And where's Hector?"

"He's inside too; chained to a fridge. Let's go get him," Kit said, getting to her feet. "And while we're in there, we probably should rescue Chucky and Liz from Guy."

"Is that who was chasing you? Hang on, isn't that strange?"

"Yeah. No idea what his problem is," Kit whispered, as they began pushing their way through the bushes. "Unless he thinks I'm in league with the bad guys. You know the bad guys: the woman who kidnapped him, and his friend who turned out to be a psycho killer.

"I'm guessing Liz forced Guy at gunpoint to crucify Charlie on the kitchen wall, and tie Hector up to the Kelvinator. But then Guy somehow managed to get the upper hand, whereon he beat the crap out of Liz and tied her to a chair."

Rabbit grabbed Kit's arm and pulled her back. "Listen," she hissed. "What *is* that?"

Kit squinted, to help her analyze the noise in the dark, and said, "Crying. There's someone crying. But it's too close to be coming from the kitchen where everyone's tied up."

Rabbit pointed to the filthy window near the top corner of the back wall. It was too high for Kit to see in, but Rabbit, with the assistance of a large rock to stand on, could just make it. She stretched and peered, lost her balance, and fell down in a hurry. Then she just sat there blinking, her mouth agape.

Kit crouched down. "You okay, Rab? What's up?"

Rabbit turned her horrified gaze on Kit. "There's a, I *think* it's a girl, chained up high on the wall. She saw me, Kit. She said 'help me.' What the fuck's going on here?"

Kit held on to Rabbit's hand while she processed all that was not logical about a woman being chained to the wall in a dingy back room of Guy Linden's fishing shack.

"This is too much!" Kit growled. "Come on, mate. We can't wait for the cops to get here. We have to go get Hector, before the other psycho hurts him again."

There was no one in sight along the kitchen side of the house, so Kit sprinted for the front, with Rabbit right on her heels. Having decided the best plan was a full frontal full-on assault, with lots of noise designed to fool all the occupants of the house into thinking there was more to the raiding party than two cranky women armed only with big sticks, Kit led the way, hollering and thumping the house, around to the now open front door.

"Wait!" Rabbit shouted, pointing at the old car which was coughing and spluttering and not getting anywhere in its getaway attempt.

Kit leaped off the verandah and ran towards the miserable excuse for a human being who was at the wheel. While Rabbit whacked at the windscreen until it smashed, Kit wrenched open the driver's door and dragged Guy Ian Linden from the front seat and threw him to the ground. In a far-off place in her mind she marveled at the sheer brute strength that pure adrenaline could give an ordinary girl, and then she kicked the bastard hard in the groin.

"Way to go, Kit!" Rabbit cheered.

Kit reached across the front bench-seat to grab one of the tools of his trade. She threw one end of the rope to Rabbit and wound the other around the still-writhing Guy Linden.

"This, here, is the Rental Killer, Rabbit. Please tie him securely to the car door and watch him. You do not have to be nice to him at all. In fact," she pulled the pepper spray from her pocket, "if he gives you any trouble douse him with this."

Kit then ran back to the house, vaguely aware that several sets of headlights were heading their way across the paddock. "Typical," she said as she ran down the hall. "The cavalry is always late."

Guy had obviously been too busy looking for her to do anything more to his prisoners, although there was a carving knife in the middle of the kitchen floor that hadn't been there before. Kit dropped to her knees beside Hector, who smiled bravely, then pouted. "Head hurts, arms hurt, knees and ankles hurt lots," he muttered, as Kit used the big knife to cut the ropes. Releasing the tension caused Hector to collapse onto his front. "Nose hurts," he added, "Want to go home."

Kit helped him to a sitting position just as an ear-thumping vibration filled the air.

"Earthquake?" Hector queried.

"Helicopter, I suspect," Kit said, holding him steady while he stretched his legs.

"Guy was about to stab Chuck, kill us all, when you attacked the house. He bolted."

"It's okay, Hector. We got him. Rabbit's out there tying him to his car."

"O'Malley?" Parker whined. Although his tone was understandable, given his position, Kit still couldn't help feeling irritated by it.

She looked up at him, crucified there on the wall, and cocked her head. "Yeah, Charlie?"

"Do you think you could get me down from here?"

"I doubt I'd be strong enough," Kit said, comparing his weediness to the only slightly weightier Guy, who she'd just thrown ten feet across the yard. "Cathy and the troops are on the way. They'll help you down. By the way, last I heard they all thought *you* were the Rental Killer."

Liz Nash, despite her completely black, blue, and swelling face, started laughing.

"Oh God, will you shut her up," Parker complained. "She's a complete nutcase."

"*Someone* has to laugh, Charlie, otherwise we'd all go mad," Kit said. "Besides, I understand why Liz thinks it's funny."

"It's hysterical. Charlie's so-called and only friend in the world is a serial killer," Liz mumbled. "I think he's got someone else in the house."

"I know," Kit said.

"Did you know he moved in next door to Charlie on purpose?" Liz ran her tongue over her swollen lips. "Guy told us he wanted to befriend the cop who'd told the nation he was a sick, sexually inadequate loser. He's been getting extra thrills out of torturing and killing right under the great detective's nose."

Kit felt like throwing up, but she snorted instead. "How does it feel, Charlie, knowing Liz and Guy, two unrelated killers, planted incriminating evidence in *your* house? You are so lucky you hired me to find out who was framing you."

Parker grunted in pain. "You still going to tell Marek about, you know? Don't you think this is punishment enough?"

Kit laughed. "I can't begin to imagine where you keep your priorities, Charlie, but you are a prize fuckwit. I'm almost tempted to untie *Eliza* and let her finish you off. For Deon."

Kit helped Hector to his feet, draped his arm around her shoulders, and headed for the door.

"O'Malley?" Deon's little sister croaked. "Why don't you?"

"Because Eliza, as Liz or Chrissie or Tina, you and Doghouse killed Sheryl Mapp—for no good reason. She was a good cop and as innocent as your brother was all those years ago. I can't let that one go. Sorry."

Chapter 33

Friday dawned all fresh and rosy-fingered like the opening of a famous Greek epic. Kit had watched the day do that, a rarity for her, because she was still awake when it happened. It was a few hours ago now, but she preferred to keep the beauty and stillness of that moment uppermost in her mind, while she finished telling Alex all that had happened out there in the bush before the sun rose.

Jon Marek's arrival by police helicopter had coincided with the skidding to a halt of Cathy Martin's three squad cars and Erin's wagon, just as Kit and Hector emerged from the house. Marek had taken Kit's advice and immediately radioed for air and road ambulances. Following a quick situation report, Cathy and four officers had sprinted to the room at the back of the house; Crosby and two others had gone inside to take Chucky down off the wall and untie Liz; and Marek had handcuffed Guy Linden to the tank stand. He left him there in the cold for the four hours it took to take everyone else's statements, and to begin the painstaking process of examining and recording a crime scene of unimaginable horror.

Andrea Chesterton, the only woman to survive the Rental Killer, aka Bubblewrap Man, was taken by helicopter to the Alfred Hospital. She'd been chained in the dank darkness by Guy Linden for only three days, but had been raped, beaten, and given no food or water in that time.

Liz Nash was transported, with police escort, by road to Maroondah Hospital. Chucky Parker was treated and bandaged by paramedics, then taken by slow squad car to a hospital somewhere between Launching Place and Bombay. His future did not look bright. Hector was checked by the medics and released into the tender care of Kit, Erin, Carrie, and Rabbit.

411

Jon Marek was the only person within cooee, it seemed, who had known all along who Liz Nash was before she grew up into a cold-blooded killer. It's just that no one had thought to ask him.

Alex Cazenove, in the here and now, clasped Kit's hand. "Darling, perhaps you need to give up your day job."

"I just need a long holiday," Kit declared, reveling in the wonderful ordinariness of the Friday morning traffic that was passing within meters of their al fresco table. Her phone rang.

"Do you want me to take it?" Alex offered, but Kit shook her head.

"Katherine, darling. Where are you?"

"Having coffee with Alex at the bookshop café near my place. Why?"

"Don't forget to invite everyone to our place for dinner tonight."

Our place? Kit frowned. "Everyone, like who, Mum? And why?" She gazed quizzically at Alex, who was looking sheepish, as if she'd forgotten something important.

"Connie wants a little party to mark her moving in here with me; Brigit says you're close to solving Angie's dead-man case; and Alex told me how you all saved Enzo's life yesterday. So I decided the whole family should get together for a barbecue."

"The whole family?" Kit said, wondering if Lillian was having a senior's moment. "Mum, that's just you, me, and Michael."

"Not that family," Lillian said. "Now, I've already invited Alex, Del, and Brigit. So you need to contact Angie and her friend, Enzo and Rick, Hector, the mad reporters, and Jon, if he's not too busy. For seven this evening. Can you do that? And let me know how many as soon as you can."

"Okay, Mum. I've gotta go now. We'll see you then. Love you." Kit set the phone down on the table. "You might have warned me."

"Sorry, I forgot," Alex grinned. "She rang my place last night looking for you. Lillian is thrilled to bits that Connie is moving in."

"In that case I'll ring *everyone*," Kit said. "Hell, I might even invite Queenie and Sasha."

"How about Julian?" Alex suggested, snatching up Kit's ringing phone before she could. "Kit's phone. Oh hello, Queenie, we were just talking about you," Alex widened her eyes.

Despite her exhaustion, that look of Alex's sent Kit all tingly, all over. There was no use fighting it, so she fell in love with her all over again.

"Yes, she's here," Alex smiled, "but I'm screening her calls. She had a horrible night and hasn't been to bed yet, so be gentle." She handed the phone to Kit.

"Morning, Queenie. Have the cops been bothering you much?"

"I haven't seen them, Kit. I've been, shall we say ..."

"Hiding?" Kit suggested.

Queenie laughed. "In a manner of speaking. Do you want this piece of rubbish that Will brought me yesterday?"

"Is it still functional?"

"For the most part. We're in the kitchen at Gerry's club. Come alone. Or bring Alex."

Fifteen minutes later, Kit and Alex were being frisked by Mr. Thumpya—for listening devices, he said—at the back door of the Moshun Club. He then escorted them into the presence of Queenie Riley. Flanked as she was by her professional biffo boys Julian and Jacko, she was looking, to Kit, for the first time like the real matriarch of a fine upstanding Melbourne crime family.

"Kit, dear, you look terrible," Queenie noted.

"Thanks. Been up all night catching killers," Kit explained.

"Well here's another one for you," Queenie said, parting the wall of bodyguards to reveal a Mark Doghouse Dixon who was seriously the worse for wear.

Kit glanced at Queenie, then back to the pummeled bent ex-cop, cop killer, and gangster murderer. She ran a casual hand through her hair and nodded approvingly. Some people simply deserved to have the shit kicked out of them. The blood-soaked bandaged hand was a bit suss, though.

"You might remember me telling you, Kit, that my taking revenge for Gerry's death, or not, would depend on whether his demise was related to the family business. Mr. Dixon here, should count himself lucky that his reason for taking my nephew's life has spared his own."

"And what *reason* would that be?" Kit asked, though immediately

413

wished she hadn't. If she wasn't careful, Doghouse still mightn't get out of here alive.

"Mr. Dixon, if you'd be so kind," Queenie invited.

Doghouse swallowed and through swollen lips said, "Sherwoods. And Eliza's brother."

"As I said Kit, drugs are not my business. If my nephew died because he made them his, then three of this murderer's fingers is punishment enough for Gerry. Had any other member of my family been harmed through Mr. Dixon's actions, however, today would have turned out differently for him."

Don't say a word, Kit told herself. She looked expectant instead.

"Julian will escort him out to your car and wherever you wish to deliver him." Queenie waved at Jacko and pointed to a pile of tea towels on the bench behind him. "Take some of them out too. We wouldn't want the useless bastard to make a mess on Kit's seats."

"Just as a matter of interest, Queenie," Alex began questioningly.

"Yes, dear?"

"What did you do with his fingers?"

"Alex," Kit cried disapprovingly.

"Well," Alex shrugged, "it's a thing I need to know."

Queenie laughed and pointed at the microwave oven next to the fridge. "Six minutes on high. *Not* a pleasant smell. I wouldn't recommend it."

"Going now," Kit insisted, nodding at Julian, who dragged Doghouse to his feet. "Thank you, Queenie. Come, Alex."

Julian seat-belted Doghouse, who was still handcuffed, into the back seat of Kit's car and then tied his feet with a bit of rope. "Will you be right with him, Kit, or do you want me to come along?" he asked.

"We'll be fine, thanks Julian."

The moment Kit pulled out of the laneway, Dixon groaned in relief. "Man, I thought I was a goner. You gotta take me to the hospital, O'Malley, before I bleed to death."

"Don't you dare bleed in my car, Doghouse. And the only place you're going straight to, is Jon Marek's office."

"But I might go all septic."

"Good," Kit pronounced. "Coz I could always take you back to Queenie. How do you think your day would end if I told her you hired Toad Ralph to beat up her granddaughter?"

"Cops," Dixon said. "Take me to the cop shop."

Alex rested her hand on Kit's thigh. "Tell me, my love, are you still thinking of inviting Queenie to Lillian's celebration barbecue tonight?"

"Yeah, why not," Kit laughed. "She could bring the dips and finger food."

Lindy Cameron

Lindy Cameron is the author, obviously, of the O'Malley Mystery trilogy: *Blood Guilt*, *Bleeding Hearts* and *Thicker than Water* (Bywater Books); and of *Golden Relic* (HarperCollins Australia) which features Special Detective Sam Diamond and archaeologist Dr. Maggie Tremaine.

Lindy is also contributing editor of a true crime anthology *Meaner than Fiction* and co-author (with her sister, Fin J. Ross) of the forthcoming true crime, *Killer in the Family*.

A national co-convenor of Sisters in Crime Australia, Lindy is also editor of the mystery fiction anthology *Scarlet Stiletto: The First Cut* (MIRA/ Australia). She lives near Melbourne, Australia.

Her latest book is *Redback*, the first in a new espionage-adventure thriller series, featuring Commander Bryn Gideon and a crack team of Australian retrieval agents (MIRA/Australia).